The
Volcano Lady
Vol. I
A Fearful Storm Gathering

By
T.E. MacArthur

The Volcano Lady
A Fearful Storm Gathering
By T.E. MacArthur

©2011 by T.E. MacArthur
Edition 1.5 (2012)

Cover Artwork/Design: S. N. Jacobson
www.snjacobson.com
Additional Cover Artwork – The Nautilus by Frank Chase
http://www.virtualnautilus.com

Published by: TreasureLine Publishing
www.TreasureLinePublishing.com

ISBN: 978-1-61752-123-2

Also available in eBook publication

www.volcanolady1.wordpress.com
www.TreasureLineBooks.com

Printed in the United States of America

Dedicated to my Mother, who brought home sheets of paper being tossed out at her office so that I could use the reverse sides to type my stories on. To my Papa, who has read every crazy thing I've written and loved them all as a father should.

Many thanks to Sharon Cathcart for the editing on version 1.5.

To Monsieur Jules Verne, the Father of Science Fiction (and Steampunk!)

Ever leave the house knowing that despite all the best plans, you just know you forgot something? Writing all your thank you's for such an endeavor as creating a novel leaves you with that same worry. So please forgive me if my list falls short.

I want thank a number of people who kept me sane and on track: Brandy Sluss and Roy Nonomura; Jay Davis - the real Professor Flockmaker; Juliana and Patrick Gaul; My writer pals Sharon E. Cathcart, Maggie Secara, Jay and Denisen Hartlove; Scott Perkins, Dre Sargent, and James McShane; Molly Burke (the Queen of Confidence); Thalassa Therese Porter and Rydell Downward; All the fantastic Downward family; Susan Bishop; Raymond E. Andre; Jeffrey Mosher; Sonya Sutton; Diane Clegg; Jessica Kelly; Karen Krebser; and David Batzloff.

To the inspiring resources: the U.S. Naval Landing Party (Civil War Naval Reenactors) and the North American Jules Verne Society.

To my inspiration for Tom - Henry Czerny, and for Nemo - the classic James Mason.

To the designer of the cover: Stephen Jacobson (www.snjacobson.com).

And not at all last or least: to Linda Boulanger and the gang at TreasureLine Books and Publishing.

A special note regarding the Nautilus on the cover: Frank Chase was the man responsible for the Nautilus you see there. He re-envisioned Nemo's great submarine by digging out every detail Verne provided in his book *20,000 Leagues Under the Sea*. While I tapped my childhood memories of the Disney film for this novel, I am inspired all the more by seeing what Verne had created in such detail. http://www.virtualnautilus.com.

Chapter 1

1856
Tahuna, Grand Sangihe Island
Dutch East Indies

A near darkness, twilight darkness, covered everything in shadows: yet it was eleven o'clock in the morning. Thick clouds, grey and swirling, shrouded the entire island. The deep greens of jungle vegetation and colorful flowers of the tropics had been buried under layers of ash and bleak flurries of the same material blew past them from a storm generated deep inside the mountain. Sulfur reeked in the wind.

The ground swelled and subsided, creaking and groaning with every shiver. Rocks tumbled down the sides of the hills, unable to lie in rest with the constant shaking. Life on the island gave in to silence and surrendered every noise to the mountain.

It wasn't the volcano's fault. It was what volcanoes do, Lettie told her father. They explode.

He wasn't listening.

Theodore Gantry picked her up: a small bundle of blanket-wrapped petticoats, shiny black curls dusted in gray, and a scalding coat of ash he tried to wipe off of her. Lettie was horrified that her father held her too tightly as he ran toward the hillside. She could run too; he didn't need to carry her. She squirmed and whined until he finally put her down. The blanket was dragged along behind. Holding tightly to his hand, she ran as fast as she could. Together they reached the hill and Gantry pushed his daughter ahead of him, up and up.

For every few steps he took, he slid back in the slimy mud, not getting anywhere quickly enough. That was her fault. If he wasn't burdened with her he'd be faster. She slipped suddenly and fell. Gantry wrapped his arms around her and lifted her from the sticky mud.

The roar behind them was growing louder by the second. Louder. Deafening. The ground was shaking harder than before. Hot, gray ash filled their mouths too. They were choking from the poisonous air. She buried her face in his shoulder grateful and ashamed that he was rescuing her.

Reaching a flat break in the slope he stopped only long enough to decide which was the fastest route to the top. She would never make it on her own: that was what he was thinking and why he had to stay with her. She knew it.

A Minahasan man, one she knew from her Papa's business, skidded down the hill to meet them. Over the roar, Lettie thought she heard him call, "Hurry, hurry!" Gantry reached out with his only free arm and let the local businessman pull him up the slope. Every step was painful, and every other step was a failure to reach safety. Her Papa tried shouting something back to him, but couldn't remember his name.

Letticia – Lettie - called out to the man, "Georgie." It wasn't the man's name, but it was as close as she could get to pronounce it. 'Georgie' never seemed to mind it, not when he'd met them at the docks, nor when he sat with Gantry discussing the price of nutmeg, nor when answering Lettie's endless questions about the big mountain.

"Higher! We must be higher!" Georgie screamed.

Gantry drew in another thick breath of air which felt like cement on his tongue. It burned. "All the shaking - I thought - they were just earthquakes. I didn't think ..."

Georgie pulled, all the while obsessively repeating, "Gunung Awu." Awu Mountain. Awu Volcano.

Lettie began to scream; shrill and terrified. She could see what Papa hadn't, yet. A wall of mud, crashing down the lush valley toward the village. The source of the deafening roar.

Gantry stopped wasting time looking behind him. He could guess what was happening.

With an arm wrapped around Gantry's waist, Georgie began pulling them both, desperately grasping trees and vines for stability. She wanted to reach out too, to help. It wasn't fair to Papa; he shouldn't have had to carry her. She was a big girl.

The mudslide hit the hill with a wave of debris, grinding down the soil with the rocks and boulders in its mixture. Trees were smashed flat or twisted out of the ground, roots and all. The three tiny humans were only halfway up the hill and not fully out of the way. The footing under both men was swept out from under them. Lettie hit an upturning root of a tree when she was ripped from her Papa's arms. The mud crushed her harder into the tree and the blanket, meant to protect her, only suffocated.

Papa grasped her any way he could and finally tore away the heavy blanket from her face. Again, his footing failed and they tumbled in the rush of mud. Gantry seized a vine and held on, calling out to Georgie. The wave of mud swept viciously over them one more time, and then subsided nearly as fast as it came.

The ringing in her ears was excruciating and she held her throbbing head in her hands, wondering when Papa was going to move. Her eyes stung from the ash and heat; the painful headache pressured them until she thought they might explode. She closed them tightly as tears formed.

The mud was flowing still but far away from them now. She reached out to Papa and he stirred enough to hold her hand loosely. Lettie used her free hand to tug at the blanket wrapped around her legs. She threw it over him and sat as close as she could. The air was hot but the mud had been cold; she would keep him warmer.

So little was left. But they'd see her if she sat up tall, as she wasn't so tiny anymore, and they'd be able to find them. They were coming to rescue Papa and her, weren't they? That's what happened in the stories Papa read to her. The good people were always rescued.

By afternoon, she was proven right. Lettie was brought down the hillside, one hand held by a local woman and the other still clutching her Papa's hand as he lay on a stretcher. He would be fine, they told her over and over. Funny, he didn't look like he would be fine. But his hand was warm and she knew this was a good sign. Where was Georgie, she kept asking?

Pretty houses, both Minahasan traditional and Dutch, had dotted the area around the village. None of them were there now. The enormous tree she'd been dared to climb by the local boys was broken in half. The top part where she'd shown them a thing or two about British girls was missing all together. Even the smell of spice trees and damp jungle was gone. There were no barking dogs; no squawking birds; no instruments being played; no exotic sounds from the tropical forest. Instead, people screamed and wailed as they found the remains of their lives, histories and families. For Lettie, it was a terrible noise punching through the constant ringing in her ears. She'd never heard anything like it. She felt nauseous. Her eyes still stung.

The little lace dress she'd been proud to wear to church was black and filthy with mud. Her skin was abraded and bruised; not an uncommon state for her. Mother was going to be so angry. Lettie looked the same as everyone, still living or dead; the same as the leafless trees

3

that somehow stayed standing. Embalmed - mummified in hardening clay. Flurries of ash still blew in the wind, but much of the initial eruption cloud was dissipating high up in the sky and drifting out toward the Pacific Ocean.

A crack of thunder echoed down the valley. Lightning was shooting out from the thickest portion of the eruption cloud, near to the summit of the mountain, still fed by the volcano's belching and heaving. Streaks of hot white and eerie blue jumped from inside the cloud, cracking and spitting sounds out toward them. A thunderstorm with no rain, no hail, no storm. How very odd, Lettie thought for half a second. Lightning? It was so beautiful.

Howling broke her mesmerized stare at the volcano. A Dutchman was crying out to God, begging forgiveness for some sin or another, seeking comfort in believing he'd been bad and rightfully punished. He was bleeding. How stupid, she thought. One was punished by being sent to one's room or made to clean the stove one's experiment just dirtied, there was nothing one person could do that was so vile that God would punish an entire village, most of whom had done nothing wrong. It was stupid. What kind of a mean bully did this man think God was, she thought.

Looking over her shoulder again at the big mountain, she didn't feel angry. Wasn't this what volcanoes do? Explode. Spit out fire and smoke? Her school books said that much. Why be mad at it? This was what it was supposed to do. She was actually on rather good terms with the mountain, as children are unashamed of being. It had been pretty and she'd liked that the boys who had teased her hadn't been able to keep up as she'd climbed its lower flanks. There had been laughter, jokes, flowers, birds, sweet and curious smells … she liked the mountain and it liked her too. It was all very simple, really.

Glancing down at Papa, she felt suddenly responsible. An adult's feeling of responsibility. He could have climbed faster if she had been able to keep up. Running around in her old dress and well worn boots was one thing, but she'd been dressed in that lace concoction with a miniature cage hoop holding the hem out from her knees and a tiny corset … just like her mother's. Instead, she'd tripped on the hem and slipped around on the slick soles of her fancy slippers, and everyone was slower because of that. Too slow. Now he might not walk again, that was what the men kept saying in whispers she could hear. She'd learned enough of the language to pick out some words and the way they moved or pointed provided the rest of the translation. And where was Georgie? He'd been the first to come to their rescue, like one of King Arthur's knights. But he wouldn't have had to do it if she had just been faster and not a burden to her Papa.

Frantic efforts were underway across the road. A boy was trapped in the mud. Lettie could see them holding up his head, which was all that was sticking out. The weight of the mud was making it impossible for him to breathe with any ease. He appeared Dutch, though that hardly seemed important anymore. In the stories, everyone got rescued by the knight; that was how things worked. The hands gouging out the mud and holding him up, the voices speaking kindly to him, they were covered in gray soot too and it was hard to tell who was from where. It mattered only that they were here, now, helping the child.

They brought the boy water and tried to make him drink. He couldn't swallow; the mud was too heavy on his chest. Crying, struggling to breathe, he made every attempt to be brave. Lettie could only stand there, and watch as the breathing slowly stopped.

She'd never seen anyone die before.

Why didn't someone tell the villagers this was going to happen?

A woman screamed and wailed. It was Georgie's wife.

Lettie dropped her father's hand and walked away from the nice woman who was trying to help her. Georgie's wife was inconsolable. She flung herself down in the mud, over and over again, wailing in agony. Their son had nothing comforting to say, nothing at all. He just sat, staring.

Lettie could hear her, through her ringing ears, through the other horrible sounds. She wanted to say something. Instead, she stood there, morbidly unable to take her eyes off the gray arm that stuck out of the mud. That was Georgie's bracelet, with its beautiful patterns of color. That was Georgie's ring. That was Georgie's arm.

She couldn't remember any story where the brave knight died saving someone. Was this her fault? Her head began to spin as she tried to understand that the gruesome object, with all its very human features, wasn't a statue of modeling clay, like the pair of hands Mother had an artist sculpt for her and sat on the front parlor table.

Why hadn't someone warned them? It was, after all, what volcanoes do.

If no one else would do it, would warn others about this sort of disaster, then she would. She wouldn't blame God or devils. But how to know? She'd figure that out. She always worked out her puzzles and annoyed her math tutors by solving their problems too quickly. She could do this: she would do this. The idea made her feel better for all of a second before she looked down at Georgie's wonderful hand: the hand that could make shadow monsters and animals on a wall.

Papa was being looked after by someone who knew what to do for him. They wouldn't let her into the makeshift hospital. So, the eight-year-old sat down next to Georgie's wife and wrapped her arms around the woman. Someone needed to do that too. It was her responsibility.

Chapter 2

An Englishman with saffron-orange hair had picked up his little cousin and carried him away from the mob. They stood with fists and sticks but only watched as their victim was carried away, bloodied and limp. The Englishman had stepped in and now it wasn't safe for the mob to seek further revenge. If he was accidentally hurt they'd all be hunted down and imprisoned. Or worse. The Englishman, with his tailored suit and stern bearing was untouchable.

No one is safe anymore, Anish thought as his cousin was carried off. But it was all necessary - a necessary evil. There was such a thing as evil, he'd seen it in all its white-skinned and bloody glory.

Anish stayed in the shadows and kept watching the white man take his cousin further and further away, considering for a brief moment that he might actually be sorry. It was just as well that Rajiv was being taken away. The little boy was useless; always had been. Between the boy's age and the fact that he'd been coddled by his parents as the golden son, the pure one, his cousin would never be anything except useless. But Anish, the less desired and not-so pure son, would do the important things as he always did. He was only five years older than his cousin but that was enough for him to have experienced the world, to see that the British were evil and they had to be removed from his homeland.

Actually, he decided he wasn't sorry in the least that the nearly lifeless, little, useless boy was being carried off. The farther away, the better. Maybe the saffron-haired man would employ him as an amusing little servant, dressed like a tiny Maharaja in silk, fanning the English visitors who'd come to gossip, sweat, plot, and drink tea or alcohol. That's all they did. Fanning their fat white bodies was all they thought his people, the people of India, were good for. Or, for laboring in the hot sun so that some worthless nobleman far away could become rich. He hated them.

Anish crept in the shadows, using the fact that he was small to avoid the angry eyes now looking for another recipient of their fury. Being a 'child' was no deterrent to the mob; they wanted revenge for the upheaval, the destruction, and the death. His cousin's wounds were proof of that. They'd hit little Rajiv while he was cowering; they beat him while he was lying on the ground: they did this to a child of five years. Whether they recognized his cousin for who he was or simply who they suspected he was, they lashed out at him. Anish was quicker and older: he got away. His stomach began to knot and something vile worked his way up into his throat as he remembered those details. No, he didn't care; he couldn't care. He wasn't sorry.

The little boy had achieved one thing after all. He'd distracted the crowd.

The people had become placated under British rule, soft and pliable to English whims. They didn't understand that his father would bring back the rightful rule of an Indian Raj. This would lead to former hopes reinvigorated, glories reconstituted and any number of desirable outcomes. All so very simple. It depended entirely on the British being forced out. They were nothing but thieves anyway. Thieves deserved to die. It was just that simple. Certainly, there would be some pain in the transition but the end result was worth any risk or cost.

He slid behind a basket and crouched down in its shadow. He was hungry. His mother had no means to feed them, nor would she until they got to France and to her family. If the French were anything like his mother, then he would be satisfied with living amongst them for a while. They didn't like the British ruling India anymore than Anish did. He wouldn't stay in France for long. He would be back by his father's side, where he belonged, fighting and killing the British. His stomach growled. Yes, he was hungry. If he could find her then he would steal what they needed to eat. And there was nothing wrong with stealing food or anything else that was needed. It wasn't really stealing. He was the only son of the Raj, half-blooded though he was, and therefore owned it all anyway. Besides, what wasn't his by birth belonged to the British and was thus the spoils of a war in progress.

A man stepped between the sun and Anish. "I found one of 'em," the man said with a thick, low-caste British accent. They always sent their lowest caste to serve in his country, Anish thought; it was yet another attempt at humiliation. The British soldier reached down and grabbed Anish by the collar, dragging him out of his hiding place. "Look at the little bit, ain't got a muscle to call 'is own."

"*Nahi!*" Anish shouted then swore at the soldier, in the language of the Kings of Bundlekund, though he knew the low-caste man wouldn't understand.

"Don' ya want to see yer mamma, boy? We gots 'er already. Look at 'em, he don' look like no wog. Mighta' got past us."

Anish bristled at the reminder that he resembled his mother more than his father.

The soldier was joined by others and the remnants of the mob. Anish stopped struggling and stood up as straight as he could. He was the son of a prince. He would act like the son of prince. The low-caste man struck him across the face, knocking him to the ground. "Come on, yer High and Mightiness."

He hated them.

Chapter 3

The swampy ground was littered with bodies, filling in the gaps between the makeshift tents. Some of the skeletons were still alive and walking: barely. A prison cell, with bars and walls was better than the 'housing' provided for the unfortunate occupants. Walls were a luxury: they kept out the flies and the stench.

The Lieutenant was no longer shocked by it. Camp Sumter, Andersonville as the Union prisoners called it, was Hell and rotting corpses were its natural residents. He'd seen so many. He'd known their names. What was different this time was that some of those bodies were Rebels. And why did it have to be two of the few Rebels that were actually decent men? Decent men, Pitkern and Reynolds, Confederate guards who were picked off by snipers and lying half submerged in the mud. They hadn't been the ones who treated Union soldiers as human rubbish. Not everyone here was like the commandant, Henry Wirz.

Was God so far away and unmoved that the better men died while evil men lived? If only for a second, while he was forced to step over the pair of Confederate men who'd once willingly given up their own rations to save a Union man's life, Navy Lieutenant Thomas Turner was amused by the irony that he might have accidentally declared himself a 'better man.' He hadn't meant to; he was far too flawed to be a better man. Now it was too late for him to have such a high goal: he was a dead man. The Lieutenant slipped in the mud, nearly losing his footing, scraping his boot against Pitkern's frozen hand. Looking down, he apologized very sincerely; he didn't want to be disrespectful, but he was not in control of where and how fast he was moving. Did he really need to care? A dead man was a dead man, and beyond any worries about his empty carcass. Still, a man shouldn't disrespect the body of a fallen enemy; it simply wasn't done.

One good thing: all the shelling and gunfire meant that neither Commandant Wirz nor any one of his minions were going to spend any time out in the open, admonishing or gloating at the Lieutenant's followers, and that was a pleasing thought. It was highly unlikely they were even in the camp. Cowards. His men didn't deserve such disrespect; they were brave and honorable. But they were good as dead, too. Once he was executed, most of them would follow. The deliberation about their lives had taken little more than an hour as to which, the leader or the followers, would die first. A lesson had to be taught. A lesson, he thought, that evil wins?

Several shots blasted out from the distance, followed by bullets ricocheting off the few solid features in the camp. The Rebs escorting the Lieutenant quickened their pace, desperate to know where the next bullet was coming from and who would be the next to fall.

It had been decided far too quickly by the Confederate officers: the Lieutenant would die first as the example to the overcrowded prisoner-of-war camp, then one third of the "Regulators" would follow. The remaining two-thirds would be put to hard labor, their nearly skeletal forms forced to rebuild a fence they'd torn down in their escape attempt, the same fence demarking a three-foot zone inside the camp wall; something they called the Dead Line. If any of them survived, they were to tell other prisoners what swift justice awaited anyone who caused disruption in Hell.

He raised his unshaved chin as he was hauled past two rows of men he'd once commanded. Honest men. Regulators. Seaman Boone was amongst them. The man couldn't hold his liquor, Turner thought, but he was most loyal man in the Navy. The others he didn't know quite as well, but he had seen their courage, and had been inspired by it. Now, they had been lined up so that each could have a clear view. In the few eyes he dared look into, he saw the same confusion, anger, fear, hopelessness. He prayed that no one saw such things in his eyes. He knew that all that was left was resignation. He didn't feel the scalding fear he once had; his muscles weren't as rigid; his stomach had quieted; his head felt oddly clear as though he was already disconnected from the world of men. Accepting. It made things easier. There was no more to fight for. It was done.

In the five months he'd been a prisoner, Lieutenant Turner had learned that there were four types of inmates in Andersonville: those who were too weak, sick or dying to matter; the Raiders who terrorized their fellow Union soldiers, the Regulators who did their best to stop the

Raiders, and those men too new and in shock to understand what was happening to them. It had taken him one week to move from being in shock to being an active Regulator. He was thin, but not yet diseased or emaciated, so he fought. Killing would never become glorious, but he did it, to stop the vultures picking the bodies of their own kind. For Christ's sake, they were all Federal, they were all Union. Desperate to survive, yes, but they were still comrades in arms. The Raiders were nothing but demons and traitors, proof that evil resided here.

He was yanked by one arm up the steps. He really couldn't feel his hands or legs anymore, which he considered an acceptable thing. His guards were in a rush, looking around frantically, expecting at any second that a sniper would put a lead ball into their brains. Perhaps they'd get him by accident, saving them all the trouble of the execution.

The stockade one hundred yards away exploded into splinters and fire as a shell hit it dead on. Everyone dropped down into a fetal crouch, covering their heads and searching for the rain of debris which could do damage on its own. It was almost funny that in the few minutes many of them had to live, they would be so concerned that they might accidentally get killed. The Lieutenant liked observing all things ironic. Maybe a little bit of God was there for him after all, allowing him one moment of humor before he was dead. Slowly, everyone stood up and returned to what they were doing, which in his case was being killed, one way or another.

The rope they tied around his neck was new, stiff, inflexible, and looked as if it had never seen other use before this particular job. No preparations had been made because no one there knew what to do. A hangman's rope needed to be stretched and softened, worked well before being used. The knot had to slide easily. But they were too hurried and the temporary hangman was too concerned for his own neck. As the rope tightened and sharp needles of hemp scratched his throat, he began to feel his stomach again, which was not good. His entire body began to stiffen and his heart began to pound. How long was this going to take? He'd been calm, prepared, but now he was losing control over his fears. The Lieutenant began quietly repeating his father's favorite Psalm, despairing that it wouldn't help him maintain the dignity he sought to keep. He would not be afraid. Damn God and every angel, he wouldn't appear afraid.

A filthy rag was tied over his blue eyes, and his fright turned to rage.

Were his hands free he would have torn it off. No one asked him if he needed a blindfold and he was no coward. He didn't want it. If they couldn't stomach the appearance of his face once his neck was broken then they could just put that rag over their own damn eyes, though he did consider for a second that it might be good if the hangman kept his eyes open and his mind on his job. But the Confederate's mind wasn't on the business at hand; it was on the increasing bombardment and gunshots.

The front gates gave way in a blast that sent out a concussive wave the Lieutenant could feel through his whole body. The scaffold he was standing on shuddered. He was suddenly aware that, despite a day of solid resolution, acceptance and courage, he wanted the trap door to stay secure under his feet. He was not willing to die if he didn't have to. He wanted to live. Union troops were on the verge of entering the camp. There was no need for them to go through with this. Was it Sherman? Had he come to free the prisoners? Screams and shouts of panic met his ears though he couldn't see what was happening. Lifting his head up, he could see a tiny bit out from under the blindfold. Confederates who were assigned to watch him hang and then to shoot his men began abandoning their assignments to race for the front of the camp. Mortar fire began in earnest, ripping out sections of the rough hewn logs that made up the twelve foot stockade wall, spraying mud and splinters everywhere. Union forces were trying to open up the camp, allowing the prisoners to escape. It was a good tactic. In the confusion and multitude of escape routes, more prisoners could get out. The Rebs wouldn't be able to wrangle them like cattle in the meat houses. Cannon, detonating shells, muskets and repeating-action rifles all blended into one deafening, continuous assault on the ears and mind.

All of the Rebel soldiers were running in one direction or another. His men were no longer guarded. They would live if only they could avoid being hit by friendly fire. He called out to them to take cover. Look for a way out. He cried out to them, run!

Irony. The only Confederate to stay his post was too rushed or inexperienced to know that the knot goes under the left ear, not at the back. A measured slackness was required in the rope. And that an average size, underweight man, like the Lieutenant, needed approximately a six foot drop to break his neck. The only Rebel stalwart enough to keep to his job didn't have the knowledge to do it right. He heard his men calling as they raced back to him: someone, it was Boone, shouting to

13

grab his legs if he falls.

The trap opened: the door crashed into the side of the scaffold. The feeling of falling, dropping, was more horrible than he'd feared. His fall stopped abruptly, with his head jerked unnaturally, painfully to the side. His eyes wanted to burst from his head; cannon fire dissolved into a freakish ringing in his ears; his body thrashed violently trying to find footing that wasn't there. The stiff rope not only strangled him, it cut his flesh. What dread or hope raced through the Lieutenant's mind as he struggled was lost to unconsciousness.

Chapter 4

1875
Darmstadt School of Mining and Engineering
Darmstadt, Germany

Lettie Gantry read her letter for the fourth time and stared. The sound of her heart pounding and a pinching sensation across her abdomen was all she could feel. She stared at the letter. Some of the words appeared to be spelled wrong or unrecognizable, only because she'd read them too often. The piece of hair she'd given him in a locket, he'd given back. The expensive watch chain, she noticed, he'd kept. But what right did she have to demand its return; it had been a gift. Gifts were to be given with no expectation as to their use or status.

Sending her this letter was an act of cowardice, but possibly something she would have done too. Neither of them liked emotional confrontation. He had waited until she'd left her father's English house in Surrey and gone back to begin lecturing at her alma mater. Lecturing was part of the process of Habilitation, the German approach to training future professors. She had been so excited, distracted in very fact. The first English woman to enter Habilitation and only the tenth woman ever. She felt like a trailblazer, a term her father had used and just appealed to her sense of what was happening. She'd been so caught up in the pressure and elation of the moment that she must have missed the signs. He, Stafford Bingham, must not have been as happy as he'd let her believe.

But then, Stafford was rarely happy watching her. He wanted to guide, protect, and even to think for her. It was flattering, really, but so very unnecessary. She was quite capable of thinking on her own and wasn't that the reason he was attracted to her? He said he was admiring of her rational mind. She always behaved well, turned to him for advice as was expected, and kept generally quiet when around his family or friends. Certainly she wasn't a typical woman, but he had nothing to be ashamed of; it wasn't as though she was out parading around London demanding the vote. Yes, she was known in the British press for some of her more colorful adventures, but that was only to be expected. No matter how unique her behavior occasionally seemed, she was a lady and would do anything to maintain that image. She never travelled outside of the company of excellent men of good reputation. Even her father had accompanied her on nearly every trip until his health prevented him. Always she demurred to the advice of learned men. Of course she broke a few of the small rules such as those that were really quite illogical: the other rules of society she kept impeccably. Didn't she?

Yet, in the three years they had courted, much of that by correspondence between England and Germany, he had tried to dissuade her from her academic goals. She always believed his challenges represented his desire for her to strive for more and better. Holding the letter, with its inelegance and somewhat lazy grammar, she began to accept the truth. Stafford had no interest in a well-educated wife. She had tried so hard to help him understand. She wouldn't eclipse him. She would do as she had been taught: she would be the ideal wife, with a few unorthodox pursuits. Or would she?

Anne. He had shifted his affections to the girl who lived on the far end of his street. She was not yet twenty, fair haired, petite, and very wholesome. The girl had become a fixture at every party Stafford attended, every afternoon visit, and most days in general. Her habit of keeping her head down meekly while looking up through her eyelashes irritated Lettie. She'd viewed it as sheepish or manipulative, yet now she would have to amend her opinion; it was calculated and intentional. Anne understood Stafford much better than Lettie had. Anne was to be Stafford's wife. And Anne had worked very hard to get him.

His letter was certainly polite enough. And, as the distance between them had made theirs an informal engagement, he had no requirement to apologize or make amends to Lettie's family. Their future had only been assumed. Stafford had maintained an escape route.

She asked him, repeatedly, though not too frequently: was he happy? Were they doing well together? Were relations good? These were natural questions that he answered emphatically, yes. The letter said differently. He had told her what she wanted to hear and not what he meant. His penmanship was poor but his ability to deceive her, for her own good no doubt, was superior.

But, how could he do that to her? She had loved him and told him so. She had kept him in her thoughts even as she crafted answers to thorny mathematical examinations. She sent him appropriate correspondences and adjusted her behaviors to satisfy him. The only place she did not yield to his demands was in her education. Was that so much? She made herself fluid and flexible in all other ways, nearly eliminating her very self. What had he done for her? Grudgingly put up with her desire to fulfill a childhood promise and dream.

In honest retrospect, he hadn't supported her dreams; not really. She could see more clearly now what had actually happened between them. Stafford constantly badgered her about how she appeared to others. He never liked her curves and really wanted her to lose weight. He had at first liked her vibrant taste in clothing but eventually changed his mind to prefer a more dulled, marriage-appropriate style for her – something he could maintain on his governmental salary and would not offend his standing with his colleagues. He criticized her expectations, reminding her that she needed to learn to live more economically. Lettie had laughed and then described the austerity required during the months she spent in the field. He would adjust her hat, saying that she needed to take better care of her skin, pulling it down lower over her face, effectively hiding her. Pieces of jewelry were taken off and hidden in pockets if he felt she was 'too well dressed for her role in life as his soon-to-be wife.' When she laughed boldly and joyfully, he'd give her a look of disapproval: she was calling too much attention to herself. Discussion of science was drastically limited to their private conversations. And while not a very good dancer himself, he insisted on attending balls with her whenever she was in the country.

There was a telling memory: the dance held by Mrs. Baucher. The winter last. Stafford couldn't quite find the beat in the complicated waltz. As they passed the quartet he announced in a rather loud voice, "My dear, I really wish I knew what music you are dancing too, but you really should try dancing to the beat of this ensemble." Everyone heard him. Mortified into silence, Lettie just giggled and ignored the judgmental glares from those standing around the edge of the room. She'd spent the rest of the night wondering how she had mis-stepped; what had she done wrong? She always had a good sense of rhythm before.

Now it was very clear: she wasn't the one off tempo.

Oh yes, and if his affections had so easily and quickly moved to Anne, it meant that they had been secretly courting while he maintained his outward interests in Lettie. No, that was too easy a way to blame him. Even if it were true, she had not gone as far as was needed to secure his love. She would only have herself to blame. And her mother would be very disappointed, though hardly surprised. That was a letter she was not looking forward to writing.

Crying was not permissible, certainly not amongst potential professors. It would be seen as unseemly, feminine weakness. Lettie had her very first formal lecture in an hour. Swollen eyes, a runny nose, shaking hands? Unacceptable. The academia watching this oddity, a woman in Habilitation, would have neither respect nor sympathy for her. Her personal life was only of interest if it provided fuel for criticism. It had no place in the lecture hall.

At that moment she did something astonishing: she blew the candle out. It was gone. The flame was gone. And it would not reignite, not if she had a say in the matter. Maintaining an outward appearance of indifference and emotional neutrality was second nature to her. Why not apply that to love? Maybe that was what she'd done wrong with Stafford: told him that there was an emotional animal lurking beneath the proper appearances. No ... that too was an easy answer. Love was a cruel joke, she decided right then and there. She felt something quite physically snap.

In the darkness she fidgeted with her skirts as she always did when feeling awkward or afraid. Her left hand swept over the rough textures of the bracelet she kept hidden under her right arm sleeve. Georgie's bracelet. A gift from his family for her tears and her sorrows genuinely given so long ago.

She couldn't tear up the letter, nor would she keep it in the little red silk envelope she'd embroidered with such care under her mother's tutelage. The red silk envelope that she made as a child to keep love letters in because that was the ultimate goal of every girl. Fall in love, get married, have children. His farewell letter she folded and stuck into one of her books, to serve as a reminder and bookmark. It might as well be functional. The remaining contents of the silk envelope she tossed into the fireplace and the envelope itself was dropped into her valise. She was done with all that. For a time she sat, watching the edges of the paper turn brown and curl up, slowly disintegrating; wisps of smoke rising up from the flames and filling the room with the scent of a forest fire.

Dressed in a scholarly black gown and wearing her teaching robes, Georgie's bracelet tucked under her cuff, she walked out into the courtyard of the building, across the garden and up toward the lecture hall. The air was seasonably warm. Her hands were cold and numb.

Chapter 5

1875
Normandy, France

Gaston was probably not the best looking man in the area, but he was the largest in both height and breadth. For that alone he was consistently employed as a laborer. Carpentry, masonry, demolition; he was 'your man.' And he was clever enough never to overcharge and never to be slipshod in his results, unless of course, you weren't Norman, or at a minimum, French. Foreigners didn't know how to appreciate quality anyway, he thought.

But most of all, he was punctual.

Anish, though locally he'd been known by another name forced upon him, had hired the team of laborers to do something he knew they wouldn't understand. He didn't care. He paid: they worked. The mental capacity of the laborers combined into one brain would not surpass his intelligence so he simply couldn't care less what they thought. He'd known Gaston for many years. Not as one might know a friend but in vicious passing. Gaston was a pig. He sneered at Anish's darker skin tone and black hair, and had done nothing to hide his contempt. Such men as Gaston made Anish's childhood a living Hell. If it wasn't the British, it was the French he hated, Anish decided. Imperialists.

Gaston, who occasionally looked over at the young man standing on the hill, must have decided that today, for the sake of his salary, he would keep his ugly, racist mouth shut. Anish was paying very, very well. Too well. That should have worried them.

Now the foul old lady was dead. She actually stank in her last days. No one had come to claim the property yet, likely because Anish had bribed the lawyers into silence with promises of greater rewards. He collected her money, and valuables were sold off. There was quite a bit, considering she never spent a franc she didn't have to … at least not on him. But the old dame was in fact excessively rich. There were items that had been in the family for a century or more, and garnered an excellent price in the market. The land was sold very quickly for less than its value, yet well enough, it was the speed of the sale that was important. By the time Anish was done, all that had been for and of the family was scattered and unrecoverable. By the time anyone else in the family arrived to claim their inheritance, it would be long gone with him. He had plans.

But first there was the matter of the house. When the old lady, his maternal grandmother, took time out from the beating and berating, she would send for a laborer to do some task around the home and naturally it was Gaston who arrived … punctually. His nasty comments about the foreign boy would be right on time - punctual; just when his grandmother or distant cousins needed to be whipped up into righteous indignation and violence. It got to a point where Gaston even suggested appropriate ways to instruct Anish on proper behavior, which was to say, total submission. None of them remembered who Anish's father was. They were peasants with cash; he was the son of a prince. But, if it wasn't a French prince, none of them could have cared less.

Exactly on time, daily, Anish found himself alone in the pantry, terrified of what the bigger, angrier boys would do at Grandmama's orders or Gaston's suggestions. It was the schedule of his nightmarish life… always right on time.

Watching them stove in the windows and shake their heads in confusion, Anish loved the sound of splintering wood and shattered glass. Every hole punched into the structure, every beam broken down, lightened him of the burden of memory. Grandmama had found him more than once in the window box, his other hiding place beyond the pantry, and thereafter decided to lock him in for hours at a time whenever it pleased her. His place of refuge became a torture chamber, seemingly smaller and smaller as each day and year passed when he was punished with hours in the box. The lid pressed on him, crushing him, the inability to move or stretch caused unbelievable pain. The punishments never fit whatever crime he was supposed to have committed. But his anger helped him to survive. In the dark or light, it didn't matter; he kept his mind focused on two things. Revenge was naturally the first, but even those thoughts could not block away the pain or the suffering his mother's family inflicted on him. Ships, locomotives, engines; these with their intricate designs and requirements dragged his thoughts down to a single, insulated point. There his mind could stay, freed from the pain of his body, just as the Indian mystics would do. He'd seen them in his father's house; aesthetics and yogis, able to endure great afflictions without registering such in their minds. It was powerful and though Anish had no formal training in their ways, he believed himself capable of discovering those ways on his own. Yes, there were things the Europeans would never comprehend.

He'd known she was dying. He came back to watch her die. He blocked visitors from the house, interrupted any attempt she made to contact family, and stood staring at her as she drew her last breath. She'd saved up enough energy to curse him, but he had abandoned believing in the supernatural some years before and only laughed at her. He could keep her death a secret for only a week, but that was more than enough time.

Anish smiled, thinking of how the despicable cousins would arrive from war-devastated Paris in a few days to find nothing. Absolutely nothing. No gold or jewelry. No money. No house. No land: he'd sold it two days earlier to a speculator who was hardly likely to sell it back at the original price. Nothing was left that had made them a family with name or importance. No safe haven from the destruction wreacked by the Prussians on Paris. Absolutely nothing. He'd erased them from the present and thus the future: quietly and almost legally. It served them right.

He would have preferred setting fire to the house, but that was obviously illegal and would have landed him in jail. Another tiny space with no air and plenty of danger. He shook for a moment. Dizziness washed over him and he fought the panic away. No, demolishing the house of pain was much more satisfying. Brick by brick.

The project was on day two and the laborers, lead by the pig Gaston, had managed to demolish the whole front of the structure.

"Stop!"

The men froze in place and glared back at Anish. Strolling forward, dressed in clothing more valuable than the homes each man lived in, he pushed past them. There, half covered in rubble was the box. The lid was delicately carved with numerous stars and a great sun in its center. The wood, appropriately, had blackened over the years. It would become the image of his past and future; his motto for life: his flag.

The window box. How he suffered in that dismal place. Looking at it made him sweat. He could feel its sides closing in.

Anish snatched the sledgehammer from Gaston's hands and attacked the carved little window box with all his strength. It cracked and ripped as he pounded it; over and over again. It had been so small. He had been so small. Once he was too big to be brutalized and locked inside, she'd handed him a purse of coins and ordered him away. The coins were payment of a debt the old woman owed his mother. He had been certain the value was incomplete and there was no doubt that the spirit of the payment was not kept.

For months after he'd left the old lady's house to seek his own way, he couldn't sleep in rooms with low ceilings. Windowless corridors made him sick. He wasn't even able to use a water closet without becoming violently ill. But he would not let this defeat him. He trained his mind and his body to resist the fear. In the process he made himself powerful. Teachers he'd sought after showed him techniques. Honing his mind, his focus, was extremely effective. To do this he would design, create, draw and build anything and everything he imagined. In short time he astonished his teachers with his exceptional mental capacity and astounding body strength. Yet, he never lost his discomfort with enclosed spaces. If he could get away with it, he would never sleep anywhere again but out in the open.

The box lasted a minute, maybe two but no longer than that, before it was reduced to splinters. Without a word to the laborers, whom he saw as beneath him, he shoved the hammer back at Gaston and walked away. Up the hill and away.

"Here now," Gaston called, then added, "Monsieur. We've not been paid."

"You haven't finished and my representative told you that payment would be received when the job was done. Not a moment sooner. Your pay is awaiting you. Just finish!"

"It had best be. We know lawyers, too."

"You are being compensated appropriately. Perhaps more so than you deserve. Stop complaining like the old woman."

Gaston winced at the comment. He had actually liked the old lady. He didn't like the foreign child she'd been saddled with.

"You'll get your money." Anish knew he was lying; that was likely one of the reasons he didn't bother to turn around, in case it showed on his face. He was lying. In two days he would be on a ship headed toward the Pacific with all the money, yet another new name, and no regrets if someone were injured or inconvenienced or frauded. They owed him.

At the top of the hill was the only friend he had; an old Oak tree with twisted branches and thick clusters of leaves. Many a time he'd gone there when he could escape the house or the window box. Few could see him unless they knew where to look. There he felt the fresh air on his face and hands, and watched birds flying free. As he was not sentimental, he did not remain to look at the tree or the house. He had a ship to catch and a branch of his family to forget. Not truly family – not before and not now.

His hand lingered for a moment on the huge tree trunk.

Six months after the demolition of the house, all that the family could claim was an outrageous unpaid bill to the laborers who had destroyed the house and now refused to rebuild it until they were compensated, harassing visits from angry lawyers, several creditors' notes including those of a Parisian tailor, and a newspaper article anonymously sent to one cousin reporting the wreck of a ship called the *Prometheus*. Under other circumstances, not one of them would have cared. The ship, it was said, had floundered near a group of South Seas islands and had been destroyed. All hands were lost, including a passenger who resembled their cursed cousin: the foreigner, the thief. Most importantly, all the money he had taken sank with the *Prometheus*. They would recover nothing, inherit nothing, had no one to punish, and were considering a midnight escape out of France, just ahead of the debt collectors.

Chapter 6

Lettie tossed the *London Herald and Observer* down with disgust and no small amount of resignation. Quickly, she recovered her composure and flattened her expression in that practiced way. The number of reported dead was already huge and still growing, and there was nothing to be done about it. The tragedies enumerated on the front page were vulgar in their publicity yet painful in their truth. Horror always sold newspapers. Georgie's bracelet was wound around her fingers, being manipulated as though it were a rosary. She fidgeted with it all the time, if not fidgeting with her skirts. Her face however was the epitome of indifferent confidence.

How ironic: the most unwomanly occupation supported her ideal feminine behavior. Science was unemotional and a lady of quality did not show any feelings.

With that same neutrality, she told the members of the British and American Geological Societies there would be an eruption. She'd written detailed analyses of her methods and how they applied to the situation. When, they asked her? Exactly when would the volcano erupt? And that was the question she couldn't answer with any certainty. The signs were there, in the reports she'd received. Ground shaking. Sulfur in the air and water. Increased fumarole activity. Changes in the amount of run-off from the glaciers and snow pack. And a misshapen portion of the crater floor. She'd fit them into the complex equations of her Prediction Model. 'Soon,' was the best she could offer. But when exactly, they demanded? The mountain had shown all those signs before and yet not erupted. Why did she believe now it would?

Those were not foolish questions.

The now famous, and unfortunately somewhat infamous, Letticia Margaret Makepeace Gantry could do no more than offer statistics, possibilities and percentages. It meant nothing to the town councilmen from the communities around the volcano that would need to be evacuated. Loss of harvesting days, potential robberies, and several thousand displaced families all needing water, food and shelter meant everything. The task was too big and too expensive to be initiated on one woman's notion that the volcano would erupt ... 'soon.' And just who did she think she was, they demanded? Why didn't she know her place? None of the real scholars, all wholesome men of learning, were making such predictions. Women are not capable of understanding the complexities of science and most especially math. And just how old was she, this unmarried female? Spinster, was she?

Think rationally, woman. That is your strength, she was once told by a rather open minded professor who also observed that she was above her sex in matters of logic. Being 'above her sex' was not a role she desired, nor did she accept that women were naturally illogical or unsuited for science. She rolled the beads of Georgie's bracelet between her fingers, repeating the words 'be rational' over and over in her mind.

Prediction is neither guaranteed safety nor prevention, she reminded herself. Scientific theories were reasoned conclusions, not some ridiculous opinion pulled out of a hat. She had done her best, hadn't she? Yet, it hurt to read about them, all the people who had died. And, in this instance, her Prediction Model had come close to working - so very, very close.

Not close enough. And she hadn't pushed her prediction as hard as a man would have, she was certain. She felt like a coward for not demanding their respect and attention the way one of her male colleagues would have. She wasn't a man.

Taking a deep breath, she looked out the window at the dull sky and allowed it to cry for her. Tears were not something a future professor could afford. Beyond the glass, bare limbs and twigs waved slowly in the afternoon breeze. The weather was clearing, enough to encourage some people to venture out of doors, including the two crazy engineers who lived nearby. She rather liked them, even if she had trouble understanding them. Drink and a heavy rural Welsh manner of speaking created some very colorful, if unintelligible, descriptions of what they were working on this time. Whatever it was bellowed steam and smoke.

The fire built up early that morning in the fireplace had died down to bright, glowing hot embers that smelled smoky sweet. She could feel the residual heat through the leather of her shoes. Was that what the victims had felt? Had they felt anything at all? Or did they know that the searing heat was boiling away every ounce of liquid in their bodies? She should have done more.

Lettie got up so quickly that she nearly knocked over the small table with her breakfast and a copy of one of the best adventure biographies written by her new favorite French biographer Jules Verne *Twenty Thousand Leagues under the Seas*; finally, correctly translated into English. Like so many of those types of biographies, it was more fiction than fact, designed for the interest of schoolboys and science aficionados. Still, there had to be some truth. At least this translation got the title right – no one went under the water, twenty thousand leagues straight down. The title referred to the distance traveled while under the water. *Under the Seas*: plural.

She balanced herself against the table. Verne's book wasn't a very romantic biography; in fact there were no women in the book at all, and if any character was actually married it was never stated, but it was well written and a break from her preferred reading materials of geologic texts or impossible love stories.

Her father steadied her by the elbow. He'd come in, quietly, probably hoping not to disturb her thoughts. He could have asked about many superficial things, as most polite families were wont to do when avoiding the discomfort of intimacy. But not him. "What are you thinkin'?" He looked as if he was bracing for the answer.

"Exactly what you know I'm thinking: my model didn't work, Papa."

"It nearly did. You were close."

"Not close enough." She allowed him to help her back into her comfortable chair. Her leg was not quite healed. "This is so utterly illogical of me. Am I being hysterical and not reasonable in the least?" She managed a smile for him.

Mr. Gantry set his cane down on the table and picked up the paper to read the headline: 'Death Toll Rising Daily.' He smiled weakly, un-amused by the report and knowing what effect it would have on Lettie. "I've never known you to be hysterical. Too self critical an' driven. You've always maintained your dignity."

Lettie reached out and took his hand. "Thank you. It's good to hear it, even from one's father."

"Did you expect me to say somethin' negative?" His American drawl was gentle and sometimes soothing.

"No. That is the point, isn't it? I daresay I'd be very disappointed if you didn't tell me something supportive. Isn't that what fathers are for?"

"I like to think so." He watched her very carefully, looking for signs he knew too well. The old bracelet was the surest sign. She was prone to anxiety; she'd never outgrown it, she'd only learned to hide it very well. In the world, especially the academic world, she never had time to be doubtful or worried. Sedentary and isolated at home, playing the role of an upper middle class lady and temporary invalid, there was little else to do but endlessly entertain curious visitors and write letters. The newspapers were constantly hounding her for the very latest in her adventures, which only served to titillate or offend the masses no matter how careful she was to present only the clearest facts.

"Stop worrying," she said a bit wryly, recognizing familiar expressions and posture. "Once I'm well, I'll throw myself back at the Model. It will work." She sat and began fussing needlessly with her skirts. "In the meantime, I will play the role of Miss Gantry, hostess and social reliquary."

"All the while plottin' your escape to academia?"

"None of this can compete with the seduction of delicious research and inquiry. Except of course, time spent with you. As it is, we get so little."

"And that, daughter-of-mine, is what the postal and telegraph systems are for."

Gantry picked up the latest Verne biography. How much was fact and how much was embellishment? Adventure-Biographers were quite notorious for filling in the missing information with ridiculous fantasy and conjecture. If Letticia didn't take the book with her, he'd have to give it a read. A good distraction for him as he would miss her so terribly. It would give them something other than rocks to correspond about, though any letter of any topic was a pleasure for him.

This recent volcanic event would be the last allegorical straw for his daughter. Now there was a fire in her, he could see it in her face. It was a relief. Her mother and the rest of the family would be mortified, but he wouldn't. And it would likely speed her recovery. The original cure had nearly done more damage than the rockslide had, but that terrible time was in the past. They did not speak of it. His daughter was neither a slight woman nor a robust woman, but she was nimble and wise enough to keep from getting killed he hoped - he prayed.

The door knob turned. The handle clicked. Lettie stuffed the bracelet in her pocket and folded her hands.

Mrs. Gantry swept into the room, a flurry of ruffles, ribbons and rose water. She quickly looked up and down at both father and daughter and smiled, quite satisfied that both appeared to be dressed and prepared for visitors. Catching sight of Gantry's cane, she scowled for a moment. Theodore and Lettie knew the look of disapproval.

The scowl remained.

"My dear?" he asked.

"Theodore, do remove your walking stick from the table and have Hughes take those dreadful papers away. It's upsetting to Letticia. I'm certain someone will be calling today. I won't be here so please ..."

She let the comment stop.

Lettie winced. What her mother wasn't saying was, "Please don't embarrass me." Even unsaid, the implication stung. She forced a soft smile back onto her face. There was no point commenting on it.

"Of course, my dear. Are you seein' Mrs. Pritchard?" Gantry asked casually. Not that he particularly cared and, in fact, was surprised he remembered the woman's name, but he was expected to ask.

"Certainly. She's finally back from London and I would be remiss if I didn't drop in. I do wish you both could come with me." Actually, she didn't but it was the proper thing to say.

Gantry nodded. Mrs. Gantry was an expert in all things socially correct. She always looked correct, knew the correct things to say and do, and the correct way of speaking – she'd forced every semblance of Welshness out of the house, which was a shame but necessary for the family's social ascent. As she put on her gloves he remembered why it was he'd fallen in love with her. Age hadn't diminished her looks, and despite all the external trappings of frigid respectability and aloof propriety, she still regarded him lovingly, in her own way. She was a handsome Welshwoman even if she didn't speak like one anymore. Proper, upper class British was only spoken now, though she had finally given up trying to wean him from his Yankee speech. Her green eyes still glittered and her black hair, though streaked in places with gray, was as shiny and luxurious as it had ever been. She was petite, which only made the pair even more amusing by appearance. He was a giant in the community at six feet and six inches. She always seemed to be looking up to him literally, if not figuratively.

"Gwendolyn dear, do you have enough of my cards?" A silly question for him to ask because of course she did, but it was the proper thing to ask. "I would appreciate your leavin' an extra for Mr. Pritchard. I hope that he and I can do a bit of shootin' when the weather lets up."

"Naturally. I will be glad to let him know." Mrs. Gantry adored it when he asked her to manage his social communications. He wasn't a buffoon socially, but he was still an American and, after all, there were just going to be limits. She whispered in his ear as she kissed him on the cheek, "Don't let her start talking about science. It bores most people. And please don't let her tell about … her accident."

"Of course my dear." It would be an impossible task as that was the exact reason Lettie had visitors these days.

Lettie heard them. "Have a lovely time, Mother." Lettie started to stand up.

Mrs. Gantry looked concerned then quickly masked her emotions. "Sit down, please. You'll never heal if you don't rest." She looked again at her daughter. "Pale yellow is a nice color for you. You really look …" she struggled for a moment to find the right word. "…pretty."

Did it have to be such a labor for her to come up with a compliment? Lettie looked down at her dress, a stylish single piece, princess-seamed gown of yellow Indian cotton. It was a walking length train covered with rows and rows of pleated, white organza she'd pulled around her feet to cover them, and the dress's neckline was tastefully cut to a pleasing depth without showing too much. No one on her Mother's side of the family seemed to feel she was a great beauty, and said so frequently in earshot, but that would never stop Lettie from making up for it with the most fashionable attire. That much pleased her Mother.

"Cook has some nice cake prepared today; be sure to have it sent up." She swept out of the room leaving a soft fragrance of roses behind.

Mr. Gantry shook his head. "She called you pretty."

"I was amazed too."

"But of course she is right. That's a nice color on you." He set the book back down. "Think anyone is comin'?"

"Only if they want to specifically ask about the accident. I doubt Mother has mentioned the … other problem."

"No, she definitely hasn't. It would be social suicide and honestly, I don't believe she'd injure you by tellin'."

"True." Injuries would be done in much more collusive ways.

He touched her hair. "She may not compliment you, daughter-of-mine, but I know she loves you very much."

"Oh, I've come to terms with that. A bit too old now to be worried what Mama thinks of my marriage prospects and the like," she lied with ease.

Hughes entered the parlor, looking rigid and efficient. "Sir, Mrs. Gantry needs you for a moment."

Gantry winked at his daughter. "More instructions, for my ears only."

Lettie winked back. "She is the expert, and we shouldn't discount the volume of knowledge she has accumulated."

Her father left the room but Hughes stayed. "Is there anything I can get you, Miss Lettie?" He always called her 'Miss Lettie' when Mrs. Gantry wasn't in hearing range. Otherwise it was the proper 'Miss Gantry.'

The fire had been lit, no putting it out now. "Would you arrange for my trunks to be taken out of the downstairs and put in my room?"

"For the Sutton house?"

"Yes."

"May I assume you'll want your research packed separately?"

"You know me too well. Yes, thank you. I'm not entirely certain when I shall leave but it will be in the next day or two."

He nodded with a slight bow and much hidden regret.

Lettie found herself alone again in the parlor, feeling as though a storm had just moved through. Her mind worked its way back to the people of Mt. Cotopaxi. She really had failed them, hadn't she?

If she had just been stronger? Braver? Aggressive? Could a woman be effective in these situations and still feminine? Lettie really despised weakness, most especially in herself.

As for the eruptions, no act of Nature was her fault and to think such a thing was beyond arrogance. If anything, the event should galvanize her and wake up the doubters. By now everyone in Britain had read of the tragedy in one or more of the papers, which were a direct result of the many innovations in communications. News travelled faster than ever by way of underwater cables; from Australia to London in a day or less via the telegraph. From Calcutta to New York in the same time. Of course, tragedy flowed at an even quicker pace.

Lettie stopped at the glass-enclosed bookcase, and stared at the blurry reflection. Too dark. Her black hair was typical of the Welsh and an exact copy of her mother's, but her sun-stained skin was not. Too thick and round in her figure, she was told. Yet, Lettie was generally in good health, plus or minus a constant series of injuries, most not very serious. Still, she looked very womanly. And her mother was right about one thing: the pale yellow was a good color for her.

Though over thirty years old, she was still young enough to do all the hard physical work that would need to be done in the field, at least once she had healed completely. Samples were always a challenge to collect and now the methods of photography were such that an amateur could take excellent pictures if they didn't mind carrying all that equipment up the sides of the mountains. It was definitely hard work, outdoors in an often treeless environment breathing in toxic air. She certainly wasn't afraid of that. It did, however, have the unfortunate effect of darkening her appearance and making her look a bit masculine.

It wasn't as though there was a husband in her life who desired to prevent her escapades, though she could say with pride that she did not adventure out without proper approvals and in the best company. In fact, the most significant man in her life provided for his strange daughter's behavior and unfeminine interests in worldly things, such as advanced education. She really was a free woman in a society that loved and loathed free women – free to take on almost anything and everything. Within reason. With approval.

Lettie limped quickly from the room, listing the things she would need to pack out loud, and up the stairs to her bedroom, leaving a confused maid and her Papa in the entryway.

Gantry shook his head. In so many ways, Lettie was like her beloved volcanoes: quiet and seeming safe, then explosive. She had a temper, which being raised as a lady she'd kept within strict confinement, but what lay beneath that proper exterior was an often well founded fury. He always wondered if she liked volcanoes because she was of such a similar existence or if it was that the mountains were ultimately equitable toward all genders. The danger terrified him, of course. When she'd been brought home this last time with no feeling in her left arm and a gash the length of her thigh, he was ready to forbid her from ever leaving the house, he didn't care how old or educated she was.

Good God, she was accident prone. Always was.

Outside, on the street, a steam whistle blew. Gantry pushed the curtain aside to see two of his neighbors from down the street pulling up a cover over the engine of what looked like a miniature omnibus. It was ten feel long, had a portion of a couch strapped to it for seating, two small spoke wheels in front, and two gigantic wheels in the back. A canvas cover was not very helpful in fending off the rain. In several places the couch appeared singed or burned. Gantry's neighbors were arguing over the source of locomotion: the basic steam engine. While Gantry flattered himself a bit by believing that he understood much of the process of steam locomotion, he wasn't arrogant enough to believe himself an expert. Despite this, it didn't require an expert understanding to see that something was wrong. Steam was jetting out in all directions. Gantry tried not to laugh. For a moment, he thought about going out to see if he could help. He would never understand a word either was saying, but much pointing and waving would do just as well. Instantly, the Misters Lewin and Llewellyn shut the engine cover, hopped into the conveyance, and sputtered off in a wildly violent and jerking motion. If Gwendolyn knew they were up to such things, she'd demand someone to move from the neighborhood immediately. And it would not be her.

There probably wouldn't be any visitors today. Most of the fashionable people had heard about Lettie's climb of Mt. Vesuvius and narrowly escaping a minor but destructive eruption. And there was the intermittent rain.

'Andean Volcano Buries Thousands.' There was more. Mt. Cotopaxi, however that was pronounced, in South America had exploded, burying villages and people in layers of ash and mud. Gantry shivered. The sound: he remembered the sound of rushing mud. The Cotopaxi eruption had been so enormous that the mud had flowed over 100 kilometers to the ocean. It was the second such disastrous eruption. Some giant of a mountain further south, called Llullaillaco - again, the pronunciation - had killed or dislodged the people living nearby.

The journalist had nothing approaching the academic knowledge Letticia had, but he hadn't let that slow him in developing a hypothesis of his own. The journalist pointed out a strange rumor of a curious storm being associated with both eruptions – perhaps a sign from the heavens that the eruption was eminent. For Heaven's sake.

Science should have been able to predict such an event: that's what Lettie would be thinking. And she would be thinking it was her responsibility. Of course she'd say it was her failure to create a simple equation or model for predicting eruptions and then to use it to warn those living in the vicinity. Simple? Perhaps to her. But her mind didn't work like other people's minds. She had taught herself to see everything through a veil of science, hypothesis, and mathematics. The rocks spoke to her and she could interpret their messages as though she were some biblical prophet. Her mother forbade the subjects of anything scientific at the dinner table.

He could hear her footsteps causing the floorboards to creak above him. The moment had come; she would take the next step: against odds, social rules, and even her family's protestations, she would head back to Academia. Back to her books. Back to her hopes and plans.

Gantry smoothed out the paper and smiled absently. This was no longer the world of limitation. If a man could circumambulate the globe in under eighty days; if miniaturized, steam powered machinery could industrialize the world; and if a man could create a submersible warship, then one determined young lady could breech the barriers of academic institutions and predict volcanic eruptions.

Gantry stretched his long back, which actually bent slightly to the right. Well over six feet tall, his spine had not been supported by a bulky torso and had begun to fatigue under the strain of a well proportioned set of shoulders and head. The injuries he'd suffered in the Indies had only made things worse, leaving him with a cane as a constant companion. His hair was gray now, and he felt no shame at any of the numerous wrinkles or lines that filled his face from years of abundant smiling and laughing. His tailor was generally at a loss as to how to build such tall trousers and long waistcoats that did not look out of proportion. But for his wealthy American client, the tailor was determined to succeed. And, he did. It was that same lanky height that attracted his wellborn Welsh wife, over whom he stood at least a foot if not more. Her only complaint at the time was that he gave her a sore neck having to stare up at him.

Yes, he'd have to re-read Lettie's monograph on volcanic ash types, which barely made it into publication but was in print none the less. That would make their soon-to-be long distance correspondence much easier. Lettie tended to forget that her father, though a scholar in his own right, didn't speak the language of rocks.

No man had greater pride in his offspring. None!

Chapter 7

The Times, both London and New York, held that the first year of the new decade had been a stunning success of human endeavor and triumph. Never mind that the decade technically began in 1881, their readers were less interested in such nit-picking than they were in finding reasons to celebrate. The Age of Invention was upon the civilized world and most people were relatively happy to brag about it but reluctant to allow such inventions to disrupt their daily routines.

The headlines had boasted that two Welshmen, Lewin and Llewellyn, had challenged both Prussian and French locomotion engineers to a race around the globe using the latest in propulsion development. It was absurd, and it had already been put off until next year due to technical difficulties faced by all the teams. Next, they would be claiming to be able to fly without gas-filled balloons to hold them aloft. The old men grumbled over and over about the nonsense, while standing outside the Club. Inside, they could neither speak nor make any offending noises as required by Club rules. And any opinion that considered progress a good thing would be offensive.

As with any time of radical changes, there would be some who felt that change was itself an evil.

One man in particular had concluded that humanity in flux was evil, tradition was evil, and the future held only one important concept: that mankind was capable and likely to destroy itself. Good riddance.

He sat quietly of course, wanting no company. His tall stature was renowned. Carefully cut, pale brown hair never crimped or bent under the constant wearing of his tall hat. His skin tended to be very pale since he spent little time out of doors. He was a manicured, tailored salute to the proper English gentleman. His hands had no signs of labor to them. His every movement spoke of British superiority. He never removed his gloves in public and kept his hat nearby as though he might leave at any moment, yet he stayed for hours at a time. He rarely changed in his daily habits, though now he was wearing a black armband.

No one spoke to him and he chose not to speak to any of them; and not only because of rules. Those members, who thought they had escaped him from the 'other' club, would glare at him from just over the tops of their papers or glance angrily over their shoulders during their silent card games.

The Diogenes Club was a place of refuge, where the slightest noise could get one expelled. Silence was far more than golden. Serving staff wore cork soled shoes to make certain that their individual footsteps were not disruptive. Members were required to change into slippers to achieve the same effect. Linen gloves were in profuse usage and newspapers carefully handled to avoid that distinctive crumpling noise.

After losing to *that* man, many of the transferred members had hoped to redeem their reputations as proper gentlemen by joining another well-established, though distinctly odd club. Thanks in no small part to *that* man, they were poorer in both money and person. Thanks to *that* man. He'd won the 'Bet': they'd lost. They had to abandon their old club for the sake of their reputations, if not their bank accounts. Embarrassment forced them to avoid fashionable restaurants and their tailors had taken to pestering them for unpaid bills for fear that they would not ever be able to pay them. It was beyond intolerable. And *that* man had followed them to the Diogenes. It was not to be borne, save for one tragic event.

Now they were gloating quietly. And they hated him as much as ever.

He had no use for them. He really had no use for the Diogenes Club either except that he couldn't bring himself to spend any time at home. His old club had asked him to quietly and quickly resign. Diogenes was picky about three things: social status, money, and the ability to be quiet. He was admirable in all three areas.

And, it was blissfully quiet, but so too would be a grave. He'd spent too much time in the cemetery. He should raze both the old club and his house and any other offending edifice to the ground: burning every effigy of his misery. That would offer some satisfaction.

Those who had lost the bet to him believed themselves to be the very best of humanity, the height of civilized mankind. They were fools, idiots, worthless. But to his mind, they did indeed represent what mankind had become. Cold. Vicious. Greedy. Willfully stupid. If he needed proof, the headline of the Times announced that someone had planted a flag at the top of the Great Pyramid of Egypt, as though claiming it for himself. A huge black flag, with a giant gold sun and scattering of stars. No nation had such a flag. As if no one had found that flag planting worthy of notice, the same someone had announced it with a blare of trumpets just in case. The arrogant man who did this was certainly clever if not brilliant, but wasted his genius planting a flag ... a flag. Such a man was able to get to the top of the Great Pyramid without notice, without sound, without a trace of footstep or equipment. For a flag?

Was this all that mankind was capable of? Mankind was incapable of evolving as rapidly as the technology. And he had had enough of it all. Mankind was not headed to Hell, it was the Devil and was home already. Mankind needed to disappear into the mists of time, extinct and forgotten.

Thus he sat alone in his club, still dressed in prescribed mourning attire long after a husband's required period of grief had passed, contemplating how this decade would be the Age of ... nothing. The 'Last' Age. And that suited him just fine. He continually checked his watch. This was a habit his wife had tried to break him of, and now that she was gone he did it twice as much. It was comforting. There was connection to the flow of life by noting every precise minute and hour.

Looking at the window, blocked by deep velvet fabric closed against the freezing cold, through a small parting between the curtains, he could see the blackened snow falling. Heavy, industrially mutated flakes cast shadows on the window that were too big be hidden from view. Ghostly waves of light and dark fell down the inside of the drapery. This was what mankind provided to the world. Industrial outrages that changed the very nature of London's weather. So-called advances that caused more damage than they solved. Ugliness: nothing but ugliness wherever humanity interfered.

Yet humanity could be damned lucky and despite its horrific behavior it survived.

Perhaps the Last Age needed assistance? He didn't believe in the Second Coming of Christ or any of the fairytales of the Apocalypse, but he liked the idea of them.

He would have to change. P. Fogg was a wreck and a relic, unnecessary for the tasks to come. First he'd need to die; certainly as far as anyone was concerned. Then he'd come back in a new guise, one that no one would recognize. He'd have his own Second Coming, but no one would want it, pray for it, or think of it as a gift from God. He quietly set down his paper, looked around the room, checked his watch and bid it a hateful farewell.

The Club Steward found a black armband lying on the floor, just under the reading table, where it had been discarded.

Chapter 8

The wind was blowing hard enough for the strands of her hair to become a whip that scraped and abraded her skin. It was the least of her worries. Ahead of her lay a stretch of volcanic ground that was neither level nor solid. Fragments of scoria and pumice covered the ground once smoothed from age. Thin layers of fine ash coated everything and created a false sense that the land was safe to walk on.

The air was moist and felt unbelievably thin. Perhaps it was simply the lack of oxygen in combat with the other toxic vapors that made it feel that way. Or that the volcano was over 1,000 meters above sea level. Her blouse clung to her chest and neck while droplets slid down her back and under her working corset. Lettie wiped a sheen of perspiration off her forehead and pushed her wide brimmed hat down firmly.

Mt. Tarumae had been busy the last month or so, with plumes of white smoke billowing from its crater, and that had local authorities very worried: the mountain was normally silent. In fact, the last time Tarumae was at its volcanic best was 1739. The entire mountain erupted then in a catastrophic explosion that caused the volcano to collapse into a deep, one and a half kilometer-wide caldera.

Lettie stared up at the summit of the newest volcanic edifice, or at least where it was supposed to be, and considered the frightening processes that had generated a new volcano inside the remains of the old one, then collapsed it, built it again and allowed a lava dome to grow deeper inside; all within 142 years. Geologically speaking, that was only a moment ago. So many geophysical structures in one place. John Milne called it a Triple Volcano. Caldera, partially collapsed vent, new lava dome: from the air it must have looked like a poorly drawn shooting target.

Her prediction model gave it a slightly better than fifty percent chance of a large eruption, with better odds reserved for a smaller event. Larger or smaller? The distinction seemed petty while standing just below the rim of the vent crater, wondering if the lava dome inside could or would explode.

She would have to include that description in her next series of articles for Punch and the Scientific Weekly. Lettie really couldn't complain about having to include such dramatic details since at the very least her work was being bought and distributed to thousands of readers. If the articles reporting her work were a little melodramatic in depiction they were twice as descriptive in scientific terms. She insisted on it. Such articles and a monograph had paid for this latest foray. They paid for many things, giving her a moderate sense of independence.

Every step started with a frightening crunch of freshly cooled lava rock and often ended with most of the material sliding out from under her foot or collapsing altogether. The path to the summit was no longer viable for the average tourist. Which was good; tourists did not need to be there. Certainly not now.

Looking back over her shoulder, she could see Professor Toshiro Murakami sifting through the rubble for the best exemplar of rhyolite, a porous stone dark with violent textures due to its acidic nature.

"Large quantities of gases," he called over to her, demonstrating his point by breaking the blood brown rock easily with his hammer. "Too much air and gas. No substance."

Gas bubbles had overwhelmed so much of the molten material during an earlier small eruption that it had created a rock consisting mostly of air pockets, with very little strength in its structure. That fact was worth worrying about. Lettie looked down at her feet, realizing that nothing she was standing on was capable of supporting her weight for any substantial length of time. And forget the ash as a plausible cushion should they slip or fall: it was too powdery fine to provide any protection against the sharp edges of the rocks.

The 'fumaroles' were belching out steady plumes of noxious gases that reeked of rotten eggs: a sure sign of sulfur and powerful geologic activity. The stones around each hole were stained a bright yellow. At best, the party of one Englishman, one Scotsman, two Japanese professors, and one Welshwoman had heavy linen pads made of layers of cloth to wear over the mouth and nose. The heavy helmets they dragged with them weren't appropriate for climbing to the crater but would be essential once down near the lava dome. The stench wasn't kept out by the linen masks but the toxicity was rumored to be inhibited by a liberal application of some common chemicals that smelled no better. At least they *hoped* the chemicals worked. Lettie wondered what she would give to have a breath of fresh air right at that moment.

Technologically, it should have been possible to maintain some sort of oxygen supply, but how to store and deliver it had not been discovered yet. Certainly not in a form that allowed it to be taken into such remote and hostile environments.

'Earthquake' John Milne kept fussing with his mask, poking a finger underneath to adjust his thick moustache. He looked over at Lettie who quickly averted her eyes and stifled a giggle. "It keeps getting caught in the fibers," he exclaimed with a great deal of frustration.

"You could always shave it off," she added quietly while walking past him.

"My wife would never recognize me." He stopped fussing. "The dog would never recognize me. At least one of the two of them has to let me back into the house."

Lettie pulled her hammer out of her satchel and began pounding at a protrusion of cooled lava. Its battered and broken texture spread out from a steaming crevice that ran up the side of the mountain several meters toward the summit. The continuously booming noise from above their position was enough to indicate that they were unlikely to reach the lava dome safely. That would not stop them from trying.

James Ewing coughed and pointed back in the direction of Lake Shikotsuko. "All this steam ... the water must come from the lake." His Scottish manner of speech was diverting in the hostile environment and he knew it.

"It's a strong possibility," Lettie called back. The sulfur smell that sneaked through her mask was quite nauseating.

A sharp chunk of lava shattered under the blows of her hammer, sending a splinter of black rock up into her face. She batted at it as though it were a fly. She held up the larger piece to see in the defused daylight. "I think we'll get some good slices from this one." She was already picturing a thin wafer of lava under her microscope. The artificial light under the slice would light up all the crystals. It was important for her to know the mineral content of the mountain's lava. Such data could explain why the volcano erupted and what kind of eruption was the average. Plinian? Strombolian? The distinction was vital to understanding the most important question: *when* would it erupt?

She was very much hoping that they would find something new, something exciting for the field of volcano research. To date, the best book ever produced on the subject was Professor John Wesley Judd's two hundred page tome called *Volcanoes: What They Are, and What They Teach*. He'd done a splendid job. He had explained everything anyone knew about volcanoes rather nicely. It was published only a few months before their climb.

A 'flat' layer of rock collapsed under her foot, and she jumped back three paces. She took a deep, ugly smelling breath of air and waited for her heartbeat to slow.

Judd had beaten her to the publisher: she had hoped to write a commonplace book to make her beloved volcanoes understandable by anyone. Well, he did do a good job and she couldn't spend time being jealous.

Lettie could be impatient and now was no different than any other time. She pulled out her jeweler's lens and stared at what could be seen outside the laboratory. It wasn't a great deal. The cloudy sky and pitch black rock didn't allow for too many details. But what she saw was intriguing: many different-sized crystals. Depending on their chemical properties, it could be significant. Such drama in so little an object. On a piece of newspaper, she wrote the time, date, location and a note to herself on what to look for, with a wide, red wax pencil. The writing was clear even over the newsprint. She then wrapped the lava piece in it and put it into her satchel. She would transfer those notes to her journal once back in her hotel room.

Above them a great cracking sound exploded from the crater and the thick steam cloud turned orange for a moment.

"Do we go up?" Milne asked, knowing the answer.

Ewing nodded energetically while Murakami simply lifted his chin.

"I don't suppose I can talk you into staying put, Miss Gantry?" Milne tried his best to look stern.

She didn't bother to reply. Slipping with every step, she walked past them as defiantly as possible.

"I'll take that as a 'no'."

Both Japanese professors exchanged glances. Lettie was aware that one of them was quite appalled that she was allowed to come at all, but had the politeness not to say anything. In fact there had been quite a bit of strained politeness within the party when they left Edo, now called

Tokio, or as some spelled it Tokyo, and the Imperial College of Engineering. British and Japanese relations were artificial at best, having grown from the Emperor's desire to modernize the country. The British happily complied by sending military personnel and academics. Not everyone welcomed their presence.

The team had sat silently and politely on train ride to the North, though once on the island of Hokkaido relations seemed a tad warmer yet, it was not until the conversation turned to geology that everyone was able to let go of all concerns beyond science. All else ... except gender. No matter how well she conversed on the subject, she was certain there was no amount of information she could provide that would overwhelm the Japanese professor's opinions regarding her sex. Like the professor who silently disliked her presence, she quietly ignored his opinion on the matter. Professor Murakami was different from his colleague. If Murakami disapproved of her presence, he did more than to keep his mouth shut: he actively altered his behavior to appear quite supportive. Lettie wasn't entirely certain, but she believed he did so with enormous effort. And she appreciated it.

She said nothing about the matter. Even to thank Murakami would embarrass him. And she would not, for all the world, do such a thing.

"This was not here a month ago when I first came to look," Murakami noted in a loud voice, pointing toward the protrusion on the side of the vent, from which Lettie had taken a sample.

The ground shook strongly for two seconds. A tiny landslide of tephra skidded down the slope near where Murakami was standing. He simply observed it as it passed him, as though it were nothing extraordinary at all. It wasn't very large. The mountain shivered again, for several seconds this time. A much larger avalanche of rock poured off the vent's rim. The party scrambled out of the way, barely avoiding it. The bouncing rocks, some the size of luggage, skipped past them, kicking up dust clouds with every rebound in the dirt. A trail of lingering dust hovered over the slide.

Between the dust, gases and steam, visibility was at best poor and at worst dangerous.

Despite the limited visibility, once they left the floor of the caldera and climbed to the rim of the vent, they could see the impressive lava dome inside, cracked and steaming. Bright bursts of lightning in red and orange flashed suddenly, followed by a roar of colliding thunder.

Occasionally, incandescent fragments escaped the steam clouds and rained down onto the crater floor.

Milne and Murakami each put on sets of thick gloves, padded aprons, and cloth lined helmets that covered them all the way down to and over their shoulders. Glass panels riveted into bronze frames served as portals for them to see out of. Hardly looking human at all, they staggered forward with small buckets containing enough water to cool any fiery bits they dared to pick up. The remaining team members donned goggles and long leather gloves just in case.

Lettie had carefully adjusted a belt around each man, specifically placing pick hammers, long metal tongs, and pieces of coated fabric underneath and in the front where they could reach them without looking. They could only see straight forward. She envied them. Bringing her along this far had been a strain on their sense of propriety: she could never have convinced them to allow her to suit up and go out to the dome. She envied them terribly.

Halfway down the interior slope of the crater toward the now sixty meter high dome, the men waited while lava was pitched at them. Murakami reached out with his tongs and picked up a large glowing chunk. Milne held out his bucket and both watched as the lava instantly boiled the water inside. Milne waved back at the party waiting on the side of the rim. It was a good sample.

Tarumae began to shake and roll violently. The output of steam from the lava dome increased dramatically, looking like a locomotive releasing the pent up contents of its boiler. It was enough of a dramatic increase that both professors looked to one another, turned, and began climbing frantically back up to the rim.

The awaiting party began shedding packs and bags to free their hands so that they could strip the two men of their heavy gear quickly.

Murakami's footing dissolved in a landslide of material down into the crater, and he fell onto his chest. He felt a strong grip on his arm, the glove pulled off, and the grip now on his bare wrist. Smart. Had his rescuer held him by the glove, there was every chance the gesture would fail with only the glove being saved.

Searing rock fragments fell on their backs as they struggled to get out of the crater. Murakami's helmet was pulled off and he looked up. The hands that held him were not his colleague's; they were the woman's. She had braced herself with one leg bent underneath her and the other foot against a solid, boat sized outcrop of lava. She was surprisingly strong, perhaps fueled by panic. He pushed with his still gloved hand against the slippery surface and climbed on his knees to where Lettie was balanced.

Alongside her at last, he gave her a sharp, gratifying nod, which she appropriately returned. They would not speak of this again.

A plume of ash and steam shot up and out of the crater with a deafening blast that sprayed dirt, rocks and fumes over them. The eruption looked like a fountain of black debris, followed by billowing clouds.

The helmets were too heavy to carry out. They left them behind.

On the downhill slope, the porters who had accompanied them were marking a trail for them to follow. Two Ainu men waited midway down the shaking trail, seeing to it the academics knew which way to escape. The earthquakes and explosive concussions forced them to stay low to the ground as they descended. Ash covered them in soot. Lettie had to constantly wipe her goggle lenses clean to be able to see. Her shortened skirt, leggings and boots were smeared in gray. This was all too familiar for her.

A hail of burning tephra and lava fragments fell around them. One tiny piece ricocheted off her arm. The heat burned a hole in her coat sleeve instantly. She reached up and pounded it with her other hand fearing the whole garment would burst into flame.

Clouds of ash and smoke exploded out of the crater, rising up toward the sky. If it was heavy enough, it would cool slightly and then fall back down on them. An incendiary cloud. It would fry everything in its path. Nothing could survive it.

Lettie didn't bother to look back again. Her satchel dragged along behind her as she fell, slipped, skidded and ran down the trail.

Ewing caught up with her quickly. "Large eruption: better than fifty percent chance?"

"Small eruption, better than sixty-two percent." Her mask twisted to the side of her mouth and she stopped only long enough to adjust it back. The fumaroles were pumping out more gas than before. Hardly unexpected.

The ash cloud kept rising.

Milne called from a meter behind them, "I think the dome is gone."

The mountain shuddered twice more. Parts of the vent slid down its sides. The whole geography of the mountain had changed. Yet as fast and dramatic the eruption was it seemed to be over. The ash cloud began to dissipate.

The party managed to get down the trail and across the land to the edge of the caldera remarkably fast.

By the time they started down the trail leading off the highest point of the caldera toward the lake, Lettie was laughing, much to the surprise of her colleagues. Had she no shame, she would have skipped all the way back to town. It was the first time she'd laughed in public in years. She couldn't help it.

With no earthquake to warn them, a great roar and cloud suddenly belched out of the vent. Another ash cloud burst into the air then, too thick and heavy, collapsed down the sides of the volcano, racing down the mountain with hideous speed, obliterating everything in its path. Nothing could outrun it.

Chapter 9

June 10, 1881
London Herald and Observer
Editorials and Letters, page One, top left-hand column

"From the Editor in Chief:

It is with some embarrassment and sadness that I must make comments regarding any person of the fairer sex, but I would be negligent not to do so now. We here in the heart of the Empire are appalled by the behavior of those who see themselves as so-called New Women or Adventuresses. Such women are abhorrent to nature and decency, and in need of a stronger hand to guide them. Today I refer to one woman, whom I will not mention by name out of respect for the departed and her family, but who is well known to the Herald's readership. This most recent, unseemly and not surprisingly disastrous adventure in Japan has proven me correct in my opinion that women should not be permitted access to higher academic institutions and the dangers involved in pursuing such adventures, such as the ascent of an active volcano. Not only did this woman endanger herself and her companions, but it was done out of sheer arrogance. Mankind, and certainly not womankind, shall never be in possession of a means to predict the acts of God beyond good Biblical reference. She has paid the ultimate price for her academic foolishness and womanly weakness.

To some degree, the learned men who encouraged her should be brought to account. It was their duty to see to it no one, not even a headstrong female, should come to harm. This editor is mortified at the prospect that a British woman has been killed in what cannot be anything but a foolish attempt by scientists to undermine and even mock the proper order of things. Her death is on their hands."

Next Day, 1881
London H & O
Page 8, Bottom inside third column

"A correction must be issued: It has been brought to our attention that Miss L. Gantry of Cardiff, Wales and Sutton, Surrey was not killed during an eruption of a volcano in Japan. No persons were injured."

June 12, 1881
London Telegraph (the Herald's immediate competitor)
Under the column concerning odd events around the globe

"An eruption of pyroclastic nature has been observed and reported by British scientists. Dr. John Milne and Professor James Ewing of the Imperial College of Engineering, along with notable colleagues, were present to witness a large cloud of burning gases descending Mt. Tarumae of Hokkaido Island. The brave British men were able to record this phenomenon which occurred a mere mile away from them.

Despite rumors, the local correspondent was unable to verify that there was a woman present during the eruption."

And ...

"A strange occurrence has been reported from America: the Great Statue now under construction and presented to the United States by the people of France has been vandalized. The citizens of New York were awakened by the outrageous behavior of some person or persons playing a loud trumpet. Thinking it a prank, many chose not to give the rude action any consideration. However, an early morning trumpet blare was to draw attention to a flag draped across the newly completed base for the Statue of Liberty. No one recognized the flag: a sun with many stars on a black background. Authorities insist it is a prank and those responsible would be apprehended immediately.

An earlier suggestion that the striking Dirigible Mechanics and Pilot's Union might be behind the prank has been dismissed. However, Trans-Atlantic Air Freight shipping remains at a standstill and the said Statue of Liberty remains unfinished – her pieces waiting in a warehouse to be assembled."

Chapter 10

May 10, 1882
Location Known Only by Those who Need to Know

"He wants more money for the fuel, doesn't he?" The Captain looked up through a tired brow at his First Mate. The fellow stood ramrod stiff, waiting for the discussion that both men knew was coming. Yet mundane issues had to be dealt with first. The Captain hated the small, the petty ... he hated the stress: it made his head ache. That was what Tom was there for – to deal with the stress. Not to cause it.

"Aye, sir. And for his silence." Turner's voice was tight.

"Of course. Goddamn British. I knew that would be a problem soon enough. He's the only one with what I need and this was just waiting to happen."

"He's not a brave sort - we could persuade him..."

The words had a real confidence that should such an action be necessary, it might also prove entertaining. Tom Turner was quite useful in that regard. There was nothing preventing the Captain from giving the order for Turner to what he'd been trained to do. It had been given in other circumstances. He knew that Turner would do what he was ordered to do, without complaint. It didn't mean that Turner liked such orders, only that he accepted his place in the ship's hierarchy and in the Captain's ambitions.

The Captain shook his head and stood to stare out at the extraordinary view. "Not yet. I ..." He seemed to swallow before continuing; dreaming for a fraction of time. "I need the fuel with as little fuss as possible. For now." He braced himself against a moment of turbulence.

Neither said anything while the ship rocked.

In response to the ship's movement, the engines flared and stability was returned. He could see the tips of the fore-propeller whipping past his view of clouds and vapors.

Finally, he turned to his man. "Late again, weren't we, Tom." It was not a question. "I failed," he spit out, curling his hands into fists. "I don't fail."

Turner waited. There was no reply that could be safely made.

"The whole thing was done by the time we got there, Tom?"

"Aye, sir."

"And we didn't collect anything?"

"Some. But not a great deal, sir. What we have will dissipate in a matter of days, as always. But, as you saw, it wasn't an eruption that we could have safely approached regardless. We were close." Turner smiled slightly with a small upturn of optimism in his voice. "We'll be cleaning ash out of the screws for a week."

The Captain nodded. "Always guessing. It'll never do, Tom. Every time I risk being observed, and not everyone will continue to attach supernatural explanations to what they see. We can't be seen. I cannot be seen!"

"No, sir. That won't happen."

He took a deep breath, forcing the tension out of his broad shoulders. "We could use a greater level of expertise, couldn't we, Tom?" He began tapping a small, leather bound book on volcanic ash content which sat on a pair of clipped newspaper articles. It was all he had to work with, all that Turner could find for him - a monograph of some cleverness, and two public, published letters to the British Royal Society of Science warning of them some eruption they ignored a few years back. Idiots. Had *he* been aware of the warning signs in a timely manner, he would have been successful. *He* would have been present for the eruption.

All he needed was forewarning, so that he could be on time and in place to take advantage of it. He resented the 'need' immediately; he should not require outside help and it was pathetic that he did. He shouldn't need anything at all. Was he not a genius? Or was he the failure they always told him he'd be? He pushed the memories away, confident his mind would provide something that would distract him from such thoughts. Focus.

The man looked back at his subordinate with a slight, purposeful smile. Turner was such an oddity, he thought, which made him amusing among other important things. The man always dressed as though he were still in uniform and only looked slipshod when the occasion demanded it. He never allowed his opinion to get in the way of necessity, but neither was he afraid to speak up. He was intelligent too, though he kept it hidden most of the time. One never quite knew what Tom Turner was thinking unless he chose to tell. It could be anything. He was always twitchy about being restrained in both the physical and philosophical sense. No doubt that was why Turner was a sailor.

"I may have a challenge for you, Tom. The services of a scientist who has already done the research I haven't the time for could prove worth the effort of obtaining."

By the suddenly tightened expression on his face, it was obvious Turner knew what he would be commanded to do. 'Obtaining' was a euphemism - one Turner didn't like yet, ironically, was a service he excelled at. Turner preferred working within moral boundaries even if they were adjustable with the circumstance. "This fellow, Dr. Gantry, with his mathematical predictions of eruptions; we need to know more about him."

"I'll make further inquiries." 'Inquiry' was a much safer word; one that required no adjustment to Turner's moral compass yet.

For a long time the Captain waited, looking out the window. Clouds were forming to the north, likely a storm front. But, for a few scattered seconds, sunlight reached his face and he marveled at the prospects of freedom. Not just a conceptual notion of freedom, but true freedom of mind and body. Nothing closed; nothing locked. Fresh air.

However, there was another matter to be discussed: a violation.

The Captain liked surprising Tom. In fact, he just plain liked the fellow who seemed to have neither ambition nor greed, nor did he suffer from the popular discriminations of the time. He was the perfect confidant with his natural reservation. First mate and only friend; moral compass be damned. But the ship's rules needed to be enforced, even if they weren't entirely clear. This was not a military vessel, subject to the laws of an organized navy. Yet there were still rules of conduct.

Thinking how anyone could dare touch the box, the most sacred thing he had, his temperature rose. Accidental or not, it didn't matter. The contents were not common or everyday. They were, for lack of a better description, holy. He had to deal with this. "That takes care of the questions surrounding fuel. You know the other reason we need to have this talk?"

"Aye, sir."

"You saw the designs on my desk."

Turner swallowed and replied firmly, "Yes, sir, I did."

"You didn't like what you saw?"

"No, sir." The remark came out too sharply.

The Captain calmly left his glorious view to look at Turner's face; to closely gage the Mate's expressions. Turner gave him nothing to read. That was usual. Perhaps Turner was simply awaiting a just punishment for his transgression. Yet for all the anger and violation the Captain felt, he couldn't look at the man, and his scar, and not consider that both men were more alike than not. They both had suffered. "I should be angry, Tom. And I am, but not so much as you think. What brought you in here in the first place?"

There was a pause, likely in relief. "Delivering those news clippings, sir." Turner nodded toward the Captain's hand. The Gantry articles were right next to his fingers.

"Even though you knew I was working on something - new?" Surprise me, the Captain thought. "Were you curious about my next project?"

"You had placed some urgency on the information regarding Dr. Gantry."

"So, you were not being curious?"

"No, sir."

"Since you've already had a brief look at them, do you want to see the design now, in good light?" It's a test for you, Tom.

Turner didn't move and almost - almost - looked shocked. "I saw them well enough, sir. I spent enough time in the Navy to know what the shape represents. The Prussians used those in France and damn near killed themselves instead of their enemies. Weapons like that, sir, always backfire on the men using them." Turner must have been feeling bold. "Begging your pardon, sir, but such things are neither worthy of you nor are they worth the risk to your person and this ship." He drew in a deep breath.

The Captain drew his hands up into fists. "These were my father's. They are all I have left of that man - that world."

"I'm sorry for that, sir," Turner said with genuine sympathy and embarrassment. Of course he couldn't have known of their nature and history. "I've stated my peace, sir. I'll say no more."

The Captain barked out a laugh. "Goddamn it, Tom, you're consistent. No more warfare for Tom. Ship and crew only. Save mankind. Good for you." He folded his arms across his broad chest. "What should I do with you?"

"You're the Captain, sir."

"And you're my First Mate. I can't punish you without risking the morale of the rest of the crew. Besides, didn't I hire you because you know how to be nosey, to gather intelligence, and to keep your peace? I don't expect to hear about this from anyone, am I correct?"

Turner's expression turned to offended. "Sir, I would never ..."

This was easier than he had expected, and the Captain was relieved. "No, I know better." He rested his weight on both hands and leaned in, adding a little conspiracy to his voice. "I also hired you because you're smart, Tom. And curious. I want to show you that design. Not for what it can do, but for its cleverness. My father was nothing if not clever, though not clever enough to live."

It took a moment for him to open a locked box that sat on his desk. His hands moved with reverence across the smooth, polished wood, hinged and bolted with brass. Sandalwood, with an ornate pattern of inlaid stones on the lid in a circle. Two brass handles waited on either side of the box, though it was unlikely they were strong enough to lift the weight of the box - purely ornamental. It couldn't have measured more than fifteen by fifteen inches square, and seven inches thick. He always wondered if he shouldn't chant some prayer or offer an obeisance before daring to open it. Inside, rolled papers were tied with twine and stacked three deep. The Captain withdrew the largest one and rolled it out to be viewed. "Haven't shown this to anyone else, Tom. You're the only one I would. A family invention. I've made necessary modifications ... for the sake of innovation."

"Bombs." Tom's tone of voice was neither that of admiration nor condemnation.

"Yes. Revenge to be rained down on the enemy."

There was a deafening silence between them.

"They're more than just bombs, Tom. You of all men can see beyond the profane to see the sacred. Look at the shape, especially in the tail section. The fins and propeller will keep it from drifting or falling sideways. These are not the crude bombs the Prussians rained down on Paris."

Turner couldn't help himself; he leaned over the drawings and noted the brilliance of their design.

"I've occasionally considered the possibility of using grooved cylinders to actually guide them to the ground. Precise destruction."

The suggestion brought Turner's eyes, wide with shock, up to his

Captain's.

He abruptly rolled the paper back into its cylinder, confused by Turner's continuing ambiguity or perhaps even disapproval now, and put the roll back into the box. There was Turner's weakness; he despised the trappings of war. He despised everything about war, and there was no doubt as to why. And yet, he committed his considerable wartime skills to the whims and needs of his Captain. Thomas Turner had been part of the American war, in command of groups of men who did God only knew what. "Oh don't worry yourself, Tom. We're not going into the weapons industry. My father can never use them, and I've decided I won't. Ah, never mind that I have more than just cause." He slammed the box closed. "But what point is there if he cannot see them, see that I made them better than he'd designed, and delivered them to his enemy? Who cares if he doesn't know that his son, his heir ..."

His first mate was doubtless worried at that moment. He had to be. Turner had a few unconscious signals that gave him away: he pulled at his high collared sweater and tried without thinking to hide the scar that encircled his throat. "Never mind, Tom. You may take my word on it; these are only for intellectual exercise. To keep my mind stimulated."

Well, that wasn't true, but Turner needed the assurance. The last thing the Captain wanted was a mutiny lead by a former Naval Intelligence officer and battle hardened Landing Party commander. The Captain was no one to trifle with, but neither was Tom Turner. "I give you my word. The past is a bad place to live. A man should only look forward, eh? Fuel is our immediate concern. Fuel now equates to freedom."

"Aye, sir." There was some relief in Tom's voice. The stiffness melted out of his stance.

Yes, Tom would believe him: would accept the Captain's word. He was loyal. "Make the arrangements." The Captain turned back toward the view.

The interview was over.

"Aye sir." Turner forced any lingering doubts to the back of his mind where he kept them. His commanding officer was amid a series of great inventions and amazing accomplishments. So what if he was peculiar in his dealings, he was going to benefit mankind. His reclusive obsession would be over-ridden by his need to advance humanity; Turner was convinced of this. Turner banked his entire existence on this isolable fact. Turner had to accept that his Captain needed seclusion and freedom. Was that so much to ask? Turner kept reminding himself of this, though he had lost some of his initial, blind enthusiasm. He had to stand true to his promise of loyalty, for the sake of something bigger than he could comprehend. Whatever it took, the Captain had to be safeguarded along with his inventions.

"Mr. Turner." The Captain never turned to face him. "No man is to touch that box but me. Am I clear? I will have no humor if its sanctity is violated. No one may touch it."

"Aye, sir."

Outside the viewing room, in the dark corridor, Turner stopped and thanked Heaven that his Captain hadn't been more angry at him for seeing those plans and having the temerity to ask. No, he hadn't asked, he'd accused, and that was intolerably rude of a subordinate. While it was true that his Captain thought of him as a close friend, something that might well have spared him a flogging for invading the Captain's privacy, there was a nagging worry that prevented Turner from thinking the same of him. He couldn't see him as a close, trusted friend. Sometimes he blamed it on his military training as a Captain rarely maintained friendships in the ranks. He just couldn't return the closeness the Captain clearly offered. He admired, respected and would willingly die for his Captain, but ...

Cold, biting wind struck him in the face as he walked across the deck to the Wheelhouse. Once he settled his hands on the great navigational wheel his mind began to focus. Sanctuary. Noises from outside were hidden by the constant rush of the wind. Here he could think. Even old Meriton, standing watch with him, wouldn't interrupt his meditations. Meriton was a good man and able seaman, which was far more than Turner could say of the rest of the crew. No, that was unfair of him; they were just sailors trapped by the need to survive. But they didn't understand what a profound gift had been given to them – a chance to serve the Captain. On *this* of all vessels. Right before their eyes were the miracles the Captain could create. They were a part of it every day.

They just didn't see it, willfully, they chose not to care.

He shook off the thoughts. The crewmen obeyed. He obeyed. That was all that was required.

Turner didn't need to know about bombs; he hadn't spied on the Captain. It was accidental, but such breeches in courtsey toward the ship's commander were not tolerated usually. He needed only his orders and course settings. He touched the old scar he tried so hard to hide and wondered if perhaps his singular devotion would be better served with a bit more flexibility on his part. Probably not. He had stepped over a line. Questioning one's Captain was just not done. He was lucky the Captain wasn't more upset. And, he had the Captain's word that the bombs were only an exercise in intelligence, something the Captain was remarkable for. Focus and determination usually resulted in success, and the end justified the means, Turner reminded himself. He would stay true and obedient. Perhaps the Captain would reward his loyalty and wouldn't make him leave anymore flags around Europe and America. Half of them hadn't been found yet. The Captain had a strange sense of humor and he risked exposure every time they planted his flag, blew that cursed trumpet, and sneaked away like school boys. Well, it was funny at first.

Staring out at the great expanses before him, his mind easily drifted off to strange memories – a habit he probably should break, he thought, along with his enjoyment of sweet cheroot cigars. He could see a vague reflection in the window. He wasn't always sure he liked the man with the blue eyes that stared back at him, but of one thing he was certain, the reflection was of an ultimately honorable man. What he did, he did with a grander vision in mind.

He remembered the exact moment he'd met his Captain. Ten years prior, almost to the day. In Baltimore.

God, what a night that had been.

Even to the present day, Turner could never remember how he got into that alley. He rarely walked anywhere near that place known too well as the site of many a sailor's death. He couldn't remember how he got there. He was brought there, unwillingly. But when and how ... those memories eluded him. Just as well.

There was another man with him; an old man. Old, simple, poor and wretched. They started with him. The Night Patrol, in their fake, homemade uniforms and big cudgels. They hit the old man, over and over, until he stopped crying for mercy.

How exactly he fought them, Turner couldn't remember clearly either. There were moments he stored in his brain of a knee rammed into a Patrolman's kidneys, a broken nose, a face shoved into the cobblestones, all visions of what he did to them. He hurt them; he wanted to break them. Now and then someone managed to do damage to him and it only angered him more. It made him fight harder.

All the fighting didn't save the old man.

What Tom did remember was a terrifying inability to differentiate between the dark Baltimore alley and the swamps of the Roanoke delta. It was suddenly all the same. One enemy was exactly the same as the other. He'd been taught to deal with enemies quickly, quietly, and finally. The Patrolman still beating the old man's corpse was in reach. Turner wrapped his arm around the front of the Patrolman's throat, grasped his head across the front, and twisted with astonishing speed. That was how one took out the enemy without drawing attention. It was fast and silent. The sound of cracking bone was even satisfying in its simplicity. The Night Patrolman was no Confederate, but at that moment, to Turner, he was. The Patrolman went instantly limp and fell on top of old man's body.

The remaining Patrol dragged one another off into the night, leaving Turner with two corpses and no proof he hadn't killed both. The real authorities of the city would be there soon enough and he would have no satisfactory answers for them.

There was nothing to be done for the old man. He'd be buried without name in a mass grave, but he would be buried. Tom stared at him, wondering if this was how he would end his days when he was too old or sick to defend himself.

He had to flee. Staggering along the street, holding a hand against bruised ribs and occasionally wiping blood out from under his nose, Turner sought the only refuge he had left: a tavern at the dockside. He could hide there while trying to understand what had just happened. His left eye was slightly swollen. His ears rang.

Sailors and acquaintances told him to get out of Baltimore, to take any job that would carry him far away. They gave him beer and bread since he could no longer afford it himself, though mostly because they wanted to hear of his misfortune. They'll hang you Tommy, they said to him, and they'll do it right this time. Don't matter what you did or why.

He remembered holding both hands up around his jaw, around his throat. He would take his own life before he'd let anyone put a rope around his neck again. Damn it, never again. His stomach was churning. What kind of monster had he become? He didn't even feel regret for killing the Patrolman, yet his heart broke for the old man.

The man destined to be his Captain had stood solidly at the back of the tavern, with arms folded; watching; saying nothing. At first Turner thought he was some sort of law enforcement searching the crowded room for faces that might match "wanted" posters. It was too soon for anyone to be looking for him but, just in case, he lowered his head down onto his arms and watched. Such searches were a regular enough occurrence in the painful years after the war had ended. One after another of such men flooded into the veteran's boarding houses, halls, or drinking holes frequented by the unemployed solders and sailors. They were sure, as was most of polite society, that this was the new criminal element. Men taught how to slaughter each other efficiently could have only one future without a war to fight. Maybe they were right.

The drinking holes had also become makeshift employment offices, especially those near the docks. Innkeepers and boarding house owners profited from the employers and the would-be employees, paid in blood money for helping to find men for the vacancies on ships and for the booze needed to numb their senses. Sailors waited in oft-times false hope. But the ship masters coming to such places tended to be only interested in the hopeless or desperate – those who would undertake horrific journeys from which they'd likely never return. The money was pathetic and the conditions worse. It was better than starving to death or dying in the hospitals, or for that matter, being arrested. In a bizarre irony, one that Turner liked to observe, there was a hidden dignity in such voyages: a wage earned, not a handout given.

The man began staring at him specifically. Since he had no minions backing him up, a standard practice of the police, Turner decided the man was looking to hire. It was his turn to be one of the chosen, one who would likely disappear and never be heard from again, and the timing could not have been better. Very consciously, Turner pulled his high-necked sweater higher to hide the ugly scar and wiped the remaining blood off his lip. He'd run out of options and was prepared to accept employment on any ship, in any filthy mail packet or stock ship, carrying anything but human cargo. There was one place he could draw the line never to cross: slave ships and prisoner transport. He didn't care who was after him, this he would not do. He'd fought against slavery and he had been a prisoner himself; no, the matter was too close to his heart. He would starve before signing onto a ship carrying either. Yet anything else, underpaid and ill fed, was acceptable.

Even resplendent in his retired naval uniform, no potential employer ever noticed the hard earned rank or the medals – only the scar. Criminals, despots, dishonest men had such disfigurements. Of course, in polite society, no one would ask. All that was left was assumption: assumption that he deserved the scar. There were sleepless nights when he thought they might be right. He'd done things in the war; things he could never tell anyone.

The Captain had approached him, said nothing, but handed him a folded diagram. The drawing was stunning, complex, impossible ...

An airship with no balloon. Screws, rotors - it was beautiful.

"She's built," the Captain said with pride. "She needs a First Mate and I'm assured you will not disappoint."

Turner stared at the drawing. "Built?" This? It was perfect in design and aesthetic. Glorious. Frightening in scope. Even were he not desperate, such a ship would beg him to sign on. "Sir?"

"I understand your name is Tom. Stay here and starve if you wish, but I think you won't. I think you want to see this creation of mine. And you would like to avoid being arrested."

The man knew what had happened? Turner wondered if he'd been followed. They said nothing more to each other.

The Captain was looking for an expression of curiosity, amazement and understanding on his potential employee, which he got.

Turner was looking for a job and a means to escape.

The document was refolded and returned with appropriate reverence. With no questions asked but hundreds racing across his mind, Turner followed the man out of the tavern, out of poverty, and into the oddest set of circumstances he could ever have imagined. His Captain never asked about the scar either, or the beating he'd taken that night, but this Turner believed was a sign of respect rather than discrimination. Once employed, and aboard the ship, he was home, he was safe. He'd found a place. Food; shelter; stimulation of his curious brain. No death and no corpses. Fresh air and purpose. For all this, he was grateful and obedient.

Chapter 11

May 15, 1882
New College of London
The Gaul Library of Science

The *London Herald and Observer* put the headline in the largest, blackest letters that would fit the page: 'Unnatural Storm Causes Eruption – Thousands Dead.' Never mind that there wasn't a single shred of evidence to conclude that a storm, natural or otherwise, had anything to do with the eruption of Mt. Merapi in the Dutch East Indies. And never mind that there were no statistics whatsoever that any more than a couple hundred native villagers had died in an avalanche of pyroclastic ash that was of course terrible and tragic all the same. One? One hundred? One thousand? It was tragic. 'Thousands' made for a dramatic headline that would sell papers.

It had been a couple of years since such a headline was printed. Rumors of a strange storm had appeared as far back as '76, but had disappeared as quickly as they had been reported. It was a recent enough memory for the journalists to re-energize it for the public.

News flowed in and out of the library through pneumatic tubes connecting all parts of the campus, but most especially the places where the students gathered. No sooner had one of the carriers, a bronze and rubber coated canister, popped into the receiver at the end of one tube then a rush of uniformed youths arrived at the Librarian's desk to know what it was, where was it from, and did it have to do with the freakish storms? The Librarian barely opened the canister, which he did with annoying, purposeful slowness, when the contents were snatched up. No admonition on his part would stop the practice.

Maybe that odd woman academic should go and study the storm, they commented, reading each report as it came in? It seemed to know more about volcanoes than she did. The laughter that followed was only between two of the young men. The rest of the students glared at them, and someone wondered ungraciously if the loud-mouthed fellows had ever listened to one of her rare lectures? Brilliant. Few in the academic world knew more about the subject. Her modeling of eruptions had successfully predicted and equally failed. Didn't they know she was held in high esteem by some of the best minds in Europe?

Didn't they know she was ill regarded by many other scholars, most of them British, the retort offered? Enough about that strange woman who thought she could eclipse her own sex by becoming a scientist. It wasn't natural. What about the storm? Was it man made? Did it have a consciousness?

Someone daringly suggested that there was a connection between the storms and the appearance of the mysterious flags: black, with its giant sun and numerous stars. He was promptly laughed at.

The students who commented and debated in the confines of the library and residences of New College were matched nearly word for word by the scholars and professors ensconced in the second floor offices. Was it a storm? How did one define a storm? And could it cause a volcano to erupt? Rubbish. Nonsense. Imagination out of control. Yet, the discussions continued until one evening when half the laboratory assigned to the lectures on Physics was nearly obliterated during an experiment to prove such a storm could be created by man. The Dean of the College declared the subject off limits to students and experimentation - though few heeded him.

Chapter 12

June 29, 1882
Yogyakarta Sultanate
Java Island, Dutch East Indies

Sri Sultan Hamengkubuwono Senapati Ingalaga Abdul Rakhman Sayidin Panatagama Khalifatullah - The Carrier of the Universe, Primary Warrior, God's Particular Servant, Priest and Caliph Safeguarding the Religion – informally referred to as Hamengkubuwono VII, was very unhappy. He'd heard the tales from his father, Hamengkubuwono VI, about the eruption of 1872, five years before his own reign had begun. It had been violent and horrible. People - his people - had died by the thousands. Today was not boding well.

Mt. Merapi roared to life again just before sunset, spraying debris over the vast majority of its flanks. A cloud of ash blasted up into the atmosphere and mushroomed out over the Java Sea to the northwest. Merapi was a restless spirit, or so the local people informed the Dutch administrators, but it was for the most part beneficent. Thus the regional governor watched intently, waiting for the amazing show to begin. It had been his policy, as well as that of the Dutch, not to dissuade any of the people from their beliefs so long as they remained loyal and quiet, and appeared to be doing the right things. Of course, the Dutch did show preference for Protestant Christianity while the Sultan encouraged Islam. There were so many religions mixed amongst the Javanese that he found the one thing they had in common was the one thing that kept the peace: their volcanoes. So, now and again, he would invite the Gatekeeper of Merapi to join him for tea and a lovely view.

The Gatekeeper had the unenviable job of predicting what Merapi might do. Several thousand people looked to him for guidance regarding staying or evacuating. It was a pressure that the Sultan could appreciate.

Thus they sat together in the growing darkness brought on by night and the ash cloud, happily sipping tea and discussing the various rituals and customs from up and down the island with an administrator from the Netherlands. The three men could not have been any further apart in dress, philosophy and language. Yet, like much of the region, drawn together by Merapi.

The Gatekeeper was a delightfully humble man with a good sense of humor, even if it tended to be a bit bleak where the continuation of the Dutch presence was concerned. Yet, there was a political line the Gatekeeper wouldn't cross, and the Sultan respected that even more.

The mountain shook the valley and roared at the administrative city. It was becoming a bit routine, as much as any massively destructive force of nature could be taken as routine in behavior. Still, there was that time, only a decade before, where the fury of Merapi was proven in a terrible night. What neither man nor their interpreters had expected was the storm.

Against the black backdrop of the ash cloud, a perfect, white vapor grew into a single white cloud, which caught the last rays of the sun and glowed in a celestial illumination. It roiled and turned with the eruption column but never mixed into it. Larger and larger it grew. Suddenly, the ash cloud lashed out, jealous of the perfection of the storm cloud. Lightning blasted toward the storm, barely missing it. After a few minutes of this, the storm began shooting back at the ash cloud and within itself, bursting in colors of indigo and pink, yellow and fiery red.

No rain fell from the cloud. It defied the ash column by remaining separate and white.

The Gatekeeper's teacup fell to the tiled floor, smashing into sharp pieces. For a second, and even his mature eyes saw it, the storm vanished and left in its wake the shape of a bird that slipped away into the night sky.

The Sultan and the Administrator saw the same event, seeing in it not a bird but a ship, like a clipper ship without sails. The hull was almost perfect and scores of masts reached up from the deck, but it had no sails. As fast as it had arrived, it too was gone.

While Merapi continued venting its extrusive materials into the late night, both men were left to wander home. The Gatekeeper would need to consult the Spirit of Merapi; the Administrator intended to consult the scholars of the Dutch instituted University; and Hamengkubuwono VIII was determined to take the issue straight to God. None would receive a satisfactory answer.

Reading his paper, the Administrator had an idea. In the morning he would contact a colleague in Amsterdam, to help him find an expert. An expert on what? He could say ghost ships in the sky and then promptly resign in shame. No, he needed another excuse. The Volcano. He would ask for an expert on volcanoes. Then he'd quietly task the scientist to devise a plausible answer to what was going on, and to send them home quickly before anyone asked too many questions.

The observations of the governing men were not the only ones to be made. It was only a matter of time before telegraph wires began to tap with the news. By the day after the event, the *London Herald and Observer* had declared the events to be cause and effect, one and the same, and perhaps … only perhaps, the work of man not God.

That was all it took to create a panic across the cities of London and Paris, through the Universities of Harvard and Munich, and in any Club or Parlor willing to take it on. Could this thing be man-made? And who would do it?

It was improbable at best. No one, not even the greatest minds, could come up with a viable way to make a floating clipper ship, which created a storm, and started volcanic eruptions. Ludicrous. Ridiculous. Impossible.

A day later, the Sultan's personal staff found a flag hastily erected at the top of the residence. A flag of no country they knew. Black, with a gold sun, stars …

No further sightings or findings were made that month, and as the news and the eruption died down, it was all dismissed as a hoax. But as the stirrings underneath an East Indies volcanic island in the Sunda Strait shook the region, a certain nervousness began to build amongst scientists from Japan to England.

Chapter 13

September 1, 1882
Université de Paris
Paris, France

"Monsieur!" The voice from the man in the second row was barely audible above the shout and fury of the crowded room. "Monsieur Professor, a question please!"

The general roar of vehemently opposing opinions quieted down, allowing the visiting professor to calmly listen. It had been a mistake to allow the old men to attend the lecture. They were against everything new and the opposition was on the verge of physical violence. All this for a little progress.

Rising from his seat, appropriately displaying the correct decorum shown in the halls of the Université de Paris, the journalist stated his question in a thickly accented but intelligible English. "Sir, if this mechanism is to become commonplace in fields of battle," the crowd began to growl and he was forced to speak louder, "would it not be better that it should be designed with heavy armor?"

Many of the European students seated in the farthest back rows nodded in approval of the question. At last, someone was asking an intelligent question in a properly mannered way, unlike the previous barrage of stupidity from the 'foreign' scholars, namely the English.

An exotic looking guest in robes and a turban, clearly a man of substantial wealth, sat in the very back left-side row, keeping his face hidden by the shadow cast from the lamps directly behind him. Resting his fingers on the bridge of his nose, effectively obscuring his face, he hadn't moved a muscle except when signaling one of three servants that accompanied him. One servant appeared to be American or European and he stared down at the Professor with cold blue eyes as the wealthy guest commented to him quietly. The blue-eyed man regularly retreated to the shadows behind his employer, arms tightly folded across his chest.

The journalist's reasonable question caused the turbaned gentleman to nod in appreciation.

It was the older men, those of higher University status or visitors with a stake in the outcome, who crossed their arms tightly across their chests and shook their heads. One commented quite loudly, "Why not have it shoot? If you're going to replace men with machines, you might as well go all out." The comment was met with uneasy laughter. The old Englishman nodded in self satisfaction.

The Professor waited until the room was hushed. In his mind, there was nothing worse than rudeness, but these weren't his students, whom he'd have little trouble putting in their place. No, these were the faculty and students of the Université de Paris, the members of the Englishman's Exploration Society – Continental Branch, and the French press. He could not afford to be anything but wholly diplomatic. It wasn't just his reputation. If that were all, he'd have no concern. It was his name or, rather, his father's name, and the reputation of the New College of London. Life was rarely simple and straight forward.

He really didn't like these sorts of presentations, but they were necessary for his work. Being the center of attention didn't bother him in the least; it was the potential for forced interaction that he disliked intensely.

Professor Rajiv Arthur Pierce knew how to hold a crowd, even if he loathed being in one himself. He had absolutely no intention of raising his voice to be heard. He was such a softly-spoken man to begin with that a certain amount of volume only sounded squeaky, almost feminine. Besides, if they wanted to hear what they had dragged him all the way to France to say, they would be quiet. And slowly, they were.

Standing with his hands formally clasped behind him, as he did in his London classroom, Pierce waited. He was glad for the lighting in the medical seminar room. The attendees of his presentation were shadowed, preventing him from having to make eye contact with anyone beyond the front row – all the better. If he could avoid all questioning audiences, he would. Frankly, he loved humanity and hated people, all in the same breath. The shadows allowed him to ignore the attendees. If only they would come to listen and learn, then go away without making him talk more than necessary.

He stood erect, shoulders back, chin level to the ground. He was not a particularly tall man, but his build was proportionate to his height, if a bit too slender, and he had been schooled from his earliest days to dress to enhance his stature. Stylishly attired in gray and black, and looking every bit the man of incomparable academic standing, Pierce was glad he'd spent more with his tailor than his butcher. Appearance was everything, especially for a man half dark and half not. He was a proud Englishman, no question, but knew that his face betrayed his Indian heritage. As such, it was twice as vital to appear correct, so that his ethnicity would not hinder his ability to interact with the academic society of Europe. Even in the Nineteenth Century, the Era of Progress, the Era of Invention, bigotry was brutally alive and well.

He wore his black hair cut fairly short and combed forward. On his face he preferred a simple, thick moustache and a narrow set of sideburns that lined his sharp cheeks and jaw, setting them off all the stronger. His fingers were long instruments he abused in his work but was glad for when the more intricate tasks needed done. Another reason he stood with his hands behind him, hidden; a gentleman did not labor. If he was considered particularly handsome, he was unaware of it. But then, he'd hardly accept a compliment on the subject with anything but skepticism. Despite his actual heritage, he was the adopted son in a significant English family and was, therefore, a sought after commodity amongst the unmarried girls of the lesser gentry who could not afford to limit their options due to something as vulgar as race. They would likely do what they did in other situations where someone was neither white, nor British, nor Christian: they would pretend it wasn't so, put up the best cloying manners and wait to speak unkindly behind closed doors. It would be his great grandson who would escape the taint of Rajiv's ethnicity so long as he appeared 'normal.' Then again, perhaps the world would change by then.

On his left temple sat a patch of lighter colored scar tissue. There was no way of hiding it through disguise or deception. Rather, he found that the less he thought of it the less other people noticed. The wound that caused it was substantial, and not something he spent time thinking about.

He spoke in that gentle voice which revealed nothing of his place of birth, only of his adopted homeland. He spoke as a gentleman would, as his father would have him speak.

"Gentlemen. May I first amend the question posed? The purpose of this," he chose to eliminate the word 'unmanned' from the title, "medical cart is not only to be used on battlefields, but more commonly in hospitals and quarantine wards." His polite correction was received cautiously by the audience. The journalist who had asked the question graciously nodded his approval, of the alteration, to Pierce. No confrontation, which was a relief. "Because of this, one can only imagine the delicate if not fragile state of mind of the patient. In considering both the appearance and mobility of this mechanism, I felt it appropriate to address the mindset of those who would see it from either the ground or the hospital bed."

The old Englishman snorted. "Then why not put an apron and cap on it?"

Pierce continued speaking, tensing as barks of laughter met with varied levels of approval. He began to pace slowly. It was a means by which to hide the fact that his hands were locking together angrily, nearly white at the knuckles. This entire, ridiculous exchange of reasoned scientific experimentation and sophomoric Eton School humor had gone on all afternoon. His nerves were fraying. But, as his father always said, "a gentleman must suffer ignorance with a smile." Pierce's smile had long since faded, but all else was under control.

"If you will allow me to maneuver the mechanism again, please imagine yourself in the position of an injured man or one who has been quarantined and is alone. Note the effect of the movement." He reached over to the controls and began gently squeezing air-triggers that set the cart forward.

Two thick cables attached to the back of what looked like a decorated steel box. Swirling brass frame braces were riveted to the base and several drawers, trays, and hinged arms remained confined to an area some eighty by eighty centimeters. The corners of the box were rounded, taking away its sharp edges. On opposite sides a pair of wheels, as large as the box itself, were attached with swivel joints. Slowly, the cart moved toward the attendees, some of whom stood to see better down the steep sides of the seminar room seating. The cart rolled smoothly, with very little sound beyond the hiss of the small engine that provided propulsion. With a soft hiss, a swivel arm moved out toward the old Englishman, who sat up abruptly at the gesture. At the end of the arm was a small tray with sweets on it.

"Normally, these would be medications, appropriate for invalid patients," Pierce's comment brought a roll of laughter from the back of the room. "But, as you can see, its motion is non-threatening. Its appearance is appealing. Every aspect that has been considered has been made to present a gentle, clean, and effective delivery."

"But Professor, why such large wheels? Surely if it is done right, small, protected wheels would not be threatening?" the journalist added.

"You are correct. Smoothness is yet another consideration. Some medications cannot be distressed before application. For instance, pills might be bounced out of their containers and thus unable to deliver accurate dosages. Rollers and wheels are familiar to most people and therefore will be the least traumatic to those already traumatized."

The journalist sat down, quite satisfied, while others in the room applauded enthusiastically.

"I wish to add that the most sensitive operation of this cart is the application of injections." Pierce retreated the cart from the old Englishman and began moving the steel arms into place to show how a syringe could be applied by distant controls. Tempting though it was, the Professor made certain that the small arc of water shot forth from the syringe did not land on the Englishman's shoes.

"Ridiculous nonsense!" The old Englishman was not going to give in. "Any man who has the courage to be a soldier is not likely to be frightened by a big box."

"Sir, referring to your specific, though narrow application of the mechanism, you must not forget that many battlefield patients have been offered Morphine, Laudanum, or other pain inhibitors made with hallucinogenic substances, which also cause mental disconnection or disorientation."

"Soldiers are not afraid. At least not the British Tommy."

"Soldiers are human," Pierce replied, becoming alarmed at the sheer stupidity of the loudest voice in the room. Could anyone be so ignorant?

"And it is humans that should care for humans. Not machines. You are trying to replace mankind with machinery and it will not do!" Half the room erupted in support while the other half began shouting him down. "A nurse can deliver medications twice as easily as that contraption."

Pierce took a deep, settling breath. He was close enough to run the stupid man down with the cart, but that would lack dignity. "Would you send a lady into a quarantined ward, locked down due to Cholera or Bubonic Plague?"

The Englishman looked appalled. "A lady? Nurses are not ladies. Only thirty years ago they were nothing but a gaggle of unemployed drunkards or actresses ... or worse. Very little has changed. Now they're staffed by New Women, who are the most unfeminine of all. And, besides, it's their job. They know the risks. That's what they are there for."

"Unnecessary risks, and I want to see those risks reduced." There it was; that strain on his voice that meant he was not keeping the calm control he wished for. Idiot. Wait until he has to be in hospital, Pierce thought. The old hypocrite will change his tune. In fact, Pierce was feeling an urge to say as much.

In the upper middle section of seats there was a small disturbance that caused several to comment, though by the tone of the comments they were not disapproving. From the vague silhouette, Pierce could make out the shape of a woman as she prepared to ask a question. While the French and Germans were at the forefront of educating women, they had yet to accept any into the inner circle of academic teachers and governors, or so he thought. She must therefore be a friend or wife of someone important, he decided. Perhaps she was a student? Or maybe a journalist; women were doing that now, too. Either way, any woman would be lucky to get into the presentation, let alone acquire a seat anywhere but in the very back of the room. This was a rarity, and indeed a shock to some who were just beginning to take notice of her.

A model of decorum, she waited for the crowd to become silent and for the professor to look in her direction before speaking. The way she stood, her understanding of courtesies in the lecture hall, the calmness in her voice; they all told him that she was no stranger to this situation. "Professor. Taking into consideration the multitudes of possibility for your mechanism, I am reluctant to limit my question to the battlefield example. You have considered walking a viable form of locomotion?"

"I have."

"May I inquire as to your conclusions?"

"It tended to totter along like a drunken insect."

The woman smiled and for a moment the whole audience was with him and laughing. "That appearance being significant though perhaps not sufficient, on what other foundations did you decide on rolling rather than walking? It does appear a bit limited in scope."

"How so?" Pierce was surprised to hear his own voice reply so quickly, but frankly he was relieved that someone was asking more, intelligent questions. Even a woman.

"Physical terrain. While a hospital ward is often relatively level and stable, exterior situations are more unpredictable and certainly not consistent in condition. For example, a mountainous region or a volcanically active area? Such places would be difficult to traverse with set, hard wheels, but such terrain would occur more frequently in nature than a level, smooth surface. Legs might prove more flexible. Drunken appearances aside. What other considerations are being taken for these situations, sir, if not legs?" Her question received quite a bit of approval, more so from the back rows than the front.

But of course the young, less established attendees, with the worst seats, would be more attracted to challenges and critical questions. And, Pierce admitted, his opinion that it was an intelligent question did not diminish. "I have for the moment limited the function of this cart to delivery of medicine, which in my mind determined a very specific form of locomotion."

"But surely you do not intend to maintain that limited function for all your carts. You may have options for collection rather than delivery. The possibilities are quite varied."

"That is correct. The cart itself may be seen as a universal tool, but much will come from the individual uses, case by case. Your point in regard to future usage and locomotion is well taken. I should like to respond in detail to that when there is sufficient time to examine specific examples. I don't believe I can give you as thorough a reply as your question deserves at this time."

"Thank you, Professor. I look forward to that discussion." And she sat down without another word. Perfect decorum.

Pierce had made a small miscalculation; he had stopped paying attention to the old Englishman, who did not appreciate it one bit. Grabbing at the Professor with a bellowing voice, he continued his tirade. "As I was saying, Nurses are on the fringe of society; always have been. Thoroughly unfeminine like all New Women. They are made acceptable by their sacrifice to their betters. We must never confuse them with the flowers of society. A real lady is incapable - of nearly everything that those women do, such as speaking in public or pretending to be a journalist or an academic. A true lady would never lower herself as we have seen so often, even today ..."

The upper tiers of seating erupted in fury. Demands for apologies were shouted down in French and Belgian at the old men in the front rows. The youth of academia and the journalistic community had had quite enough of the fat foreigners and uncouth antiques who felt that they were above good manners.

Several of the older, senior academics stood and began shouting back. The whole scene was absurd.

"Excuse me, sir." It was a feminine, but stern, voice from the upper seats: her pitch helped to carry it above the din of masculine anger. Pierce could still barely see the woman who addressed the seated man due to the men standing protectively around her. The Old Englishman's dismissal of her had not, by appearances, diminished her dignity. "Excuse me," she said, not raising her voice beyond its normal volume. The gentleman in the turban seemed to smile. If the blue-eyed man had any reaction, it wasn't visible from his place in the shadows.

Some mumbling remained but for the most part, the audience calmed down. She continued undeterred. "Those nurses who serve the injured and sick deserve our respect and gratitude, not contempt." And with that statement, the woman gathered her things, of which there were few, slipped past a pair of rather supportive men who quietly complimented her statement, shook an offered hand, looked back briefly at the professor and walked up the stairs with a practiced air of cool confidence. The rules of society would not allow her to remain to be subjected to further insults, even if she chose not to acknowledge them. It likely wasn't the first time she'd been forced to leave a lecture due to one man's bad behavior. Unfair as it was, the responsibility of keeping the lecture civil and focused on the subject and not on her presence fell completely to her. She was the odd factor – the intruder. It was not fair, but it was as things were. Pierce knew how that felt. He was grateful and assumed that before she'd allow another minute, another second, to be wasted, she would exit the hall with her dignity. Besides, she received her answer and probably knew the lecture was just about done. Perhaps she didn't want to be caught in the rush for the door anyway. She looked back one more time.

In that moment, Pierce thought he saw green eyes despite the poor lighting, which really was no more than illumination from the lecture stage, and a look of disappointment ... disappointment, he was sure, with him. Her expression of frustration and defeat followed. It lasted a second before she cleared her face of any considerations and turned away from him. He wondered if anyone else caught the expression? If anyone else knew what it was like to be the outcast?

All that Pierce could see of her then, as he hurried to the base of the stairs, was the sweep of a silk bustle as it rustled out the door and down the corridor at a stately pace. A low grumble of voices buried the sound of her footsteps. Many of the conversations were centered on translations of what she had said amongst those who did not speak English. The exotically dressed man shook his head in amusement and his servants retreated further to the shadows. The blue-eyed man leaned out of his shadow, smiled in approval behind his employer where he would not to be seen. There seemed to be a general confusion: approval compromised by social distaste.

What a dreadful morning, Pierce thought, turning his anger toward the old Englishman.

Chapter 14

Paris Gare du Nord, the Paris North Rail Terminus, was a stunning example of the post-Prussian era in France, occasionally referred to by the overly romantic as the Second Empire. In 1871, Paris was bombarded from the land, the river and the air. Before long, it was occupied by Prussian forces and the Emperor had fled to England with his family. Republican and Royalist Parisians alike were left to clean up and rebuild once the enemy had departed. The lovely rail station was one of the first targets of the newly created Prussian balloons armed with guns, and explosives being dropped from above, half of which were surplus from the American war of the 1860s. Primitive in design, aerial bombs were a dangerous yet formidable weapon of terror. The bombs were crude hand-thrown balls of gun powder, at best inaccurate, and often destroyed the balloon they were to be thrown from with too short a fuse or too volatile an explosive charge. But two such bombs did make it to the rail station and wrecked a gem of French architecture.

To the relief of many, aerial bombs were abandoned or out rightly banned by several treaties. No one wanted anything to do with them.

Paris rebuilt itself quickly and the new station's design closely resembled the old station's, being based on the triumphal arch. Thick, sand colored stones were used to give passengers a faux sense of antiquity. Eight enormous statues, each representing the major cities the rail served, topped the dramatic façade. Above the passenger's heads towered iron arches supporting lattice-work glass panels by the hundreds. The effect was spectacular but left an impression that the building was designed to keep birds in. A cage. A cage of fabulous size and beauty. A cage nonetheless.

By 1880, the number of passengers overwhelmed the capacity of the grand terminus and plans were put into place to add five more rail lines into a freshly constructed part of the station by 1887. The train for Calais was waiting on one of the first new lines, away from the chaos that echoed inside the existing structure. Rajiv Pierce was happy for that.

The railway station was active as usual and packed with travelers: some heading North toward the English Channel or Brussels, some heading South toward Italy and the Mediterranean. One could tell who was going short distance and who was heading far away by their manner of dress. Ladies and gentlemen of society, many of whom were escaping to warmer winter climates or embarking on the Grand Tour were obvious standouts from those who used the trains on a daily basis. The tourist women tended toward fancy, expensive suits with ridiculous layers of ruffles, pleats and lace. It was a time of social competition, where one's very quality was worn on their back. Thus was dressed the over-stuffed couch that had been chattering away for several minutes at Pierce.

To his horror, he discovered that she was the wife of the annoying old English explorer who had given him such grief during the presentation. Pierce was loathe to allow the conversation to start, but it had begun so auspiciously with her general apology for her husband's behavior. It didn't take long for Pierce to realize that she was doing so out of habit and not really for him in particular. Clearly it was her routine. Several of the attendees at the Université de Paris had departed for the railway station at the same time. He had hoped to avoid everyone, but in his usual manner, he'd lost his ticket. He could remember the tiniest detail of an engine design, but keeping track of a piece of paper eluded him. Pierce had been forced to stand in line for his new ticket with the old Englishman glaring at his back. The wife simply recognized her husband's behavior and knew where to direct her socially corrective efforts. Pierce had to admit at first, it was refreshing to find that someone had an interest in decent manners.

But it ended as quickly as it had started. She launched, with an appalling assumption of familiarity, into a catalogue of who was who, as though Pierce couldn't have cared less. There was someone by some name he'd already forgotten. She was determined to show him how much she, an Englishwoman, was connected in Paris. Lord "so-n-so," from somewhere in Essex, was newly married to someone's daughter, who came from an old French family - he just couldn't remember, nor did he want to.

It was the worst situation he could imagine. The old Englishman had gone on ahead to see to the luggage and was rudely taking his sweet time getting back to them. Likely it was an act of revenge, Pierce thought, leaving him to stand with the nattering wife. Did she never stop to draw breath?

Even worse, she didn't actually look at him while talking, which usually happened when people were being forcibly polite to him but unable to look at the color of his skin or his overall Indian appearance. It was also possible that none of that mattered to her; she just didn't care to whom she was talking so long as she was talking.

Women had changed over the years. Gone were the pretty, petite girls who let a man open doors for them or read to them only those articles in the newspaper that were suitable for their dispositions. Those who sat quietly, listening to every word and laughing at just the right moments. Those who understood that the world was an ugly, vicious place and had the good sense to want no part of it. Now there were New Women, who did anything and everything they wanted to. Not that that was such a bad thing, really, when he thought about it, but there were limits, Pierce decided. Light, curly hair; small lips; dark eyes, sweet smile; short, tiny-waist and delicate – that was his idea of beauty. That was everyone's ideal of beauty, was it not?

A newspaper boy wandered by waving the latest editions of several Parisian publications. Each had a headline regarding the Dutch Indies, and some sort of supernatural bird. Pierce thought for a moment, not that again. How gullible were people these days? Man made eruptions ... it couldn't be done. Of course, he, himself, knew absolutely nothing about volcanoes. Nor did he have any interest in learning. Rocks had no appeal to him.

With Mrs. Old Englishman staring off into the distance, going on about something she found quite scandalous regarding the French, a pair of women, drowning in lace and satin and whatever else they could combine, strutted by. Talk, talk, talk, all in that same high-pitched voice that grated on the nerves and said nothing in particular. Pierce's head began to hurt, especially under the patch of scar tissue. Children squealed and ran around his legs, only to be shouted at by a plump woman who was clearly the nanny. They would likely be headed for the Second Class car: let them take the chaos with them, he prayed. Here and now, he needed calm. But the chances of getting it in one of Europe's busiest rail stations were near to impossible. Blasts of steam shot out of the engines; Conductors shouted out warnings of immediate departures; and baggage men vulgarly commented on the wear and tear of individual pieces of luggage. All of this echoed and doubled in volume under the high, glass paned roof.

Through this, Pierce heard one sentence spoken. A gracious yet assertive voice, a touch on the low side without being unfeminine, asking for the appropriate track.

It was *her* voice he heard, as though he had desired it so much he would have detected it across the city. The idea that he wanted something - someone - this badly disturbed his priorities and proprieties. Yet, Pierce remembered it quite clearly for reasons he couldn't fathom. Looking around the crowded train station, he wasn't entirely sure how he would even recognize her if she didn't continue to speak. All he'd really seen of her was a look of disappointment and her dress, from the back, as she left the hall. Green eyes he remembered easily. She had green eyes. He couldn't count on identifying her by her clothing. She might have changed to another costume if she was so inclined. It was something that women were always doing. He, himself, had changed into a sack suit of light brown wool tweed, but that was for practical reasons not vanity - wasn't it?

Walking around a rather animated family of eight, leaving Mrs. Old Englishman to chat with someone she actually knew, he was surprised to see the back of the woman again - the bold speaker from the Université de Paris.

How he discovered it was her was the most objectionable thing. The old Englishman had stopped her and was quite rudely blocking her way. "If you are not a journalist then tell me Miss, from what academic institution do you claim to come from, that you should be given access to such important, scientific forums?" He looked as though he'd won a bet.

Calmly, she replied to him, slowing her speech deliberately. "I am an academic with interests in Professor Pierce's work. My initial schooling was the University of Edinburgh."

"So you attended university ..." His voice was dripping in disbelief.

"And, graduated with recommendations to attend lectures at the Paris School of Geology." Before he could make some other comment, she continued, resting her hand gracefully on the tall handle of her parasol. "Lastly, I received my doctorate in Geological Sciences from the Darmstadt University of Mining and Engineering. Habilitation too."

"Well ... well ... Miss ..."

"Doctor, if you would, please." She was patient. She spoke slowly and deliberately, almost as though she thought it might help the Englishman understand her better. Her grip on her umbrella, however, tightened to the point of drawing the leather of her gloved hand tight across her knuckles.

"Never heard of such a thing, not ever. A woman academic? You're not too far gone or too old to have a natural life, you know. Take my advice, Miss; you should find a husband who will clarify the meaning of your life and give it prudent direction. You clearly require a firm hand and guidance."

She calmly raised an eyebrow and smiled in that purposely gracious way. "I don't believe I shall ever be in need of one such man, when so many good-natured fellows like yourself are so brilliant and quick to offer me the advice they think best." Now her words were dripping in sarcasm. She could not be rude, not if he might impact her career later on.

He entirely missed her point, thought himself the best man standing, and wished her a curt, "Good day to you - Miss!" He walked away, half lifting his hat and looking straight at his wife who had heard nothing. The woman, the doctor, reached down gracefully, picked up her valise and something else with her right hand, and walked away with a triumphant swish in her skirts.

She strolled along with determination, at first stopping to inquire of a man selling newspapers something regarding America, then seeking the train, headed north to the coast, which was blissfully out from under the cover of the main station, in an area yet to have its construction completed. As luck would have it, no one was working in that area at the time. Compared to the rest of the terminus, it was peaceful.

Pierce quickly completed his transaction, fumbling a few times when entering the destination code on the mechanical ticket agency. The large box had a sign that indicated the various stations on the train routes and listed a set of numbers next to them. Keys protruded from the face of the machine and one entered the code. Once the weight of proper coinage was achieved in the coin box, a paper ticket was spit out. It worked most of the time, but left first and third class travelers alike standing in long queues. Regretting the distraction his replacement ticket was proving to be, finally Pierce followed her out to the new rail line.

Sitting in the midst of the track was France's newest locomotive and a short attachment of passenger cars, something Pierce would normally have had a keen interest in. Everything was painted in a matching burgundy, beige, and gold. The Number 18 Engine was the foremost in short excursion locomotives, made from new alloy metals that made it lighter and thus more fuel efficient. A 020+021 axel configuration according to the French designations for locomotives, or as the British preferred to call it, a wheel arrangement of 0-4-4-2. Inside its large, cylindrical, bronze body were three British Wimshurst Electrostatic Devices linked into a Norwegian-built Sandvand Alternator. Heavily insulated and bound into the engine's body by thick, shiny steel straps, the electrical generator assembly was intended to provide energy to gigantic copper coils that heated and boiled the water for the piston engines. As was the nature of new technology, the Number 18 maintained a short boiler and coal car for emergencies, adding five meters to the length of the engine. It was huge and thus quite impressive, as intended. It wouldn't do to slow commuting traffic in and out of Paris due to a malfunction in the generators; not with all of Europe watching. And, well, it happened frequently, regardless of who was watching. This did not stop the Rail Authorities from celebrating the new locomotive in every newspaper and broadside and billboard. Its stack was pouring forth slightly gray smoke, and one of the engineering crew was looking particularly put out as his hands and trousers were covered with soot. Number 18, this trip, would be a standard, coal-driven ride north.

The object of Pierce's interest didn't appear impressed with the locomotive as much as she might have been. In her left hand, she carried a folded parasol with a stick long enough to be a walking cane. She held it rather gingerly now, almost too loosely, as though she might drop it. In her other hand, she held two pieces of luggage: an overstuffed valise and what appeared to be a rifle case, which was ridiculous as no woman would be walking through Paris with a rifle. There was no reason for her to be carrying such a thing. It must have been something else. The weight of the two caused her to lean slightly to her left to compensate. Why did she insist on carrying all the heavy items in one hand, he wondered? Not very smart of her. Certainly not for a Doctor of Geological Sciences, if she were to be believed.

Turning sharply toward the Porter, she apparently asked him to take personal possession of the rifle-like case. He did so with mixed curiosity and pleasure. He took it to the waiting first class car and copiously noted its owner and destination on a small notebook. The baggage man, he handed it to, said something nearly inaudible of which Pierce still managed to pick out the French word for 'lock.' The lady understood and thanked both in clear, metropolitan French. In that brief moment she looked out toward Pierce.

She was not what he had expected. She had an athletic look to her, not delicate at all, and yet she had very womanly curves. She looked masculine and feminine at once, deliberately so.

Did she see him? Perhaps? Yes! Yes, she did see him. His stomach began to knot.

The lady looked him over for a second, raised an eyebrow, and allowed the corners of her mouth to arch up slightly. She turned her whole body toward him. His stomach knotted tighter.

As the train was not set to leave until the stroke of six, there was just time enough to make proper introductions. His invention had been re-boxed and sent ahead with the rest of his luggage. All Pierce had to worry about was the ticket he'd likely lose again if he didn't remember to put it in exactly the same place in his travel case. He rested his hand on top of a mahogany cane, which his father had given him along with several 'lessons' in its proper and improper usage. As she took a step in his direction, he was grateful to have something to occupy his hands, otherwise he would have to stand there and fidget. Very undignified. Oh God, what was he going to say to her? A panic was rising in his chest.

A low rumble from the sky drew everyone's attention upward. The clouds had formed quickly. Too quickly. They were dark against the brighter sky and, if one was poetic enough to think it, sinister looking. A louder rumble filled the railway station, followed by a burst of rain and hail directly over the waiting train. Men and women in the open cried out and ran for safety. Pierce lifted his travel case and covered his head. He maneuvered in her direction, careful to place himself under what cover there was before his case was ruined by the rain. Would she allow him to guide her out of the inclement weather? Would he find the words to ask her if she would allow him? Would he be able to speak them? Oh God, did he actually have to talk with her about something other than his invention?

She opened her parasol and stood in place, glaring at the clouds with absolute defiance. Of all the foolish things? But there she waited, as if demanding greater action from the storm. She looked angry and yet, perhaps, a little afraid. Her taffeta petticoat became splattered with mud. And yet, she stood perfectly still. If he didn't know better he would have

79

assumed she had been bullied to the point where either she had to cower and take another beating or stand and fight. For a moment, Pierce knew what that felt like, intimately.

But that was rubbish; she was a lady, not a schoolboy.

Slowly, as though in response to her defiance, the clouds cleared.

The whole storm lasted less than three minutes. It was meteorologically impossible, wasn't it? Nonsense. Such things must happen all the time in France, Pierce assured himself.

The lady, affecting an unfazed expression, irritably shook off her parasol and meticulously folded the cloth portion back into place. Lifting her chin high and her skirts just enough to clear her now muddy shoes, she marched victoriously over to the waiting train. In two graceful strides, she climbed into the car.

There was something oddly beautiful and intriguing about her. It was not the nature of women to be so openly bold. And, as curious as he was about the lady, he was equally interested in why she had reacted to the storm as she had. She also wasn't the type of woman he usually found attractive. He wasn't certain he liked a woman who appeared more comfortable in the outdoors than most; more than he did. Yet, she intrigued him.

Pierce looked at his first class ticket and decided that being in the same car was exactly the chance he needed to corner her, to see what she thought of his lecture, his machine, his conduct under fire. And yes, what about the storm? Good, now he had something to talk to her about. The knot in his stomach remained, but the rest of the panic and cold sensations were evaporating.

By the time he actually reached the stairs to the first class car, he had come up with fifteen very good reasons why she wouldn't talk to him and why he shouldn't bother her at all. Yet, he felt the imperative to meet her.

First Class Salon cars tended to look alike on the haul up and down the Continent. They provided superior individual seating in an open parlor or salon, hence the name, of which there were two per car. Each salon was separated by a connecting corridor and refreshment service. Since so many used the line for commuting or quick travel to the north coast, the Pullman had been redesigned with business efficiency in mind. In a very French egalitarian manner, there were no servers but only those who tidied up or maintained the two enormous carafes of tea and coffee. Pierce preferred the openness of that type of car, not being fond of tight spaces. If only the other first class passengers could restrain from staring, or worse – striking up conversations with him.

Like any ocean cruising ship there was pride of service and presentation which he greatly appreciated. The rail system of France ran on time: not quite as obsessively as the British railway, but on time and steady. Pierce entered the car to find it half empty. First Class tickets were an extravagance for most travelers. Pierce maintained the notion that after a typical, academic showdown, of which he'd seen his share, the expense was worth it.

The Conductor called out the final opportunity to board. After a rush of people to the third class car, he turned and signaled an all-clear to the Engineer and Fireman. Inside the cars, it felt like an earthquake with two distinct jolts, and then the roughness began waned as the train picked up momentum. Until it was well into the countryside, the Engineer would not open up the throttles and let it race along at top speed. The back-and-forth jostling was now replaced with side-to-side swaying and a bump or two where the rail itself was not in perfect repair.

In many ways, it was too bad that the electrified engine wasn't working. On coal steam alone, the train would only make a top speed of twenty miles per hour. Pierce had hoped to see the electrified engine in action, with a potential of up to forty miles per hour if the Engineer was so inclined to take it to full chisel. Now that would have been something to experience, he thought.

The individual, overstuffed chairs were lined up in sets along the windows, every other one being paired up and placed with a small table between them. Such a layout was perfect for businessmen who had leftover work to be done. As this was not an overnight journey, no accommodations were made for sleeping. And, since the journey was so short, no separate smoking car was provided. It was a high-class café on wheels.

Where was she?

A burst of laughter from the opposite end drew his, and a few other's, attention. A tall, slender man topped with wild reddish hair and holding a cigar was noisily making his admiration for her wit well known. He stopped only to drag deeply on the cigar and to allow the smoke to slither out. She stood with her fresh cup of tea, trying to avoid the smoke and to keep her balance against the increasing sway of the car. Couldn't he see that it was bothering her and he was keeping her from reseating herself in a more favorably situated chair, Pierce thought? Vulgar, that's what it was. The man was ill-mannered and ridiculously loud. She nodded politely, as much as she could stand to. Twice she attempted to disentangle herself from the conversation only to be blocked by the rude fellow. That made two men who felt free to be inconsiderate to her that Pierce himself had seen; was it because she was alone? Could she expect any different treatment while insisting on such independence? But when she tried to stifle a cough brought on by the smoke, it was clear to Pierce that she had had enough. The smoker then committed the worst faux pas possible: he reached over and stroked her arm with the same hand that held a smoldering cigar. Her eyes went wide.

No one in the car moved to her aid.

Pierce couldn't tell what was exactly said or done in the next instant, but the cigar smoker suddenly found the front of his waistcoat and trousers covered in tea. Hot, scalding tea. He leapt back and she innocently apologized for her clumsiness with vigor. Perhaps too much vigor. He waved her off; assuring her it was just fine. Grumbling, he walked to another car of the train to seek an appropriate amount of privacy to clean up.

The inhabitants of that half of the car glared at her, not him. They likely thought she should have just suffered it like a lady, or in the minimum, waited for one of the gentlemen present to assist her. For a lone woman on a train, it was beyond socially acceptable for her to react in such a way. Never mind that he deserved it.

Pierce realized how confused he was at that moment; she was a lady, but not a lady. He couldn't decide. Part of him was appalled at her unfeminine behavior while the rest applauded her for not allowing such outrageous treatment. The lady sat her empty cup and saucer on one of the tables and attempted to ignore the low grumbling complaints and unkind stares around her. She was embarrassed, no doubt. If Pierce approached her wrong, in the mood she was in, he could be the next one wearing a beverage. She wouldn't hesitate for an instant. No, she was not a lady. He had been mistaken. She was not someone he should converse with. A so-called New Woman. What would his family and colleagues think of him?

His opinion must have shown on his face.

She was looking at him, her smile faded and she seemed rather disappointed if not discomfited. For a moment, a look of genuine hurt crossed her face before habit forced a more neutral expression to cover it

He turned away, not wishing to make eye contact anymore, a habit of his own.

From the sound of her skirts he could tell that the woman in red had walked to the other end of the car, likely seeking a place to sit where no one disapproved of her.

Surely he could still come up with some excuse to talk to her, could he not? He would only need walk up and say 'Good evening.' That was all. A wave of panic swept over him and he spent his every effort keeping any emotion under control and appearing to be just fine.

All the way from Paris to Calais, Pierce stayed on his end of the car, engrossed in his sketchbook, consuming brandy-laced tea and ignoring everything - and everyone - else. And, feeling oddly ashamed.

Chapter 15

September 2, 1882
The English Channel Ferry
Calais, France

The steamer that served as England's main link to the Continent was a lovely, if well-worn, edifice of earlier technology. The application of the steam engine and dual paddle system had cut the travel time from Calais to Dover down from four hours to two. It still surprised those unfamiliar with the crossing that such a short distance could take such a long time. Weather conditions, tides, currents, other ship traffic, and obstacles normal to docking all contrived to slow things down. What remained was a miniature ocean voyage which, while it could be quite dangerous, was nonetheless made pleasant by the steamer company and was as brief as could be.

Once he was satisfied that his mechanism was safely packed on board, Professor Pierce set out to find the Adventuress. Yes, he decided that "Adventuress" was just fine. He needed to be more open minded, yet "Doctor" was a bit beyond his reach for the time being. A fitful night's sleep had not done anything to sooth his exhausted nerves and strangely he couldn't shake her from his thoughts so easily. But it had given him time to think and re-think his approach to the extraordinary woman. She had been allowed to attend the presentation, thus she had some prestige. If that was the case, then her opinion was all the more valuable. What did she think of him? Not the man who turned his back on her in the car, but the man who had presented a unique invention in the midst of an august body of academics. He really desired her opinion. Well, at least he thought he did. There were those abdominal butterflies again.

As time for the first crossing approached, dozens of travelers began gathering closer to the steamer. Pierce searched the crowd as they passed him where he sat, having tea and pastry. Near the end of the flood of people, the Adventuress strolled by, reading a small, pressboard bound book and leaning to her left in compensation for the heavy valise and rifle-shaped case she carried in her right. It looked like she was reading one of those foolish, romantic novels women so loved. He thought she should put the book down and wait to read until she was on board. Then she could carry one of her bags in each hand, to balance the weight. For that matter, why did she insist on carrying them herself? Were there no porters to be hired? A small pair of reading glasses were balanced on her nose, which he took to be a sign that she exhausted her eyes with abundant reading.

Pierce left enough money for his bill, took up his gloves and cane, and followed as inconspicuously as possible behind her. What would he say? He'd forgotten what he'd planned already. How could he speak to her without giving away his previous judgment of her or the fact that he likely didn't remember what it was he'd decided to say to her in the first place? Damn the panic.

Pierce managed to keep his head down and stay no more than thirty yards behind the Adventuress. She'd changed her costume to another simple wool suit, this time in dark brown tweed, which made her hair appear a bit more brown than black. In fact, it gave her an overall warmer appearance, which was so very contrary to the dictates of fashion. He knew all about that, being himself darker than was fashionable.

A man sitting on the ground near, but not too near, the ferry held out a cup; he was ignored by all. All except the Adventuress. He kept his head down, blacked by shadow, probably out of shame. His clothes were dreadful, yet had once been those of a sailor. His beard was thick and blotted out much of his face. "Help a seaman," he whispered hoarsely, pulling his collar up around his throat.

"A British sailor in France?" she said kindly.

"Bit trapped, Miss." He kept staring at the ground.

"Are you looking for work?" She stopped and leaned down toward him. "I know some people who might be able to help." She looked away for a moment, digging into her valise.

The sailor looked up at her with a startled pair of very, very blue eyes. Immediately, he dropped his head. "Yes, ma'am. Honest work for an honest sailor."

She set down her valise, pulled a pencil out of the spine of one book, and actually tore away a page from the back of her novel. She quickly wrote out a name and address, folded the paper in half and in half again. After slipping a substantial value of coins into the pocket of paper, she handed it him. "Go to Barking. There should be enough here for a ticket and something to eat. See a Mr. Thomas Fezziwig IV at that address. He is a tea importer; an old family business. He's always in need of help."

A dirty hand reached up to take the gift. He held it for a moment, looking at it, almost treasuring it. "God bless you ma'am. I swear, I won't spend it on drink. I promise."

"Your promise is good enough. What will the world have become if you can't trust the word of an honest sailor looking for honest work. I wish you luck."

Whether she actually believed him or not, Pierce didn't know. Surely she wasn't so naïve: the chances of her money being spent on liquor were appallingly high. Yet she walked away without looking back to check or to see what the man would do. The sailor watched her as she walked away. He was stunned. So was Pierce, who hurried to catch up.

The ferry waited, bouncing in what might have been an indication of a rough crossing. Waves rocked the boat back and forth, banging it into the sides of the pier and threatening to damage its new white paint. Finally the captain brought up pressure in the boilers and began stabilizing the vessel. The power of steam forced into pistons near the aft of the boat flushed through long coated, tubes that narrowed as it reached its destination. The effect caused a squeal and groan that startled everyone. As the tubes heated, any condensation vaporized and floated away as a strange fog. The pipes popped and snapped as the metal reacted to the cold morning air. The pistons turned the turbines, which in turn whipped up the seawater. Carefully and expertly, the captain used the propulsion to hold the boat steady against the pier. Passengers began boarding again.

She handed her rifle-shaped case to a ship's Purser, who broke with customs regarding first class travelers and asked her some rather pointed questions. What caliber was it? Was it a French made gun or Italian? She smiled at him and kindly answered each and every question. An old model 1869, lever-action, .44 caliber rifle, made by the now the famous American gun manufacturer owned by Mr. Winchester. It was a 'Henry,' named after Mr. Henry, the prior owner of the New Haven Arms Company.

So, it was a rifle after all. How absurd, Pierce thought dismissively. And a bit of an antique too by comparison with current weapons designs.

"Lettie?" a voice called from the crowd. "Excuse me, Professor Letticia Gantry?"

"Are you making fun of me?" she said, looking past several heads to find the man who was addressing her. At first, the way she smiled, Pierce thought the man must be her husband. He felt surprisingly disappointed. But no, their physical language said otherwise; they shook hands and he kissed her on the cheek. Such behavior rarely occurred between two married people; it lacked the dignity of the aloof married state. Besides, what man would let his wife run around Europe, attending lectures and speaking in public? An equally extraordinary man, that was who would allow it. And, did he call her 'Professor?'

"My dear, you look refreshed."

"Do I, Professor Moore?"

"Travel has always suited you." Christopher Moore took Lettie's hand as only a friend could and held it. He was considerably taller and much broader in the shoulder than most of the men around him, and he wore his size with confidence. This was not to say that Moore wasn't fit, rather, that he was one of those muscular men who simply defied the current fashion for slenderness that bordered on frailty. With a full head of light brown hair, a peppered beard and strong hands, he was a model of masculinity. He was also entirely useful as he stepped between the bright morning sunlight and her eyes.

"I think this was one time my travels haven't been successful. Entertaining and exhausting, but not successful. I don't suppose you have *the Times* or *the Herald*?" She stopped removing her glasses and looked at him hopefully that she might need to keep them in hand.

Moore could now see the dark circles under her eyes, which led him to look for more signs of fatigue. The lines near her eyes appeared a bit deeper than he remembered and his friend, who would never appear slovenly in public, had clearly rushed styling her hair and had mismatched a pair of pearl earrings. He then noticed the way she protected her left hand, the tired way she held her head, and the general lack of enthusiasm in her voice. He wouldn't, however, contradict his earlier statement. "Yes, I have those newspapers: thought you might like to get caught up. Tea?" he asked, taking her arm and starting to escort her in the direction of Ferry's passenger deck.

For her part, Lettie didn't resist. She slipped the reading glasses into a pocket in her skirt and held onto his arm. "I'm rather concerned about some people, and I'm looking for an indication that they are alright," she said with a rise in pitch in her voice.

It seemed that only Moore could get away with such indulgent behavior as taking her arm without asking; he knew it and took advantage of it. "Let's get settled first, then we can peruse the news of the day."

The deck was crowded but not noisy. On a day as clear and sunny as it was turning out to be, naturally everyone wanted to be outside. The coastal fog was burning off quickly and the temperature had become rather pleasant in relative terms. Pierce seated himself where he could hear but not appear to be listening in. The clichéd use of a wide copy of *the Times* actually served him quite well. Certainly, she would recognize him if he didn't take some precautions.

For her part, Lettie was eagerly turning the pages of the newspaper handed over to her by Moore. She held it so tightly while snapping the pages back and forth that she wrinkled them.

Moore felt obliged to take the paper from her hands and to lay it down on the table so that she could not destroy it before he had a chance to read it. He helped to keep the pages flat in the breeze as she scanned through the headlines. "Now, explain to me why you think this journey of yours was unsuccessful. Let me see if I have this straight ... Portsmouth, New York, Philadelphia, Baltimore, Paris, Dover, home. Did I miss anything? All those places and no luck?"

Lettie leaned back in her chair as far as decorum and her corset would allow. Whatever she was looking for hadn't made the news that day. "Oh, a great deal of fun was to be had in each city. I daresay the best was Philadelphia," she said, pulling the glasses off her nose.

"Ah, the missing Weldon Institute members? I knew it!"

"Has anything been reported?" she asked with anxiety in her voice. "There was nothing in the Paris papers except the bizarre business in Java. I can't find a single issue from America." She was forcing herself to whisper even though her level of urgency was rising. "I've been cut off from any information out of the United States ..." She hesitated as Moore closed the newspaper, and folded it very carefully and crisply. "Christopher Moore, tell me."

"The Weldon fellows got away from their abductor by sinking his ship, no more than three weeks ago, but beyond that they won't say a word about what happened. It's become a huge mystery and quite a sensation in London. But we have always loved our mysteries and scandalous adventures. The Continentals seem a bit less impressed, probably why you didn't see anything in the newspapers. But you know what happened, don't you?"

Lettie leaned her elbows on the table and rested her face in her hands. "Thank God." There was a deep sigh of relief before she finally looked up. "'Sinking his ship?' They're lying, Christopher, though I daresay I'm not surprised. And, yes, I know what happened. And I have nothing but bruises to show for my effort to prevent it." When Moore's face showed more than polite concern, she added, "nothing dreadful."

"Not quite what happens in the romances, eh? Tell me what happened. As I said, it was all through the papers in London up to about a day or so ago. When I read about it and saw the name of the institute, I wondered if you were involved. My telegrams didn't catch you? I knew I should have sent a 'Tipsy.'"

"No, but thank you for sending them all the same. And don't you dare spend that much money on a Tipsy. You are such a dear friend. No, it was horrid and I really found myself out of my … league."

Moore waited and listened. Damn the authors and preachers who said otherwise; women had the same pride as men, and Lettie was especially vulnerable when she simply wasn't able to do everything she wanted. "I presume the balloon enthusiasts were not helpful?" he asked.

"Not in the least, but they themselves were rather entertaining."

"Start at the beginning. You and I both know where it stands. I want every detail leading up to today."

Chapter 16

Three months earlier: June 12, 1882.
The Weldon Institute
Philadelphia, Pennsylvania, United States

The Weldon Institute was no institute of higher learning; nor was it a place of greater technological development. It was a gang of uncouth Americans unaware of their own rudeness. Lettie was not in the habit of casually dismissing Americans, nor anyone else for that matter, having found most to be of excellent character, bright wit, and dynamic courage. But the balloonists of Philadelphia were sadly none of the above. They had built the world's largest balloon, called it the *Go Ahead*, and hired someone to fly it for them. It seemed that their courage only held when arguing with each other and spending cash so that others could be brave on their behalf.

She knew she had made a terrible, and expensive, mistake in approaching the so-called center of aeronautic invention when she met the men running the Institute. First off, the balloonists were led by the most simple-minded, stubborn old fool who called himself Uncle Prudent. Prudent was obviously the family name, but it hardly was a family quality. Uncle, as he insisted on being called, was an overstuffed chair with legs and hands, a man who filled his pockets with that curious American paper money. Why he did this seemed to be a minor mystery, though Lettie guessed that he probably liked to be known as the on-the-spot fellow who could pay for 'a round,' or to hand out to needy children in hopes that his apparent generosity might earn him admiration. Thin strands of hair were drawn over his broad scalp in an attempt to appear as a full head of hair. His hands darted about when he spoke, indicating a certain nervous desire to distract a listener from the fact that he knew little about the topic he was expounding upon. His nails were bitten down too, another sign of uneasiness. That was the President of the Weldon Institute.

The Vice President was a man named Phil Evans, who, by all appearances, lived for the sake of being in opposition to Uncle Prudent. He was much leaner, better dressed, and always took the Devil's side in any argument Prudent participated in. It was rumored that he should have been the President, but missed the appointment by a strange question of measurement. It was all very confusing. There was something at once interesting and repulsing about Evans, as though he desired to be in opposition to everything and everyone, so long as it kept life interesting for him. If it should harm your life, well, he couldn't have cared less. Lettie estimated that Evans was no more than ten and no less than five years younger than Prudent. His pale hair was thicker, his moustache more grand, and his command of certain topics far greater than Prudent's. Overall, Evans seemed to have been born to torment and tease Uncle. But, what a small thing that was, frustrating a silly old man. Evans, she suspected, had grander plans but no means to achieve them.

So there she sat, in the front room, waiting for them. Doctor Letticia Makepeace Gantry, future Professor of Geology, Explorer of the erupting Mt. Tarumae, Survivor of Mt. Awu, having arrived exactly on time for the evening's meeting, only to find the doors barred to a woman. It took Prudent, Evans, a Mr. Forbes, and several others half an hour to realize that in the Institute's rush to create rules and regulations for every little thing, they had forgotten to consider if women could attend meetings. Things were made worse by the simple facts that Lettie was better educated than all of them combined and she had the means by which to become a significant benefactress. She could not, in simple terms, be ignored and sent home.

She'd dressed for the affair in simple black wool surah, tailored but not ostentatious. Underneath the fitted body of her cuirass jacket and un-bustled skirt, an underskirt of pleated grosgrain peeked out as she walked. Downright scholarly, in fact. She had even gone so far as to wear a matronly looking bonnet of blue silk velvet instead of her usual preference for a beautifully crafted hat. She kept her belongings to a bare minimum: a pair of gloves and her valise. Thinking she would be in a room full of people, she left the extra mantle in her hotel. Alone in the frigid room, she decided that was yet another of her mistakes. The fire was low. It was chilly, even for Eastern America in the summer. There was no tea to be offered. Americans were notorious coffee consumers and besides, it was not an afternoon visit she was attending. She liked coffee and would have gladly accepted it had it been offered. No such luck.

Her chest began to tighten in response to a rising sense of panic.

Breathe, she reminded herself. Just breathe. If she could contain her fear and keep her composure, then all would go well. It had to go well. It would go well. She repeated that thought several times. She needed their help. Well, at least she was alone. No one was witnessing her panic.

Alone? Lettie had the sudden feeling that she was not alone in the room. "Hello?"

A figure of a man moved in the shadows cast by the streetlights. Backlit as he was, she couldn't see his face. He moved stiffly, with his shoulders solidly set in place. He seemed to bow slightly then turned away from her to look out the window.

Before she could ask him any questions, the Steward arrived to announce that special dispensations had been made and that she was to be allowed into the meeting. Lettie turned to see if the man was still at the curtains, but no one was there. It might have been her imagination. Then again, it might have been a ghost. She did believe in ghosts and thought it foolish of the scientific community to dismiss them without study. She knew a couple of ghosts.

Contrary to the hauntingly quiet mood outside the meeting hall, the inside was full of shouting voices, name-calling and papers being thrown about. Uncle Prudent called the room to order, at one point resorting to the use of a steam whistle.

All eyes turned toward Lettie as she entered the room and was shown to a seat, near the back of course. The roll call of attending members was completed in some haste and all else was quickly set aside.

"Members of the Weldon Institute. We are privileged tonight to have a guest among us. As you have been informed, we have a proposal to consider regarding the use of the *Go Ahead* for a great scientific purpose." Prudent hesitated for a moment then directed his comments to Lettie. "Madame, it is our usual policy to ask the proposer to speak on the subject. However, we would never wish to put you in an uncomfortable situation requiring public speaking."

Leap in woman, before he cuts you off, she thought. "Thank you Mr. President." She stood up but instantly signaled none of the men to respond in kind. The balloonists, confused by the moment, didn't even attempt to stand when she did. She didn't really expect many of them to, to begin with. Still, she was here to address them, to make a request of them, and she would be the epitome of proper behavior. And they had their pride too. She deeply swallowed hers, while setting her gloves onto her chair.

"Mr. President, Mr. Secretary, honorable members of the Weldon Institute. Good evening, gentlemen. First, I must thank you for your graciousness in allowing me to intrude upon your deliberations. And to you, Uncle Prudent, my deepest appreciation." She calmly folded her hands. A feeling of nervousness washed over her and she was determined not to allow it to affect her speech. Even to her own ears, her speech was quite clipped and exact, thus she deliberately softened the tone as to not sound too officious or superior. That was a lesson she'd learned when first attempting to lecture in Germany. "I'm afraid I'm going to cause a bit of shock, yet I think there isn't a man amongst you that is not quite capable of enduring it." A low rumble of genial laughter followed her remark. "I am a scientist – specifically a Volcanologist, with an advanced degree from the Darmstadt University of Mining and Engineering. This is all very new, to have a woman put the letters of DR and SC after her name, but I ask you to humor me for but a moment longer." Mutters rose from the crowd, but they were entirely anticipated. "I am certain each of you gentlemen is fully aware that it is the path of some to remain safe and quiet, and the path of others to risk all for a greater purpose. The latter path is the purpose of your Institute, your development of the *Go Ahead*, and your robust discussions. Please allow me to say that I can appreciate that passion and in fact request your assistance in bringing a seed of purpose to bloom."

She hadn't expected applause, but for some reason, a majority of men felt inspired to do so. "It is my most earnest desire to discover a means of prediction for volcanic eruptions, wherein lives may be saved. If a predictive model can be found, its implications for peoples all over the world, even here on this continent, will be profound."

Evans, not to be outdone by Prudent, stood up. "Members, this learned and well meaning lady has come all the way from Europe to learn if our magnificent balloon can assist in the goal?" He swept a pale, thick lock of hair off his forehead in an easy if not rehearsed manner.

The question of, 'how' was immediately shouted around the room.

"Aerial photography," she simply answered. "Photography of volcanic structures such as craters, vents, and lava flows."

The room immediately erupted on its own, with debate of such vigor that Lettie was at first taken aback. Prudent's gavel started pounding and then that dreadful steam whistle. What in the world was the matter with these men? Did they have to argue over everything?

It was Evans who stepped in again. "Members. Please. We have a lady amongst us. Decorum, gentlemen, decorum." The roar quieted. "I feel that we may need more discussion on the matter, Madame. Perhaps we could derive a list of questions that may be answered."

One fellow didn't wait. "Miss Gantry," he said loudly, ignoring her academic title as pleased him. "Do you believe that it is safe to attempt such a thing?"

"Most certainly not, or I would have asked this of the French." It was unkind to say such, but she understood the odd if not indiscernible relationship between Americans and Frenchmen. Laughter, however, was a potent counteragent to fear and the Weldon Institute men were laughing heartily now. "I need American courage." Too much? She would have thought so, but the membership of the Weldon Institute readily accepted the compliment.

Someone began pounding on the hall door, startling the Steward who rushed to see who was making such a noise, none of which slowed Lettie down. "The greatest danger is found when one is on foot and attempting to take photographs from the ground, while a balloon can, as the saying goes, rise above it all. Many have lost their lives while ascending or descending from an active crater. To learn, we must collect information."

The Steward rushed back to Prudent with his silver tray. "A communication!" said Uncle Prudent. "A stranger, my dear colleagues, vehemently asks to be admitted to the meeting. We had not yet voted on his admittance but now he specifically desires to add to this discussion."

What in the world? She picked up her gloves and hid her nervous hands with them. She really hated arguments and now someone new was going to join in the potential riot. He could either be helpful or hindering. She took a deep breath and met Evans's gaze strongly.

"Madame Scientist?"

"I welcome intelligent discourse, sir." It was a stretch of the truth, she was in no mood to welcome any interruption, but she also knew it was only right. True discourse was one of the greatest tools of scientific discovery. Besides, whoever it was might well have something useful to say. This was not about her pride but the predictive model.

"Never!" replied every voice.

So much for that, she thought.

"He desires to prove to us, it would appear, that to believe in balloons is to believe in the absurdist of Utopias!"

"Let him in!"

My, how the wind quickly changes direction around here, she noted.

"What is the name of this singular personage?" asked Secretary Evans.

"Robur," replied Prudent.

Robur? Wasn't that Latin for 'Oak?' Or was it American for 'the Devil,' she wondered, looking back to see the most extraordinary man enter the room; so full of himself; so confident; so arrogant. He was of average height but the upward tilt of his chin made him seem taller by far. He was broad in his shoulders and slender through the waist. Dressed in a light gray, military style tunic, trousers and highly polished boots, he walked down the steps of the hall, taking his time. A smile curved his thick lips, perfectly centered between a trimmed moustache and goatee, as he stopped for a brief moment and stood next to Lettie. He bowed his head slightly in what might have been deference and she decided that it must have been he who was her temporary ghost. What nationality or race he'd come from seemed impossible to detect. He was at once dark and light. Perhaps a bit more light than dark, and that conclusion might have been more drawn from her observation of his attire than fact, she admitted to herself. She returned a polite nod and watched him descend to the platform below, where Prudent and Evans were waiting. He seemed to be scanning the room for someone or perhaps trying to better gauge his audience.

Prudent and Evans scowled at him, then at each other. They hadn't invited Robur to stand in the center of the room. But then, they hadn't invited her to do so either.

"Citizens of the United States. My name is Robur and I am worthy of the name."

Lord of Mercy, she thought, as he described his excellent health, strength, and digestion. Why did men always brag about their digestive prowess? His speech wasn't English, nor was it French, nor any nationality she could recognize. His pronunciation was perfect, but she had the feeling that he was working purposefully to maintain a carefully accented voice, closer to the vocal habits of his hosting Americans.

He continued: "And now, honorable citizens, for my mental faculties."

Must you, she almost said out loud.

By the time the Aviator, as she was mentally referring to Robur, had finished, he had managed to esteem his intelligence above all others' in the room, including hers, to insult them, and to challenge everything they believed in dearly. It was extraordinary. During the entire exchange, in which Robur bragged and insulted and the Weldon membership shouted and interrupted, Lettie kept looking at his eyes. They were the most important objects to observe, or so she had found through the years. Much could be told of a man by his eyes, regardless of his speech. It mattered how he looked at objects and people, what he looked at, and where he looked when thinking.

This was very true of Robur. Whether or not he believed his own bravado, he knew his audience would overreact wildly. He knew they would hold to their ideas of aeronautics without the slightest care for the logical arguments he presented. And, they were very good arguments, for the notion of a Heavier-than-Air craft. When he wasn't speaking of himself, he was actually quite interesting and persuasive, at least to her. He would occasionally look her way but never did he address her directly. His black eyes told her everything; he was there neither to convince the members nor to persuade them. He was there to play with them. A cat with a mouse - a stupid, ill-behaved mouse at that.

"... and the bee, which gives one hundred and ninety-two beats of the wing per second ..."

"... One hundred and ninety-three, actually!" she said, the words slipping past her lips before she could stop them. It was the smallest trivia, so inconsequential, and certainly nothing so vital that deserved correction, but it was something she happened to know. Lettie simply wasn't patient with men who ignored her, but her correction was also a tad rude and she blushed a bit.

Silence filled the room, and a reluctant smile crossed Robur's face. "One hundred and ninety-three. Yes, Citizeness, you are correct." It was the only correction he would allow. All others shouted at him were ignored. As he spoke, he occasionally looked over at her, seemingly disapproving and yet grudgingly allowing for some admiration. Each time Lettie caught his glance he erased all but the expression of arrogance on his face.

Heavier-than-Air ships were his proposition, and none of his arguments had anything to do with her proposal, she realized with immense frustration. It was an intriguing idea she had to admit. Balloons depended on their lightness, and as had been debated hotly since her arrival all that kept it from becoming the transportation of the future was a means of controlling its direction without relying on the wind. The Aviator was proposing something radical, unique, unheard of ... plausible.

"Mr. Robur," she finally said far more politely, rising from her seat and waiting patiently in the proper manner in which these things should be done. The room hushed. This Oak had taken the conversation away from her proposal and she needed to get it back. There were lives to be saved, if she was successful. "My request of this august body was to consider the use of their balloon in aerial photography." Robur opened his mouth to speak, but she continued unfalteringly. "Sir, your proposed flying machine will clearly have speed and maneuverability, but in context of my proposal, will it have stability? For photographs to be useful in my research, they must be sharp. Clear. Would you not agree? Will your invention have the necessary stability?"

He narrowed his eyes at her. "Madame, I gather from your accent that you are not a citizen of this country."

"That is correct, Sir. But that is not an answer to my question."

"If not a Citizeness, what shall I call you?"

"You may call me Doctor Gantry, for I have earned that name,' she replied, lightly mocking his introduction a bit, "and you may feel free to use it as you answer my question."

The room hummed with a low laugh from most of the members.

For a moment, Robur was silent and his gaze reconsidered her. There was a look of triumph on his face for a fleeting second. "Madame Volcanologist," he replied, unshaken and unwilling to acquiesce to her. "My flying vessel is not merely a proposal, it is a fact. It is built! And yes, in answer to your question, its stability is greater than a balloon, as it will create its own placement in the air rather than hanging like rotting fruit in the breeze." He turned his full attention toward her before anyone else could comment and allowed a slight smile. "My airship will provide a perfect platform for your photography. If you are serious in your desire to photograph your volcanoes, then it, and I, will be at your disposal. Such advantageous pictures will make your predictive model more accurate, will it not?"

"You suggest this ship of yours is built? I doubt it. Have you even ever aviated?" Evans demanded, realizing that this Robur was going to steal their new benefactress. In fact, the whole room was growing restless, as though they had adopted Lettie and had no intention of sharing her.

For a moment she found it very amusing, considering that they had almost blockaded her from entering the building in the first place. And the saying held that women were fickle and ever changing? She tried not to laugh.

"Well, Mr. Aviator, have you?" Evans challenged again.

"I have," Robur said, not taking his black eyes off Lettie. It was momentary at best, yet he seemed to be amused with her.

"And made the conquest of the air?"

"Indeed."

"Hooray for Robur the Conqueror!" shouted one of the members, apparently a bit more inebriated than his fellow Institute members.

"Well, yes! Robur the Conqueror! I accept the name and I will bear it, for I have a right to it!"

A cheer went up from the crowd and shouts of 'Robur the Conqueror' rang inside the hall. Lettie broke the mutual gaze she held with the Aviator and shook her head in disbelief. They were throwing fuel onto that fire and if the cliché held, someone was going to get scorched. And, it wouldn't be Robur.

Some fool named Chip introduced himself as a vegetarian, whatever that had to do with anything. Oh yes, men and their digestion. "Sir, I refer you to a respected inventor, one Doctor Pierce of New College. While he is accepting of numerous theories regarding flight, he has yet to accept the principles of design you suggest. While I'm sure you've accomplished some form of aviation ...well I must be blunt, sir. If the most preeminent inventor of our times has not developed this unusual and doubtful type of flight, why should we take your word that such a ship exists? Who are you that we should believe you?"

What this Chip fellow said was different from all the rest and it set off Robur's temper, likely more the fault of being called, rather politely but nonetheless, a liar. Threats issued from him and were returned in kind. Before Lettie knew what was happening, the membership was rushing the platform to beat Robur quite possibly to death. "Stop!" she cried to no one who was listening. "Stop it!" She even tried to hold back one member who shook her off rudely.

Evans ran against the tide of angry balloonists to her side, to try and protect her, something that angered her all the more. "Mr. Evans, I don't require your assistance. Forget me, if you are a gentleman, you will save that man ..."

Suddenly there was rush to violence. Robur had put his hands into his pockets and now held them out at the front ranks of the mob. Lettie drew in a breath, as did Evans. In each of Robur's hands were a set of custom-made, short-nosed, Colt Navy revolvers, shiny and without a doubt, fully loaded. The immediate silence in the room was staggering. Robur said something, almost certainly insulting, that Lettie could not quite make out for he had said it through clenched teeth and with a low, angry voice. It was not a comment for her ears, but she could guess its meaning.

Four or five shots cracked out, fired into space. Not gunshots; something else. The room lit up so brightly that everyone shielded their eyes. Evans brutally pushed Lettie behind one of the folding chairs and held her down. As the light returned to normal a low mutter arose from the crowd. Both Evans and Lettie waited in silence, staring in the direction of the Aviator and the mob.

No one was hurt, yet, amid a blanket of smoke, the Aviator had disappeared. Robur the Conqueror, Engineer, Inventor and Aviator, had vanished. Borne into the air by some apparatus of his own design no doubt, Lettie thought. What an amazing sight.

"Mr. Evans," she finally said, "he's gone now. You may get off of me."

Evans sat back on his knees, amused to find that he had nearly crushed her with his own body. "I'm terribly sorry Miss Gantry." His voice lacked the certain sincerity she would have preferred to hear. He stood up and then assisted her to her feet.

"I know you meant well, but did it ever occur to you that bullets can as easily go through one of these little chairs as through a window."

Evans stopped and looked at the chair resting under her gloved hand with its tapping index finger, then up at her irritated face. "I ... I was ..."

"... Being gallant. Thank you. I'm just glad that no worse was done here tonight."

Chapter 17

The Same Evening
Fairmont Park, Philadelphia

"Miss Gantry ..."

"Mr. Prudent."

"Oh, please call me Uncle."

"Only if you call me Doctor," she said with such a smile that the assertiveness of the remark completely escaped the Weldon President.

Evans, Prudent, and Prudent's valet had all insisted on walking Lettie to the hotel. Philadelphia was not filled with hansom cabs as were London, Rotterdam and Paris. It was eleven o'clock at night. While Walnut Street was finally quiet once the Weldon Institute membership had broken up its lynching party and headed home, one simply did not send a lady out into the night without escort. Not even a volcano climbing, public speaking, photograph-taking lady.

Neither Prudent nor Evans could stop talking about Robur. And Lettie could not stop thinking about him. The two men snarled at each other, then apologized to the lady, then went back to jostling for her admiration. She had neither the heart nor the energy to inform either that neither of them was likely to get that admiration returned in any kind. Once in a while, she and the valet, named Frycollin, would exchange knowing glances and try helplessly not to roll their eyes.

The hotel was located on the other side of the Schuylkill Bridge and Fairmont Park. No one else seemed to be about, but Philadelphia still made the noises of a growing city.

"Perhaps Miss Gantry will do us the honor of attending another meeting?" Uncle Prudent interrupted her thoughts.

"Only if you promise that it will not include a public lynching."

Both men tried to laugh it off and the valet looked disappointed in both of them. But, as a good valet and a patient man, Frycollin said nothing to embarrass his employer.

"It was a meeting fraught with unusual circumstances. We'll set up rules to assure that no such thing shall ever happen again. We shouldn't allow just anyone into the hall."

"Mr. Prudent. I don't believe that more rules will serve you nearly as much as being open to new suggestions. While I admit I loathed Mr. Robur's outrageous bravado and self-serving language, his ideas were not unsound. And calling his honesty into question? Really? It only caused consternation ..."

Evan hid his laugh, but Prudent didn't even try. "Miss Gantry, you must leave such discussions to men who know their science," he said with a condescending tone. "That is why we should blockade ourselves from such ... inappropriate or uninformed persons." Then, he made his error. "But, while others of your gender will not be allowed to meetings, we will maintain the special dispensation for you."

"What?"

"Well, we can't have everyone coming to meetings, especially those who are ignorant of science or useless in advancing it."

"And because someone is a woman, she must therefore be ignorant?" Lettie stopped walking. "And useless? Mr. Prudent, do you really comprehend just how insulting that is?"

He stopped abruptly and Evans nearly walked into the back of him. "Oh, my dear Miss Gantry ..."

"... Doctor Gantry ..."

"... I was not referring to you in any way."

"Am I not a woman?"

"You are a lady." He smiled at her, hoping the compliment would placate her.

It didn't. "And yet, by virtue of that feminine status, I am relegated to being ignorant and useless – unable to ask reasoned questions or to make observations? Sir, are we not well into the nineteenth century and beyond such notions? Surely women are proving themselves to be of great benefit in those areas once reserved for men. I realize that the concept is rather new, but I believe that science is a realm desperate for all persons driven by passion and logic. This is the very heart of the membership of the Institute, is it not? I should hope that you wouldn't lock your doors to women for no other reason that they are women?"

"How absurd. For an average woman, it would be unseemly and unthinkable. Science is entirely unfeminine. But you, dear lady, have been given special dispensation," Evans added. "On account of your unique gifts of intelligence."

"Why? Why have I been granted access that you would give to any fool who could provide the hot air necessary to fill your balloon but not a curious, interested woman ... average or otherwise?"

"Because you ..." Evans looked from Prudent to Frycollin and back to Prudent in a minor state of panic. "Because you have advanced degrees. You eclipse your sex in all things regarding logic and worldly understanding, and ..."

"... And I have money," she said very flatly. Yes, there was the truth. Her words of logic were falling on deaf ears. No matter how much she believed what she said, a voice in her mind told her it was utter nonsense, against nature. Surely, that too was what Prudent and Evans were thinking. This whole situation was about money; not exploration or innovation. Money.

The men stood perfectly still.

"I have enough money to make it easy for you to finish the *Go Ahead*, to make another such balloon, and to involve you in an attention getting endeavor that could make the Weldon Institute famous. Oh yes, I did some research before sending you my proposal, which I now feel I must withdraw. Clearly, I failed to do enough, otherwise I would have found the lot of ..." She stopped herself. A loss of temper would do nothing but brand her unladylike. She couldn't bear the thought of that. Lettie turned heel and started back toward the bridge. "I am certain that I can find a cab on my own. Good evening."

"Madame ..."

"I cannot imagine, Mr. Evans, that you would desire my company. Therefore I shall spare you the distress and find my own way."

Evans thought frantically, hoping to invent something to save the situation. "Miss ... Doctor Gantry. Please. You require our *Go Ahead* and we require your assistance in many regards. You are very correct in this. But we need each other."

Lettie stopped, drew in the deepest breath, as her mother had taught her, and turned to face the two men. "Mr. Evans, I must disagree. While the use of the *Go Ahead* would be of enormous value to my research, it is not the only component. As one of your members pointed out, there is Doctor Pierce, a noted and respected inventor, whom I plan to petition for assistance as well."

Prudent looked as though someone had struck him. "Madame, you wouldn't abandon such a noble project as the *Go Ahead*? Does Doctor Pierce have a flying apparatus? Have you communicated with him, as you have with us, and has he agreed to help you? Surely you can see how foolish it would be to give up our guaranteed mutual assistance for a ... a man who makes toys to satisfy the unenlightened masses."

She was astonished that he couldn't see the greater good of her research. "Mr. Prudent, Mr. Evans?" She paused, holding back whatever comment waited to be said. "I am too tired to argue with you here in the park. At best, we will end up disrespecting one another and at worst ... I wish you three a good evening. I have visits I must make before leaving this city. My ship leaves Baltimore in two days." She knew she would regret cutting them off without another opportunity. "I believe that the *Go Ahead* is not the resource I need. I genuinely offer you my best, most sincere hopes of success. I must focus on my Predictive Model and the immediate means by which to achieve it. Good night." Her mother would have been proud; well, perhaps not. She told a man 'no' and that was not in her mother's inter-gender vocabulary. Exhausted, she walked down the hill toward the bridge at the bottom.

While Evans and Prudent began blaming one another, it was Frycollin who approached her. He was a black man, born in South Carolina according to Prudent, who had worked, with patience and diligence, his way up to the position of valet. It had not been easy. He understood all too well what she was feeling. "Excuse me, Doctor Gantry. I would feel terrible if no one escorted you to where you're going. If it's a hansom cab you want, then please let me get it for you."

Lettie looked into Frycollin's eyes and for a moment they shared a mutual frustration that neither Prudent nor Evan would ever understand. "Thank you. Yes, if you please."

"Let me tell Uncle Prudent that I'll see to this. If you would wait here for just a moment?" The man walked quickly back up the hill.

She liked him. She knew nothing of him except that he was abundantly patient, even tempered, and willing in kindness. These were traits she wished she herself had more of. Her temper deflated faster than a balloon.

As Frycollin approached the pair, Evans was making a fist and clearly hoping to use it. His face was contorted with anger and it was well that Prudent seemed to be cowed by it.

Standing there watching the discourse, Lettie felt a touch embarrassed by her own behavior. She was too defensive about her gender. Walking a few steps back up toward the bickering men, she was resolved to end the situation more convivially and, perhaps, with more cooperation. The closer she got to them, however, the less she believed such a resolution was possible.

"I am the President!" She heard Prudent shout. "You are not." He seemed to be emboldened with each statement. "Were you as clever or wealthy as me, then maybe you would be more than the Secretary."

"You miserable little ... You just cost us everything! Your nonexistent wealth won't fix that."

"I'm the President! I am!"

The argument stopped immediately as the valet approached them, with Lettie only a few yards behind him. Evans stuck his fists in his pockets and turned away, wrestling to control his temper before a lady.

While Frycollin was in much quieter, yet animated, discussions with Prudent, a whistle was heard. A flash of electric light shot across the clearing of Fairmont Park. It was a signal. Lettie stared in horror as six men leapt out of the bushes and attacked the three unarmed men at the top of the hill. Why she ran toward them, she didn't know. What could she do? She had to do something!

In a moment that would seal an even higher opinion of Frycollin in her mind, he turned from his captors, stopped struggling to his own detriment, and shouted to her, "Run! Run for your life!"

Lettie stopped cold.

The leader of the attackers turned and from his expression, was surprised that she was still there. Bright, pale blue eyes lit by the park's gaslight opened wide. He had miscalculated; he thought she was long gone when he'd given his signal.

She stared at him for only a second, unable to make out anything but cold eyes in the vague light, then turned and ran as fast as her clothing would allow her. If it was all she could do, she was going to get assistance. "Help! We need help!"

"Oh hell, get her back here before she wakes everyone up."

The bridge was too far away for her to outrun the men coming down the hill after her. She couldn't gather in enough air for a sustained run because of her corset and heavy skirts. To the right was a stand of trees and shrubbery that sloped down toward the bank of the river. If she could get into their shadows, she could possibly elude the men. With only a moment's hesitation, she let go of her precious valise and pushed herself through the bushes with a silk-tearing crash.

The ground was muddy and slick, but there was a path that she could see now. Her balance changed too suddenly and she fell.

It was darker in the trees than the open hillside and the men hadn't seen her fall. She lay still, wondering if her black clothing would look like rocks and mud in the night. If these were thieves, then they would search her valise for money and valuables. They'd find nothing but a sixpence, a few American nickels, all of which she could live without. It was otherwise filled with papers, charts and diagrams that were only special to her. They likely wouldn't come after her at all. Being hurried, afraid she would rouse the neighborhood, they would leave the valise behind. And, they might leave the men alone too.

Yet, she couldn't take a chance on Weldon men's safety. As soon as she could, she had to get help. Damn it, she had to get help. It was so quiet. Even the river made no sound. She could hear her heartbeat though and if it were practical would have stopped it for fear of its being heard by the thieves. Her hands were so cold and her skin clammy. She couldn't focus, thinking that every tiny sound was something far more.

The bushes cleared loudly, and two men stepped through them. They rushed down the hill, past Lettie, who held her breath and turned her face away from them. Two more men entered the stand of trees. One went half way down the hill to Lettie's left. That was the leader of the thieves, the man with the cold blue eyes. The last man stayed at the top of the hill. Walking forward, slowly, he stopped his foot just short of her gloved fingers. A glow of light reflected off the pair of polished, elegantly made boots. She couldn't move her hand, for fear of making a noise, but if he were to step on her hand, could she keep from crying out?

"Madame Volcanologist?"

It was *him*.

"Madame? This will do no good."

Silence.

"Madame, please come out. I had extended my hospitality to you before, and I do so again. Allow me to prove that my offer is genuine. I will assist you in your photography. Surely your prediction model would benefit? But you need to reveal yourself and come with us now."

A dog barked in the distance. Lettie remained frozen.

Robur stepped forward, missing her hand by an inch. She drew in her breath preparing for the worst pain. He heard it, but wasn't certain where the sound came from. He began looking in front of him, pushing aside bushes.

"Tom? Up here I believe ..." He turned his foot and caught her hand under the sole of his boot. Lettie cried out and pulled her hand out from under him as he jumped back. He was on the edge of hill and she grabbed his ankle with her good hand. Had he been on solid, level ground, her effort would have been laughable. But he wasn't. His balance swung backward and down the hill. Robur grabbed at several branches before he regained his footing ten feet down the slope.

It was the only chance she might have for reaching help. Lettie pushed herself up with both hands, one now throbbing, and pulled her skirts nearly to her hips to clear her footing. She knew how she got down the hill; now, she would get back up the hill the same way. Out to the clearing. Down to the bridge.

Robur was disadvantaged by not knowing exactly how slippery the hillside was. He looked up to see her climb onto her feet and flee back up the hill. He swore loudly and started up after her. She had but a moment's lead, yet he was Robur and had no intention of letting her go.

The ground on the hillside was emphatically not aware that he was Robur and in nature's indifferent way, hindered him at every step. Leaves, moss, and muck slowed his pace. As it would seem, the lady had a better idea of where she was going. The thought amused him for a second.

Robur's man raced past his employer, knowing that the Aviator neither wanted nor required any assistance. Gaining his footing, Robur himself soon passed his man. It wouldn't do for the Aviator not to be the primary in pursuit.

Lettie reached the clearing and looked up the hill. There was no sign of Evans, Prudent or the kindly valet. She couldn't stay to look more. She kept hold of her skirts and ran down the path toward the bridge, shouting, gasping for breath, and praying she could make it. She could feel Robur and the blue-eyed man not more than a few feet behind her.

"Hey! What's this?" shouted a man standing, smoking a cigar, on the bridge. A large American waved to his friends who were approaching the bridge to meet him.

"For God's sake! We need help!"

A hand grasped her shoulder but she shook it off. The move, however, was enough to cause her to stumble. It was Robur who caught her around the waist and pulled her to the side of the path. That was all the Americans needed to see. They rushed toward the hill to do whatever harm they could to this man who dared accost a woman in their park.

With a brilliant frown, Robur reluctantly let the lady go and turned to jog easily up the hill, meeting halfway with the blue-eyed man. The other two men came out of the stand of trees and disappeared into the night with their master. Robur's man stopped to look down at Lettie, confused and annoyed, then followed into the darkness.

"Miss? Miss? Are you all right?"

"No." She could barely catch her breath. "There are three other men who… are being … attacked. Please, you must … help them." She clutched her left hand and moved her fingers, amazed that through the pain, she could count on one good piece of news; her hand wasn't broken.

One fellow stayed behind with Lettie, who was determined to rush to the aid of her, un-illustrious, companions. The others raced up to the hilltop and stopped. One turned to shrug his shoulders and to shake his head.

"'Ain't no one up here. They're gone!"

With those words, Lettie's heart skipped a beat and she sat down heavily where she was. She had run away. Excuses be damned, she didn't know how to fight and couldn't have helped anyway. She had ultimately been useless.

Chapter 18

Lettie sat for a moment, vitally aware that she was back on the Ferry, sitting with Christopher Moore, and no longer lost in her vivid memory. She couldn't help wondering how much time had been gone by while telling the story; she'd lost track.

"No one believed you about the Weldon members being kidnapped?" Moore asked, incredulous that anyone with a modicum of good sense would dismiss her.

"Not at first. They thought I was being hysterical and imaginative. One of them offered me laudanum," she said looking knowingly at Moore. He tensed but otherwise said nothing. "Then I showed them all the places, the footprints, the broken branches. Only when they couldn't locate the Weldon fellows at their homes did the alarm go up. You know the rest, I think."

Tea had arrived and she was clearly holding her cup to keep her hands warm. She hadn't removed her gloves, and now that they were steady and close to one another, it was obvious that the left hand was significantly larger than the right. Her hand was still bandaged. Moore shook his head slightly, wondering if he would ever know a time when she wasn't bearing some sort of physical damage. The woman was positively accident prone. It was going to kill her someday. At least it appeared that her hand wasn't broken. He decided not to comment.

"Christopher, I was ... unable to help them. If not for the grace of God, they might have been killed, or - or - I don't know what. They're home by no effort of mine."

He shook his head. "That is no fault of yours. Had I been there, I'm not sure what amount of help I could have provided. And, as you say, they are now safely home, safe and sound."

"Don't humor me." She picked up her cup.

"I'm not humoring you." He rested his hand on her arm as she set her cup down. "I know you. I know what you're thinking. You're thinking about how you failed those men, but the reality is that you came very close to saving them. You were fearless…"

"I was terrified!" she snapped, immediately sorry for her outburst. She started to apologize. She must have been too done in and weak to keep proper control over her emotions.

"My dear friend, you are your own worst critic. And, I would say you are quite exhausted. If you were that frightened then its all the more heroic that you kept your head and did what you could. I suspect the men of the Weldon Institute would have avoided all of this had they been better hosts to this Robur, or at least better behaved amongst themselves."

She looked up over her lashes and said, "He knew they wouldn't be. He was playing with them. Picking a fight. And playing with me, too. Though I simply don't understand why."

"Because you're beautiful and intelligent?"

Lettie made some "tush-ing," dismissive noise and took another sip of her tea.

Pierce had listened to her entire description and barely remembered to breathe the whole time. What an amazing tale. He had remained within earshot the whole time, a feat not easily done as he was certain she would recognize him. Pierce thought about what Moore had said, too. Moore was right about Miss Gantry. That was perhaps why this Robur fellow had interacted with her, even attempted to entice her to his airship. There was an uncomfortable thought. An airship, one that had been built and one that Robur made ready use of, or so he claimed. Pierce shook his head a little. His own invention was so small now by comparison. And did he have such a reputation in the United States?

"I doubt Robur's interest has anything to do with me, personally," she said into her tea cup, trying to sound unaffected by the topic. "I'm sure it has everything to do with the Weldon Institute."

"Aren't you tempted to find out?"

Lettie's eyes grew wide. "That isn't even funny, Kit. I would never … Do you really think I'd allow myself to be shipped or flown off to parts unknown, alone, with a man I barely know? A man of dubious reputation and character? "

"Of course not. And I would be greatly disappointed if you did. But aren't you just a little bit tempted to know why? Maybe he's madly in love with you?"

"Ha!" she said much too loudly. Covering her mouth gracefully with a gloved hand, she hid her laughter. "I think that giving Mr. Robur so much credit for adoration beyond himself would be too generous, indeed." She began straightening out the folds of her skirt that did not require any tidying. Of course, she was tempted.

"And that gun case, the one you handed over to the Purser? You got *it*, didn't you?" Kit very kindly changed the subject, amused by her fussing over her skirts; a reaction he recognized immediately for what it was.

She nodded.

"Winchester?"

"Henry. The older model from the New Haven Arms Company. Before Mr. Winchester took the company over. Don't ask me why, it just felt better in my hands. It's a drudge to load when compared to the Winchester, but, well, it did feel better to my estimation. Oh, I know it's a couple of decades out of style, but what can I say. Use what works." She sipped her tea.

"Why not an Enfield or a Martini-Henry? We build good firearms in England, you know."

Lettie shrugged. "When in America, buy as the Americans do? It changed the outcome of their war. I heard someone describe the Henry rifle," she added quickly, "not to be confused with Misters Martini or Henry of England, as the one those 'Yankees' could load once on Sunday and fire all week. The caliber is huge ..."

".44 if I recall?"

"Yes, which is about all I can manage. The hammer was adjusted to accommodate Mr. Winchester's new ammunition for his new model gun. There's too much heft in the newer Winchesters for my liking."

"That could break your other wrist."

She said nothing to the comment. "You will let me come up and practice, won't you? I'm still a hideous shot."

"The family would never forgive me if I didn't."

"I'll tell you something else, Christopher."

Pierce sat up and held his breath again.

Lettie sipped her tea, and then set the cup down. Her voice lowered considerably. "I've seen him again. Robur. But not him. Not exactly."

"That makes no sense, but it makes me all the happier you bought that American gun."

"You know my habit of observing physical language? I've seen

Robur's eyes, on someone else."

"Who?"

"I don't know. I only know that I've had that sense of déjà vu since attending the Pierce Lecture." She stopped and smiled for just a second. Moore had no idea why, but something amused her for a moment. "I got so distracted by a fool seated in the front row that I honestly don't remember who it was that looked so very much like Robur. And of course, there were the storms that came up later. I believe Robur is behind the storms. I can't quite put my finger on it but I just know that he is behind them. Creating them, somehow."

Now she was thinking out loud and Moore was starting to feel left behind. "Storms? What storms?"

"They'll never believe it at New College," she said, ignoring his question and abruptly changing the subject.

Moore lowered his head in frustration but he wouldn't be put off. "You're a dreadful storyteller. First of all, my dear, when you become New College's newest professor, you are going to have to speak: to tell your students through narrative form everything you want them to learn. You simply must become a better storyteller."

"I won't be telling stories, Christopher. It's science." She ran her finger around the lip of her cup. "Besides, I'm not a professor yet."

"It's a given."

"Possibly. We must not forget that my Predictive Model isn't what one would call accurate. Not yet. It certainly didn't work in Japan. I could have gotten us all killed. So, you see my dear friend, I might not gain that prestigious title of Professor just yet."

"Lettie, they adore you at New College. You're exactly the thing that will bring the right sort of students and benefactors. Doctor Hauer is your strongest advocate, and he can move the Board of Academics in whatever direction he wants. Your appointment as the first woman professor at New College is assured." He leaned back, feeling very satisfied. And he was right. The Board of Academics, tasked with hiring and disciplining staff at the college, was seventy-five percent in her favor. She had undeniable credentials and some extraordinary theories.

His smile faded a bit as he recalled the point he originally meant to make. "Now, back to my original question, and please don't change the subject. What storms?"

Lettie picked up her cup and smiled on the far side of it.

Chapter 19

June 25, 1882
Steamship SS Atlantis
Atlantic Ocean

The *Atlantis* was bound from America to France, before the English ports, and then back to America, heading straight out again from its home port of Baltimore, Maryland. No one knew her on board, except perhaps for the charming ship's doctor who had taken a great deal of trouble to re-bandage her left hand. He had also been quite considerate in not offering advice to her as so many men felt free to do. She had grown tired of the loud noises of Philadelphia: the crowds and the demanding investigators – both professional and journalistic. At the time of her departure from Pennsylvania, not a word had come regarding the fate of the Weldon members and after ten days she could offer no more to help them. Packing her bags and purchasing a special item that made her feel safer, even if she had no easy access to it, she made her way to the Atlantic passenger ship. By the time she reached Maryland, one by one, the intrusive reporters dropped away until she was able to board the ship unhindered and anonymous.

After a splendid dinner of American beef cooked in a French style, all Lettie felt able to do was to walk the deck, pacing, as was her habit when feeling angry and helpless. She'd left Georgie's bracelet in her cabin and she shouldn't have. Tonight, the anxiety was acute. Where was Mr. Frycollin? Was he being treated as well as Evans and Prudent? And why did Robur take them away? She couldn't answer the questions and while she knew she was no longer of help, she felt her lack of presence in Philadelphia to be a bit cowardly.

Stopping at the starboard rail, she looked out over the ocean. It was calm, more so than when she had first traveled over from England. That had been a harrowing ride. But this time the Atlantic was being kind, perhaps out of respect for the ship that bore its namesake. The air was cold but felt soothing, at least in the short term. She rubbed her left hand, which still hurt a bit. Elbow-length gloves of fine cotton and a lovely silver bracelet hid the difference in size due to the bandage. Dining on board was a formal affair, and she had of course dressed the part as expected though she had no interest in socializing. She should have insisted on taking her dinner in her cabin. With her hair swept up and held in place with jeweled pins and a silver comb, she appeared a bit taller. Her dinner dress of bronze velvet fitted her exactly through the waist. The bodice ended in four long points in the front and a flowing train in the back. Underneath this she wore a matching velvet bustled skirt parted in the center to reveal a bronze taffeta petticoat. The sleeves fitted tightly to the elbow, which opened up to a swath of black net lace. The neckline was one she had chosen long before the events in America, wide and plunging, as much as a decent woman might allow. Her collarbones and throat were displayed in the latest style, with a tasteful amount of cleavage revealed. It was all very dramatic, though she hardly cared if it met with anyone's approval. Her mother would have approved. She'd planned to dine by herself, but the ship's doctor had other plans, and she found herself seated at the Captain's table. The formality doubled and for a brief time, she was relieved to play the quiet, demure lady.

There had been an honest attempt at friendly banter amongst the ladies at the table. Lettie chose to say as little as possible. She wasn't always certain what to say to other women. She couldn't spend time with those of equal experience or thought as there were none on board. She was the only woman academic she knew, she wasn't married, her social status was contrived by her own education and not that of her father or some male in her life. She had nothing in common with any of them. When her mother passed away, her female relatives had attempted to govern her, but had grown exasperated at their failed attempts to take over directing her life. She just didn't spend time with women with one exception: Miranda Gray. And they saw each other minimally due to their conflicting schedules. Male friends and colleagues were those who surrounded her at any given time. She strived everyday to gain their approval or to glean vital information from their experiences.

When the genders parted after dinner, she desperately wanted to go with the men to smoke cigars, drink port, and to join in the discourse. Yet, she wished deeply that she could sit with the women and enjoy the gossip; to discuss the challenges of husbands and children. Lettie could do neither.

The ocean was rather inviting, to the point she wondered when the

Siren songs would start. The rhythm of the ship plowing through monotonous waves was soothing. While she was no Ulysses, she had to wonder now just when she would, if she could, return home. The whole of the summer had been one fools errand after another.

A tiny light showed in the distance; vague and blinking. She wondered if that was one of the twelve T.P.S. stations, the "Tipsy" as they nicknamed it, floating dangerously in the Atlantic. The Trans Pneumatic System provided what the company called "all but instantaneous communication." Anyone could send a telegram from the United States to Europe via the Atlantic telegraph cables, but it was a statement of importance and futuristic thinking to send a message written in your own hand, which would then arrive at its destination within three days. Twelve stations, called "Apostles," dotted the ocean between London and Maine, floating free in the waves except for the pneumatic tubes coming in and out. Superior engines powered the pressure containers which would blast the steel bullets through the tubes, on to the next station. Inside these thickly insulated bullets rested delicate communications and excessively expensive letters. The bullets themselves didn't tend to last long: neither did station employees who took the monikers of 'apostle' and 'gospelites.' She wondered, as the light faded away, just how lonely it would be, working on a Tipsy station? Tipsy. How funny, she thought, as it occurred to her that someone very drunk must have invented it. Yet, it worked wonderfully. The Tipsy didn't break the news of President Abraham Lincoln's assassination; that was for the speed of the telegraph and Mr. Reuter's news agency. The Tipsy's fame came from the delivery of Queen Victoria's handwritten letter of condolence to Mrs. Lincoln within days of the tragedy. If anyone knew how it felt to lose a beloved husband, the Queen most certainly did.

Couples began wandering in and out on the deck and for a moment, Lettie's chest began to ache. That should have been her, on a gentleman's arm; that should have been her life.

A little vapor cloud formed out over the waves, little more than a one thousand meters away. Tiny, white, nearly perfect as any artist might want to paint into a romantic portrait of the seas. Lettie adjusted her simple necklace, which sat on her chilled skin.

The cloud had grown substantially when she looked at it again. And, more threatening. While still white, it was far more dense and layered. Lightning, which didn't come out of the vapors, turned the cloud purple and pink, and sometimes a searing yellow. And it moved, with the ship. Looking around, almost frantically, she realized by the flags waving in the breeze, that it was moving opposite the wind. She backed up, as the storm grew larger and closer. It was too cold out and the weather was changing, she said to herself, trying to be one of those sensible ladies the doctor kept speaking of.

Lettie stopped at the door to the interior, and glanced back. The cloud was gone. There was no sign of it.

Twice more, after dinner, under the cover of twilight or darkness, the storm formed itself right in front of her. Then vanished. The third time, something was different. The sun had only just set. She'd sat for the first dinner serving and was hoping to be out on deck just a bit earlier, perhaps to test a theory or to see if it would appear at different times.

The storm appeared as she walked to the bow of the ship. It flashed and roiled. But this time, she did not move. What was it going to do? It was a storm, correct, she asked herself? It moved closer to the ship, but had no effect on the waves below it, she noticed.

Suddenly, it vanished, and in the fading light she saw what was underneath: a ship. No, a flying ship. Like a Yankee Clipper. Its hull was like any ship on the oceans, but she saw no sails, only masts. It turned just a bit, and disappeared into the indigo sky.

Chapter 20

Christopher Moore leaned back in his chair and tried to calmly digest the details she'd given him. He'd never actually crossed the Atlantic and the tiniest voice in his head wanted to know more about the Tipsy system. He quickly silenced the voice. "I don't suppose you informed anyone on board the *Atlantis*?"

Lettie sipped her tea. "And just who would have believed me?"

Pierce finally turned a page of his newspaper and thought, I would have believed you. I do. As his lips moved slightly, he suddenly worried he'd spoken out loud.

Lettie shook her head. "No, I've kept this to myself. If it is Robur and his airship, then it only brings up the question of 'how.' How does one create their own storm?"

Moore sat forward again. "Now we're in my area of expertise. I think it has something to do with water vapor. If this madman has created a ship that flies without hot air, and I must say if anyone else had suggested it I wouldn't believe them, he'd need a crew. Men must have water. So too must the engines. I think the vapor you're seeing is excess steam. He's powering this ship with steam, which is the most powerful engine we have, and he has to vent it out if the pressure or volume becomes too much."

"But would steam last long enough to appear as a cloud?"

"I think it would depend on the air temperature, quantity of steam - he could be venting out tremendous amounts of pressurized vapor. There may be more in the steam than just water. The potentials are endless."

"There was no precipitation either. No rain at all. Except in Paris ... then we got a hail storm."

"Paris? This happened in Paris, too?"

"Well ..."

"We must work on your communication skills, my dear. Fine, he can either dump the steam once it's cooled, or keep it to power his ship and water his men."

Pierce thought quietly, what about the hail?

"What about the hail," she asked.

Good question, Pierce thought, turning another unread page and smiling slightly.

"How high up was he? How high up had he been? It's cold in the upper atmosphere; he may well have allowed some of his water to freeze. Ha, that's it!"

Moore suddenly stopped and looked out over the Channel, searching the sky for something amiss. "If he followed you across the Atlantic and into Paris ..."

"No, no. We're in the middle of the daytime and there are neither clouds nor fog. There's nowhere for him to hide, unless he wants to be seen. Which I don't believe he does. Not really, or at least not by anyone in general. Besides, I think he's played enough with me. I'm not so very much fun these days." She sipped her tea. "Madman, you say? Maybe. But he is a genius if nothing else. If he has actually made this airship and I wasn't suffering from the dinner wine, then he has done what few dare dream of." She set her cup down abruptly. "We've been missing something important here."

Moore stopped looking around at the sky.

Lettie continued, "if my guess is correct, I believe he made that airship five or more years ago and has been sailing ... flying ... it ever since."

"I don't follow."

Nor do I, Pierce thought.

"This has to do with the storms seen near the volcanoes. I swear to you, that storm which followed me across the ocean matches the description of storms that heralded the eruptions. What if the sequence of events has been reported wrong? What if it's Robur and he is only present at eruptions, not causing them? Or can he? But why? What would be the point of endangering such an amazing piece of technology by flying them near eruption clouds? Oh Christopher - none of this is truly happening is it? This is all in my exhausted imagination, isn't it?"

"I don't know. But – no matter what anyone may suggest – you are one of the most sensible ladies I have ever met."

She slouched as much as possible and closed her eyes. "I'm seeing things and accepting reports from the *London Herald and Observer*. That is distinctly not scientific thinking on my part. And hardly sensible."

He set his hand on hers, in a brotherly way. "If you don't trust your own observations, then what hope have I? You need rest. Come up to the house on Sunday. We'll make a nice day of it. Mother would love to see you. And I want to see that Yankee gun you purchased."

"Yes. Yes, I think that's what I'll do, but not Sunday. But I need to head home first. Papa would never forgive me if I went to another family's home before his."

"Then come Monday, re-examine your evidence – your experiences and knowledge. Do a little research – you're a 'Swell' at that ..."

Lettie only raised an eyebrow at the coarse term he used for her. Heavens, he called her a 'Swell,' but then she had to be honest with herself, it made her feel accepted as one of the fellows - the intellectuals and scholars. Yet, it wasn't a term for a lady.

"... and then decide. No more storms until you get rest. Do we have a deal, Professor?"

She smiled and offered him her hand. "We have ourselves a bargain. And a date set to meet at your Mother's." She leaned forward. "Thank you, Christopher."

Instead of shaking her hand, he kissed it. That genuinely surprised her.

"Marry me, Professor Gantry?"

"And ruin our friendship?"

"How many times have I asked you?" he said with a smile, all the while anticipating that she would tell him 'no.'

"I've lost count. Oh, ask me again next week."

"You'll tell me 'no' then too, won't you?"

"Of course. I like the stability of it."

Pierce didn't understand what was happening ... why didn't she say 'yes?' Not that he wanted her to do so in particular but it seemed so very simple. Despite being brilliant, she was a woman and a woman needed to get married.

"Speaking of," she said in a slight whisper, "how is William?"

Moore only smiled.

Pierce still didn't understand who William was or what William had to do with anyone, but Letticia Gantry did. She understood and accepted it without judgment.

Chapter 21

London had always been known for poor weather, mostly attributed to the fog, but freakish thunder storms set against relatively clear night skies were not normal. Not normal at all. Naturally that drew people out by the hundreds. September wasn't known for rain, either.

Pierce stopped his welding at the first flash of lightning and waited. Experience over the past week had told him not to expect a long lasting storm. And now every time a cloud formed in the sky, he was suspicious. He moved the worn pair of goggles off his eyes, as though the view out his windows would change to the better without the protective lenses. The storm was still there. Pierce walked quickly to the old doors and stepped out onto the three feet he generously called a balcony and stared at the roiling clouds - no, cloud - singular cloud. One huge cloud, reaching up into the atmosphere. Flashes of light from deep inside the vapors showed the layers and depth of the storm. Was it even a storm, in the proper sense of the word? Yellow, gold, red flashes burst and flickered angrily within the confines of the cloud as though trying to break out of a prison. All the while, not a sound; no thunder, no rumbling, no crackling. Silence.

Resting a hand on the balustrade, Pierce pulled down the cloth mask that kept smoke and flying debris out of his nose and mouth, revealing that strong chin in need of a shave.

On either side of the storm, stars twinkled in a clear autumn sky. Voices rose from the street below. Two men, likely neighbors, were calling to one another and pointing upward. From their tone, they were astonished and frightened by its abnormality.

Pierce was neither. Well, perhaps a bit frightened. But storm clouds like this one were becoming old habit, just a bit too familiar. They were written of in the newspapers, spoken of in the pubs, and he himself had witnessed at least one. In fact, were he a superstitious or primitive thinker, he might have been tempted to claim the storm had followed him from Paris to Calais. But Professor Pierce was not prone to superstition. Even the Hindu myths his father secretly told him were presented as descriptive metaphors, as reminders of his heritage and nothing more. Pierce preferred science over all and had no intention of letting a vivid imagination get control over his nerves. It was 1882, damn it, and the days of fairy tales and miracles were long past. He planted his hands on his hips and scowled at the dissipating cloud. Perhaps he would inquire at New College in the morning about such weather phenomena. Surely someone had a theory or explanation for it. Whatever the explanation, Pierce was entirely certain it was quite mundane and had absolutely nothing to do with him, the Lady, or airships. For a brief moment, he remembered Doctor Gantry and her defiance of the storm in Paris. Almost as defiantly, he turned his back on the storm and walked back into his workroom. Scratching the day-old growth along his jaw line, he decided a shave could wait until morning.

Whatever sense of British supremacy and scientific arrogance rested in Pierce was shattered by a roar of something dreadful from deep inside the storm. Pierce was blasted back from the balustrade with a blow that knocked the air from his lungs. The windows of his workroom rattled and cracked, one pane shattered, and equipment shuddered as though the city had been rocked by an earthquake. Expensive glass tubes and delicate wires crashed to the floor. It was a concussive explosion of air that might as well have been artillery fire.

Silence.

The night sky, with a waxing moon, cast an eerie light over everything, as though a painter had washed the world with a glaze of blue and indigo. Even the gas lamps from the workshop could not warm the iciness in his hands, and he would have to relight them before the gas suffocated him.

Dogs began to bark and people began to cry out to one another frantically. Neighbors rushed into the streets, some wearing the day's work clothes and others in bed clothes.

Church bells were clanging, not ringing purposefully, but slamming into one another. The noise began to subside almost immediately.

Pierce pressed his hand down on the floor to lift himself up and found that sharp pieces of glass were scattered everywhere. Slowing climbing to his feet, he saw that his medical trolley was leaning oddly against a cabinet, two tables were pushed against each other, and his best

– latest – miniaturized engine was lying in several chunks in a back corner.

Beyond the howling and screaming panic below, there was only an eerie silence. By all standards, considerably less damage had been done than he thought was possible. His chest hurt and he heart was pounding. Would there be another concussion?

Looking out at the night, the cloud was gone. The Reuters Heavy Hauler dirigibles floated by as though nothing interesting had happened. The pilot of the flying train wasn't slowing down to look. Pierce wondered for a moment, why hadn't the haulers been affected? Was it possible that the concussive blast had been directed toward him? Impossible.

"Professor! Professor!"

Pierce peered over the rail to see one of his students, who was a neighbor as well, waving up at him.

"Professor, what in God's name was that?"

He shook his head in bewilderment. Not prone to the use of many words, Pierce said nothing. What was there to say? What had happened was impossible, was it not?

Chapter 22

September 8, 1882
5 Cater Lane, Sutton, Surrey
Residence of L. Gantry, Dr.sc.geo

On Friday morning, Lettie stepped out into a chill and slightly overcast day. It was early. The fog was likely coming but there was always a chance she would be finished before it cloaked the city in a suffocating gray.

She had appointments. One appointment was making her stomach tie in knots and she considered going back up to her water closet. She simply had to learn to be steady when appearing before the Academic Board. Though it was tempting, she was beginning to question her decision to avoid the medicinal bottle, addiction or not. No, it wasn't a new question, it was one she had always asked herself before taking the prescribed laudanum, both before she knew how easily it would overwhelm her and after she'd broken its hold on her body.

Not today. Not ever again. She would depend on nothing but herself today. And she wouldn't be afraid of the Academic Board either, a group of men, most of whom knew her from repeated presentations, and most of whom were open to the outrageous notion of a woman professor. It was the few individual hold-outs that gave her the vapors and she despised meeting with them so much that it made her physically ill.

What if she did go back upstairs and shut the door? No one would blame her. She was a frail woman, the weaker sex, the soft gender. They would just say it had been a matter of time before she crumbled under the challenges.

Closing the door, Lettie saw her reflection in the glass panes. Her eyes had a tired, hollow look to them. And she knew from the handful of hair that came out in her brush that she was starting to see the ravages of time, or the stress of it. Several of the hairs were gray and she hated it. She wasn't ready to get old. She hadn't even begun the life she desired.

Lettie turned away from the reflection and marched down to the waiting brougham cab. The less she thought about it, the better her chances were that she'd make it out the door.

Volcanoes! She'd willingly stood in the path of flowing lava, nearly been incinerated by a pyroclastic cloud, and damn near boiled herself alive in steam vents. But the mountains never judged her. They would not question her intelligence or her fitness. They would not call into question her femininity, her goodness, or her moral decency. No more than any other human foolish enough to challenge the volcano, it would never deny her right to life and love.

Sanderson the cabbie was sitting, half asleep, in the driver's seat. He had been asked to come by and pick her up at this time, which in itself had become a bit of a ritual. He didn't mind the hours, since this lady was very generous in her payment. With five children at home he needed the money. Even at that time of the day he took the effort to see to it his older yet elegant carriage was polished and tidy. The average brougham was not designed for conversation between driver and patron, but he had still managed to glean a brief story or two of exotic places from her and her household staff. Those he took home to his children, to regale them with tales that otherwise would be found in the books he couldn't afford to buy.

"'Mornin', Mum."

"Good morning."

He was the prompt and professional driver who took her to the West Sutton rail station nearly every time. Her butler saw to it. It was likely that he made her his favorite patroness because she tipped well, she thought. That made him a smart cabbie, too.

"The station, if you please."

"Yes, Mum."

Reflexively, Lettie looked back at her house as the horse pulled the brougham sharply out into the street, avoiding a man pulling his cart of gardening tools. It was her father's house, not hers, and she wished that she could have afforded to buy it all those years ago. Now the funds were possible though she'd have to tighten her purse considerably to do it: to purchase the home from him. He wouldn't hear of it. Despite being one of the most forward thinking men she'd ever known, there were a few places he maintained a more common, fatherly stance. The house was something he felt deeply about and there was no discussion over it. Until she had someone to provide a house for her, it was his job, his responsibility, his duty to keep a roof over her head. While marriage was becoming less likely by the year, she had to admit one more drive to

123

achieve the position of Professor was that she could then point to a profession and claim it in place of a husband. He might - perhaps - accept that.

The only argument they ever had was over who should pay for the staff. That time she won - barely. Looking back at the two-story, quaint but new home, she longed for a time when she'd know that she had earned it with her own hands. Such a fantasy was ridiculous, of course: she was a woman and women didn't own homes they hadn't inherited. Her father had already been too generous and too indulgent. Had he not been a successful businessman, all her intelligence would have gained her nothing as she could never have afforded the schools and travels abroad. Now the books, monographs, occasional lectures and newspaper articles provided more than enough for her to see to every bill and her obsession with good fashion. Enough for everything except purchasing a home. He wasn't being unfair to her dream: she was his daughter and he felt such an expense as a house near London was expected of him. So he willingly obliged the duty. For him, it was such a small thing.

They almost argued over the location. Greater London was no place for a woman on her own, he had said and believed, until she pointed out that the side of an erupting volcano was no better. "My dearest daughter," he said after he thought about it. "There seems to me to be a general respect between you and your mountains. I would not assume such a convivial bond between you and a criminal."

He had her there. Sutton was chosen because of its closeness to London and all the academic institutions, and yet its distance. The village was not crammed full of multi-story apartments and shops. The land was generally flat, rich with old trees and tributary rivers flowing into the Thames. Gardens and sweet houses dotted the area around the rail station. It was as though she lived away in the countryside and yet housed in the heart of the metropolitan monster that was London. It was the best of both their hopes.

The house was situated sweetly on a curving lane fronted by a tidy cobblestone street. The trees were few but tall and old. Most houses in the moderately fashionable area were on the small side; nothing such as the mansions found on in Belgravia or Chandler Square. The Gantry residence was narrow with high ceilings and a tiny but well kept garden. Sutton was a quaint and logical place for an academic lady.

The trip by rail was usually pleasant, in that Lettie chose to travel at very early hours, thus avoiding the commuting businessmen. In the quiet of the rail carriage, she could read if there was enough light or rest her eyes and meditate on the events she was to face. The advantage of being a lady was that few ever pestered her, though she did look this morning to see if a certain red-haired fellow was there.

With a single transfer at a station midway to London proper, she soon found herself over the river at the insanely busy Victoria Station. The echo of voices calling, negotiating, commenting and hawking were nearly deafening.

A lady did not hail any mode of transportation on her own, which would be considered an act of gross indignity; thus it was easier for Lettie to hire a cab quietly from the row of drivers waiting for a customer. She could be unobtrusive or secretive. It was her main reason for off boarding at such a horrendous place. Due to the immense traffic coming in and out of Victoria, a special set of controls were put into place to encourage the maximum efficiency for drivers and riders. Hansom cabs were licensed to have free entry to a lane at the front of the station, where a manager would ensure smooth hiring and no cutting in line. It was an experimental effort only to be found at Victoria. In reality, the station was one stop shy of the closest station to New College. But her dignity absolutely needed to be maintained and her reputation protected.

The cab manager signaled the next driver forward for a pair of gentlemen too caught up in a legal argument to be bothered with acknowledging the human beings around them. One yanked his tall top hat from his head in such a way as to suggest he was not pleased with the direction of the argument, or that he was losing. As each driver moved his conveyance, horse or horses all, moved up in the row, it was easy for Lettie slip in and take the next cab. She could not afford to be picky or to wait for a brougham. A few seconds after she received a nod from the manager, who had grown used to her routine, Lettie was settled and back in a cab headed to New College.

Ladies generally did not hire hansom cabs. They truly were a transport designed to move gentlemen with active lives from place to place. Barristers late for Court; bankers running home at noon; young men escaping to the Clubs and Theaters; the cozy two-wheel, semi-enclosed cab was ideal. As two could fit well inside, often stylish couples would make use of the thousands of cabs available, happily sandwiched together.

Rumor had it that mechanized vehicles were coming. Miniature trams with room for no more than four people. Perhaps when the mechanized cabs were in place, men would choose those and hansom cabs would become more appropriate for ladies?

The cabbie whipped up the horse to a gentle trot and headed deeper into the city. The local tradesmen were out and about, even at that early hour. Everyone seemed to be shaking off the sleep of the previous night and focusing on the day's tasks. The cabbie steered his conveyance routinely between carts full of industrial equipment and goods, ridiculous new inventions that seemed only to clog the streets, and around careless pedestrians. A steam-engine drill started to hiss and pop as it was prepared for roadwork. Something that resembled a carriage but without an animal to pull it had stalled, leaving one man banging ferociously at the engine with a mallet and the other sitting in what appeared to be a couch strapped to the contraption. A woman with a handcart filled with breads and tea was rolling along toward the busier thoroughfare where she could do a better business.

With a sudden laugh, Lettie looked back at the horseless couch. It was her neighbors. For Heaven's sake, it was Lewin and Llewellyn. They'd made it to London after all. There was no time to stop and chat, which was too bad. She really liked them. She hadn't seen them in years.

Drifting in from the South, just passing over the river, were the international mail and cargo dirigibles. Heavy haulers. Almond-shaped bags of helium, with armored baskets hanging underneath, were tethered together like a parade of circus elephants, so that only the first and last of the gigantic balloons needed fuel to rise or sink in the often treacherous changing winds of the Channel. Fuel was heavy and the line of floating mail ships would never be able to carry enough cargo to make them profitable if every dirigible had to have its own supply. One of the great balloon bags had the name of Reuter's International News and Mail Service painted in gigantic letters. This was the cheap alternative to steam ships, telegrams, and the Tipsy pneumatic tube systems.

Lettie stretched her bruised hand, pulled an envelope out of the reduced contents of her valise with the other, and read the address with a soft smile. Mr. John Milne, Imperial College of Engineering, Tokyo, Japan. 'Earthquake' Milne. He had the look of one of those heroic men, and acted the part too. If only geologists were considered worthy material for romantic novels, she mused. They could use Milne as the inspired hero. She would gladly read that story. Ah, but no, scientists weren't what romantic authors had in mind for passionate love affairs.

My dear Miss Gantry,

I hope this letter finds you in excellent health. I must express to you again my great satisfaction in the ascent of Mt. Tarumae. The event is still spoken of with much enthusiasm. Mr. Gray and Mr. Ewing are currently completing work on the new seismometer, which I am looking forward to putting into operation. Of course, as I had mentioned before, the damped horizontal pendulums have given us some challenge, but it has been met with no small amount of determination and (as you will recall from your visit) laughter. In the meantime, I have enclosed a copy of my design for the Horizontal Pendulum Seismograph. I should also add that Mr. Gray, Mr. Ewing and Mr. Murakami wish me to extend their congratulations on your superior report of the Tarumae climb as they were not available to do so before your departure from Yokohama. And of course, each sends you both their general well-wishes and their letters of admiration (here included.) Never fear any setback in your progress toward a Prediction Model of Eruptions. Much is gained in failure that cannot be obtained in easy successes.

Before this becomes so long that I shall have to overstuff the envelope, let me conclude by also offering my support and a letter of recognition in the hopes that it will be of some value in achieving your position at New College (included here.)

I look forward to hearing about your efforts to develop aerial photographic opportunities and other technological advances to the science of Geology. Please consider me a great supporter and do not hesitate to contact me if I may be any assistance whatsoever.

With warmest regards,
J. Milne
Tokyo

Written in a different hand with a more flowing and elegant style, a little note was scribbled into the last half of the page. From Mrs. Milne.

The dog nearly chased him from the property. John's promised to grow back his moustache.

She opened the included sheets of paper to find an excellent drawing of Milne's Seismometer, as well as three letters of recommendation and support for her application for a professorship.

It was times like this that Lettie missed having her father close by. He would have gladly gone with her, sat quietly in the corridor outside the Board's room or gone to fetch lunch. If the meeting went too long, he'd stroll out onto the campus and light up a deep, meerschaum pipe filled with sweet tobacco. The aroma would be pleasant and Mr. Gantry always chose his tobaccos with those who would have to smell it in mind.

Frankly, she was too old to have her father sit with her and he was too old to be so required. Not that he would mind ...

Mr. Gantry was in Cardiff and not of travelling health. If it meant keeping them together, albeit via telegram and post, for just a bit longer, she could forego his immediate presence. The day he dies, she thought, I'll be unfit for human company and not likely to recover for a long, long time.

Her mother, however, had passed three years before. Hypercritical of everything Lettie did, her mother was not so much a cruel woman as much as she was brutally practical. In her mind, as so many believed, Lettie could never become a whole person, a true woman, without a husband to make it so. Mrs. Gantry firmly believed that a woman was meant to suffer the ills of the world with quiet, modest behavior and to never see or hear anything distasteful. So when Lettie didn't turn into the marrying kind, and held a particularly odd interest in things that should only concern men, she was determined to push her daughter out of such dangerous thinking. The result was that Lettie was a strange mix of social demands and new ideas. The blend was hardly seamless and most of the time proved to be very uncomfortable.

Of course Lettie desired a husband. Part of her dreamed of a tranquil domestic life, with children and a home. But no man was likely able to live up to her demand that he be either perfect or fully supportive of her dreams of science and exploration. It was her private, lonely road. The only man she'd wanted to marry had been so repulsed by her academic ambitions that he married someone else. Once she had reached the age of thirty, she was officially a spinster and unlikely to be wed. She had married her science and found it the only worthy husband. A husband with demands of his own.

"West gate, Mum." The cabbie said, pulling her from her daydream.

She paid him quickly and set her focus on the next few hours at New College.

The place was aptly named. It was new, fresh and exciting. Less emphasis was placed on theory and more on practical application. That did not stop the architects from trying to give the place a wizened, ancient appearance. Designed and constructed in 1815, New College's façade was a collage of Tudor brick, Greek Revival, and Egyptian nostalgia. Ivy was growing but hadn't quite made it past the second stories nor had it grown so dense that buildings appeared to be swallowed whole. Only the pneumatic tube system poking out of the walls and thrusting into the building next to it managed to resist the plants.

Lettie began to open the folding doors only to find it being done for her and a hand being offered by a student for her to use to climb out of the cab. It was not an uncommon practice. Many of the younger fellows were tasked by their upper classmen to wait near the street for hours at a time, to provide such services. The upper classmen called it character building, the hapless lower classmen called it routine, and Lettie called it safer than some of the older practices. To her delight, amongst the boys was a girl.

The girl, in her school suit of gray wool skirt and bodice, no bustle, and plain cap, walked up to Lettie. "Good morning, Ma'am. May I be of assistance?"

"I know my way, but thank you all the same."

"Yes, Ma'am."

For a moment, Lettie was deeply curious and grateful for a moment's distraction. "What program are you enrolled in?"

"Blackwell School of Medicine, Ma'am."

"Brava. Thank you." Another lady doctor? Wonderful, Lettie thought as she strolled down toward the center of the campus.

Chapter 23

"Miss Gantry." The Chairman of the Board of New College, William Congher Ashfield, looked over his narrow glasses at her and tried his best to find some fault in her. He couldn't, unless he could insist that her arrogance in wanting to be a professor in his college was a fault - which it was, though he was not able to say so. Damn her, she had dressed very carefully for this interview. Nothing overly masculine, yet nothing so feminine as to suggest the weakness of her gender. Her patience and quiet while waiting between questions was frustratingly wise. The fact that she had long since won over his colleagues was maddening. "There is no question that you have the academic credentials necessary. A professor in this college must be more than accredited. A larger view must be taken."

Lord of Mercy, she thought. Here we go again.

"Our school's reputation, academic standing, stability. There are many factors ..."

Another man on the board jumped in. "What he's trying to say, Doctor Gantry, is that we are financially supported by many men who may or may not find us to be a solid investment if we hire a woman professor."

"Doctor Hauer!" The Board Chairman turned to him in disgust. True though it was, there was no need to say it out loud. That was crass, vulgar. And it might be too political for the woman to understand.

"No," said Lettie, "please don't mire this in correct rhetoric. I appreciate your candor. I am not so naïve that I would believe a piece of paper is all that one needs to become a professor. Most especially in this institution which relies heavily on endowments."

"Doctor Gantry, I do believe the benefactors of this institute were wise enough to invest in a new approach to education, and thus are likely open – if a little skeptical at first – to the placement of a suitable woman in such an esteemed role." Hauer glared at Ashfield, effectively silencing him. "Your qualifications, in my mind, make you a very suitable candidate for the position."

Several others nodded and smiled. This was not Lettie's first time seated before the long table, with its Board on one side and only Lettie on the other.

Hauer noted the positive reaction from others on the Board. "I cannot see any particular reason why we could not move up your candidacy. I believe we should vote now to support further steps."

"Excuse me, Doctor Hauer, but I am the Chairman of this educational Board." He looked furious. "And I do not believe a vote is called for yet. There is one vital question of qualification that has not been satisfactorily answered for me: field experience."

A groan rose from the ranks of the Board. Hauer shook his head. "Doctor Ashfield, we have reviewed Doctor Gantry's field record a dozen times."

Ashfield turned condescendingly to Lettie. "I'm afraid we need to do this again. You see, your field work is distinct but always under the tutelage of another academic. The question might arise as to who did the actual work, whose concept and skills lead to specific conclusions. You must understand that we have no proof that it was you ..."

"What!" Hauer shouted. "Doctor Gantry, I must apologize."

Lettie lifted her hand to signal he needn't. "Gentlemen, I would prefer by far to answer Doctor Ashfield's concerns."

"You have no provable leadership experience in the field." Ashfield said bluntly.

Hauer looked as though he could melt into the table. "Leadership? Define leadership."

"I define it as being in charge of an excavation or exploratory mission. Miss Gantry can be commended but also criticized by the singular fact that as a woman she has had to be supervised in the field by a man. We therefore cannot connect any specific advancement or innovation to her exclusively."

God give me patience, Lettie thought as she drew in a deep breath. "I would like to answer this. While I have not been the identified leader of any exploration thus far, I have taken a position of leadership each and every time I have been in the field. Not only have I consistently been placed in charge when the mission leader has been away, which is quite frequent, but I have taken teams into field to conduct multi-site evidentiary gathering."

"But your name isn't on any such explorations. The gentleman in charge is."

"No, Sir. My name is not on the final report in a leadership role. My leadership is however identifiable. This is quite common with large scale expeditions."

"Well?"

"Nor, might I add, are any of the names of gentlemen I've had the honor of leading who have since been placed in excellent, thoroughly deserved teaching positions. Only one name ever appears on the reports or issued papers, but many contribute extensively. I would venture to cite precedent in practice with other, less famous scientists being placed in professorships. I believe this precedent is well established and therefore will satisfy benefactors ..."

"In this, my dear, you are wrong."

"May I ask how," she asked, trying not to correct him in his calling her 'my dear.'

"You are a woman. This is not a casual, usual, established posting for a woman. If we are to break with convention and place you in a position that carries the highest honors on this campus, you must be as the Emperor's wife - above reproach," then he quickly added, "academically speaking. You need more field experience, in your name." He cleared his throat. "And there is this matter of your Predictive Model, for which you are noted, having failed."

Again an uproar seemed likely until Lettie raised two fingers, as though politely gesturing for silence. "You are quite correct. My Model did not accomplish the task for which it has been invented. Not, at least, during this last test. Prior predictions have proven to be in equal measure successful and unsuccessful. Doctors Milne, Gray and Ewing, along with a handful of other geologists from the Imperial College of Engineering were with me on Mt. Tarumae. If anyone had just cause to complain, it would be those gentlemen." She drew out the letters of recommendation and offered them to Hauer. "As you can see, they are not of a mind to either complain or condemn."

While Hauer smiled triumphantly, Ashfield reddened as he vaguely noted the signatures of the preeminent scientists. Why she couldn't be more feminine, accept that New College was no place for her, and go find a husband to take care of her was beyond his understanding. Of course, there wasn't a doubt she was a fine geologist, but that only made things worse. Ashfield kept looking at the signatures and calculating the potential damage.

The meeting went into the early evening with only a brief break for tea, leaving everyone annoyed, conflicted and exhausted. For the latter half of the discussion, Lettie was relegated to a seat in the waiting room, as though she were an errant student waiting to see if they had been expelled for their bad behavior. Her life and dreams were being altered without her being present. She was used to such things, as all women were. But sitting in the cold, dark waiting room, she realized just how tired of such inequity she was. Raised voices made it all the way to her ears. When it was all done, some of the professors took the back exit to avoid looking or speaking to her. To say it had not gone well was far too obvious.

London's ugly fog returned from a day's hiatus and settled over the campus, making it nearly impossible for a student to see the building opposite where he was standing. Hauer and Lettie bundled themselves up appropriately. The 'pea soup' fog placed a disheartening gloom over the entire College and city. The general depressed haze was barely a match for Lettie's mood.

"He's shut the book on a vote," Hauer said miserably. "We once again must wait to have you in our ranks. Doctor Gantry, I must confess to you that up until this moment, I thought your appointment only a matter of getting through the interview process."

"As did I." She continued to stare ahead, hoping to see the lively campus through the fog. "But if there is any disappointment on my part, it is only because I took it for granted that I had the job."

"I find this hard to say, but he may have ultimately won. And New College will have ultimately lost."

Lettie sighed. "I haven't given up." She looked up at the glow of a gas lamp and considered how welcoming her lit parlor fireplace was going to be.

"I know. But, while you may not get a position, we are losing out on your qualities which would serve our students exceptionally, and we still are short a professor in the School of Geology and Mining."

"Thank you all the same."

"Are you still lecturing outside of the school too?"

"Oh yes, at every opportunity I get. In hope of success, I wish to hone my presentation skills. One must be used to public speaking if one wishes to teach."

"Where to after that?"

"The field. I have every intention of developing my Model, academic position or no. I have some hope that I will be able to show significant progress by the summer of next year."

"I hope so. I have to wonder if Ashfield will declare the open position as a detriment to the School and will fill it with a temporary appointee."

"Can he do that?" The wind blew wisps of fog past them.

"Yes. He can't appoint a permanent teacher without the Board's consent, but he can place one temporarily. And I can say that such people have first right of refusal when the job is eventually offered. It would effectively cut you out." Hauer pulled her into a shaded area. "Lettie, you must get that field experience ... now - without some damn ass of a man claiming it for himself. Forgive me, but you must stop being a woman and be a scientist."

Lettie winced but controlled her reaction as much as she could.

"I'm so sorry to say that, but it's true. You are a lady whom I admire greatly, and I hope I am not embarrassing you to say so."

"No, not at all."

"There, see. You are the perfect woman of kindness and graciousness. That's why it is so hard for me to beg you to give it up and risk all on being the scientist I know you to be. Not very kind of me to demand androgyny of such a feminine creature. You will forgive me?"

"Could I do anything less?"

"No. But you must put Science ahead of all you were taught or this dream of yours ends here and now. Or better still, get that damned Prediction Model working. That would certainly do the trick."

"I have plans ..."

"Make them happen, sooner than later. Where are you going to go?"

"Have you been reading about the substantial activity and strange phenomenon around Mt. Merapi and Mt. Bromo in Java? There is also something going on in the Sunda Strait. The East Indies is where I will go."

"I don't think I approve of the location, though having said what I have; I doubt I should stop you. Dangerous stuff, if the papers are to be believed."

"And, intriguing stuff too. I'm determined to go there. Oh don't worry so much. Remember, I lived in that region briefly and I'm prepared for the climate. I have already arranged permission from the Dutch, now all I need is a particular piece of equipment. Then I can go."

"Go without the equipment. Damn the equipment."

"No, Lesley. The equipment is partially my design. Adding that to the mission will further my professional goals but, far more importantly, it will help remove much of the danger imposed on staff."

"Who are you taking for your staff? Tell me you're getting that wastrel Kit Moore on the boat with you. His reputation ... well ... no one will think you've compromised your own reputation. I shall just leave it at that."

Lettie allowed the comment regarding Christopher to go without acknowledgement. "The Dutch want me to hire locally. Part of the reason they granted me entry into the territory in the first place was that I promised to employ locals. I tend to prefer locals as they know more than any of us know-it-alls from the other side of the world. I've also contacted a former colleague of mine, Mr. Rogier Verbeek, a mining engineer with interests in Java's volcanoes. He and his wife have offered me a place to stay while I'm in Batavia."

"Be careful Lettie. I've read all sorts of nasty things about those volcanoes."

"I will. I promise."

"I mean, I've been reading about them ... recently."

She thought for a moment. "You mean the volcanic island in the middle of the Sunda Strait? Yes, yes, I know about that. I'm not going to be anywhere near that place, as I haven't heard anything yet to make me think it's on the verge of an eruption. Just a great deal of steam. Nothing urgent. Mt. Merapi is showing much more promise at the moment. And it is located in the middle of Java Island, quite a distance from that other volcano." She smiled sweetly, knowing all the while that if the Sunda Strait volcano showed even the slightest bit of increasing activity, she was headed right for it without delay. Prediction required observation. Though, the likelihood of an eruption anywhere but Merapi was improbable according to her experience and her modeling. She'd watch all the same, as it would serve her right to presume where Nature was involved.

Chapter 24

Sir Richard stood in the doorway of his library as his son was let into the house. Rain poured down from the nighttime skies but such a thing would never have kept Rajiv away from dinner at home. The rains were arriving early this year. Professor Pierce smiled up at his father while dismantling his protection from the weather: hat, scarf, gloves, coat, rubber boots, umbrella, a small package in extra wrapping … it was all rather funny, actually. Pierce was just as happy to be freed from all the weight of it.

Sir Richard waved his son into the warm room. There was a familiar aroma of cigar smoke and old books that was comforting. A man of middling height and athletic build, even in his late 50's, Richard was still a good catch as far as the ladies were concerned. Ginger-red hair had faded quite a bit, and the lines around his eyes and mouth were permanent, but he maintained a handsome appearance; vigorous, bold, assertive … one Rajiv was envious of.

"God, what a night. It'll be interesting to see just who will drag themselves out for this little gathering."

"Well, you know I wouldn't miss this," the young man said. "Father's birthdays are to be celebrated."

"Not sure I want to announce I'm a year older, but any excuse for a party, eh?" Richard said, shaking his son's hand warmly. He couldn't reach out and wrap his big arms around the boy anymore, since Pierce was no longer a boy.

Pierce accepted the handshake. It was always welcome. "I have something for you."

"Good. I have something for you," Richard said, handing his son a glass of brandy. "Drink up. And accept my apology ahead of time."

"Whatever for?"

"Mrs. Devereux and her two darlings will be here shortly. Invited themselves. Couldn't un-invite them." Richard was amused when Pierce emptied the glass in one gulp.

"Apology accepted."

"The trouble with birthdays. Everyone feels entitled to show up."

"Including your son."

Richard barked out an easy laugh and patted Pierce on the back. "Start off my evening right, son. What did you bring? Home made?"

Pierce handed him the package with a look that said what else would it be? The elder Pierce sat down and un-wrapped the box. In it was a miniature engine, with a tiny water reservoir and pressure valve. Richard burst out laughing. "Good God, my boy, how much smaller will these things go?"

"Who knows? But so far, that's the smallest."

Like a child at Christmas, Richard pushed the toggle switch and the engine started up. A few seconds into it, and the valve let off a hiss of steam and a vapor cloud no bigger than his thumb. "I'll be torturing the cat with this, I'll have you know."

"Oh do leave the cat alone." Pierce said half heartedly, knowing perfectly well his father would never do such a thing. "If you must, scare Mrs. Devereux with it."

"Too easy." Richard switched the tiny marvel off and looked at it. In all the years he had watched invention and industry grow, he never imagined that such a thing was possible. And it was his son who did it. Carefully, reverently, he placed it in the center of the mantle, where he'd cleared a space for it. It was their private ritual: Sir Richard would age exactly one year, and Rajiv would bring him a working model of something fantastical. The younger Pierce would always come up with something new.

"Happy Birthday, Father."

"Thank you." He looked back at his son, feeling something mixed of pride and gratitude. "Remember that?" He nodded his head in the direction of a wooden boat, with a propeller that worked from a piece of rubber tube twisted and released.

Pierce's jaw went a bit slack at first. "My God, where did that come from?"

"Found it the other day. I remember when you made it."

Pierce looked a little sad at first. "I wish I could. I mean, I do remember it, but not all the details …"

Richard walked over quickly and poured another glass. "I shouldn't have put it that way. Of course you don't remember. You were only five and - well, those were times I wouldn't want you to remember fully anyhow."

"Oh, I think anything post-Bombay is worthy of remembering. And - I have come to terms with not knowing anything prior. I've long since decided that it's best that way." He tapped the patch of scar tissue on his temple.

"See, smarter than your father."

He sipped the brandy this time. "No, no. Just more damaged." He tapped the glass on his forehead. It was so easy to talk to his father. When words failed him elsewhere, here, at home, he could converse easily.

"Damn good thing you healed so well. How else am I going to sell you off to one of the Devereux girls?"

Pierce nearly sneezed the liquor out of his nose. "That's not funny, sir."

"It's a riot. Especially since I'll have to pay them, as they haven't a penny to their name."

"No, sir, you'll have to pay me. And I won't go without a fight."

"Now that's my son!"

"Was there ever any doubt?"

Richard stopped smiling altogether. "You know that you're my son, no matter ..."

"It has been thirty years. I think you can forego any worry that some family from Calcutta is going to show up to claim me."

Richard didn't smile. "It - it isn't very rational, is it? But I keep wondering ..."

Pierce set down the glass and leaned up against the mantle next to Richard. "I wouldn't know them even if they did show up. I have only one memory, and plenty of scars – which would have meant my death if you hadn't taken me out of India."

"Do you? Do you still have that much memory?"

"It shows up as a dream - a nightmare every now and then. But yes."

"And the business with the tree?"

Pierce looked at the floor and tried not to grin too much. "Probably the same memory every boy has. One minute I'm sitting in a tree, a Bodhi tree as I recall, the next I'm on the ground with a broken arm and someone is laughing at me. A man in a blue turban, picks me up, and tells me not to cry. Princes don't cry."

"I've always wondered if you were royalty and I stole you away from a life of luxury and exotic dancing girls." Both men laughed out loud.

"I think it was just my name. 'Rajiv' does mean prince or something rather like it. And frankly, I wouldn't trade anything of my life. I'm happy with what I have. I'm a Professor, an Engineer ..."

"... An incredible toy maker..."

"Yes, and a toy maker, but only for you, Father." Pierce picked up his glass and saluted his father. "You are the only father I've ever known and have memory of. Happy Birthday."

Richard returned the salute and a thank you that couldn't come close to truly expressing how much hearing those words meant to him.

Chapter 25

The year 1864 had not proven to be a good year for Union Naval action, at least not as of May. Why Turner was thinking of this when he finally fell asleep would remain his private mystery: it had been eighteen years since then. He had put particular energy into forgetting as much as he could. Yet, the more he forced the memories aside, the more vivid they became.

Despite all the substantial wins the Navy had achieved for the Union, most especially in New Orleans where the battle would have been lost without them, the Army had both numbers and public relations on its side. Accolades were printed in every newspaper in the North about how important the Army's victory had been at the mouth of the Mississippi River. And it was an important victory, though unachievable without the men of the sea. The Navy did receive some comment and compliment. But, with fewer than 200,000 men and a public mandate from Lincoln regarding the Anaconda operation to cut off the South from supplies and foreign aid, the media had decided the only role of the Federal Navy was to administer and enforce the droll blockade. It wasn't very newsworthy. And what the media printed the average Yankee believed. Rear Admiral David Porter was said to have made a thoroughly unprintable remark.

And, it didn't help that May had not been a good month for the Navy.

Turner's arm tingled with numbness as it was his habit to sleep on his side with that arm crumpled back over his neck. A protective position. His fingers and his eyes twitched like a cat in deep slumber, chasing a mouse or escaping a dog in its dreams.

Turner's dreams were not so mundane.

The ironclad Confederate ship *Albermarle* had taken control of the Roanoke River and more than one attempt to battle her had ended in disaster. Three Federal ships, the *Sassacus*, *Wyalusing*, and *Mattabesett*. had tried to take her together and failed. Control of the river was important for a variety of reasons, not the least of which was public relations. Every day the purpose of the war was challenged and its costs were reconsidered. Every Rebel victory was cause for concern and doubt. There was also the problem that it signaled, rightfully or not, an advance in Confederate naval technology and design – though provided by the French or British. "Interested foreign parties" were getting too involved where they were not wanted.

Orders had come from Admiral Porter, "enough with the large scale attacks - send a Landing Party to take out the *Albermarle* with a hand delivered torpedo." A brash young Lieutenant, William Cushing, wanted the assignment. He was too new to the game. No, this called for a level of stealth and cunning no pup could know. It needed an older dog, a fighting dog, with obsessive obedience. One so loyal to the cause of the Union that he would do anything – anything they asked of him.

Turner's fingers twitched.

As they had rowed quietly up the river, Turner looked back toward his ship, the USS *Sassacus*. Neither he nor his ship would leave the North Carolina swamps as they had arrived. Once on shore he had directed them to move with absolute silence. Eight men and Turner. Small, fast, deadly. Two of the men who took orders from him were older and more experienced than he, but that was a bonus. Their hard earned knowledge proved vital more than once.

Biting mosquitoes and thick patches of foul gas greeted them in the swamp. Their uniforms, which he had insisted they wear so that no charges of espionage could be made should they be captured, quickly became matted with soil and sweat, and clung to their bodies. They had carried two revolvers each, except for the Gunner's Mate who carried in a haversack the components of a torpedo. Each also had their weapon of choice: a Bowie knife or just their bare hands. Shots were to be fired only if there was no other choice.

The Landing Party could go where the ships and armies couldn't. And they could go with complete invisibility. That reputation was well known and the Captain of the *Albermarle* had been wise enough to place sentries on both shores opposite the boat.

One by one, they crept up on a Confederate sailor on guard, and removed him like a chess piece. The quickest way was to break the neck, but it wasn't an easy task. It took practice; hours of practice to be fast enough and strong enough. As commander of the party, Turner chose the first man and demonstrated his unhappy mastery of the skill. His other men tended toward seizing their victim by the mouth and cutting his throat. It was not a method that guaranteed silence, but it was practical enough.

Turner rolled over, trapping his arm under his body, fitfully still asleep.

Four men. He killed four men within a single hour. They were the enemy. They knew the risk they took joining a rebelling military. The Rebels knew they were wrong; they had to. No honest man fought for slavery, mob rule, and the destruction of the Union. No honorable man could ...

Before leaving with his men on the mission, he'd read his father's latest letter. His father was an absolute abolitionist and yet despised the war. To his son, he confided his fears of divine retribution on those who killed their brothers. His father wasn't wrong. But his father wasn't there, in the thick of the war, seeing comrades die or lose limbs in bloody hospital tents.

His mind was not in the moment. He was distracted though how, with his blood pounding through his body and his every nerve on fire, he would never understand. In that second, Turner had doubted his purpose and broken his focus. The fifth sentry escaped his reach.

For that long minute, the two men stared at each other. The 'Grayback' was fifteen, if that much. His eyes were huge and blue, like Turner's. He held his rifle in unsteady hands. Farmer's hands. He had something that resembled a moustache. It was too thin, too sparse, too new. Beige blond hair hung down his head and curled at the ends. He was a boy, fighting for a cause that would never benefit him. Abolitionists in the North weren't the source of his poverty and social mistreatment: rich plantation owners banking on free labor from slaves were. He didn't even have shoes. His feet had become mangled from the years of unprotected laboring in the fields and he was only fifteen. He might not have been fifteen yet.

Lieutenant Turner just stared. Hesitated.

"Mister?" the boy said in a slightly effeminate voice.

Turner's Boatswain dropped down behind the boy and nearly removed his head in a single cut.

Turner awoke, sweating. Every drop of moisture appeared to be from the spray of blood that coated him when the boy was killed until his senses regained knowledge of the actual place and time. It had been eighteen years ago but now he dreamed of it regularly. Why that boy? Why was it he and no other Grayback that drove a spike into his confidence, skewing his moral certainty? At that moment? Why did he dream of it so much?

He slowly rolled onto his back, shaking his arm to try to start the circulation to his fingers. Life was not as he had expected it. Young William Cushing had followed in Turner's footsteps, achieving what Tom couldn't: the destruction of the *Albermarle*. Cushing went on to become a famous man, beloved and decorated. Yet there too was a lesson: Cushing eventually went mad. Turner wondered if perhaps he too would surrender his mind to oblivion before he lost his life?

What should his life have been? There had been hopes that with his college education, he might form a merchant company with his father as chief Ship's Master, with a fleet of vessels supplying the gold fields of California and the Pacific Northwest. They would hire the best seamen in New England, veterans of wars, and outfit the fastest clipper ships. They would have broken speed records around the Horn and up the Pacific coast carrying goods to the remote but exploding populations in the west. Doubtless he would have been married before too long, giving his father a set of grandchildren to fawn over.

But the war broke out. Against his father's hopes, though with his reluctant blessings, Turner joined the Union Navy. His education and a bit of hard cash brokered him a commission. He wasn't too old, at the age of twenty-five, to be a Lieutenant. He'd move up. He was bright.

And he had a knack for the games of intrigue. That was something he did not tell his father. He told him only that he participated in sea battles. The rest was unfit for the eyes of an honest sailor like his father. Most of the war was unfit for anyone's knowledge. But that was war. Always had been.

His father died thinking Tom had been killed as a prisoner of war. Thinking his only son had died before him. The knowledge had probably been what brought on the stroke.

At least he never had to explain to his father about the scar. Turner reached up and put his fingers on the unnatural feeling tissue, wishing he could tear it off his body. He never went back to sleep that night.

Chapter 26

As was her habit, Lettie arrived early in the afternoon in the hopes of avoiding most of the callers Miranda Gray might have at the fashionable visiting hours. Once the flocks of ornately dressed sheep started to appear, she could easily retreat from the endless gossip regarding who was marrying whom, who had which misfortune, who was having difficulties with the servants, and all the other topics that served no purpose for her. Not that she hadn't initially tried to fit in with Miranda's other visitors. At first the gossip sessions made her feel normal and acceptable, but soon the topics tired and annoyed her. It was the meanness, the thinly veiled insults, and the complete lack of understanding of worldly topics that pushed her further away.

Miranda, on the other hand, was a genius in the art of patience.

The early timing would also alleviate the need for the awkward question of staying for dinner, especially if Miranda was distracted by her other guests. Otherwise, Miranda would insist, and then they would stay up talking until the earliest hours of the morning. Then Miranda would be obliged to wake her butler to send for the carriage and Lettie wouldn't get home at a time appropriate for ladies. Or worse, she'd be a nuisance when Miranda would insist she stay in the guest room. Then they would start all over again in the morning and Lettie would never get home to do her work. And she'd have far too much pleasure in doing so. Miranda had gone so far as to suggest that the two 'spinsters' should share the house and simply grow old together. It was a tempting idea.

When she and Miranda got into the same room with no interrupting outside parties, they suddenly became sisters, best friends, and scientific colleagues. Neither could shut their mouths nor hold back their opinions. If anyone outside ever heard them, they might be inclined to think they were fighting.

Lettie had so few women friends. It was as much due to her career goals as to her perhaps unreasonable expectations that anyone she called 'friend' should be able to engage in intense scientific discourse. In thinking about it, Lettie realized she hadn't many friends at all. She had excellent colleagues with whom she could talk about most public topics. But those she would deem 'friend' were very, very few.

Not wishing to embarrass one of those few friends, Lettie indulged in her vanity and dressed the part of afternoon visitor just in case she might be observed. Not that she really needed an excuse to exercise her feminine skills. To show up in anything but the most well thought-out costume would be insulting to her hostess and her mother's memory. The fashion magazines announced the return of the bustle in all its fullest and most outrageous width, and Paris had been responding with vigor. The couturiers were fawning over every lady who offered her figure as an ambulatory dress dummy and advertisement.

Conversely, the reality of outer London communities dictated a modicum of fashion restraint. Just because they printed it or the French made it did not mean that Englishwomen were ready to wear it. Sutton was, by all appearances and practices, a quaint English village … one that sat on the precipice over which one might fall into the chaos of London life. The community was growing as those accustomed to a slower pace, or seeking it for the first time, fled the city and settled in places like Sutton. With them, they brought their slower, more conservative lifestyles. High fashion was for Londoners. Lettie compromised her flare for the dramatic rather reluctantly and chose a simple silk gown of intense glacier blue with a new fashionably large and beautifully draped bustle. Her hat was a tall, flat-crowned straw with the brim raised in the front to show off the lining in heliotrope silk plush. Blue and lavender flowers, along with an array of ribbon loops, completed the hat's decoration. Her kid gloves were a lovely shade of lavender. All in all it was a lovely suit of clothes she would be proud to wear in Paris and ashamed to be seen in on a work site. Such was the easy hypocrisy of her life. It was the difficult hypocrisies that exasperated her.

She'd left her valise at home, which made her feel absolutely naked. She would need to keep a free hand for her umbrella. Certainly in the last six months there hadn't been a day when she was without the valise. But, in the last six months she had made only one afternoon call, in Baltimore, at the home of the very lonely Mrs. Barbicane whose husband was away on this latest obsession with all things lunar. A further compromise was accomplished in that underneath her glove she could feel the beads of Georgie's bracelet. It was her comfort. Her other hand was filled with books and paper-wrapped gifts she'd brought from her travels. One did not arrive at their first afternoon call after such an extensive trip without gifts for the hostess. Regardless of how close she was to Miranda, to arrive empty handed would be grossly uncivil. Since Miranda lived very close and the weather was quite obliging for the moment, she decided to walk. The wind scattered the first wet, browning leaves of autumn around her feet and whipped the slightly damp hem of her skirt against her ankles. Huge trees swayed and dipped their thick branches with each gust, often losing handfuls of leaves and twigs. Such a wind suggested another storm front moving in and Lettie was glad for having thought to bring her sturdy umbrella. A dog began barking as its human children scurried around in the garden, kicking at leaf piles and pulling berries off the bushes before they had ripened. They would all be soaking wet from the remains of the last evening's storm. A squeal of laughter escaped the mouth of the little girl and, covering her lips with both hands, she looked to see if anyone had heard her.

The Gray home was a perfect edifice of upper class living and middle class envy, and had in its own time held more secrets than Whitehall. It was one of the larger houses in the village, with an extensive, well kept garden. So close and yet far enough away, it was the perfect place for unspoken truths and things that shouldn't be known to be kept. But wasn't that just how one expected it to be? Sir Charles and Lady Gray had long since departed the Earth, leaving behind seven girls and no boys. Though society had dictated that each Gray girl either marry or perish, they had proven themselves greater than the demand. Of the seven, the younger three had entered foreign educational institutions just as Lettie had, the fourth had become a successful writer, sisters five and six had married interesting though improbable men, and Miranda had become matron over the entire Gray estate.

A maid, in crisp apron and cap, conducted Lettie into the parlor. She had been expected any day, or so the gossip above and below the stairs had indicated. A warm but small fire was burning and the shades had been put up. The room was very welcoming, with a hint of flowers drifting in the air. Everything matched in some way, even if it was by the tiniest means. Stuffed chairs on tufted rose-pink velvet. A pair of footstools embroidered with bouquets of silk flowers. Draperies were swept into cascading folds of fabric, in textured pink and heavy gold fringe. Correctly mismatched wallpaper with a flurry of design and color.

Even the ceiling was papered in bright teal, beige, gold and red. The molded plaster crown from which the gaslights hung, was painted in pinks and greens. No horizontal space lacked for something evocative of some family memory. Each surface was clean of any dust and neatly covered with embroidered cloths and runners. Multiple pillows were piled onto the chairs, offering a person in a tightened corset support while they sat. It was extremely fashionable and yet an assault on the senses. It was a woman's room.

Miranda swept into the parlor with her usual flair and held out her arms to embrace Lettie. The gesture was not one she'd offer to any other afternoon visitor. "Welcome home, dear."

"Thank you."

Stepping back from the embrace, Miranda looked her friend over very carefully. "You're not taking off your gloves or hat, so I presume you can't stay." There was a genuine sadness to her statement.

"Not this time. But I promise I will soon."

Miranda frowned. "Work, isn't it?" She waved at one of the more comfortable chairs for Lettie to sit and ignored the damp mark on her friend's skirt. Lettie would not appreciate having it pointed out. The silk taffeta Miranda wore made an alluring rustle when she sat opposite and rested her arms on her knees, eyes wide and ready to hear what Lettie would share.

They were contradictions in some ways, identical twins in others. Miranda was quite tall for a woman and too thin to be fashionably pretty. She could easily wear styles that put emphasis on layers of draped fabric around her hips, something Lettie knew better than to do. To compliment her dark auburn hair and blue eyes, Miranda always chose to wear wine or burgundy. Always.

"Work," Lettie replied.

"You only just returned, and though I'm sure not nearly as exciting, there's been plenty going on around here." Sometimes it was hard to tell when Miranda was being sarcastic. She looked over at the pile of gifts Lettie had brought her.

"Such as?" Lettie could be sarcastic too.

"We've finally become a Local Government District. The 'Sutton Sanitary District.'"

Lettie screwed up her face in confusion. "Finally? They finally approved the Local Government Act from '58? It's 1882."

147

"We seem to be moving at the usual pace."

"Is that all?"

"Indeed it is. See how progressive we are? Did you bring me anything nice?"

"Yes. But I have plenty to tell you, too."

It was sometime around three o'clock when the first regular visitors arrived. Until that moment, Lettie had carefully repeated the story she'd already told Christopher Moore on the Ferry. Adding to it, Lettie also relayed all the nonsense of her meeting with the Board.

"Truth," Miranda demanded. "You do want to go with this ... what did he call himself?"

"Robur." Lettie stared at the tea cup waiting for her, yet she hadn't touched. Only Miranda could ask that question and not get a shocked or offended reply. "Every thought or instinct tells me to have nothing to do with this man. I'm not sure if I am actually tempted anymore. Perhaps for a fleeting moment I was, but no more."

"I'll say this only as a good measure, since I've said it before ..."

"Get a man?"

"Get yourself a man. Marry Kit Moore if you must, he'll never stop you from running all over the world. He might even join you. And he certainly won't be a difficult husband unless you object to sharing?"

Lettie shook her head and thought of William, Kit's friend. "No, I don't think I would like to share. Perhaps that's not very fair of me. But I daresay I don't think ... he ... would want to share Kit either." Lettie carefully chose her words all the while knowing that Miranda was aware of the situation with Kit. "Ultimately it wouldn't be Kit that would stop me. It would be the demands of society that I stay put and portray the good wife. And, I'd want to. If I marry I will do so fully aware of the - the sacrifices I would need to make. I really do believe I couldn't marry unless I expected it of myself. At least if I'm not ..." She didn't finish the sentence, but instead straightened out her skirts unnecessarily.

"Do you still swear there's no such thing as love?"

"Often. I've decided that if I repeat it enough times I'll stop wondering if I think otherwise."

Miranda leaned against the arm of her chair. "A husband, unloving but respectful, is better than none at all. One of these days you're going to have to choose between your professional dreams and marriage. I hate that thought, but it's true. And for all you've done to show the world

148

what a woman is capable of, the painful truth is that nothing has really changed for us and we'll have to choose a man, even at our ages." She truly did look a little depressed for only a second before the maid entered to inquire if Miss Gray was receiving. With a deep sigh, she continued, "In the meantime, keep doing what you are doing and tell me every little detail. If it has to end someday, I'd like to live vicariously through you in the meantime. Now sit still. You won't be able to sneak away until you've at least said hello."

"Anyone I should know?"

Miranda's voice dropped with an edge of disdain. "Oh, you know them. I don't suppose I could ask you not to ..."

The door opened and an older woman entered the room, followed by a girl in her later teens. Additionally, a rather matronly-looking woman in blue, sporting either a wig or dyed hair in a color not found naturally on women her age, followed right along. The girl spotted Lettie right away and beamed brightly behind her grandmother. Her small gloved fingers made a secretive wave in friendly greeting.

Lettie carefully hid her sigh. Yes, she knew them. And this, she thought, could be either very entertaining or a complete disaster, just as Miranda feared. She really needed to go.

Miranda graciously met them at the door. "Mrs. Kingsbury, Amelia, how are you both? Mrs. Emerson, please do come in."

Mrs. Kingsbury looked across the room at Lettie with an expression unsure of what to think at that moment. "Better than I think some of us are, or have you managed not to injure yourself, Miss Gantry?"

"Good afternoon," Lettie said, equally unsure what would come next. "To my own surprise, I have managed to stay whole and unbroken for an entire year," she lied, grateful to have kept her gloves on.

Mrs. Emerson stopped so abruptly that her false hair almost slid forward. Her lips pursed and she actually moved back a bit, as though something of Lettie's unladylike behavior was viral and might infect her. To date she had always refused to speak to Lettie.

The three visitors stood facing Lettie with varying degrees of approval in their expressions. Two of three were clearly, and had always been, looks of disapproval in the highest degree. Lettie picked up her reticule. "Miss Gray, I have enjoyed this greatly. I hope to call again soon."

Miranda, her patience fully engaged, nodded.

"Good afternoon," Lettie said vaguely to the others. Amelia would be sorry she was leaving. She quickly swept from the room. Behind the parlor door she could hear Mrs. Kingsbury and Mrs. Emerson loudly protesting that Miranda even received her let alone allowed her to still be present when they arrived. The volume of the comments was clearly intended to be heard by those outside the room. Cruelty bred itself in the boredom they faced daily. Sadly, Lettie allowed the front door to be opened, and stepped out into the fading light. Clouds were building over the river. Her heart sank. This was what she knew, intellectually, was the cost of being a scientist. But that was no salve to the wounds inflicted by the small and petty minded.

How very true it was that the matrons of the neighborhood, especially the widowed ones, were bored beyond human ability to withstand. They turned their disappointments into bitterness and lashed out at the weak or obvious targets. Eton School bullies would be humbled by such behavior. For the remainder of her walk home, she couldn't decide whom she felt more sorry for at that moment.

That night she had every vertical surface covered with paper, black boards brought up, and plenty of lights illuminated in her study. She scrawled every equation she knew somewhere in the room and kinetically bounced from one board to another rearranging the notes and details.

Chapter 27

September 9, 1882
Brunswick Gardens, Kensington

Everyone wondered where his income came from. As a British gentleman, he had no occupation. Yet there was no family fame to supply him with funds, nor did he claim to any investment that could account for his private wealth. Most assumed that he got it from a well made investment.

Everyone was wrong. The family fortune had been made in the most inappropriate way: the trafficking of such items that few would openly speak about. The weapons of war. It was a shameful business unless one was selling to the winner; then it was considered quite laudable in the business world. Of course it often happened that such sales were to governments not British, hence the secrecy. Had he not been such a recluse in his youth, or disgusted by what his father and brothers did, he might well have entered the family 'business.' He certainly knew all its details and benefitted monetarily. But some sense of propriety had always kept him at a distance. He'd chosen coldness over human warmth. Time over substance. He was essentially harmless. Terrible to work for, but otherwise quite harmless to the world. And virtually invisible. The worst he'd ever done to threaten the façade was to wager now and then. Because of one wager, he met his wife, and the Universe changed. For her sake, and the promise of a world she believed in, he abandoned all history to be just another gentleman of means, a husband, a hopeful father, a better employer and an active member of his community. Someone suggested a run for Parliament.

In a matter of seconds, all that had ended. The world she so diligently strove to improve turned on her. It killed her. And it left him with nothing. Nothing, except a fortune of ill-gotten gold and family secrets.

If he could not bring about a world worth living in, then he might as well profit by its self destruction. He might even help it along. Would it be so bad if everything ended?

On the bill of sale, filled with euphemisms and false legalese, he signed 'P. Wickham.' The whole document was so full of lies that it barely mattered that Wickham wasn't even his name. Twelve thousand pounds remaining on the account. It would be paid with that standard, German precision and timeliness. All for a little mechanism that kept bullets from jamming in the barrel of a gun. Killing would be so much more efficient now.

Wickham wanted something bigger, something worthy of his attention. Something worthy of his desire for the whole world to go to hell. He carefully blotted the signature and folded the document. A fancy wax seal made it look like an official document. No solicitor had touched these papers. But, it had to look right. Wickham knew how to make things appear as though they were something else. It pleased him to do so.

He pulled out his watch and checked the time. His entire evening had been spent on designing and completing the document, as well as concealing the diagrams inside an ancient Greek amphora jar. Naturally, such an item would be sent to a German university for study, or so customs inspectors and clerks would think. Such an antique would never survive too much handling by customs officials, and not one of them would want to pay for damages; thus, the jar would sail safely into the hands of the buyer.

Mr. Winchester of America would be fine without profit from the patent. Americans were notorious for not respecting copyright laws in Europe, but then Europeans were dreadful in failing to respect American copyrights. Patents, books, and texts were stolen and plagiarized with wild abandon back and forth across the Atlantic. The venerable Charles Dickens spent half his later days suing to get paid for books published and sold by the Yankees. But their Mark Twain was finding the same problem in London book stores: hundreds of copies of his *Huckleberry Finn* with not a penny coming to his pockets. So, a little mechanism for rifles would hardly be missed.

Well, at least not until a German gun was being fired with great rapidity and absolutely no jamming. Who knew who the Germans would be shooting at? It would likely all happen in Africa. The Dutch in a minor way were interested in the interior of the Dark Continent, but never so much as the Belgians, British, French and Germans. The Turks were even glancing in that direction. Happily, the Americans were too busy establishing their own borders and subjugating the savages they ran into along the way.

Wickham opened up his copy of the *New York Times*, only two and a half weeks out of date. Transatlantic travel and post were getting better by the year. Not much was reported, except a now fanciful event somewhere out in their western territories. A gun fight. At a stable. Family against family. The McLowery and Earp families. Wickham scoffed. Irish sounding surnames. Of course. He wasn't surprised that the Irish were involved since everyone knew they were all violent. Or perhaps Scottish? They were violent people too, weren't they? Did it matter. They were in America being Americans: Americans killing Americans. He'd eventually have to see if there were some business opportunities there.

"P. Wickham" was actually quite fascinated by the "Yanks." If discarded or dismissed by the great European nations, "America paid no never mind," as they were fond of saying.

The Weldon business. Now that had some merit. Three men kidnapped by a man they called Robur. And that nonsense about escaping him. Anyone could tell that they were lying. Still, a madman with the ability to snatch these men out of a public park and to take them to the other side of the world in an implausibly short time? While the Weldon men said nothing of how, except that this Robur had a flying ship, the newspapers were filled with interesting drawings of fancy balloons. A balloon couldn't fly that fast. No, there was something not being told about the incident. Or, it was completely fabricated. Either way, amusement or business potential, it was worth watching, listening, and learning.

Chapter 28

September 10, 1882
Moore Family Estate
Kent, near Joydens Wood and Old Bexley

The butt of the rifle settled neatly into the pad draped on her shoulder. Slowly she closed one eye and centered the sights on the old archery target. Taking a deep breath, she slowly blew the air out past her lips until her entire body had calmed and settled. It was at that moment she pulled the trigger. It was just after that moment she remembered that she should have squeezed the trigger, not pulled.

At the very last second of the shot, her effort with the stubborn trigger raised the barrel slightly and her shot only tore a hole in the top right corner of the paper target and caused the rifle to slam back into her shoulder. Lettie sighed in exasperation.

"You need to have the trigger loosened. It's calibrated for a stronger hand." William Smythe pushed his long legs out in front of him and crossed his feet. "But you are hitting the target. That's better than Kit was doing."

Moore looked up from pouring tea. "Oh, I think I deserve better than that. It's the first time I've ever shot an American rifle."

"Excuses."

"All right, you two. It's my weapon and I need to be able to use it well." Lettie intervened. She flicked out the lever and snapped it back into place. The brass cartridge from the spent shot popped out of the top opening and a new cartridge was pushed into its place. At her feet lay the remains of an afternoon of practice, empty shells in a pile. One had been a bit too hot and singed a mark on her skirt. Gently setting the weapon back against her moderately sore shoulder, she lowered the barrel in alignment with the target. Another deep breath, followed by another slow exhale. This time, Lettie tightened her fingers on the foregrip and lowered the barrel tip ever so slightly. Squeezing the trigger, the barrel popped up again, but this time it was compensated for. A hole was ripped out of the outer black circle of the target.

"Well, now, that's much better. Take your aim just a bit more to the lower left and I think you'll have it." Smythe sat up. His long, blond hair fell slightly into his face and he flicked it away without consideration.

Moore set the teapot down and poured brandy into his cup. "You are taking it with you to the Indies, aren't you?"

"Of course," she said, chambering another round and aiming again. "With everything that has happened recently, I think I'd be an idiot not to."

"I should come with you."

"You can't. You have classes."

"Damn them!"

"Language, Mr. Moore. Language." She wasn't in the least bit concerned about his cursing, but an honest, forthright lady should always insist on the best manners. Down and to the lower left. Squeeze the trigger. The bullet ripped the target slightly off the center circle.

"Bloody good there, my dear." Smythe reached over and purposely took Moore's cup of tea. "That's the sort of thing that will keep the natives off."

"The natives are not what I'm … being aware of."

Moore casually took his cup of tea back from Smythe, as such gestures were not uncommon between the two men. "You meant to say worried about, didn't you? Well, I'm worried too. The reports from Java aren't very soothing to the nerves. The locals are becoming vocal again about the Dutch presence; no less than three of the volcanoes are showing activity, and then there's the weather."

Lettie took aim again, and hit close to her prior shot. Still not a bull's eye. "The mysterious storms have ceased. I haven't even seen one around here. I daresay that the Conqueror has become positively bored with me and gone off to pester someone else."

Smythe slipped a bit of the brandy into his new teacup. "Not a peep from him?"

"Not since he rattled a few windows in London."

"Are you so very sure it was him?"

"Sure, as in positively certain? No. But experience and eyewitness accounts of an unnatural storm convince me it was Robur."

"Robur? Sounds like a name in one of your silly woman's books."

"Romantic novel. And yes, they're silly; they are expected to be. And yes, Robur does sound like a name they'd use. He looked the part too. But he's quite real. I'm actually curious about how he broke so many windows. Something concussive, I suspect. They're still talking about that at New College." She wanted one more shot before taking a rest from the exercise. The rifle might have been the lightest and most comfortable of those she looked to purchase, but it was still heavy. She'd have to get used to it. And her left hand still hurt.

"Say there, speaking of New College ..." Smythe started to say. Moore made some noise to catch his attention and signaled him not to continue. Lettie knew what was transpiring behind her.

"It's a 'no,' William. I'm not in the employ of New College ..."

"... yet?"

"Possibly, never." She lowered the gun and turned to face the two men making the effort not to allow the barrel to point at them. "I have to make that Model accurate more than half the time. Can't save lives without accuracy. And that will take more fieldwork. That's what they want, William, more fieldwork."

Smythe was positively amazed. "Just how much more do you need? For God's sake, you've done more than most."

Moore shook his head. "That's the paradox – she almost never can do enough."

Lettie smiled kindly at two of her three most favorite men. "But I will, all the same." Returning her attention to the target, she chambered a round, lifted the weapon and fired. All in a matter of seconds. To her surprise, the bullet tore through the center circle. By no means was it a bull's eye, but it was close. Perhaps she needed to think about it less? Just act. Just fire. "Miranda Gray says I should find a man and settle down."

Smythe sniffed loudly. "She wants to be married, so of course that's all she's thinking of. It's all that she and her class think of."

"Don't be uncharitable. She has a brilliant mind. She's not afraid to use it either."

"Wait 'til she has to ask her husband for permission to have an opinion." Smythe folded his arms tightly. "Don't do any such stupid thing until you're a Professor."

Lettie lowered the rifle and stared out at the distance. "Then they'll expect me to quit, so I can be at home taking care of the family I'm too old to have."

"You're not thinking seriously ..."

"No, no, William. But, you have to understand how very hard it is to do what I'm doing. I've been taught all my life that there is only one way for me to be a whole and complete woman: get married, bear children, take care of a house. The expectations of others who neither care nor comprehend what it means to be – different. As much as I fight that and can tell you every logical reason that is not my destiny, there are times when the struggle hurts very much.   I know you understand that, William."

Smythe waved dismissively at her.

"Why not take one of those darling little American pistols? The Derringer, instead of that rifle? You could fit that in your reticule and no one would know." Moore changed the subject abruptly. He knew where things were headed. This was a continual conversation.

Accepting of the change of topic, Lettie replied, "That's the point. If I'm seen with something *this* large, most who might think of me as an easy target will think otherwise. Its presence is a deterrent. And if I'm ever forced to use it, it's as excellent a close range as a distance weapon. Holds more cartridges too. More shots."

After the sun had set and a soft breeze had come up to toss around the autumn leaves in the "Garden of England," a lovely dinner was had. She loved the Moores. They made up the bulk of those she considered genuine friends. Like Christopher, they were larger than life and full of joy. Lettie gathered herself and her rifle up sometime after midnight, kissed her friends goodbye, and was assisted in climbing into the family's carriage that Moore insisted she use for the trip home. The wind was actually blowing rather steadily now and as the carriage rolled down the slope of the hills, heading toward the road to Crayford, it seemed to pick up considerably. The framework of the carriage rattled with each gust.

Several times, Bourne Road came close to the riverside and matched the wind through the trees with at beautiful, flowing sound that soothed and calmed the soul.

Pulling the blanket around her all the tighter, she settled herself in for a fairly long and bumpy ride. Her thoughts were of Java, a green jewel on the eastern edge of the Indian Ocean. Deep, rich fields of tea, coffee, and sugar were punctuated with sharp volcanic peaks. Strange music and the smell of spices in the air. Ancient ruins with fearsome creatures carved into the stones sitting next to Dutch-inspired towns of white-washed architecture. Incense and cooking fires. Organic smells of the tropical jungle. Birds calling out in an array of songs. The low rumble of the mountains …

No.

That was the low rumble of thunder.

Lettie's half-dozing mind awoke suddenly as she realized the thunder was not in her half-achieved dream. She sat up and pushed off the blanket, her heart pounding. She drew the window curtain back and looked up at the sky. A flash of lightning made her jump and to cry out.

"It's all right there, Miss. Storm's a bit off to the East. Been buildin' all day, it 'as. Should'n' come no where near ta us." The driver had that lovely, comfortable Welsh lilt to his voice. She'd heard such speech nearly all of her childhood.

"Thank you," she replied, not sure if he'd heard her. The carriage itself was rather large, able to seat all seven of the Moore clan, and completely enclosed from the often wet weather. She settled back in her seat, hoping to catch her breath and calm down. It had been such a long time since she'd seen the storm she attributed to Robur. As she'd said earlier, he certainly should have grown bored with her by now, as most men did. That notion disappointed her. She ought to be honest with herself. She really did want to go on some wild adventure where her status as a lady was not constantly under siege, where she could forget manners and pretense, and part of her had hoped that the reason for Robur's interest was romantic. Illogical and unseemly as that was, her desire was fueled by her reading too many romantic novels and a part of her that wanted the attention. That was honest. She had to admit that much and move along with her life.

The carriage started uphill, past a tavern on the edge of Crayford where music and laughter were still pouring out the windows and doors. Naturally, they were not stopping. Sutton was only two hours from the Moore house.

To satisfy her curiosity, or perhaps to verify that Robur was nowhere in sight, she drew back the curtain. The driver was correct; a large, rather normal rainstorm had formed to the northeast and was rumbling along the Thames estuary and plain as should be expected. The Moore house might be drenched by morning.

The tavern's lights warmed the reflections on the polished carriage doors, and Lettie looked over at the quaint country inn wondering what was happening inside. Standing at the gate, leaning up against a stone wall, a man lit a cheroot and looked up at the passing contraption. In the light of the match, she could see his eyes looking up toward her, his strong face and thick hair. She'd seen him before. Hadn't she?

Quickly, she fell back into the seat hoping he hadn't seen her looking – rather, staring - at him. She pulled the blanket up around her, all the way to her throat and set her hand down on top of the rifle case.

The man with the cheroot drew in the smoke and exhaled slowly, all the while enjoying the view of the carriage returning its passenger to where she needed to be.

Chapter 29

Robur's head pounded the more he thought about the Paris lecture. 'Rajiv Pierce.' Whatever the Professor was called. It didn't matter. He was brilliant, but not more so than Robur. That would be impossible of that much he was absolutely certain. He enjoyed the satisfaction of knowing that few if any were capable of the mental gymnastics and gyrations that he was.

Robur rubbed the temples of his head, hoping the throbbing would go away. Stress and fatigue. This was what he got with stress: migraine headaches that could reduce his powerful body and mind to that of an invalid. The room felt too close. Small. Smaller. Too enclosed. He would need to go up on deck; to the fresh, open air.

Copies of newspapers created a pile on the right half of his table. Report after report on what atrocity was committed, who was threatening whom, and established scientists berating new ideas and those developing them. What the hell was wrong with humanity? Had nothing changed?

He opened his box again and pulled out the designs which had so upset his first mate. They now included a set of maps: London and Paris, which he would never show to Turner. It was only by divine providence that he'd not put those maps into the box before Turner saw. And Turner would never again look at without permission. Had he lied to Tom? Yes, but that was his prerogative. Turner just wouldn't understand until the very last moment; then he'd adjust his perspective due to loyalty to Robur, and all would go according to plan. The plan wasn't going as assumed, but it was in motion. Did it matter what humanity did to itself, really? Some deserved to die, but there were some who did not. Thinking of the potential still untapped, Robur's head actually felt less painful.

Pierce owed him and Robur would make him pay; and that was enough to keep him alive. Gantry was a woman; God help the world. She was a sign of things to come. She, perhaps, should live. Turner was horrified at first when he learned of the Doctor's gender. He dealt with men, not women. He was very old fashioned that way; never mind that she had no difficulties in presuming her place amongst male colleagues. Turner still disliked the idea of involving her.

Robur gave the order to follow her, as though she were any of her male colleagues. Tom did what he was told to do. Was Tom becoming dubious, maybe even disloyal, over this? Robur was beginning to doubt his decision, was no closer to finding his unlimited fuel source, and had to depend on a woman - a woman - to gain it.

He was sure that the longer he stayed in Europe, the more likely the British were to discover him. Or perhaps worse. There were those Turner would catch word of, that would sell to anyone the fruits of his brilliant brain. Weapons mongers. The British could afford top bidding on weapons and innovations. But so too could the French, the Belgians, and the Germans. He would direct Turner to gather more information on those arms dealers as well as the usual agents of the Empires. That command Turner would be happy to obey.

He'd have to leave off the flag planting pranks which amused him greatly. Since he'd not had what one would generously call a childhood, there were times when Robur needed the immature laugh. No more. His avoidance of capture was now too vital and urgent.

Cause and effect: a very Buddhist concept, and a scientific one as well. Robur rubbed his temples as they started pounding again. He hadn't had so many migraines in such a short length of time. They were, perhaps, a result of the Weldon Institute men, their escape and subsequent attempt to destroy the *Albatross*. Yes, since having to rebuild sections of his ship they so clumsily damaged, he had become less humorous and twice as prone to bursts of temper. Here he had given the Weldon men the perfect opportunity to advance their knowledge, improve their technology, and to provide the sort of worldly assistance that would make Turner proud. All they had to do was keep quiet and learn. Their bag of gas was no match for his airship and he would prove that to be the case.

Now his head was really pounding. Just thinking of the irritating cretins made him feel ill. Ungrateful idiots, whoring after Doctor Gantry's money and fame but not her science. They didn't have the mental capacities to recognize how much she could provide them. Robur laughed gently recognizing his hypocrisy, hoping not to cause his head to explode. He pulled his box closer. The cold wood and stone felt soothing. He laid his head on it for a moment, feeling the chill on his skin. This box contained his life. Sacred. Powerful. The life that should have been ...

Underneath where the designs and maps were kept, Robur had replaced the other, unimportant documents with a green bottle, a crystal glass, several lumps of sugar and a neatly wrapped square of brown paper. A crewman had brought him nearly frozen water which he demanded on account of his headache. The contents of the brown paper was getting harder to obtain and, he felt a strange shame and need to keep knowledge of it from Tom. This he would have to arrange for himself. Another secret from Tom.

This was a concoction that his teachers had used. He'd seen it work. The mind expanded as the pain subsided. It was risky, but he could easily maintain complete control over its effects. Filling the lower half of the glass with the green liquor, he cascaded cold water over a sugar lump into the glass until the liquor turned a milky color. Finally he added the contents of the brown paper envelope and stirred.

Chapter 30

Despite outward appearances, the Professor of Engineering was not by nature a tidy man. Keeping himself organized and controlled took monumental effort and training. There was a balance involved, as any attention given to neatness took energy away from the flow of inventive thought. The only logical solution was to designate zones within his life and abode, to define them, and to keep them under the strictest control. All things directly affecting his father, both their reputations and social standing were to be confined, by near violent means of persuasion if necessary, to the realm of calm – the front parlor. That meant he would never appear in his father's presence nor when officially presenting himself as a Pierce in anything less than the most perfect attire or with the excellence of a gentleman's manner. His parlor, where he might receive guests, including his father, was an image of simple, elegant, refined taste. With not a speck of dust to be found. Few if any decorations that made reference to his occupation were to be found; after all, a gentleman occupied himself but did not have an occupation … a job. Everything was elegantly English. Not one element spoke of the Indian continent. It was kept that way at all times.

Pierce almost never spent time there.

The zone of chaos, as he called it, encompassed all else of his life. His workshop, bedroom and office were all an alarming mess: clean but cluttered. The bedroom was on the first floor with the Parlor, cut off by a substantial door. Amongst his books on the over stacked shelves was a beautiful, brass Ganesha – the elephant-headed god and son of Shiva. A few books of serious study on the subject of Hinduism were kept in a dark spot near his reading lamp. The English Church's Book of Common Prayer was displayed openly, out of habit and safety. He was the respected son of a baron: inventing was his one and only allotted eccentricity.

Other stray books, monographs, diagrams, memoranda, newspapers;

they covered most of his bed, allowing only enough room for him to sleep. Half burnt candles, two gas lamps, and an old lantern surrounded the edifice, threatening to set the whole thing on fire after any late night inventive jag. The workshop and office were on the upper floors that had been at one time an attic. His father had never been in one of those chaos zones, even though he had expressed an interest in seeing the workshop.

Pierce could never decide which zone he preferred, so he happily lived with a foot in each. His landlady saw to it he never had to spend valuable time cleaning. She did an amazing job, under what could be trying circumstances. The bedroom only received her attention when linens needed washing. The workshop was off limits by her royal command, not his.

Pierce was a bit of an oddity in Brompton, which said something in that it was a locality better known for its Bohemian tenants. Artists and writers flocked to the borough for its pubs, post-Georgian architecture, its location near to the center of the city, and mostly for its acceptable rents. The fashionable Belgravia had become too expensive and quiet a decade or so before and the creative minds had migrated a bit to the south. The densely-packed, five-story buildings with their brick facades and long windows appealed to those who liked to watch the world pass by. Since the landlady had a choice between temperamental authors, drink-prone painters and a well-behaved inventor, she chose Rajiv Pierce.

There was one afternoon Pierce learned about the cholera outbreak of '69; how it killed his landlady's husband of thirty years; and how it came so close to killing her. Everyone had been so afraid of becoming infected that few would come to offer her comfort. None of the many 'brave' physicians were located in her ward. There was no money in her neighborhood, or at least not back then.

As she had described the details of her agonizing recovery, the Professor's mind wandered up to his workshop. A cart? A trolley? An unmanned and controlled from a safe distance mechanism that delivered the comfort of life saving medicines and letters from loved ones. A steam – piston engine, of extremely reduced size, could do the trick. A nurse or a doctor could be halfway down the hall, controlling each patient stop through a series of pressure or even electric cables. Would a modified Wimshurst Electrostatic Device provide sufficient power? Not without several of them linked together and boosted by an alternator, just as Pierce had seen with the French train.

He had his landlady to thank ... or maybe curse, as the development of the medical cart instantly engulfed his every waking moment. Sitting in coffee houses, he would let his cup grow cold while scribbling down notes and ideas until one day the thinking stopped and the activity began.

Pierce buttoned his waistcoat of blue and gray wool tweed, checked his watch against the parlor clock, and began slipping on a sack coat of similar cloth. There was a knock on his door that sounded the same as every knock his landlady made. "Come in?"

"Sorry to interrupt you, Professor. But there's a young lady who wishes to see you regarding a professional question." She handed him a card. Her voice intoned a certain doubt. Among her many assumed duties were the monitoring of the home's moral standards. She liked visiting cards, especially those of Lord Pierce. A nobleman's card was distinct among others by quality and simplicity.

The latest card was very charming; ivory, textured paper with an elegant print type. He read it, swallowed then read it again: Miss L. M. Gantry, Dr. sc.geo. Volcanologist. "Please show her in."

"Certainly, Sir." The landlady walked out of the room, leaving the door open. Normally she would shut the door, but a woman wouldn't want to be found behind closed doors in a gentleman's rooms, even with a professional question. The open door made it all proper. She could then vouch for their behavior by listening in from the kitchen.

What is she doing here? Pierce felt a touch of panic rise in his stomach. The book of geology, written by an Oxford professor, lay out where he had left it the night before. Philip Striker had managed to obtain it, though how was best not considered for too long. He rushed over to the table, closed the book that had been opened to a description of Mount Etna, and pushed the volume out of sight.

When Lettie Gantry walked in, he got an answer to all his fears and questions: it didn't matter why she was here, only that she was. Now that it was the two of them who stood in the room, he could more effectively gauge her. She was of his height and pleasantly round through the bosom and hips, while still the very image of health that he had originally recognized. She was, as before, dressed exquisitely, this time in rust-colored wool. A soft, silk tie was knotted in a masculine way at her throat and set into place with a plain, gold stickpin. The lapels and cuffs of her bodice were trimmed in warm, dark brown velvet. Perched high on her glossy black hair sat a fedora decorated with ribbon and curled feathers.

Her eyes, her most outstanding feature, were somehow greener than before; soft green and large under heavy eyelashes.

"Miss Gantry?"

"Thank you for seeing me without an appointment, Professor. I hope I'm not interrupting you or making you late?"

"Oh, no. Not at all. Would you care to sit?"

"I would. Thank you."

Pierce watched her sweep across the parlor to take the chair he had indicated. She carried that small but overstuffed valise he'd seen before. In sitting, she effortlessly maneuvered her bustle and skirts aside to allow a graceful descent onto the cushion. He'd forgotten how lovely he thought she was, and yet so ... he let the negative thought slip away. "Would ... would you mind if I asked you a question, Miss Gantry?" His voice was barely above a whisper.

Lettie thought about it for a moment. "Please do." She watched him, but also began to unlock her valise without looking at what she was doing. He was really a nice looking fellow, but she had promised herself she would not inject any silly notions of romance into the situation.

"Are you the same lady who attended my lecture in Paris?"

A slow, soft smile filled her face. "The very same." She turned her attention to the contents of her valise, but kept talking. "I believe I owe you an apology for leaving your lecture too early. I hope you'll accept my explanation of fatigue."

"Of course." Fatigue? No, she was shamed from the room and he wanted to say something comforting to her about it. His mouth remained closed.

"I'm also the same woman whom you followed at the railway station and the same whom you sat near on the Channel Ferry."

Pierce turned dark pink. He hated confrontation of all sorts yet any complaint she might choose to issue would indeed be warranted.

"You have a memorable face, Professor. You should realize by now that you are quite recognizable." The tone of her sentence was complimentary.

He sat down opposite her. "I hope you did not take me to be improperly following you."

"Of course you were," she said bluntly, with a wider grin. "I would have followed you too had I seen or heard what you had." Her voice had a merry laugh tucked away in it. It was deeper than most women's voices.

Pierce looked at his hands and carefully, with each controlled breath, crafted a full and complete apology in his mind. If he ever wanted to know more, he needed to assure her that he was respectful and not a man who was stalking after her. But before he could say anything, she pulled a set of sketches out of her valise and thrust them at him.

"Never mind explanations, sir. If you want to make good by me, you need to be the same Rajiv Pierce that I've observed. You're curious, I daresay, enough to follow me. You're clever enough to invent brilliant mechanisms. Now, I am hoping you are brave; brave enough to help me." She pushed the sides of her valise together in a vain attempt to close it. The case reopened under the strain of the paper load. "Professor, I've had a rather bad month of long ocean voyages and disappointing adventures. Along the way I have dealt with the most appalling men, who have neither a respect for me nor a respect for my science. I can excuse the former to a point; I am after all an anomaly in the scientific community. The latter is not open to ridicule."

"I overheard something of the Weldon Institute and your ... unfortunate dealings with them. I assure you, I am not one to take any honest scientific endeavor lightly." He couldn't look directly at her; he was still mortified that his behavior had been called out.

"That is a relief."

He didn't meet her eyes, but could only look out vaguely across the room. "Please tell me how I can make amends for my overactive curiosity."

She watched him for a moment, attempting to look into his eyes.

He was surprised when he realized she was so closely scrutinizing him and he had to turn away again.

"It's a pleasure, I assure you Professor, to work with someone of broad intellectual interest. I traveled on the Eastern Seaboard of the United States and also in Europe, all in search of inventions and inventors who could see the value in creating an effective Volcanic Prediction Model. What I found, instead, were half meant promises, personal danger, and no small amount of rudeness. I hope you will excuse any assertiveness on my part, but you have become my last hope. And for reasons I don't believe I need go into at this moment, I'm also running out of time."

Pierce perked up to that. "Madame, tell me more." Now, he could make it up to her.

"It had been my intention to discuss with you your medical cart while in Paris, but those men of the Exploration Society ..."

"They have no place in their world for un-manned mechanisms. I understand them; they are threatened by all the changes. If un-manned, then what use is there for men?" Where did all those words come from he thought? He never made such comments before. He never talked that much.

"Well said, sir. Please look to my drawings. They are amusing, I'm sure, to an engineer, but to this volcanologist, they are the future. I wish to ask you to make another cart, with several distinct modifications, as you can see."

Pierce looked up at her for a moment, then back at the sheaves of paper.

"Sir, I would like you to create for me a device, not to deliver medicines, but to take samples. It very likely cannot roll but must walk, for it will be needed to collect samples of volcanic gases and debris from the most dangerous and inaccessible of places."

"Inside the volcano," he said frankly. He stood up and took her drawings to the window to see them in better light. She was correct; they were not the sort of thing that an engineer would prefer to work with, but they did the job of describing the mechanism she needed. The cabling for the controls would be a problem. To make the mechanism viably safe it would need to be a long way from the controller. And, as resistant to heat as possible. Lacquered or steel wire wrapped bronze? There were significant challenges to start with. "Are you a Neptunist or a Plutonist?" Yes, he got the terms right, didn't he?

Lettie was genuinely startled, in a pleasant way. "I don't believe I've ever seen myself as either. It's been quite sometime since anyone actually chose sides."

Pierce began to blush a bit. It hadn't occurred to him to check the date of the publication he'd read. His data was out of date.

Lettie didn't seem to mind. "It is rather interesting, the history of a science. Sometimes one looks back and laughs. Historically speaking, I've not yet found anything decent to say about Herr Werner nor his Neptunist concept that all rocks were formed by sedimentation in the Great Biblical Flood. The fact that he maintained the unreasonable belief that the Earth is a mere 6,000 years old is simply cause for a chuckle, don't you think? He was far too vocal about any disagreement. I cannot abide rudeness, especially within the scientific community. Debate: yes. Good wit: most assuredly. Vulgarity: never."

Pierce cleared his mind of all but the text he had devoured in a day regarding geology and volcanoes. He had been hopeful. "Yet, James Hutton was as vehement that the Plutonist theory was correct. That the source for all rock formations is fire. Why is Werner so disagreeable where Hutton is not? It can't simply be a matter of manners."

"Because Werner was wrong. And he said there was no value in studying volcanoes. Such an opinion is contrary to my heart. How could I find him anything but disagreeable?" She grinned coyly. Keep to business, she reminded herself.

"You don't fully believe in the Plutonist theory?" He didn't really expect her to say yes.

"Oh no, I don't believe anyone is wholly Plutonist or Neptunist anymore; the field has grown up a tad since those two men set at each other's throats. Lyell's work on the uniformitarian ideas of Hutton and the Plutonist theory ultimately lead to the compromise theory generally accepted today. Most rock formations are from molten material while some are created by sedimentary processes."

"So it isn't layer after layer of sedimentary rock down to the very core of the Earth?"

"Now you're just teasing. Of course not. We understand today that there is a molten layer of rock under the Earth's crust. How large or deep that layer is, we don't know yet. And, according to the German explorer, Professor Otto Liddenbrock, there are pockets of life found in cave-like, under-crust structures. I'm not sure how much I accept Liddenbrock's theory, but it might prove interesting to explore. If such places do exist, then it may be possible to examine the molten layer through one of these pockets."

He nodded soberly. "Such a layer of molten rock would have to be dense in order to support the weight of the crust."

"Indeed." She leaned on the arm of her chair. Most scientists took a very long time to develop a comfort in speaking with her. This was going well and her heart was beating a little faster at the idea that she'd found a competent and enthusiastic resource. "Does that not suggest a fascinating concept?"

"How so?"

"Will you accept the principal of Hutton's uniformitarian theory, which is to say that rocks are broken down by environmental processes, such as erosion, melted in their reduced state, combined with the molten layer and driven out by pressure onto the Earth's crust?"

"For the sake of this argument, I will." He smiled slightly. Surely there were no other women to be found like this volcanologist. How had he been so lucky? He kept smiling, but his stomach knotted again. His father would not approve. He couldn't let her know what he was thinking.

"Will you also accept that this indicates motion on an enormous scale?"

"I accept that too."

She smiled, revealing small lines near her nose and eyes from the times she allowed her manic energy to bring her pleasure in life. "The crust cannot weigh more than the molten layer beneath it; otherwise continents would sink, yes?"

"Yes."

"Constant motion under a light layer of crust, convection if you will: what do you think would naturally happen to that crust?"

Pierce had no idea and quietly said so. He had been doing so well up until that moment.

"Professor, consider ice flows in the Arctic. The motion of the water beneath the ice that has not frozen into a hard shell is reasonably constant? Yes? What has happened as a consequence to the sheets of ice above?"

He thought for a moment, considering the illustrations in the Times of Admiral Sir George Nares's Arctic explorations. Cracks. As far as the eye could see, broken and cracked sheets of ice. "The ice is shattered into islands."

"I would suggest rafts rather than islands. Does the water come up between the ice rafts when given sufficient energy? Or, when they press into each other?"

"Naturally." He walked back over to her and sat down, clutching the drawings in his hands. "The denser material, such as sea water or molten rock, would rise up through those cracks. You believe that's how volcanoes are formed?"

"Yes. Precisely. It would account for Island-Arc chains of volcanoes, such as those found in the South Pacific, all sitting neatly in a row. It would account for similarities in volcanic activity between neighboring mountains. It would also account for nearly all types of earthquakes."

Pierce looked at her incredulously. "Miss Gantry, volcanoes and earthquakes may go hand in hand, but earthquakes do not require volcanoes, as was proved in the 1815 earthquake on the American river, the Mississippi. There are no volcanoes in the region."

"Professor, consider a raft the size and weight of France. Then consider what would happen were that raft to bump up against another, the size of Prussia. The result would be?"

"But we know France does not regularly 'bump' up against Prussia or Germany, except politically. There have been no reported earthquakes in that region."

She wouldn't be silenced. "It's a hypothesis, a generalized question. Something to suggest the sheer size of what I'm talking about. These rafts are constantly bumping up against each other. I simply have no complete understanding of the size of the rafts. But I suspect one need only look to a map. Surely one raft is Africa and another is Europe. We may be looking at as few as four or six geological rafts. Or maybe thousands."

Pierce leaned back in his chair. How had she done it? She'd managed to get more words out of him than he'd said outside of lecture halls all year. "Radical."

"That's why I'm not prone to shouting it from the roof tops. Besides, before I entirely reinvent the science I thought it best to obtain the evidence. Scientific method is always the correct process to use."

He waved her drawings in the air, almost triumphantly. "I like your proposal," then he added, "Miss Gantry. I can see some problems with an exact copy of what you describe here but the overall concept is both sound and possible."

Lettie's eyes lit up.

"Yes, Miss Gantry. I do believe I can build this."

"Professor, I must say, this is the best news I've had in a long time. And to think, I needn't have left England to do it."

He wondered, out loud, "If you hadn't come to Paris, you wouldn't have seen the medical cart. We wouldn't have met, in our odd way."

She began forcing her valise closed, which took some effort. "If there is any question as to funding for such ..."

"… I think we needn't worry about that just at the moment. For the immediate future, I need to consider the basic design, especially the footing of this mechanism."

"I would also offer to bring you rock samples and some limited but useful photographs of the terrain it will need to master. You will then see why I suggested walking rather than rolling. But, I will concede my theory in favor of your practical knowledge in areas where my imagination has attempted to exceed reality."

"Madame, it is the nature of imagination to exceed reality. Where else does invention and growth come from?"

Chapter 31

Robur grasped the debris which had lodged itself in the exposed rotor of the fore-screw and yanked it out. The violent action caused the gigantic propeller to vibrate out to its tips. Sitting back on the rotor shaft, he rested his shoulders and head against the hull and held up the offending clump of grass. "We are capable of flight, Tom, when the rest of humanity must trudge along in the dirt. I've designed the ship to maneuver at the highest speeds, to survive in extraordinary circumstances. Yet the clippings from a farmstead have nearly brought us down out of the sky." He sounded more frustrated and amused than angry, to Turner's relief.

Turner, straddling the rail and holding onto a secure line around Robur's waist, tried not to laugh, just in case he was misinterpreting his commander's mood. "Mix a North Sea storm with Dutch farmland and we were bound to come out of it wearing a piece of Holland. Could have been worse sir."

Tossing the clump overboard without a care for who might be far below them or how they might explain dirt clods falling from the air, Robur climbed off the fore-screw and up over the rail. He didn't even attempt to dust himself off but set about untying Turner's knot in the line. "So," he said, much quieter, "They'll be working together now. That's superior, you know. Their genius put together. We can use that once we've returned from America."

Turner couldn't help smiling. The brief but potentially satisfying detour to the States would be a welcome respite. It might ultimately distract Robur. Once he was in a better mood, Robur would be more amenable to his suggestions.

A visit to Philadelphia for the launch of the Weldon Institute's big balloon wasn't the very best of ideas. They might be discovered. Yet Turner believed that a mysterious nighttime raid would put an end to the constant public bragging by the Institute's President, Prudent. Not that Prudent or the Vice President, Evans, had given particulars to the press that came close to describing the *Albatross* accurately: to do so would put the balloon's technology into question and therefore, its investment worthiness into doubt. But they had told the world that a madman and his faulty flying ship existed. Whether they were laughed at or not, it planted in the minds of many the notion that such a flying ship was out there. If the *Go Ahead* failed, the story would be doubted even more.

Turner's wartime skills would find good use again. Sabotage was in fact a very interesting exercise in planning, stealth, and timing. While he hadn't discussed with his captain what would be done, Turner had already designed a triple method of causing the balloon, the *Go Ahead*, to fail before leaving the ground. Prudent and Evans, and all the others, were fools and braggarts, but not deserving of death. The *Go Ahead* would not leave the ground.

The *Albatross* crew would have to be careful, of course. No room for error if they were to remain unknown.

"Aren't you looking forward to this?" Robur asked.

Turner perked up. He must have been frowning. "Considerably."

"Well, we won't be able to enjoy it for long. We have other work to do."

"Sir, with regards to the volcanic model, I still recommend," Turner started carefully, "that we simply take the model from Doctor Gantry and make it appear to be a robbery."

Robur's good hearted mood began to dissolve. This was a conversation they'd had already. "I want its creator too." He threw the line back into Turner's arms.

This was where Turner had to be artful, he knew. He respectfully lowered his voice. "It's nothing but an equation; something you'd master in a short span of time ... if that long. I think we may risk too much of our independence and anonymity in trying to kidnap ... a lady. You know the problems we faced after abducting Prudent and Evans, and they were nothing but a pair of idiots from the States. This time, sir, we're talking about the abduction of a woman: one with friends and resources as well as being known to the public."

Robur kept fussing with his uniform. "So tell me, Tom. If the equation is incomplete, or if she is working with the British government and is purposely concealing the most important details ..."

Turner could only think how unlikely that was.

"What do we do then? I need to have its creator here. There's no more time to be wasted, we need that 'model' now." He stopped and stared out into the distance. "We'll put her back, Tom. I'm not interested in killing women," he snapped. His hands were shaking slightly and his migraine was returning. "And now that 'they' are conspiring together we'll have to deal with both of them. She should have taken me up on my offer. That would have been the sensible thing to do."

That much was true. "She's a lady. I doubt she can ever accept your offer without ruining her reputation."

Damn it, Turner was right. And he was beginning to doubt. But Robur knew what to say to get his first mate back in line. "Imagine what we can do with no more ties to the Earth; no fuel demands, no governments watching for us. Freedom to live, to create ..."

Turner's expression stiffened. The Captain was right. A brief annoyance for two people, but with a benefit to his crew and likely many more; if he could persuade Robur to share his creations with the whole world. The implications for mankind were staggering. Freedom from poverty or disease would end the need for war. His thoughts must have shown on his face.

"Yes, Tom. We'll inconvenience two people, but they will have their rewards for their contribution. They might even thank me in the end. There is so much good we can do, but first we must ... break some rules."

There was no persuading his captain otherwise. The decision was made. Turner looked around the deck and considered what might happen if Robur sent someone else to do the job? No, it was his duty. He knew exactly what to do, and how. He simply had to erase the discomfort in kidnapping a woman: to treat her as though she were a Confederate spy. There had been plenty of women who spied during the war. They knew the consequences. Surely this Doctor must know the consequences of living a worldly life? "May I suggest sir that we wait until Doctor Gantry is in route to wherever it is she's going next? Fetching her from a train going through the American West or India would create less distress and attract less attention."

For a moment Robur seemed to approve of the idea. "Pierce ... if he's like most inventors he's prone to disappearing without warning. Common place." Robur's face hardened. "Pierce. I can have him anytime I like."

"But perhaps we should wait until he actually accomplishes his task for the geologist?'

Robur didn't hear the comment. "Take whatever crewmen you need."

"Thank you, sir, but I prefer to hire on the spot." When Turner received a questioning glare, he explained, "What we're doing is risky and I want the men with me to have as little knowledge of you and the ship as possible. The less they know, the less they are connected to you, the better."

Thinking for a moment, Turner's philosophy seemed good to him. Sound. Loyal. Robur nodded in approval and headed toward the Afthouse. God, he needed something for the pain.

Little Meriton had waited nearby. "Do you want me to come with you, Mr. Turner?" The stout, aged sailor looked up at Turner with vigorous grey eyes.

"No thank you, Josiah. Stay as far from this business as you can." Then he added, "Watch the ship. Keep her safe."

The deck was busy with work. Though Turner had a deep worry: he had not hired them, the Captain had. Neither Meriton nor Turner knew any of them.

Both men looked out over the deck, at the other crewmen and realized that they knew less of those men then they had when they had first come on board. They'd been with Robur for years, but who they were and why they stayed was something not discussed.

Chapter 32

The great wooden box was being loaded on the cart: it was his greatest success, humbly transported. The nurses had commented gratefully and most of the doctors nodded in full agreement. Pierce's medical trolley was a triumph. Oh, of course there were suggestions and some criticisms, but on the whole it was a day well spent.

Pierce was feeling rather satisfied with himself. This was a giant leap forward for the trolley and it would now leave him more time to work on Miss Gantry's project.

His heart stopped briefly, or so it felt, as the box nearly slipped out of the grip of the workmen. But it did not fall and he took a deep, satisfying, calming breath and his head became too light. Adjusting his scarf up his throat a bit more, to both warm himself and to protect the silk cravat he'd worn, he decided to walk home in triumph. The brisk air would do him good.

The sky was alive with flashes of light and loud thunder. It had driven off the bulk of the fog for now. But none of it compared to the freakish storm above the Paris rail station or the one that had cost him twelve shillings to replace his workshop windows. This was much too beautiful a display of electricity to be the work of - what had she called him - Robur. Putting up his umbrella and keeping close to the buildings, he strolled the mile home, stopping only to purchase a packet of excellent writing paper and a pound of coffee, ground finely. The bundle of brown, waxed paper smelled wonderful. But he needed to keep it apart from his new paper or every letter would smell of roasting beans and old tea leaves.

As he stepped from the tea and coffee shop into a low-lying mist of steam and aggressive fog, he passed a man who'd turned the notched lapels of his short wool coat up around his ears and wrapped his head in a scarf. The man walked past him, narrowly missing him by an inch and without slowing down or saying something polite.

"My apologies," Pierce quickly offered.

The man waved him off curtly and continued on his way down the street.

Pierce retreated a step, restraining the urge to comment on the man's rudeness. His day would not be ruined by something so common. He closed his eyes, took a good breath, and let go the anger.

Looking down the lane, after the man, Pierce was surprised to see him standing at the crossing, looking back. The man glared angrily, as though it was Pierce who had behaved offensively. A pair of black eyes: all that could be seen of the man's face, stared, unblinking.

It was possible Pierce was about to be confronted, something he loathed.

For a good four minutes they watched each other. Finally, Pierce took a step toward him, hoping perhaps the man had not heard the apology that had been given and that any insult might be reduced if it were offered again.

A moment later, the man disappeared around the corner.

Chapter 33

Philip Wickham had studied the professor and the woman academic for a month, with absolute, machine-like precision. At best they were droll in their regular habits. At worst, they were ignorant of what was happening. He needed to step in and get things under control, before they got themselves killed or caught up in the middle of business that wasn't theirs. Not that he cared what happened to them, only that such events would draw too much attention. Besides, his old colleague Monsieur Jules Pierre Hetzel had asked him to help. Hetzel's requests often lead to profit. Hetzel had become his greatest resource. Of course Hetzel didn't know all the aspects of his business. Perhaps he didn't care to know.

He looked at his watch several times before satisfying himself that the time was absolutely accurate. Such was his daily ritual. He then placed the packet of letters he kept in his locked drawer desk, tied together with one of his beloved wife's ribbons, up to his lips. It was the only gesture of feeling he permitted. Putting them back in the walnut and leather desk, he wiped any expression from his face and erased any concern from his mind. He was a machine by all other standards, human only when he allowed himself the rare emotional release over the letters and other memorabilia that connected him to her, to the only creature that had ever stirred his heart.

For a moment, he felt a bit sorry for Pierce and the woman scientist. They had no idea what strange circumstances they were being drawn into. He folded Hetzel's letter an extra time before sliding it into his pocket. Pierre-Jules Hetzel, a former French naval officer and now a publisher, had asked him to look in on Pierce and - what was her name? Gantry? They might be creating something of importance. Hetzel had asked him to see just what they were up to, and in Hetzel's melodramatic style, to see if they were aligned with any great evil. Probably only a potential evil, as Hetzel tended to be frequently paranoid about such things. Anything or anyone that kept Hetzel from being at the center of all technological advances of value was considered a great evil. Occasionally, though, Wickham had to admit, Hetzel had been right. And, since the two of them had deemed it appropriate to intrude on everyone's business just in case there was something valuable to be had, for separate reasons of course, he would comply.

As a gentleman, he had no desire to maintain a profession; however, his existence required a steady income. He'd long since detached himself from the affairs of individual nations, petty and ridiculous. Wickham really no longer cared what they did to one another, so long as they battled incessantly. But to Hetzel, the details were apocalyptic. Hetzel made certain no one had the upper hand of advanced technology. In his mind, that meant the avoidance of war.

Such a foolish notion. War was part of being human; why pretend otherwise? Why not derive sustenance from it? No, Hetzel wanted to save the world.

Well, he thought, it is a distraction. Hetzel could be amusing, if only Wickham allowed himself amusement. Nothing got past the machine's logic. Nothing amused, confused, or surprised Wickham anymore.

The woman would be an important contact though he suspected she was one of those irritating "New Women." Always going on about equal pay or educational opportunities. Riding velocipedes. Going about without consideration or temperance. Smoking in public. She was likely one of those. Yet, she had seen this *Robur* up close – and that gave her value. Wickham couldn't count entirely on anything the Weldon Institute men had to say as he was convinced that they were liars. But this woman, a New Woman or not, could hold keys to his discovery of who and what Robur was. She probably didn't understand how much she knew.

Leaving his study, he stopped to make certain that all his artifices were well done: the hair, the moustache, the clothing. He slowly adjusted his expression from cold and blank to one of dull self-satisfaction. Well-dressed, willful ignorance. His look implied nothing of what calculated, generated, and observed from underneath. It was not the same man who stared back in the mirror's reflection five years earlier. Though flesh and blood, he chose to be a machine. As a machine, he could do as he pleased, caring nothing for results that did not immediately impact him. Flesh and blood had a tendency to care - he refused to do so.

Chapter 34

Seeing Rajiv Pierce that close had upset him far more than he'd expected. What had he anticipated? Why did he even go to see the inventor? Sometimes Robur made decisions even Robur didn't understand. He simply needed to see the man he was dragging into his world; to look at him and potentially size him up; or rather to diminish him, thus making it easier to commit such acts against him. Instead, the encounter had brought up memories and doubts he couldn't afford. Pierce had been in excellent spirits and it was no wonder; his invention was a success.

For a brief moment, Robur felt a bit sorry for the professor. The thought did not last.

Robur held the box cautiously, perhaps wondering if its contents would either spill out and spring to life or turn to dust before he could put them back. And he held it reverently. It was a metaphor for his early life. Dust, ashes, loss. It could be said that he'd dealt with no more childhood afflictions than any other contemporary of his. Everyone he'd known had a similar story to tell. Times were hard but had been harder before. Children would always bear the brunt of social or economic disaster. His father had allowed life to have power over him, had allowed outside forces to drive him, had allowed himself to be reduced and eventually to be destroyed. A typical story, was it not? This would not be his life, not Robur's.

Never!

Placing the box down on the desk in a satisfying, sacral way, he made his decision. No, that wasn't true, he'd made his decision before this, when he'd given the nearly disastrous command to attack the *Go Ahead*, the Weldon Institute's gigantic balloon. Turner had warned him not to be open and obvious: someone might see him. To simply sabotage the Weldon's balloon and therefore to make fools of its President and membership was more than enough. But Robur's temper had taken control when he saw Prudent and Evans again, with their smug faces and bragging words. Damn it, with an assembly of Philadelphian balloon enthusiasts in attendance, Prudent regaled the crowd with the now famous, malicious tale of how he'd destroyed the *Albatross* and its inventor. Destroyed? Prudent? That witless fool? But the Institute's President didn't stop there. He went on to spin a fabric of lies that ended with how Prudent had outsmarted Robur.

Worst of all was the claim Prudent made regarding Robur's treatment of the valet, Frycollin. A lie. A god-dammed lie. Prudent had blissfully described Robur as a bigot who referred to Frycollin in the most hateful of terms; terms usually used by angry plantation owners who lost everything in the American war and needed someone to bully or to blame. Of all the things Robur imagined himself being accused of, vile racial epithets and behavior associated with slavers was beyond impossible. Turner was disgusted too. As the crowd had cheered Prudent, Robur's self-restraint was annihilated.

Turner was banned from carrying out his plan of sabotage. Robur locked himself in his quarters and seethed until the anger was explosive. He wrote a single letter, an announcement, scrawled out with every ounce of hatred he could muster. When the next day the *Go Ahead* launched, Robur was ready.

Turner said nothing, but obeyed the commands given to him.

Above the clouds, where few if any could see what was happening, the *Albatross* struck. The *Go Ahead* couldn't maneuver; it was helpless. Time after time, pass after pass, the *Albatross* broadsided the balloon with swivel guns and compressed air. No more than five minutes and the *Go Ahead* careened toward the Earth.

Why he let Turner talk him into saving Prudent and Evans, he couldn't fathom. But he did. And he handed the warning letter to Evans to be read publically once they were on the ground safely again. Oh yes, he would follow through with his threat to kill them if they didn't read it aloud. To the very same crowd that had cheered the lies Prudent told. *Mankind is not ready.* Through Robur's letter, they were forced to admit that his ship was superior to theirs, that they had lied about Robur, and that mankind was not ready for what Robur could create.

Not entirely satisfying, but with the crash of the *Go Ahead* and the public humiliation suffered by the Weldon men, he decided it was time to put his plan into motion. He was not entirely unknown anymore. Complete anonymity could no longer protect him. He would have to have complete freedom from the earth to remain safe. Not one of his better decisions.

It was time to stop watching and begin his plan. He'd been waiting for far too long. The vengeance would be divided amongst his targets, those who had to pay for what they had done to him. He had to attack them first, before they could abandon their hatred for each other and combine their efforts to destroy him. To attempt to destroy him. Even combined they hadn't the genius he did. They didn't have his ship.

Tom Turner would object; he'd been hoping that Robur would change his mind about many things. Tom was intelligent enough; he would soon understand the necessities of the plans he kept locked in the box, Robur assured himself.

The box opened easily enough. Inside was the set of plans he'd been developing quietly. In some ways it had always remained a fantasy, but Rajiv Pierce changed everything. Now he knew how the Professor would pay him back.

Leaning back in his chair, he sipped the milky green liquid that had become his one indulgence. Intelligent men drank it, in moderation. His teachers had been prone to its use for opening the mind, though he eschewed their other vices of women and drunkenness. He had no use for women around him. If the urge became truly distracting, he had the means to find a willing woman and to afford one who was clean and discreet. And there were willing women, for he was quite attractive to them. Besides the obvious wealth, he was handsome, fit, free of disease and not interested in talk. A wife would be tedious and unnecessary, and he had no time for courtships. Women had little or nothing worth talking about.

No, not all women. A very few had intriguing minds and might even be considered downright brilliant. Not the sort of brilliance he demanded of himself, but a reasonable facsimile. And one in particular … yes, he could consider her acceptable. She was not ugly, but perhaps was better described as handsome instead of beautiful. Yet her equations and hypotheses were attractive, especially since he could put them to use right away. Perhaps …

He stopped the thoughts. It was the so-called 'Green Fairy' that was causing him to lose sight of his purpose; a fine example as to why he planned to indulge infrequently. The infrequency was also attributable to a logical concern regarding the opiate he added, in response to an ancient prescription he'd learned. Too liberal a use of this mixture and he would damage his body and his superior mind. If the said green creature was to be of any benefit, which it had been before, he needed to leave off the ideas of a woman and to focus intensely on his latest technical problem. The absinthe and opium mixture had proved to free him from conventional thinking and to envision remarkable concepts hidden deeply in his powerful mind. He simply had to keep focused and not allow the little, unimportant distractions to divert his enhanced vision. He held up the glass and gazed into the liquid asking it and himself, how do I control the power? How do I manage it and not destroy the whole goddamned ship?

Smiling, he sipped a little more. A vision was coming to him; something like a giant bird. No, not a bird: an insect. Its wings thumped through the air, pounding out a rhythm. Wait, they would fold up tight to the body - the hull - but not flap. That would take too much energy from the engines and might even weaken the wings. Yes, he could see it. Clearly in his haze of green.

His right-hand man was out on the mission and would be successful no doubt. Turner did not fail.

Once the captive and Turner were retrieved, every plan would be ignited and launched into a motion that could not stop. It would start with Rajiv Pierce, and likely end with him too.

Chapter 35

Twilight was Pierce's favorite time. The whole world was cooling down in a blanket of blue, balanced between the day and the night. The colors and the light were gentle to his eyes, and hid away all the details that made men argue or worry. A soft wind blew up from the river and through the trees of the Park. So soothing to his fears. Fog was being pulled down in strings from the sky by extra moisture that would likely turn to rain by midnight. If the temperature kept falling, it might become snow. With the madness of the weather these days, he wondered, anything was possible.

At home waited his latest addition to the trolley he was building for Miss Gantry: a grasping armature that could hold greater weights than any other appendage he'd created thus far. It worked due to a delicate balancing act. The arm had to be made of a strong metal, which meant it was heavy. He'd also crafted a triad of bronze fingers that clamped down firmly on the material to be picked up. Perhaps it held on too tightly; he would need to test that with differing types of rocks. All in all, he was feeling proud and quite accomplished. A stroll was well earned. Perhaps a dinner at La Rochele's would be in order? Wine? Roasted Lamb? Yes, he could celebrate.

Pierce strolled along the cobbled pathway. It was still rather early in the evening, but winter nights started much sooner and lasted longer in London. In the twilight shadows, no one could see his skin, judge his height, question his motives, challenge …

Stop it, he thought. Even in this comfortable time of day and his celebratory mood, the anger from old wounds could still rise.

A dry day in late October was a blessing as the month tended to be the first of the wettest months of the year.

Considering the season, it had started out as an uncommonly warm and unseasonably dry day, thus all the couples and groups of young people had ventured to stroll, in case this was the last clear evening until spring. Once the fog rolled over the city, it was evident that the weather was about to change, but that didn't stop anyone from seeking the last outdoor moments. Gas lamps hissed and the occasional policeman assured a feeling of safety. Even some ladies were daring to walk out at this time. Two lovely girls, dressed in promenade gowns, furs and tall hats, passed by him and giggled coyly. Pierce slowed his pace, touched the brim of his bowler and bowed slightly. They both nodded sweetly in his direction. Naturally, being un-acquainted, all three were prohibited from saying more than "Good evening."

After the girls passed, one looked back at Pierce, and then began chatting with her companion in earnest. The words were inaudible but the tone suggested admiration and quaint pleasure.

Pierce sighed. It was exactly what he needed. A boost to his esteem. He gripped the cane his father had given him and felt all the more grounded. The lamps flickered and reminded him that there were some ideas he wanted to try on his volcano machine. That seemed like a good thing to call the trolley. His "Volcano Machine."

The twilight was fading into darkness and a foggy haze was getting lower to the ground. Pierce could feel the beginnings of a mist falling on his face. He followed the path around a tree-canopied corner and found himself generally alone, admiring a sweep of hill that just seemed to blend into the darkening sky. Much further ahead, he saw two working men walking his way. They seemed engrossed in conversation and one had lit up a cigar or cigarette. Pierce decided that they were married men. They were of that certain age most men had a wife; their clothes were worn and unfashionable, but they were clean, neat, and pressed. Someone saw to it they were cared for. Someday he would have to have some such person in his life. Naturally, the future Lady Pierce would not be expected to do the sewing and washing, but to run the house as a well-oiled machine, taking pride in her work as he did in his. And, she would have to be socially savvy, making up for his greatest weakness. A lady who could speak graciously and eloquently, and fearlessly on his behalf. Lettie Gantry slipped into his mental Utopia, as she had frequently over the past weeks, and he didn't fight the notion. Could it ever happen? She was an adventuress and scientist, and would hardly think becoming a domestic-bound spouse a satisfactory life. Yet, that was exactly what women aspired to, wasn't it? Honestly, he believed he might provide her with a good home. She would rule over his zone of calm.

But, this was his momentary fantasy, and perhaps here he could desire such a thing without believing that he had crushed such an amazing spirit by taking her away from her volcanoes. Besides, would she want him? Or was she far more drawn to Christopher Moore? Why hadn't he married her: why had she refused him? Was she a New Woman who had no interest in common, womanly things like marriage and children?

Pierce pushed that idea out of his head. If he admired her as much as he believed he did, then he couldn't think so disrespectfully of her. Still, a thought, a picture, of her standing in the doorway of his workshop reminding him that it was late and time to go to bed, warmed him against the rising chill of the evening. Tomorrow would be rainy and cold again.

And if he didn't bring her up to date on his progress, none of this fantasy would ever come to pass. She was quite meticulous in her details to him. The samples had been sent, photographs delivered, and itemized lists of what the trolley would need to be capable of, prepared. Every fourth day she sent a letter inquiring as to his progress and providing the most concise responses to his prior questions. Yet, she had been so precise and complete in her replies that he found after a week or two that he had no real questions to ask. He has so engrossed that he barely gave the landlady, who read the letters to him as his hands were often full, one or two sentence responses to Doctor Gantry. Surely she must think him rude or annoyed, but in honesty he was so intrigued and energized with the project he simply couldn't take the time to tell her so. That would have to be corrected soon or he was going to cause too great a rift between them. That's what he would do when he got home, he'd write a long, friendly … yes, friendly … letter to her.

"Sir, I'll have that cane."

Pierce turned around to see that the two workmen were in front of him, two more had come up behind him and he was sandwiched between. He grasped the stick in both hands.

"Come now, sir. You'll not be needing it." The workman dropped his brown cigarette and put it out with his foot, rather casually.

At a signal, all four moved closer around Pierce. He twisted the cane until he heard a small snap. This was the moment he knew was someday going to come; the reason his father had given him the cane in the first place. "I have nothing for you. Go on your way," he said as calmly as possible. He looked around quickly; other than the five of them, no one was near. He'd wandered too far from the popular areas, seeking solace in his thoughts and escape from the very people who might have helped him now.

The spokesman for the group of men motioned for the others to wait. "We're not thieves, sir. You'll be coming with us now. And I would prefer it if you've not got that cane in hand."

The man's language was too refined to be working class, and it lacked any British pronunciation. Was he American? The clothing was a disguise.

One of the men held a length of rope; the other had long pieces of cloth. The leader reached out to take the cane and Pierce reacted.

The cane slipped apart into two sections: the strong walnut stick and a sharp steel long-knife. The blade flashed in the gaslight and the sudden glare made them step back. Pierce brought the knife closer to his body and held the stick out further, as he'd been taught. His stance was weak and no amount of control was keeping an expression of fear off his face. Trained, yes; experienced, no.

The leader moved first and received a blow across his back as he swept past. Pierce saw the opening left by him and rushed to escape the circle. It was a ruse, one he didn't know to recognize. One man wrapped thick arms around Pierce and tried to force him to the ground. Pierce slashed one of those arms and broke the hold. He turned and began to swing wildly at anything that moved. But it was, as the cliché said, too late. The remaining two leapt on him, grasping legs and wrists. The recovered leader wrestled the knife from Pierce's hand. His jacket was pulled off, with something said about other possible weapons. The slashed man then knelt down on the small of Pierce's back.

He was trying to shout for help and adding a few more rude comments before a twist of cloth was finally stuffed into his mouth and tied at the back of his head. A bandage was wrapped around his eyes and his arms were painfully pulled behind him, long enough for one of the men to bind them.

Unceremoniously, Pierce was picked up by several hands and half carried, half dragged off the path. Dirt and mud were replaced by metal under his feet. Soon he was climbing up some sort of walkway into a confined space. Voices echoing inside the space told him how large the structure was, and sometimes how small. The floor shook violently and a rush of light headed-ness overtook him. His knees weakened with the sensation of floating, his ears rang with a strange *whir* and the noises of a powerful engine. A door creaked open and Pierce was pushed past it. He landed painfully on a cold floor. He attempted to sit up once he realized that no one was trying to hold him down. That was when he felt a bruising blow across the back of his shoulders, from his own cane he was sure, and through the burst of pain he heard a threat issued against any further disobedience.

The door was locked and he lay quiet, partially holding himself still as the floor shook and slid underneath him. Everything hurt, and the cool of the metal floor offered him an odd relief.

Chapter 36

New College was considering a temporary posting for the Professorship in the School of Mining and Engineering. That meant that she was being pushed out by bureaucracy. Lesley insisted that she need not worry, that such a decision was very political and wouldn't happen in the immediate future. Get to Java, predict something accurately or test one of her mechanical designs - anything, he told her. Thus the travel arrangements were hastily made.

To make things worse, Pierce had become impossible to work with. At first, he communicated, mostly about what he'd done or was doing. Then, the letters and telegrams drastically reduced to terse or incomplete responses. Finally, her requests for updates and any needs he might have were sporadic at best. Now, he'd stopped communicating all together.

Pierce was a strange man, shy and introverted. She'd hardly expected eloquent speeches and multi-paged replies. In fact, she was a little surprised at how much he did initially say, though it tended mostly to be about his progress. Polite chitchat was absolutely ignored, and that was fine, at first. If he wanted to focus on the job, Lettie was content.

Late in the week, she sent him a note asking if she could come to visit. Not a word was sent back. Deciding that she'd somehow lost his interest, after all that was what always seemed to happen to her, she boldly arrived at his doorstep at a reasonable hour.

The landlady had no idea where he was or where he'd been for the last month. His luggage and much of his equipment had been missing for a week, perhaps more. It appeared that he had gone away to finish his project. It was unusual, but not completely out of character for the very quiet man. He had done so once before.

Lettie was devastated. Had she pestered him too much, and he felt he had to hide from her? No, her requests and discourse were completely within the bounds of such a relationship between scientists. She had done nothing more than she had when arranging to visit Japan. Doctor Milne had never said anything that might indicate her assertiveness or directness was in poor taste. Yet, as she sat going through all her notes and correspondences, she couldn't stop asking herself what she'd done wrong.

There was another possibility, which she tried in vain to avoid, but despite its foolish melodrama, it was a potential reason Pierce was nowhere to be found. Robur. Oh, but that was a ridiculous notion. Why would the Aviator want Pierce? Was he not a man of equal cleverness? Could he not design and create any mechanism he wanted? No, Lettie thought, there was no reason for Robur to even be aware of Pierce, let alone be interested in him. Sadly, she wondered, if it was she that Robur seemed temporarily interested in. And now there seemed to be no interest at all. How odd that she even cared?

What if she took Robur's offer? Could he do what Pierce wasn't doing? Was there any chance that Robur still wished to help her? And, of course, the hardest question was, what price would Robur ask in return for his assistance?

Lettie was mortified at the idea. How she even allowed such a thought to occur was - was inappropriate. She would lose her character. A woman's reputation, her character, was all she really owned, despite reforms in property and inheritance laws. The truth was it would be a long time and many reforms before women could even claim ownership of their own bodies. Thus, it fell to a woman to protect her character with as much vehemence as was required. And thus, Lettie pushed the idea of Robur's offer out of her head, with much appropriate disgust. Her father would never approve, New College would be scandalized, and even Christopher Moore would question her sanity. Of course, she had to reasonably admit there was a bit of logic to it. Robur could, if his grand aeronautic invention was real, kill those two proverbial birds with one airship. But, how could she allow herself further contact with him and not ruin her already vulnerable reputation? Not even to gain the position at New College? No, not for any of those things could she ruin herself by traveling with a known kidnapper and criminal. But, could she do it for the sake of Georgie, and that Dutch boy she'd seen die? Was her reputation more important than the lives imperiled every day?

What sort of man would Robur prove to be? Arrogant. Selfish. Did he want more than scientific adventure with her? Was he honorable?

Chapter 37

Date unknown
Location unknowable … yet

The door opened, allowing engine noise and the cold air to rush into the room. The sounds had become familiar but yet unseen. Pierce's captors kept his eyes covered the entire time. Forced to sleep in a chair, he felt exhausted, as though he'd been exerting himself physically. Perhaps he was simply emotionally expended. Either way, he was neither in the mood nor strong enough to offer any resistance.

His hands were freed periodically, but only while under supervision and always while blindfolded. No one would speak to him, which also took a severe toll on his nerves. The food had been cold but good, and certainly not requiring any utensils that might be turned into a weapon. Although unsure, Pierce was convinced that there were three men who would come at a time.

It was one of the two meal times, which now were becoming routine. Two meals a day was likely better than he should have expected, and in reality provided more than he normally ate.

Pierce sat in his chair, blind and restrained, wondering if today any his questions would be answered.

As before, his hands were freed, but the blindfold was not removed, and he was led to a table where simple food waited.

This time, two pair of shoes left the room, leaving one person behind to watch him eat. Pierce felt around the plate. It was metal, though not thick or very heavy. And it was sharp around the edge, perhaps because it was a cheaply made item. Sounds in the room indicated that the remaining man was sitting down behind him, on a bed or bench he himself had not yet been permitted to sleep on, and lighting a cigar or perhaps a cigarette. The man who led his capture? It was possible. The smoke made its way to him, and it smelled something like pipe tobacco. The American? Americans smoked cheroots, which often used sweeter tobaccos. Yes, it was the American. Had he been taller or more muscular than Pierce? Yes. He kept that in front of his mind.

He had to try something. His body would never take another day of sleep deprivation and immobility. "I'm sorry," he said softly, weakly. "I can't - can't eat. Not yet."

The man sighed and stood up, the furniture creaking as he lifted his weight off of it.

Pierce swept his hand across the plate, freeing it of food, grasped it with one hand and pulled on his blindfold with the other. He swung out the metal and struck at the man approaching him. It wasn't enough of a blow to knock him down, and in fact, he seemed to duck at the right moment. But the unexpected maneuver was effective. Pierce threw all of his weight against the man, landing on top of him, pinning him to the floor. He jammed the sharp edged plate against the man's neck and ordered him to keep quiet.

Cold blue eyes glared at him. The man Pierce had subdued was indeed taller and broader in the chest as he remembered, but hadn't expected the assault. First, he lifted his chin as if to pull his whole throat out from under the plate. The man's skin was exposed instead, and it revealed something normally hidden by the high collar of his sweater. The edge of the plate sat on top of a long, ugly scar that stretched from ear to ear.

Pierce took a second to observe his surroundings. The room was tiny, sparse but clean. The blue-eyed man began to struggle, but Pierce put more weight on the plate. While it might cut his own hands, it was worth it to keep the man still. No one else was there.

"Where am I?" Pierce whispered.

The blue eyes kept staring and nothing was answered.

"What in God's name do you want?"

The door opened, and the returning men were astonished to see their prisoner crouched on top of their colleague. An alarm went up. Pierce took his weight off the metal plate, resigned to the fact that he couldn't fight all of them.

To his surprise, everyone who pulled him off the blue-eyed man seemed amused rather than angry. Even the man himself wasn't entirely upset; if anything, he was embarrassed. Pierce was held by his arms and the man took the plate out of his hands with some disgust.

"Can't leave you alone, can we sir?" One of the others joked.

"Funny," he replied, tossing the plate down on the table, collected up the cheroot that lay where it fell on the floor, and pulled his collar higher to hide the scar.

193

Without warning one of the comrades back-handed Pierce, knocking the Professor to the ground. The others were still joking as they picked Pierce up.

The blue-eyed man wasn't laughing and the glare he gave his colleagues was a far worse threat than he'd given Pierce. "Help him up. Never do that again."

"Aye, sir, Mr. Turner," one ventured to say with a slight laugh. When Turner failed to laugh with them, they became immediately silent and one assisted Pierce back onto his feet. Any remaining sense of amusement vanished as a fourth man entered the room. Pierce didn't recognize him, not entirely, though there was something memorable about him. Ignoring the question of familiarity, Pierce was feeling foolhardy enough to not give up on gaining some sort of answers.

"Why am I here? Where am I?"

The fourth man said nothing, but stood examining Pierce. His distaste was obvious.

"What do you want from me?"

Walking slowly, confidently, over to Pierce, he leaned in and whispered one sentence.

It was in Hindi, Pierce was sure. But what was said, he didn't know. He didn't speak Hindi anymore. That was a long time ago and the vocabulary had vanished in disuse.

"Give Professor Pierce something to help him sleep. He looks terrible. We'll need him to start work soon. Every man earns his keep here, isn't that right, Tom?"

Turner did not look happy at all but signaled for the others to take action, and stood by as they forced Pierce to drink a concoction that tasted like whiskey and something revolting mixed together. Pierce had heard of it, what it would taste like, how it was mixed with other distillates to help administer it. Laudanum.

In half an hour he was asleep, sedated and exhausted. They allowed him to sleep on the small bed. Turner watched over him, guarded him, clearly unhappy with the situation but determined that all should go exactly as designed. There was a greater good, he kept saying to himself. As he had justified all he had done for the Union during the war - there was a greater good.

Chapter 38

New Year's was not one of Lettie's favorite holidays. For one thing, it reminded her of time slipping by while she waited for the next leap forward in her life. It was as though sitting on a precipice, looking out over a crater, wondering if something, anything, was going to happen. It was not permissible for a lady to invite herself to parties and, though she didn't like them, she did like being invited. Miranda was throwing a fine gathering and yet it was the same gossiping old creatures Lettie was desperate to avoid. She certainly could not arrive at a restaurant to dine alone. Unthinkable. Definitely not her favorite time of year. This New Year was not boding well.

Still no sign of Pierce, no trolley, no appointment at New College.

The police had been called for, asked the usual questions, and had made no headway in their case to find Pierce. Had Sir Richard Pierce not intervened, Lettie was convinced that nothing whatsoever would have been done. The Police barely believed her, dismissing her as prone to womanly hysterics and overwrought imagination. And, unlike her episode in America, she had no proof at all that Pierce was the victim of a kidnapping.

No ransom was ever asked for; thus it was concluded that he'd simply wandered off somewhere to work in private.

The explanation was unsatisfactory to both Lettie and Sir Richard.

New Year's celebrations had to be put off by a slight but still worrisome illness in her father. Lettie's first reaction was sheer panic. Influenza was the cause of her mother's death and she was not willing to let it take her father too. But in a day or so, he recovered, too late to follow through on his usual plans to join her in London. So long as he was recovering, she maintained, she would miss him this year.

As she stayed put for the season, her energy began to drop and the looming depression was only barely held off. She tore through three romantic novels, only finding the love scenes, the passionate letters and looks between the characters, and the requisite happily-ever-after endings to be a reminder of the disappointment of her own love life.

What love life? Did she have one? Despite her adoration for romance stories, she knew their wild, exciting, passionate adventures were purely the imaginative work of the author. People didn't fall in love that way; she'd already learned that hard and cruel lesson. There was no such thing as love at first sight. That was reality.

Lettie preferred the fiction.

Miranda Gray had visited on one of the better days, but even the sight of her friend in the latest fashion of enlarged bustle and tall hat, burgundy of course, didn't strike her fancy. Try as she might, Miranda did not manage to improve her friend's mood. The truth was, when Lettie wasn't travelling and working, she wasn't happy.

Out of kindness, Miranda kept the conversation on the latest innovations, which fascinated both of them immeasurably, and off of the topic of marriage - even her own, which was now just as unlikely to happen. There had been a man, a potential, who arrived in her life as if a Yuletide present. But it didn't last. The fellow had made other promises to other women. The last thing Miranda wanted was to discourage her friend from a goal she herself thought so very honorable. The last thing Lettie wanted was to remind her friend of a hurtful failure. They stayed off that subject, except in their own minds.

Chapter 39

January, 1883
Residence of L. Gantry, Dr.sc.geo
Sutton

Snow was still falling when, at two in the afternoon, someone knocked on Lettie's door. The maid answered it and was surprised to find a footman at the doorstep with a card. She hurried to bring it to her employer, who was feverishly writing and rewriting a mathematical equation on a large chalk board.

Lettie held the extremely expensive linen card, with its simple but elegant type. Sir Richard Pierce. He was apparently waiting outside in a carriage; awaiting her response if she was receiving.

"Please have him come in," Lettie instructed the maid.

Bobbing a curtsey, she turned from Lettie and stopped abruptly. Sir Richard was standing in the doorway of the parlor; his hat in hand and his eyes deeply sunken from what Lettie perceived was a lack of sleep.

"Maddie, will you please take Sir Richard's things and bring us hot tea right away?"

The maid bobbed again and took the elder Pierce's coat. She held out her hands for his hat and gloves, but he declined.

"I would not like to presume to stay more than is appropriate," he said hoarsely.

"Nonsense, sir," Lettie was quick to reply. "I insist you stay for luncheon. You've traveled too far in this weather. Maddie, please set his hat aside, and see to it that the kitchen is made available to his staff, if they should care to come in."

Richard watched her appreciatively. "Not exactly by the book? I think I like that."

"Social books are written by those fairly unaccustomed to reality and rather unhappy with society as it is. Would you care to sit?"

"Thank you." He wandered over to the seat near the fire that she indicated, stopping for just a moment to stare at the incomprehensible scribble on the board. Kindly, she sat down quickly so that he wouldn't have to stand waiting for her. He was a gentleman after all.

He cleared his throat. "I have heard nothing of my son, and from your reaction to my arrival, I can assume neither have you?"

"Not a word." She leaned forward, her elbows resting on her knees.

He stared at the fire. "It's not like him, you know?" Realizing his assumption, he added, "That is, I should tell you that it is not like him to disappear. He's very attached to family. Though he travels often, I never go a week without some contact. Two months ..."

"It's unlikely that he's gone on his own. If I may presume, I believe he would have mentioned to you that he had made such plans."

"He'd never worry me like this. Not his way." Such pride was welling up in his voice. He suddenly looked up at her. "You said in your testimony to the police and your kind correspondence with me that you believed this 'Robur' was potentially behind his disappearance."

Lettie nodded and sat back. "Yes sir. But I have no proof. And there are reasons I think it could be equally unlikely that Robur has your son. For one thing, this Robur is an inventor himself. I cannot believe that Professor Pierce would provide any expertise that Robur would not think himself already superior in. That does not indicate that he is a better scientist than your son, only that Robur might not recognize such brilliance in another man. When I met this Robur, he was arrogant and self serving. No, he didn't strike me as a man who would acknowledge another man's genius. "

Richard stood up and began pacing. In many ways he seemed to be cut from the same cloth as her own father. He was perhaps a bit younger and smaller in stature, but they held the same fatherly values by all appearances. "From your letters Doctor, for which I am extremely grateful, I would assume the same thing regarding Robur. I have ..." he hesitated. "I have another concept, one which would be wasted on a policeman but one which I believe you might understand."

Lettie couldn't help but like him. He had yet to examine her parlor as other visitors so often did. There had been no judgmental look at her rather casual attire. No scoffing expression barely hidden from view once the chalkboard had been observed. He presented his case as though speaking to any intelligent person. She really liked him.

"Doctor Gantry, I should like to give you some information regarding my son, but I would like not to presume that you should want to hear it."

"I do, sir. If it will help to find your son, I should like very much to hear it. And you may depend upon my discretion."

Richard nodded. "Thank you. As you may have guessed, he is not my natural son. That is, he is not biologically my own, but in all other ways he is. I have no children of my own, and my wife passed away very early on. I've never chosen to remarry. I have had Rajiv legally recognized and, named as my son and heir. There is still some legal nonsense regarding my familial titles but all else is his upon my death."

He waited patiently and silently while Maddie brought in tea and cake, and quickly exited. The hot tea soothed to his throat and he found his voice much clearer as he continued. "I believe this disappearance has something to do with his birth. In '57, I was traveling on doctor's orders. Get out of England, he told me. My wife was gone and I'd lost two sisters the year before." Richard smiled briefly at Lettie. "I have been blessed with several outstanding women in my life and was at the time missing them all greatly. It was affecting my nerves. So, off I went. A Grand Tour without the bride. But, turns out my doctor was right. Travel did me a great deal of good.

"It was that awful year that I arrived in Bombay. You cannot imagine the chaos in the harbor. With the rebellion running amok in the North, everyone was in a panic. Those that could were trying to flee the country and the violence. Those that couldn't, or who had been sent there, would battle each other in the streets. No one was safe. That's when I found Rajiv.

"A mob was up. People who had been displaced by the fighting but were loyal to the Crown had heard that some of the families of the rebellious Rajahs were attempting to escape. In those days, some of the Indian royalty had connections in Europe and were sending family there. In particular, I recall the story of one Prince who actually had a French wife. Certain that she would be killed by either side, he sent her away with his children. They never made it to French territory.

"The mob attacked anyone who appeared to be associated with wealth, the rebellion, oh whatever the excuse. Rajiv was five years old, dressed up like a little Prince himself. Five years old ..." He sipped his tea trying to comprehend the abomination that was violence against children. "He'd been struck so hard in the head that most thought he was dead. I could see he was breathing. I picked him up, walked to the first departing ship and never looked back."

Lettie sat perfectly still, waiting.

"He has no memory of the event, though occasionally he would recall something from a bit earlier. Something about falling out of a tree, or some such thing children do. We have no idea who his family is. No idea about his connections. I suspect that he is half English, or at least part European. He understood both English and French in addition to Hindi. But I'm not sure what his lineage was and he simply does not know. I never asked. I just saw a child and ...

"Doctor, I have always maintained a fear that his family would come looking for him and today I am convinced that they have."

She waited a moment or two, to see if he was done before she commented. "Sir Richard, what purpose do you think they would have in kidnapping him? You've not received a ransom request; thus, I believe money is not the issue. If he is with his former family, and they do not have evil designs, then I see no reason why they would prevent him from communicating with you."

"There is one possibility. They have killed him."

Lettie gasped before realizing it was a sound not indicative of calm and reason. Straightening out her skirts, she forced herself to remain calm. "I've never considered death to be a viable explanation for his absence, and I refuse to do so now," she said with a bit too much determination.

Richard smiled at her. "No, my dear Doctor, I would not think you would. I however fear that, if he has not fallen victim to a robber or madman, he may have fallen victim to the events of twenty-six years ago. Rebels or extreme Loyalists? It could be either. That Rebellion left unhealed wounds that still fester, even today."

It was Lettie's turn to stalk the room. "I - just can't accept that. His equipment and luggage were missing from his home. A common thief would have only taken what was valuable and a madman would have no notion to go to his home and take such items. No, sir, someone wants us to believe that Professor Pierce has gone traveling or into seclusion."

"This does not preclude murder. The murderer may be trying to hide the deed."

"How many murderers would think to do such a thing, such as taking his notes and equipment? Luggage perhaps, but not all the rest? No, it is someone who has the Professor and doesn't want us looking for him."

The speculation continued over lunch, though less and less toward the conclusion of murder. Such proved to be a relief for Sir Richard, who seemed to be of a clearer mind when he finally took his leave from Lettie.

He took back his hat, gloves and coat from Maddie. "Your work? I confess to not knowing a great deal about it, except that it may save lives?"

"That is my hope."

He stopped to think for a moment. "Yes, you must concentrate on that. You must. Leave it to me and to the police, to find Rajiv - go to Java."

Lettie began to shake her head. "I can't go …"

"My son thinks your work worthy and important; otherwise he would not have agreed to make one of his contraptions for you. Trust me, he told people 'no' more often than 'yes.' If he believes your geological work to be vital, you must respect his opinion and continue it. Go to Java. I insist you keep me informed of your whereabouts - please. I should not like to think of the two of you missing."

Chapter 40

February was not the beginning of spring and its promise of renewal for her. She felt trapped in winter with all its gray, and cold, and fear, and doubt. Lettie remained hopeful, however, and her mindset was rewarded quite astonishingly, if circuitously.

First, a substantial storm, a natural one she concluded, based on its enormous size and abundant rainfall arrived with all its fury. It was too big for Robur to have created with his airship. Thunder shook the house. She adored thunderstorms even though they frightened her terribly when they arrived at night. In its own strange way, it calmed her and comforted her. No, it was not Robur making all that noise; it was only the pleasing sound of rain on the roof.

Yet, there was a sinking feeling in her stomach when she considered that it still might conceal Robur and his airship, unlikely as that was. The idea that she should risk everything on a hope that Robur might still want to assist her was gnawing away at her patience. That and a prevailing notion that Pierce's disappearance was directly connected to her work. As both her father and Sir Richard advised, she needed to continue with her plans in the hopes that something might be revealed that could help find him. And, that her model was too important to forsake. "Take your gun," Christopher Moore demanded. "Befriend persons of good character at every opportunity so that they may be of assistance if needed," advised her father, who was surprising her a bit with that. She would have thought he'd rather she came to Cardiff. Sir Richard wrote to her requiring that she communicate with him by telegraph twice weekly and promised to maintain complete contact with her father. The sheer quantity of support from so many boosted her spirits. And she needed it. Her stomach was tight. Pre-travel jitters, she decided, while locking the rifle case after cleaning her Henry.

Sitting on her oak desk, slightly buried under piles of notes and scribbling from a particularly good evening of work on her model were

the most amusing letters she had ever received. They were not intended
to be funny. Philip Evans, the retired Vice President of the Weldon
Institute had decided he needed to travel, and where better than London?
Would she not wish to dine with him? Perhaps it was unfair of her to
make the comparison, but his ridiculous attempt at courting her by
correspondence was all the more laughable when set side-by-side with
other such attempts. It was amusing and quite clear he had taken each
phrase and copied it from any one of the manuals written for the middle
class man desiring to move up in the world. While she could laud his
awkward effort to be gentlemanly, Lettie couldn't find any comfort in the
lack of personality. It was all by the book and not from the heart.

Lettie could feel her muscles tightening at the thought of having to
generate a response that was at once definitive yet considerate. Men
always needed some sort of comforting when being told no. Miranda had
explained that notion to her. Dispassionate men, men who wanted to
change her, men who wanted to use her: was that all she would know?
Did she have to choose from that small a pool for a future husband, if she
were to choose at all? She should have chosen a long time ago.

Evans's letters suddenly ceased to be amusing.

She needed good news, and she got it.

Within a day she was informed that Sir Richard had received a
telegram from his son. Lettie was elated. The telegram had explained to
his father that he shouldn't worry, all was well, and he was on the
continent - working. Further, he requested his father to contact Doctor
Gantry and to say that she would hear from him soon. It would seem that
the sample trolley would be ready for her and he would send it to her in
Java, which struck Lettie as expensive and difficult, but there were mail
packet ships sailing everywhere and at all times so the notion wasn't
impossible. Sadly, she thought, it would be much better if he were there
to instruct her on its proper usage and maintenance.

Still, the telegram was such a relief, if a bit sudden and simple, yet
she could hardly contain her excitement. She frightened the Cook when
she burst into the kitchen to announce the good news. She wanted Pierce
to be safe, she wanted to believe all was well. She could go to Java
without thinking she'd abandoned Pierce. She'd never stopped chastising
herself for leaving America before knowing the fate of the Weldon
Institute men. Lettie considered that an abandonment, and not something
she would ever do again.

Chapter 41

Delays, a return of her father's illness, restrictions from the Dutch, and three more interviews at New College had all conspired to block her passage to Java. Her shoulders had become so tight that she had tingling sensations up and down her arms. Her temper was tightening too, though she'd not lost it, yet. But that, she reminded herself, was in the past. Today was a much better day.

She sent out for every newspaper that could be found. Cooped up in the house, she was going slightly mad. News of the outside world would help her escape the boredom of isolation.

Parisian papers focused on the debate over Mr. Eiffel and his monstrous tower. At this rate, she thought, he'll have to pay for it himself.

The *London Times* reported that the Dutch, Egyptian, Italian and French governments were nearly at an agreement, a singular impossibility before, that the Trans Pneumatic System would be extended along the same route at the Eastern Telegraph. The cost would be borne by everyone who benefited by it. And most certainly, the customer of the Tipsy. Yet, the concept made the world feel a little smaller.

An odd report came from the American newspapers, which of course the British news agencies disbelieved. The Weldon Institute had lost its balloon, the *Go Ahead*, sometime in the fall and was just now reluctantly discussing it. While the old President of the Institute swore it was shot down by a mad man on the ground, the new President and other Institute members claimed an aerial clipper ship of magnificent and brilliant design was responsible. Such a story made for sensational headlines. Lettie stood with the British newspapers in believing it was likely that the gigantic balloon was destroyed by its creators via human error or incompetence. Robur won't have bothered, would he? If he did, he was becoming very public in his activities.

But today was the perfect time for her to forget Robur and the

Weldon Institute, and to concentrate on her efforts toward completing the Prediction Model. Things were going to get better.

Even Professor Pierce had begun to ask when she would be leaving. Always the questions came through telegrams sent to his father, but as long as he was well she didn't care how he communicated. Only that he did. It created opportunities to correspond with Sir Richard. At last, her mother's insistence on lessons in proper letter writing had proven not only beneficial but pleasurable.

The most spectacular moment came when an invitation, in beautiful handwriting, begged her to come to Paris to meet the celebrated, though sometimes vilified, Professor Aronnax of the Paris National Museum of Natural History. He wished to meet her and to receive her opinion on volcanic rock samples. It was indeed one of the greatest compliments. It was not something she could turn down, nor did she want to. Too excited to save the invitation for later, Lettie shot off a quick letter to Christopher.

Lettie began to transform dramatically as she prepared and packed. There was something frantic about her efforts, as though she anticipated at any moment one more cause for delay. But gone were the dark circles under her eyes.

It was with great astonishment that, on the eve of Lettie's departure, one more extraordinary event occurred.

A letter. Dated only a week and a half earlier, it was from Uncle Prudent; certainly the last man she expected to hear from. Lettie was still in an optimistic mood when she tore the envelope open, hoping to find a report of the good health of his valet, Frycollin. The 'love' letters Evans continued to send never mentioned Prudent, but one did note that neither man had retained his position in the Weldon Institute after the *Go Ahead* was destroyed. Perhaps Prudent would be more open and provide better details. Immediately, she was disappointed.

The paper was thin, slightly rough, and not very expensive, such as one might obtain at a second-class hotel. Prudent's handwriting was dreadful.

Miss Gantry.

It was a bad start. 'Doctor', she winced, 'Doctor Gantry.'

Please excuse the short length of this communication but I must earnestly beg you to reconsider your opinion of the Weldon Institute and its superb balloon, the Go Ahead II. It has been brought to my attention that Professor R.A. Pierce, upon whom you have placed your entire hopes, has abandoned you and gone abroad without fulfilling his promises to you.

The *Go Ahead II*? That was illogically optimistic. Just who was going to pay for it, she wondered with much sarcasm.

"Pierce has abandoned you ..." How Prudent had concluded this, Lettie couldn't begin to fathom. Pierce had initially gone away without a word. It had not been, however, common knowledge. That concerned her. And clearly, Prudent didn't know that the trolley was being completed. She felt downright defensive of herself, her important work, and Professor Pierce.

As I am certain that you mean to continue your research unaided by such inventions as the Professor had promised to produce, it is my honor and pleasure to resubmit the Weldon Institute as the most reliable partner in your endeavor.

Partner? Nothing in her previous discussions had suggested such a status between them. She would have been a benefactor and been, by virtue of her investment, allowed to make use of the Institute's gigantic balloon. But a partnership? Never! They expected her to fund the new balloon?

I would ask only that you cancel your excursion to the East Indies and return with haste to Philadelphia. Without the Go Ahead II any effort will be wasted.

What nerve, she thought. As if I cannot succeed in my research without the aid of toys: not the Weldon's and not Pierce's.

Please return to the United States. Do not go to Java Island.

Calmly breathing, deliberately, carefully, she counted backward from ten, determined that she would do nothing Prudent suggested, and folded his letter in half. She'd read enough.

Pulling paper and pen from her desk, she quickly jotted down a brief but committed telegraph reply. She would send it on her way to the Calais Ferry.

It is with regret that I must decline your kind invitation to return to the Philadelphia.

No need to be rude. Prudent's arrogance was no excuse for her to forget herself.

Thank you. L. Gantry, Dr. sc. geo.

Chapter 42

May 14, 1883
On Board the English Channel Ferry
Dover

"Welcome aboard, Miss Gantry," the Purser said, bowing slightly at the waist. He quickly refolded her ticket with a sharp crease that duplicated the one that ran the length of his trousers and blouse. "It is a reasonable day for a crossing, but we expect the trip to be a bit rough all the same. And most decidedly chilly, as usual."

She nodded politely and allowed him to direct her into the main gallery. Her travelling companions, which included a sweet but precisely moral physicist named Henderson, headed off to the comfortable seats. She had promised not to be too far away from them. As kind as they were, they did not move at the same pace she did and it made her wonder why she had allowed herself to be so restricted. "Above reproach - Caesar's wife ..." Yes, she remembered Ashfield's words quite clearly and had changed her old habits to include what amounted to chaperones.

As she remembered, the Channel Ferry was well maintained but hardly a first class cruising steamer. The primary level was for all sorts of travelers, goods, and conveyances. The second level, toward the bow, was for the gentle yet not wealthy. Its environment was a mixture of card players, smokers, and exotic foreigners. The enclosed stern section was reserved for the higher priced ticket holders, and appeared more or less like an average parlor. The carpet was fading a bit, but cleaned to the baseboards. The walls were not of any particular wood, but polished brightly. The room felt mature and well used, yet proudly kept at its sparkling best. The trip across the Channel was brief and the practicality of expensive décor was - well - impractical. The stern was also where outdoor seating was provided. For Lettie, it was worth the extra cost to have a bit of comfort and quiet, either going to or returning from the Continent. The stern section, however, had a distinct drawback: it was a social minefield.

Lettie swept into the stern gallery quickly. Several men looked up from their papers and, several women began intimately whispering and glancing her way. It is hardly due to my looks, she immediately thought. Her temporary impact on the room had more to do with the unknown nature of her identity and her beautiful clothing. Her fellow travelers were likely sizing her up as to breeding, social standing, and potential companionship for more than the next moment. She tried not to shiver, nor to roll her eyes. She might have to interact with any one of them. This was becoming an old habit as part of the crossing. And of course there was her promise to her father, to find persons of good character to associate with - for protection.

Her eyes fell immediately to a black haired man, in exquisitely tailored clothing, delighting in drinking his tea. He sipped deeply from the cup he held gently, eyes closed as if in meditation for the brief moment it took to fill his mouth with its pungent sweetness, and before he was interrupted by a fellow passenger. He was a foreigner, perhaps French or Spanish, she guessed. His clothing was European, his appearance quite bohemian and yet his manners appeared impeccable. The details were in his physicality. He politely made eye contact with his fellow conversant while listening with much attention, nodding now and then to acknowledge some point of interest, whether interesting or not. He clearly did not interrupt the other speaker. He held his cup and saucer lightly, and used his free hand to gesticulate each sentence. Every gesture suggested superior schooling in the art of discourse.

He must have sensed he was being watched, something likely familiar to him, as he looked up and noted her existence with a polite lowering of his eyes and tilt of his head. Lettie, blushing deeply at the idea of being caught staring, smiled and graciously returned the nod.

The stern had an outside deck that just called to her, begging her to escape the hanging fog of smoke to breathe the cold salt air - and to abort her not-so-covert observation of the foreign gentleman. She couldn't decide if her mother would have been appalled by her interest in such a man or pleased by her dignified retreat.

A steward quickly stepped up to her and inquired her preference of tea. She requested in a whisper a hot cup of coffee instead and informed him she would take it on the deck. The steward was clearly expecting a lady to order tea, so he felt obliged to ask her again. Lettie was used to this. Her American father with his Yankee ways had addicted her to the taste of coffee, at an early age.

With her order placed, she headed quietly outside and into a place of relative peace. It was not nearly as cold as one might think thanks to the Ferry's extensive use of water pipes under the decking, which carried the still-scalding hot steam from the engines around the body of the boat, warming the floors, and then expelling it out the back. The result was a strange but welcome mist, like that over a hot cup of tea, which never rose more than an inch off the carpets. An hour after running the boilers, the carpet would be dry and the mist gone. An awning of striped canvas covered most of the deck and trapped the warm air around the seating. Humid as it could be, the effect created a much more comfortable journey.

For a moment, she saw herself in a window's reflection. She was too round and someone, such as that foreign fellow, would not find her attractive; surely not.

"Oh, stop it," she heard herself say to the reflection. "I shall not think on such things today."

Besides, the prospect of indulging in the science of Volcanology had erased many of the lines around her eyes, as well as the dark patches underneath that were genuinely unattractive. It had brought back the sparkle in her eyes, which she knew would be ageless even if she weren't. The rest of her reflection was at least satisfying. As was the highest fashion of the day, she wore a tailored, seafoam green wool suit, fitted in the waist but looser in the chest and shoulder. The color was perfect for her, giving focus to the depth of her hair color, a brightness to her green eyes, and a paler cast to her skin which was so very fashionable. The skirts were straight and plain in the front, but beautifully and artfully bunched up into a bustle in the back. Underneath the wool, and revealed by a purposefully missing off-center panel, was a lovely silk underskirt. Tabs made from black velvet stretched across the gap in four places, buttoning on the other side. None of this actually touched the ground, but grazed the top of her highly polished black boots, a requisite when walking in muddy streets or on soggy carpets. Under all that she wore a linen chemisette, a ruffled traveling bustle sans wires, a pair of petticoats, and soft wool stockings. Perched on her upswept hair was a medium crowned, black hat with a rosette of ribbon and a wide brim to shade her eyes. Silk ties knotted and bowed at the back of her head held it in place and two precisely thrust hatpins nailed it down against the Channel wind. If necessary, she had a long knitted scarf to tie around her hat and head, in case of substantial wind. She would not go back inside, even in those conditions, as she valued the quiet above comfort.

Lettie set down her valise, draped herself neatly into a deck chair, and covered her skirts with a heavy blanket provided on each chair. Across from her was the table that she and Christopher had used the previous year. Professor Pierce had been sitting one table away. For a moment she began to recognize how much she was looking forward to seeing him again. She had, of course, shared her itinerary with her father, Sir Richard and Christopher Moore. Sir Richard promised to inform his son of her plans so that they could coordinate the delivery of the trolley.

The lined, soft kid gloves were preemptively donned. She would read as it always made the trip much more tolerable. She had the latest book by a notorious author which promised to break all the rules. Rumor had it that the author, a scandalized woman, had written in love scenes - "realistic love scenes," not just a kiss and then suddenly someone was putting on his boots to leave. No, the author had placed intimate details into the pages. To get her copy, Lettie had had to send Christopher and William to obtain it from the book seller in Cheapside. She couldn't possibly have walked into that shop. What if she had been seen? Poor Christopher, he indulged her too much.

And she had a tour book. Not nearly so exciting as a romance.

Unable to decide between the two choices of reading material awaiting her perusal, she blindly reached into her valise and pulled out the first book her hand fell upon, a book on travel through the French Alps, along with the pair of narrow reading glasses. The loss of clear, crisp eyesight was probably the most galling aspect of aging. For a woman who read and wrote hour after hour, the need for reading glasses was aggravating and problematic. Until she started the habit of consistently placing them in her pocket or in her valise, it was a constant struggle to know where she'd left them.

A string of dirigibles was floating toward the French coast. Mr. Reuters's Heavy Haulers – they were as common as clouds in the sky. Poor weather slowed the mail from the Continent generally, so any day that offered potential or relative calmness was a profitable boon. The leading balloon soon fired up the pressurized, gas fueled flames that could be seen for miles and the entire group followed its ascent to higher, faster moving winds.

The ship's horn blasted and Lettie tried not to jump in surprise. Perhaps it was the slight ringing in her ears that caused her not to hear him at first. Lord of Mercy, she thought. She couldn't afford to be that easily surprised.

"Excuse me?"

Lettie looked up to see a dazzling gold watch chain with a strange fob dangling from it. Even with her reading glasses, she couldn't quite make out what it was. Removing her glasses, her eyes took a second to refocus and to allow her a better view of the gentleman who had removed his hat and was waiting for her permission to continue speaking.

"May I help you," she asked?

"Did I overhear the Purser correctly, you are a Miss Gantry?"

Lettie's eyes narrowed a bit in suspicion. "Yes."

"Would that be Miss Gantry, the Geologist?"

A feeling of warmth flooded onto her cheeks. "Volcanologist, technically speaking, but yes I am. And you are, sir?"

Tucking his wool top hat under his arm in a very precise and practiced way, he removed a card from his waistcoat pocket and offered it to her. His coat flapped in the breeze and he chose to ignore it. While accepting the card, Lettie decided he was the strangest man she'd ever seen, which was perhaps not fair to him as it wasn't his look so much as the uneasy feeling he gave her. Aged too soon. Eyes narrowed from years of unsatisfied inspection. Yet, a smile that glazed over the cracked pottery of an angry facade. She more rationally observed he had to be about six feet tall; even taller when he placed the hat on his head. The man was faultlessly dressed in coat, waistcoat and trousers of fine deep burgundy wool so dark as to be nearly black, all cut to excessively fashionable perfection. An edifice of the latest style not yet announced by the magazines. A customer to be cherished by his tailor. His tie was of a patterned and elegant gold silk, his shirt sported a spotless celluloid collar and un-worn cuffs, and his Dogskin-Brown cloth gloves fit his long fingers exactly. That he wore a pair of glasses intended for constant use was apparent by the red marks on either side of his nose, but vanity had caused him to hide those spectacles and to squint at her instead. He trimmed his whiskers to the latest style, which was substantial in the cheek and cut precisely to the shape of the jaw with the intention of displaying an ultimately unworthy chin. By its thickness she could imagine him sporting any number of fashionable beards and considered that her first impression of him said that he would not hesitate to adjust his facial treatment to be up to date regardless of the result. A moustache of inconsequential size was curled tightly and meticulously on either side of his mouth, yet coated with that despised colored wax so many men felt was necessary to hide gray hairs without admitting to the use of dyes. Everything about him spoke of a well-enough gentleman of leisure, with one exception: his hair. His fading, light ginger hair was excessively long, drowned in pomade and worn slicked back over his broad forehead, yet allowed to twist at the nape into greasy corkscrews. It was not his natural color, which was to say he had made a deliberate effort to alter himself. He was likely a Dandy or one of those middle-aged men who couldn't bring themselves to wrestle with time and age. The cemented-into-precise-form style for hair was en vogue amongst the younger gentlemen and in many ways appeared almost pathetic on a man of his years.

Her first inclination was to offer him the small pair of scissors in her valise and advice on who had the best skills to return him to his natural state. She did not like Dandies as they tended to be selfish, difficult, and slavish to fashion dictates that made little to no sense at all. In this particular fellow's case, he appeared not to have a coat, but then such an item of clothing would have hidden the fine figure his tailored attire showed off. It was cold and anyone with some bit of sense would be bundled up. Tact prevailed and she quietly accepted the card with a gracious nod. 'Mr. P. Wickham, Burlington Gardens, Kensington.'

"I hope you will allow me to introduce myself, seeing as there is no one to do it for me." He was very practiced and dramatic in his speech, lilting where no natural lilt was present in his pronunciation, which was the mark of the Dandy.

His demeanor was certainly assured and very pretentious. It was nearly amusing were it not for the fact that he made her feel as if he wanted something very specific from her.

"May I," he continued.

She replied, "Of course, as there isn't another to do so." Now Lettie was curious.

"Philip Wickham," he announced with flair, as though she ought to know it. He seemed slightly amused when she offered him her hand to shake. How very liberal of her. "A pleasure to meet you, Miss Gantry."

"And I you, Mr. Wickham." She neatly folded her hands back in her lap, covering the title of her book. Her second inclination was not to give this stranger any indication of her plans, as he seemed to know too much already. "May I ask how you recognize my name, sir?"

"Of course. I did not mean to cause you any distress, though it is unlikely that a woman who climbs erupting volcanoes is easily distressed at all."

"Ah, the dispatches published in the newspapers?"

"I read about your ascent of Mt. Tarumae in the *Telegraph*. It would seem that the editor was more than a bit shocked." Wickham mocked, smiling slightly.

Lettie sighed. "That was nothing compared to the shock I instigated in many other quarters. My aunt ceased to speak to me for two weeks; a former acquaintance wrote a five-page letter to scold me by saying that had I married him, such an outlandish thing would never have happened; and New College nearly locked its doors to me. So, as you can see, Mr. Wickham, such publicity is neither desirable nor advantageous. My dispatches are mere attempts to correct erroneous science often printed in the papers. Please allow me to assure you I did not seek the attention."

"I would not think otherwise. I have received some ... unwelcome attention myself while attempting to do right. Promised myself never to do that again."

"Was it worth it," she asked, looking up at him. He shifted his weight, compensating for the Ferry's motion away from the pier and turn of the bow toward Calais. "Was the cause, for all that attention and all that came with it, worth it?" she repeated.

"Was yours?" His voice was suddenly serious, until a smile returned to his face.

The Ferry's horn sounded again, and with a rush of noise, the steam engines pushed the ship away from the White Cliffs. "Please do sit down, Mr. Wickham. I am only the slightest bit accustomed to crossing the Channel, but I do know that clear, sunny skies are no guarantee of a smooth sailing."

"Oh, I think I can ..."

"And I'm craning my neck to see you."

Wickham tried not to grin, but it came out on both sides of his mouth, and turned the waxed ends of his moustache even tighter. He nodded politely, set his hat down on the small table between them - after all, wearing a hat in Channel wind was simply foolish... and folded his long frame into one of the deck chairs, forgoing the blanket. And his hair was going nowhere.

"Much better," she said, adjusting herself to see him.

"Tell me, Miss Gantry, what adventure are you off to now?"

"Nothing exciting I daresay, just a visit to a colleague." She would say no more than that regarding her destination. "He is allowing me access to a particularly fine mineral collection from various Italian volcanoes. It is my passion, you see."

"What in Heaven's Name causes a young Welshwoman to forego all social norms to climb mountains that are like as not to kill you? I promise I'm not offering any criticism at all, rather wishing to understand something I confess to admire."

That was curious, how did he know she was Welsh? "How very kind of you, Mr. Wickham. But I assure you I've not done anything worthy of admiration just yet. I hope to, but nothing at the moment. Why, you ask? My reasons may seem a bit droll, but they are what they are. As a child, my father took me to the Dutch East Indies. While we were there, I - I witnessed an eruption and its aftereffects on life."

Wickham waived over the Steward, who was looking to deliver coffee to Lettie. "And of course, you decided you would dedicate your life to learning about what happened."

"And, perhaps, to prevent it through logical predictive methods. Quite boring, isn't it," she asked, raising the cup of hot coffee to her lips and looking out over the rim.

The Steward poured another cup for Wickham and left them to their discussions. "Not dull a bit. It's the very thing that drives us all – curiosity. I am always keen to learn more."

"It seems to be working for you, Mr. Wickham. And what of your travels currently?"

"Nothing in particular. Meeting a friend or two." He waved vaguely toward the distance, indicating the rendezvous was off somewhere. Lettie began to ask another question but Wickham changed direction. "Do you play Whist?"

"Not that well, but I can survive a hand or two."

"Good enough." He reached into his pocket, withdrew a simple gold watch, marked the time, and put it away. "Plenty of time for a game or two." There was a bit of a twinkle in his dark hazel eyes. "I insist."

Wickham very kindly assisted her out of the chair she preferred and offered to take her valise inside, presumably with her right behind it. Lettie felt trapped. She couldn't say "no" to his offer of a round of cards without being rude. But there was one thing she would say "no" to and that was his taking her valise. It had been around the world with her, and rather showed it by the scratches and faded spots on the leather. No one was taking that for her, she could see to it just fine.

Well, a hand or two of Whist wouldn't hurt. Pick your battles, she thought, giving in to his request. And it was warmer inside the ship. All the way into the salon, Wickham kept prodding her for information. For a moment she thought she was back before the examining board at Dharmstadt School of Mining.

The entire trip followed along similar lines: he would ask questions about her current travels, specifically where was she going and how was she getting there and she would answer vaguely, unwilling to state anything specifically. Charming and entertaining as he was, he was still a stranger and she needn't provide him with private details about her schedule. She would ask about his current travels and he would evade the question with another round of Whist. She was enjoying neither game.

Two gentlemen had joined them to make it the required foursome; to her surprise and pleasure one of them was the foreign man she'd watched earlier - the Franco-Iberian gentleman, by his own admission, with his elegant taste in clothing.

Monsieur Armand Guy d'Saint-Amand, the foreigner she decided henceforth to think of as "the Frenchman", was softly spoken, but had a face full of experience and diplomacy, and expressive, small, peridot-green eyes. She now had a closer look at the Frenchman. At a distance she'd failed to see the unusual, likely provocative, personal style he cultivated. Like Wickham, the Frenchman was tall. His hands were quite elegant and he spoke with such clarity and knowledge that she was reluctantly compelled to doubt her own intelligence by comparison. It was surely not his intention: that would be rude and impossible for him, she presumed.

The other fellow was a genial yet eccentric man in the most delightful way. He was a lively and chatty academic whose very energy seemed to fill the room. He had a German sounding name, Flock – something. Flockmocker; that was it. Phineas J. Flockmocker III. Sparkling white whiskers bounced every time he laughed, which was pleasantly often. He seemed to be completely at his ease, unaffected by pretense or any fashionable requirements. Flockmocker was a Professor, an honorable title; one she coveted. He had a working man's hands, which immediately reminded her of Pierce. He was an outstanding whist player, who now and again exchanged knowing glances with Wickham. There was more to the pair of them then they were willing to comment on. She was quite glad that not a penny was involved with their card game, as she was certain she'd be poor before the trip was over.

Wickham clearly lorded over the table, as well has having some sort of established relationship with the two men, which she wondered about. She could see it in his body; the way he spoke to them with his chin raised, forcing his comments down his nose. He also used sharp looks, as one might expect a commander to do in the field. But the other two gentlemen seemed to give little credence to Wickham's aspirations of control, and were perhaps willing to go along with the farce if only for the amusement.

Surely Wickham must have seen that his behavior was cause for ridicule, not respect? Why would any intelligent man continue to act in such a way, Lettie wondered. An odd thought occurred to her; was he play acting? Did he want to be purposely underestimated?

The Frenchman was considerably nonplused by Wickham's behavior and Lettie concluded that it was because he knew Wickham was conducting a failing imitation of him. Where Wickham was well dressed, the Frenchman was equally dressed and more comfortable in his clothing. Wickham spoke little and when he did it was a continuation of his apparent arrogance, while the Frenchman's words were elegant, refined, and intelligent with a ring of complete satisfaction to them. Wickham's waxed moustache was a duplicate of the Frenchman's, except that he had not developed a proficiency in the use of wax, or the choice of curl versus straightness. The Frenchman was the master in this arena. His black hair was an excellent contrast to the olive tone in his skin, no doubt a result of his Iberian origins. He too used pomade to control his hair, but in the right quantity. It appeared that he had quite a bit of hair but hid it under his collar, possibly in a long tail, which she certainly couldn't stare at. Very curious. Handsome and provocative.

Wickham was his pale imitator.

Wickham changed the subject of the conversation, forcing the Frenchman's adventure to be related at another time.

If Lettie had been one of those heroines from her romances, she would have easily imagined being in love with the Frenchman. It was stuff and nonsense, as she didn't believe in 'love.' Not anymore. It was something that gave fiction an added dimension, nothing more. She suddenly felt herself flush through her cheeks and felt a pang of pity for the inadequate Wickham.

Three hours and a moderately rough sailing went by curiously but quickly. Wickham was a dedicated player, rather intense, and unmoved by either a win or a loss. Paired up with the professor, he tended to win. The gracious Frenchman was closer to Lettie's skill level, which was to say very moderate. They shared a smile or two as hand after hand fell to Wickham and the Professor.

Of particular interest and entertainment, Professor Flockmocker provided the majority of the conversation by continually commenting on his inventions. Not a single one had any practical use, though that hardly dismissed it from being worthy of creation. It was his enthusiasm for the very nature of invention itself, as though it didn't matter what he designed so long as he could design it. He had more interest in the process and industry of each item than he did in what might become of it once it was completed and patented. He reminded her of what Pierce might yet become.

As the Ferry docked, Flockmocker bid everyone a pleasant journey, nodded to Wickham specifically and headed officiously into the crowd to depart, clearly searching for someone. Monsieur d'Saint-Amand was much more confined by the rules of society.

"Madame. Sir. It has been a pleasure," he said with his accented English. He bowed ever so gracefully, shook hands with Wickham, and then accepted Lettie's hand for a moment. "I wish you the greatest success with your work, Madame. I shall maintain high hopes that it is you who will provide the world with a bit more safety."

Lettie blushed deeply. "Que vous réalisiez votre souhait d'un retour sans histoires." It was a saying her Grandmother used to good effect and there was no reason for her not to use it here. She hoped that the rest of his journey home would be as uneventful as he wished it to be.

"Je vous remercie, chère madame."

As both Lettie and Frenchman took their leave, Wickham reached out and held her by the elbow. She was about to ask him what he meant by such an impertinence, when he stepped much too close to her for comfort. "Miss Gantry. Before you leave …" He hesitated, only long enough to calculate his next comment. "Believe me when I say this is neither a criticism of you nor an expectation that you will fail in your endeavor. In fact, it is very much because I believe you will not fail."

"Fail at what?"

"Do not go to Java. And do not seek ... inappropriate assistance in obtaining your goal. Stay on this ferry and go back to England. Or, if you must, stay in Paris and go no farther. Stay and buy dresses, or whatever it is you do."

Lettie stepped back, pulling her arm away from him. She had been cautiously vague in her answers. She had given away no indication that she was going to the East Indies. "I beg your pardon." It came out of her mouth too sternly, but she felt her temper rising.

"You must not go to Java, and certainly not in disreputable company. I will not tell you why, but I must insist. I will make arrangements for you in Paris. It is the least I can do since you will not be going to Java. But you will not be going ..."

"Mr. Wickham. We have only just met so I hardly think it appropriate for you to give me such advice. Further, I must tell you that I am alarmed at the amount of knowledge you have regarding myself and seem to feel that you can freely bandy it about."

His hand reached out to her with such speed she had no time to react. He gripped her upper arm resolutely and painfully. "Yes, I know quite a bit about you, and again, I cannot tell you how it is possible. I can only tell you that if you go to Java ..."

"Yes?"

"I cannot be responsible for you if you go all the way to the Indies. Should you go there without assistance and protection, disaster will be the most noted and probably the only outcome of your work. I'm certain that is not a bit of the publicity you wish."

Lettie's face burned red. Her voice dropped to a frighteningly low level. Her eyes never left his, and she drew herself up with her shoulders back. "Remove your hand from me immediately, you are hurting me."

Wickham was a little surprised and let go immediately.

"Either tell me what you know or get out of my way."

"Miss Gantry, you cannot understand." He reached out to take her by the arm again. "I insist you do not go to the East Indies. Shop in Paris: find some new hat or such ..."

"Good day, Mr. Wickham!" She twirled around, avoiding his grasp. The silk of her skirt swished back and forth as she all but ran from the room, clutching her valise. At the doorway, she stopped. It was inexcusable of him. Who did he think he was? Did he think he was Robur, with that arrogant behavior? Did he imagine she would wreck her reputation by aligning with such a man such as Robur? Or with him - with Wickham? She was not so easily tempted. Her arm hurt where he'd held her, bruised no doubt and the throbbing fueled her anger.

She turned around to take him to task with all the energy her temper was providing. To Hades with social propriety; the man deserved all that she was willing to throw at him. He'd been playing her like a hand of Whist. The questions. The knowledge. How dare he?

Wickham was not there.

No one was in the room. The deck was deserted. He wasn't there, as though he never had been.

Lettie's knees felt weak and her heart was pounding.

Chapter 43

Wickham's intrusiveness and audacity, certainly his sheer rudeness, had shaken her nerves more than she would admit. From the Gare du Nord to the Hôtel sur la Seine, she was hyper alert to every voice and every movement that might be a strange man. It was delightfully warm in Paris that day and her fur muff was almost unnecessary. Almost. The sky was streaked with high clouds that were beginning to turn pink from the tiny sliver of sunset escaping from the horizon. "Tomorrow," the railroad Conductor had warned her, "it may rain." Thunderstorms, the very sort she liked, weren't exactly common in late spring, but they weren't unknown either.

The Hôtel sur la Seine was not ostentatious as some of the other, newer hotels of Paris; it had maintained its slightly medieval character despite the overenthusiastic building and destruction of France's 'Second Empire.' Somehow the Hôtel sur la Seine managed to elude Napoleon III and his engineers, and their vision of the futuristic Paris. Parisians as a whole were non-committal; Paris might be losing its ancient charm, but nearly anything French designed was better than that of the Prussians after the war in 1871. Of course, there was some remnant anger even in 1883 over that dreadful period in French history: a decade was not enough to heal the wounds. Now it seemed that to erase the past was to free Parisians from the pain of maturation. The avenues leading to the center of the city were lined with construction equipment, workers, and debris. Agonizing as it was to lose the old, the new meant employment and modernization.

Her cab rolled past a number of the newer projects. In the distance she could see the base of La Tour Eiffel which looked at that moment to be a puzzle of iron spider webs and concrete. Not due to be completed for a few years, it appeared more like a child's room where something had been broken, discarded, and not tidied up due to immature refusal. Two balloon ships, larger than the cargo dirigibles running mail back and forth, held an iron girder between them, lifting slowly until workers could align it and weld it. Unlike the *Go Ahead*, they were elongated bags of helium with human-driven helixes that controlled direction. The screws acted like an ocean vessel's paddle wheel but with less efficiency. They were more airship than balloon. A miniaturized steam engine, such as one Professor Pierce could build, would eventually replace the human powered motion - and then what? And did it matter? Robur, the Conqueror, had made any of those innovations outdated before they could be put into use. Times were changing faster than most people could keep up with.

Twenty years ago, it was unthinkable for a woman to consider a life beyond marriage. Now Lettie was proof that women were untethered from the old expectations. Almost: yes, well, almost. An adoring husband was still a tempting desire. She closed her eyes and let the tight feeling in her chest pass, while reminding herself that there was no such thing as love.

There was Les Travaux de la Vapeur Nationaux de France, the French National Steam Works, a building dedicated to France's contribution to power generation and locomotion. Pipes and conduits shot out of the walls and bent back into the brick building, giving it the look of the inside of a ship's engine room. Parisians had made many complaints of this particular edifice.

She stepped out of her cab, quite pleased with the hotel's location. An advantage of the Hôtel sur la Seine, quite apart from being a lesser known establishment and unlikely to attract men like Wickham, was that it sat in the northwest of the Fifth Arrondissement, home of the Musée Mécanique, the Université de Paris, the Sorbonne, and the Jardin de Plantes. It simply sat amidst the intellectual heart of the city and, arguably, the whole of Europe. Such renowned institutions would fill the two spare days she had before leaving for Brindisi. The Steam Ship *Mongolia* was not due to leave for Bombay until the twenty-seventh of May and there was little reason to get to the Italian port too early.

A trolley rolled by, puffing out vapors from its overtaxed engine, sounding more like an old fashioned locomotive than the quiet modern form of urban transport they were originally touted to be, and carrying a full load of worn out commuters. The sun had set, the temperature was falling, and the museums were closed for the evening. Lettie agreed with her exhausted brain, it was time to retire until the morning. Oddly, beyond verbally fencing with Wickham, she'd done so little and yet was so very tired. The nature of travel, she supposed. She remembered being amused when escorted to a lovely single room with a view of the river seen through a break between two buildings – hence a legitimate though exaggerated claim to the view. The accommodation had a dining table, a writing desk, an attached room for the commode, and the most welcoming bed. By 10 pm, when most of Paris was just getting itself energized with the evening's activity, Doctor Lettie Gantry was asleep and dreaming of the lush jungles of Java.

By morning, Lettie was rested, clearer headed, and far more confident that the Wickhams of the world had other things to do with their time than pester the likes of her. She logically and rationally acknowledged that she would not be so hostile to the Frenchman who left such a shining impression on her despite the fact that he was in some fashion an associate of Wickham's. A shame, she thought, he had such a pleasant speaking voice, an interesting look that could be intriguing, and remarkable eyes. And his hands were so elegant.

Yes, it was a shame; at last she'd met a man who didn't want something from her or to change her. He was beautiful to look at too, perfect in his graciousness, brilliant, and sadly, nowhere to be found. Was that her luck? Knowing how things went for her in the area of romance, the Frenchman was probably married to a wealthy aristocrat who had already given him ten glorious children. Yes, that was more like her luck.

Think about the day ahead, she reminded herself. Stay on track; get through the day.

The hotel provided its lady travelers with a temporary maid, one of the owner's five daughters, which was welcome. She was a cheery thing, eager to gather gossip or tales from those who travelled. It was exotic to the girl as she had never actually been outside of central Paris. At fifteen, she had all the attributes that would either attract a good husband or gain her employment in a grand household, either as a parlor or lady's maid. By the efforts she was exerting on Lettie's behalf and the tales she was gleaning, Lettie decided that the girl was not yet looking for a marriageable man. The girl seemed quite content where she was.

Lettie was quite capable of dressing herself: such skills were imperative when on a geological worksite – anything else would be absurd and completely unsupportable to the other members of the expedition. But today, she had formal visits to make and welcomed the assistance. The girl was quite the marvel with the art of hairstyling.

Carefully refolding the invitation and sliding it back into its ivory envelope with the exquisitely written address, Lettie set off very early in the morning to the Musée National d'Histoire Naturelle, the foremost natural history institution in Europe. The card included with the invitation she kept reading over and over was printed on excellent linen paper stock, with simple Copperplate lettering. It made her chuckle a bit to recall the difference in handwriting between the lovely invitation and the scrawl of a signature. It was clear that her host wisely employed an assistant who took great pride in the formality of presenting his employer in a professional light. The linen card was yet another example of simple elegance, assured by the efforts of said assistant.

Professeur Pierre Rene Aronnax
Directeur
Musée National d'Histoire Naturelle de Paris

She had dressed to meet him and, hopefully, impress him. Although they had never met prior to this, she felt very familiar with his life. This was more due to the publication of the Nemo Chronicles by J. Verne than Aronnax's original paper on the submarine mountains of the Atlantic, which after his adventures he was forced to retract and revise. Despite his fame, or infamy, he was a man she needed to know professionally and a man she truly wished to engage in conversation. His knowledge base was wide and now very experienced. That he invited her to his institution was a compliment she intended to return.

This was a time for first impressions. She'd chosen a dark wine colored wool costume with plush cuffs and waistcoat. She knew that to look too feminine would undermine her desire to be respected as a scientist. She chose a crisp white shirt and dark silk tie, in the masculine style, as well as a camelhair notched collar jacket. Her bonnet was in the latest fashion, called a Conquistador for the peak at the center front brim that mimicked the helmet of the Sixteenth Century Spanish soldier. Curled and combined feathers in olive green encircled the crown and it tied neatly under her chin with a pair of watered-silk ties. Over this she wore her wool scarf and hid her gloved hands from the brisk spring air in a fur muff. Only one hand at a time could be warmed as the other held tight to her beloved valise. Beneath her sleeve was her comfort, her agnostic rosary: Georgie's bracelet.

Of course, once she was done with her stay in Paris, she would ship home all the clothing and purchases appropriate to the cold, European weather and would travel lightly to Java and its tropical environs with only those things that served the environment and the work.

Before she was to arrive at the Galerie de Minéraux et Géologie, a part of the Museum, it was her intention to breakfast at La Belle Patisserie, situated halfway between the Hotel and her destination.

The hour was early enough that Lettie could take her time and stroll to the delightful bakery she'd known during her last visit to the Société Géographique. The street was one of the newly widened by Haussman's great plan to modernize all of Paris but most especially those areas nearest the museums and universities, where foreigners tended to venture. It had rained overnight, leaving even the lamp posts dripping off the last droplets before the day warmed up. It looked like it was going to rain again, by the afternoon.

Looking at the well heeled and working classes mingling on their way to work, and seeing the whole in that gentle light filtered through thin clouds in the morning and sporadically lit by gas lamps, Lettie thought of a Jean Beraud painting. The moisture and spring temperature had brought out some of the brightest blooms of flowering plants hanging above the streets in baskets dangling from the lampposts. The day was yet young enough that the hiss of the gas into the lamps was still audible and would be until they were shut down - one at a time.

Her goal was to find something small but satisfying to consume for breakfast, the alternative being that her stomach might grumble during the vital interview. La Belle Patisserie awaited her needs. It was too fine an establishment to attract cash poor students, but appealed to professors, curators, and the ladies acquainted with them.

The waiter who escorted her into the Patisserie seated her near the window facing the street and in full view of the pedestrians. Such a fashionable woman would attract customers, so long as they didn't mind her being a foreigner; her attire was distinctly English in his opinion. He could hear it in her pronunciation too when she thanked him. Her French was good enough that it didn't annoy him, but he could just tell she was British. He was always alert for foreigners, especially tourists, as they were notoriously bad tippers or only ordered those items which best resembled their own customary foods. Worse - they saw themselves as superior to the staff - to him. Such bad manners. Paris was after all, "the birthplace of equality."

The dining area was relatively bright. Mirrors on nearly every wall made the place appear much larger. The decorative scheme of taupe paint, pastel wall paper, and gold detailing lent the bakery a rich, sophisticated air.

Even at such an early hour, Lettie found herself in plenty of company. Elegantly dressed women made their selections and filled their plates from the delicate choices arranged along the pastry bar. One was free to choose whatever delight struck their fancy. Some ladies chose to remain standing near the bar, nibbling lightly, while others brought their small plates back to their tables. Lettie slid her valise near her feet and pulled her reading glasses out of her deep pocket, setting them on her nose. Over the top of the rims, she noted who else was seated in the café. A cadre of young, well-off ladies were also seated near windows, and they were engaged in a lively discussion regarding men, fashion, and a new display at the Palais d'Art Moderne. An older couple were seated to Lettie's left and a gentleman of late years was enjoying his coffee and newspaper. Two ladies sat with their selections while a third mindlessly fed bits of her food to the poodle standing on her skirts. One man had just been seated and now sat with his back to her with a stylish, low-crowned, "Homburg" hat, which she suspected he had just purchased, set in the chair next to him. The hat was too perfect and appeared as if taken right out of the box. The assortment of people was actually quite delightful, especially as it did not include Wickham. It would have been rather pleasant had the Frenchman, Monsieur d'Saint-Amand, been there.

A waitress, in a crisp white apron over a fitted black dress, poured coffee or wine into glass cups at each table. A gravity press coffee machine at the end of the bar was tended by another uniformed woman.

Eschewing coffee, Lettie enjoyed her cup of chocolate, a rare treat, with a touch of orange. The pastry was small, just enough to keep her from feeling faint in her tightly laced corset, which she had done out of nothing more than vanity, and she knew it.

The man with the hat looked briefly over his shoulder at her, returning to his cup and a book. She couldn't quite catch seeing his face, but thick brown hair covered the back of his head, cut short at the nape and natural in tone. Definitely not Wickham. Along with the new hat he wore a new suit. But of course, he was in Paris and would want to purchase such a thing. Men were no different from women in this regard.

His hair had just been cut too, and though she couldn't see his chin, he was likely freshly shaved. He pulled lightly at his collar, drawing it up to its fullest height.

Sipping her fragrant beverage, she found herself thinking of Pierce and his father. She would need to send a telegram to Sir Richard, letting him know that she had arrived safely. With any luck, he would have more news regarding the whereabouts of his son and perhaps the progress on the sampling trolley. The trolley was of lesser importance. She had to admit, she was hoping that Rajiv might contact her while she was in France.

After paying her bill, she started down the avenue toward the Jardin des Plantes. There she would meet with the luminary Professor Aronnax, which frankly speaking, made her quite nervous. Her hands were cold despite gloves and she felt some queasiness in her stomach regardless of the meal. Yes, she was indeed, very nervous.

A couple passed her, the woman holding delightfully onto the arm of her gentleman. He whispered something and she allowed herself a bright laugh that broke through the increasing gloom of a gathering rainstorm. In Paris, such behavior was not inappropriate. Neither of the couple appeared to be of questionable character; they were simply a happy couple strolling out of doors in the morning, before the weather trapped them inside for the rest of the day. Perhaps he was on his way to work somewhere in the maze of intellectual institutions?

Lettie envied them. Before their happiness distracted her from her purpose, she looked away and tried to predict the interview to come.

Chapter 44

The Paris National Museum of Natural History
Paris

The Musée National d'Histoire Naturelle de Paris was not one but many museum facilities, each in its own building; each with its own character. Her appointment was in the Galerie de Minéraux et Géologie, home of the d'Dolomieu collection with its extensive samples of unique minerals, precious stones and volcanic rocks. The entrance was a grand combination of Neo-Classical and modern architecture. A Greek revival lintel was held up in the air by a quad of thick fluted columns, allowing the steps and foyer to be filled with light and air. Yet the building was dull in color, from the gray stone to the aged wood doors. Those doors were quite huge, as was the standard for such designs, and clearly were meant to display the seriousness of what lay inside.

The man who answered the door was a youngish man, thirty five or forty, with a little gray hair, a slender build, and superior taste in his attire. Superior, but by no means expensive or outlandish. He was an assistant professor, she guessed. Inquisitive eyes stared back at her. Ladies did not come to the museum during working hours. They came for shows, presentations, and social events.

"Bonjour. Je m'appelle Docteur Gantry. Je crois qu'on m'attend?" Lettie handed him the invitation and her card.

"Ah! Oui! Yes." The fellow straightened up and found a broad, sweet smile to offer her. "Madame is here to see my master, the Professor. He is, with much apology, a ..." He stopped to think of the correct English word, " ... a little tarty? Tardy? Oui. The Professor suggests that Madame peruse the collection until he arrives and thus has sent his servant should Madame have any questions."

"And does the Professor's assistant always speak in the third person?"

"Oui, Madame. A habit of years. I ..." he struggled for a moment to move the conversation both into English and the first person. "... find that all things in their proper order are much clearer. A certain formality is essential. I am known to be a bit formal. I hope Madame is not put off by this?"

"Not at all," she said as he showed her into the first hallway before the grand gallery.

"A good servant should never eclipse the master, no?"

"Even when he has better handwriting?" she asked coyly, rocking the invitation he'd just returned to her in her fingers.

He colored deeply but smiled again. "Madame took notice?"

"Madame knows when she sees a signature not of the same hand as the rest of the document, which I believe I have you to thank for?"

"No, no," he quickly replied. "It is my master's pleasure to meet you at last and his servant's to make any necessary arrangements."

"What may I call you?"

"Conseil."

"Then, thank you, Monsieur Conseil. For the arrangments."

He bowed at the waist and smiled. Folding his hands behind him, he strolled beside her as they moved in from the foyer to the anteroom. Near the doorway was an impressive painting: a volcano with a vertical column of ash bellowing out of its crater and spreading out at the upper altitudes, looking like a furious mushroom. The painting was quite beautiful but was also quite wrong. There was no ashfall, no pyroclastic events, and the column itself was too clean and precise.

"Ah, does Madame know this painting?"

"I must confess, no."

"A recent donation from Monsieur George Julius Scrope. It is entitled 'the Eruption of Vesuvius as Seen from Naples, October 1822.' Perhaps Madame can tell me if this is an accurate des - dis - description?"

Lightning was shown shooting forth from the ash column. "To a degree, yes, though most ash eruptions are much bulkier and ... well ... fluffy, despite its actual density." She gesticulated the shape of the cloud with several circulations of her hands. "And most assuredly such an amount of ash particles would indeed create friction."

Conseil nodded gravely. "And from that, a static electric charge ... lightning."

"Indeed. You know the concept."

"Despite what Madame may have heard or read, we are not without scientific basis here." Conseil's voice was suddenly sharp but not angry. "My master was so very happy you accepted his invitation. There was some concern."

Lettie stopped in the door frame to the main gallery and looked up at the now unhappy assistant. "But of course I would. I am flattered beyond words."

He shook his head. "No, Madame, not 'of course.' I fear my master's reputation has suffered in the past years and now - But I will assure Madame that Professor Aronnax is an excellent scientist, a man of reason and logic."

"You're very good to him."

"He is all these things I say."

"Oui. I know. I read both his papers, the one written before and then - after - the incident. I was looking for references to marine volcanoes which, as it turned out, there were none. I enjoyed those papers all the same. His conclusions were superior. You needn't worry; my opinion remains quite high. I know of no reason why I should feel otherwise. This is a great compliment to me that the professor will take the time to see me."

Pierre Aronnax appeared at the far door and waved. He was not quite what she had expected. Tall, with curly graying hair, and a delightful countenance. In several great strides, he made his way through the main gallery and to her, hand outstretched. Very continental.

"Welcome, welcome Doctor Gantry. Bonjour! What a singular pleasure it is to meet you at last. Come in! Come in!" He was almost out of breath with excitement.

"This is a great pleasure for me, Professor. I cannot thank you enough for seeing me."

Aronnax waved off the comment as though it were said between two old friends and quite unnecessary. He wrapped her arm in his and began chatting about this subject and that … all as though they'd simply not seen each other in a couple of months.

If Lettie had any reservations about her host, which she did not, they would have been quickly dismissed and replaced by the impressive array of skills and experiences that set Aronnax beyond comparison to other scientists. Every word he spoke doubled in importance simply because he was saying it. But for all the prestige she heaped on him, he was humble, witty, and exuberant.

Her heart was pounding and her head spinning with all the questions she wanted to ask him. The whole time, he did the one thing she hadn't dared to hope for: he called her Doctor Gantry with a tone that indicated respect and equality.

Before her lay the collections of Professor di'Dolomieu, whose interesting history and extensive work had earned him the distinction of having *Dolomite* named for him. Conseil was quite capable of reciting the origin and classification of every stone. Aronnax would simply smile and offer some anecdote about where the stones came from and how they managed to get into his museum. For her part, she commented and questioned, always leading to an ever-increasing sense of enthusiasm in everyone.

The tour ended, much to Lettie's disappointment, but she knew both men had important things to be doing. To her surprise, Aronnax sent his assistant away to fetch some coffee and escorted Lettie into his private office. It looked like Pierce's home, cluttered yet creative, an intellectual nest of books, papers and chalk boards.

"Would you mind, Doctor Gantry, if I asked a question?" When she nodded affirmatively, he continued. "I suspect Conseil regaled you with some details about the incident?"

Lettie didn't know how to reply.

Aronnax nodded. She must require a little more directness, clarity. "As you probably can imagine, I am referring to my misadventure with Captain Nemo and his submersible boat. Conseil still places great energies on the matter. For myself, I prefer to live in the present and not the past. Did he not mention it?"

She shook her head. "No details, only a general comment."

Aronnax was visibly relieved. "He makes more of it than I do. As a scientist, you know too well how there is an ebb and flow to one's status in the community. Because of the - falling out – is that the right phrase in English? No. Let me say it this way: my reputation has suffered somewhat from 'the incident.' I do not see this as a long term problem. This is but one time I must be patient and continue my work while moderately isolated from the scientific community as a whole." He leaned back to sit on the edge of his desk, in front of where she was seated. "I believe you may have heard some of our tale; we went to find a sea monster and found far more. Nemo's research and collections, which he kept in his salon but allowed me complete access to, were astonishing. I resolved that I must tell the world about everything, in solid, scientific terms. A thesis that could be discussed and considered. After our escape, we returned here, to my offices in Paris and I began to write - ma thése -

my thesis. Of course, I had to report to the French and American governments, who initially funded our hunt for the sea monster. There were also journalists who asked many, many questions. Public and academic reaction was overwhelming. Next thing I knew, there was this book - our lives were instantly changed and I had not yet finished my thesis. I will admit I came to think of this place," Aronnax waived his hand at the walls of the office, "as my refuge. Even Ned Land is still with us in our refuge. He hates the attention the book brought him as it showed him in an unfavorable light. He is much more clever than he is portrayed in - what did they call it?"

"20,000 Leagues under the Seas."

"Oui. A silly name. But, my thesis, once completed, was not so well named or publicized, or timed. The book came out first, then my often contradictory thesis, and the rest is history. My history. I became for a while a fictitious person. Me? A real man, and my life was reduced to an adventure biography. And not even my biography. So, I let go of my anger and rededicated my self to my work."

"A wise decision, if I may say so."

"Thus speaking of Mr. Land, I had hoped he would be here. It is not like him to be so very late."

"I'm sure he has good reason. Professor Aronnax, you told me your story for a reason ... I should hope you aren't concerned that I am one of those academics who has isolated you. I will freely admit that I am deeply flattered to have been invited here and was very nervous about meeting a scholar whose work I greatly admire."

He blushed a little and tried to find, in English, some way of dismissing her compliment. He was unused to such things. "Forgive me if I gave you the impression that I was seeking your kind words. This is in fact a reason I am telling you this: you must not be afraid of what others may think or say. You must strive onwards," Aronnax said earnestly. "Your work ... and I say this having read your monograph on ash content ... is quite important. If it is not ... ah, peu approprié ... inappropriate of me to say, I suspect as a lady in the scientific world, you have encountered much of the ebb and flow of opinion. Do not allow it to cause you grief or doubt. I have offered other scholars this advice and it has fallen on deaf ears."

It took her a moment to draw up the courage. "May I ask you a question? What was 'he' really like? You are clearly not the same man that was called Pierre Aronnax in the Nemo Chronicles. Was he? Was he the same man or different, as shown in the book?"

"Captain Nemo? Not such a blind villain as that biography purports. But he was a harsh man, cut off from the world for his own purpose. There is a price to be paid when one abandons all that it is to be a social human being. The first cost is one's humanity. His ... singularity of purpose combined with his passion ... his hate ... it was at times overwhelming. Now I hear rumor that Monsieur Verne is finishing the last book of his Chronicles. It tells us that Nemo has ... passed."

"Dead?"

"Oui. He was one of the deaf ears I begged to enlighten the world around him. He could have made such a difference. There was another brilliant mind, a long time ago. He was more inclined toward engineering. An orphan who I thought would make his way in the world."

"What happened to him?"

"He too died. But a long time ago. In the Pacific. Chased away by evil relatives, the likes of which you and I would not know. He confided in me, which I believe to be a remarkable thing, as he did so with no one else in this world. But that was a long time ago. Neither Anish nor Nemo will change the course of humanity, as they should have. As you will," he said, changing the tone of his speech.

"Is that why you want to encourage me?"

"Oui. But not all my reasons. I see myself in young scientists and I wish that someone had been persuaded to offer me the wisdom of never giving up. Such life lessons ... we ask ourselves when we're older, why did no one tell me this or that?

"I have long since given up my search for the guidebook to life - real life - day to day life. I never found it."

"Some find it religiously."

"And I did not. Perhaps I will yet."

He allowed his whole face to brighten up. It was clearly a new pleasure for him, as Conseil brought in the coffee, to speak frankly and earnestly with a woman scientist. Who would have thought it ever possible?

Chapter 45

Musée National d'Histoire Naturelle de Paris
France

Outside the Museum of Natural History, Lettie waited while her mind swirled with all the ideas, details, and encouragement she'd received. Frankly, she felt giddy. Wonderfully, alarmingly, giddy. A light drizzle of rain started and yet she decided to walk. Pulling the muff over her forearm, she extended her folding umbrella, grasped her valise, and headed off into the gardens, using every ounce of control not to skip like a child. At one point she caught herself swinging her valise to some inner song and swishing along in an almost unladylike way ... almost.

Aronnax had liked her and had been impressed with her work. What a sad thing that he, or Conseil, felt his reputation was so damaged. He deserved so much better. But his attitude and good sensibilities were infectious; Lettie's mind was racing through everything he had said and how hopeful it made her feel. He had enjoyed their discussions on rock formations, ash fall, and eruptive materials. She could drive a person insane with the subject if they had no interest in geology. But both Aronnax and Conseil had been as enthralled by her knowledge as she was with theirs. After a bit, she thought she must have been showing off. If either gentleman perceived her that way, they thoughtfully concealed those notions. It had been an afternoon of intellectual discourse and mutual admiration.

Nearer to the street, she passed a man who was well-dressed but terribly uncomfortable in his attire. A large man, with big hands and a considerate smile. He lifted his hat as she walked by and completely forgetting where she was she offered him a good day, in English.

He stopped immediately. "Madame, are you the Doctor of Geology that was visiting Professor Aronnax," he asked in a mildly accented but clear voice.

"I am."

"Madame, I must apologize to you then."

"Whatever for?"

"I should have been there. I'm quite inexcusably late and now it would seem I've lost an opportunity. The fault is mine; entirely mine."

"Pray forgive me, but feel a bit lost ..." At the gate to the gardens, she saw someone had stopped, covered himself against the rain, looked at her for a long moment, too long, and then walked quickly away.

"Edward Land - Ned." He tipped his hat again, not sure what else he was supposed to do. "The Professor asked me to relay to you some of my observations regarding an eruption I'd seen in the Kamchatka Sea." He scrounged around in his pockets. Carefully lifting out a square, bulky package wrapped in brown paper and twine, with an excellent knot, he presented it to her. "I'm no scientist, just a harpooner. But I wrote down everything as best as I recalled it. I'd picked up a piece of rock that was blown onto our decks. If it isn't offensive to you, Madame, I would like you to have it. Lightweight stuff, full of holes. I saw some of it floating on the water. Didn't make sense for rocks to float so I mentioned it on my return to the Museum."

Lettie smiled, inspecting the package. "Mr. Land, a good harpooner has excellent eyes; I should be surprised if your description is not full of useful observations. Thank you, sir."

Land put his hat back on, his hair being somewhat wet now.

"Do you think that the Professor would allow me to inspect the sample you've given me under his microscopes?"

"I think it would be worthy of asking, Madame."

"Then I think we should return to the Museum and ask. The worst he can say is no."

The harpooner wasn't certain what to do next, but he offered her his arm and to take the umbrella for her. "I do really, really apologize for being late."

"No need to. I think this turned out quite fortuitously."

"It's those damn, free running trams Paris seems to be in love with. No horse, no rail. No direction. It's a wonder accidents aren't happening every day." Land continued his description of a collision between two such steam powered trolleys, the annoyed yet not injured passengers, and his inability to get around the crowds that came to see what the under-carriage of such transportation looked like. Even without the horror of a rail accident, people were drawn to it and stayed out of what Land considered outrageous morbidity. Of course, that same morbidity didn't stop him from regaling her with every detail all the way back to Professor Aronnax.

For the rest of the afternoon, she sat welcomed in Conseil's workroom, eyes focused on the piece of volcanic pumice, and deliriously discoursing with three of the most charming men of varying scientific degree about everything from Parisian architecture, to volcanoes, to how to be a better passenger on the sea. And to think, she had planned on wasting the afternoon shopping for things she likely didn't need.

Land's description of the tram accident put her in mind to travel on foot all the way back to her Hotel. It was dark but Haussman's streets were generously lit.

Four blocks from the Hotel, she noticed a man lingering at the curb, somewhat shadowed by the lamp itself, placing a cheroot lightly between his lips and keeping himself bundled against the chilled evening. As he lit the cheroot, his illuminated light colored eyes, possibly blue, stared out at her from under a new Homburg. She recognized the hat and had decided a quicker pace was required when he suddenly slipped back into the shadow, turning his back on her. She couldn't quite make out all the details of what the man looked like. She was in little danger as the streets were full of people, horses, and the occasional policeman. But that man brought back several memories where it could have been him watching her, although she was forced to admit that it was unlikely to be the same person from the tavern in Kent now here in Paris. He simply, logically couldn't be. But he was the man in the restaurant that morning; the restaurant wasn't that far from where they were and he might be a tourist staying near by. It was possible, but she couldn't help wondering.

It was safe. For heaven's sake, it was Paris. There were choices for her, but only one that would give her immediate satisfaction. No waiting for a gentleman to assist her. Gripping her valise tightly as though it were a cudgel, Lettie turned toward the man with the new hat and marched straight for him. Approaching within a few yards of his lamppost, she was prepared to demand his name.

The man tossed his freshly lit and smoldering cheroot into the street, turned heel, and marched away. His departure was so sudden Lettie was startled out of her righteous anger and left a bit embarrassed. He was just standing there, she reminded herself, doing nothing at all. Her indignation dissolved the more she considered how ridiculous her paranoia had been. Taking several deep breaths of the moist air, she slowly retrenched herself in thoughts of the day and what might pass for an excellent dining choice.

Looking back, she noted that the man had put some distance between them, walking deeper into academic Paris. He hadn't even finished his cigar. That was her fault.

She was just being silly, that was all. It was the giddiness of the day. That was all.

Wasn't it?

She locked her door that night, bolted all the windows, and lay awake for hours rummaging through her memory. Where had she seen that man before? Why would he be following her? Wickham?

Lettie decided that once she was on the train, she would be safe. She lay on her side, pulling the covers around her body and thinking her feet were too cold. Shadows and unfamiliar light made the room too empty, spacious, filled with places where danger lurked.

Stop it, she thought. Review your day. Think clearly. Be rational.

Her trunks were packed and ready for two different destinations: one set would go back to her home with items she wouldn't need in tropical Java. The other, much more austere and dedicated to her science, would follow her East.

Counting sheep was not her method for inducing sleep. Instead she continued reviewing her itinerary: Paris to Brindisi, via the French-Italian Alps. She would be alone for that leg of the trip, something she was not entirely used to being while in a foreign country. Yet, nothing would happen on the train. At the port town of Brindisi, she would board the steamship *Mongolia*, meet with a Dutch Professor and his wife, and sail in their company through the Suez Canal. They would naturally stop for customs and provisioning once through the Canal. She could send a telegram to her father and to Sir Richard while they were docked. After that, it was a long way to India. She had been told that much of that journey would be out of sight of land. Once in Bombay, she would change ships and sail to Ceylon, then straight to Java. They would pass through the narrow Sunda Strait between the islands of Java and Sumatra, around to the capital of Batavia. She'd almost come full circle. A few hundred miles Northeast from Java was the island of Sangihe, Georgie's home.

She'd never forgotten him.

It was early in the morning before she finally fell asleep. It was going to be a very long but worthwhile trip. Everything depended on her actions now. There was no room for failure.

Chapter 46

May 22, 1883
The French Alps
Approaching Frejus Rail Tunnel

Dearest Papa,

I am quite well and have no occasion since my crossing to believe myself in anything but the best company of fellow travelers.

I believe that I cannot adequately describe the French Alpine countryside. It is breathtaking. Should I use any other clichés I doubt they would fail to be true as this is some of the loveliest country I've seen. I read a bit on the tunnel we are about to enter as it is a marvel of construction. The Frejus Rail Tunnel, sometimes called the Mont Cenis Tunnel, is eight and a half miles in length and passes beneath the Pointe du Frejus (something close to 3000 meters above sea level) and the Col de Frejus (only a mere 2500 meters.) While I am sorry not to see these extraordinary sights of the Alps, my greatest curiosity is for the engineering miracle that has taken some hours off the trip between France and Italy. I cannot wait to tell you about the Great Roundhouse and Turntable at Bardonecchia.

As you know, it was opened not long ago, in late '70s, at a length of 12.8 kilometers, but in '81 it was extended and reinforced – naturally on the French side, for I have found that the French never seem to accept when things are done. Even as we approach the structure, I can see continuing work being made to the rail and the area surrounding it. I understand that Pneumatic drilling machines, well orchestrated explosive charges requiring a differential calculation machine to coordinate, and even electric detonation devices have made this whole spectacular effort possible. The tourist booklet you kindly gave me says that it was scheduled to take twice as long as it actually did, no doubt in part due to the invention of new construction devices and the demands of the Tunnel's German designer.

We shall soon disappear into its depths to emerge in Italy, at a town called Bardonecchia, then on down the Boot to Brindisi on the coast. I expect to have some time ...

The letter went unfinished.

Lettie set her pen down gently and slowly, not wishing to make any gesture that might be misinterpreted.

She had just begun her last sentence when a man entered her carriage unbidden and turned a short-barreled, American revolver on her. This was exactly what her father feared might happen. She should not have been alone.

"My apologies, ma'am," he said with a slight twang in his pronunciation. Shoving the compartment door closed behind him and drawing the curtains, he set about an attempt to make himself comfortable, which was an impossible task in the tiny room. With a supreme effort, he set a calm expression on his face, intending to convey confidence. "I would appreciate it if you wouldn't scream. That could prove very unfortunate."

Lettie swallowed hard but looked him over quickly, to see what she could possibly learn. The gun was distracting. Terrifying. Was he a thief or worse? He was staring at her, not at her belongings. He was a handsome man, in his late forties, with medium brown hair and pale blue eyes - stunningly blue eyes. His clothing was in that typically American style, with a simplicity that didn't attract attention amongst international tourists. It was new. So was his hat. Dark blue sack suit of winter wool, a lighter blue jacquard waistcoat, spotless celluloid collar, and a pale tie. Just above the collar, peeking out, was a discoloration of his skin, a hideous scar. He set his new Homburg down on the seat next to him, revealing the fullness of his thick, straight hair and a high, intelligent forehead. And he had a smell of sweetened tobacco.

His hand was steady and he didn't blink excessively. His eyes darted up and down as he tried to assess her too.

She recognized him. Wasn't he the man in the café? Yes, he was, and he had followed her to the Museum, to the Hotel, and now to the train. She should have been more careful: she should have followed her instincts. "I carry very little money," she said in almost a whisper, knowing instinctively that he was not there to rob her.

"I have no interest in your money, jewels, or possessions," he said sharply, insulted. He forced the charming smile again. "I simply want to start by making your acquaintance, on behalf of my employer."

"At gunpoint?" She drew herself back from him, as much as the tiny compartment would allow, and took off her reading glasses.

"Well, you've already rejected his advice. We wouldn't want you doing so again."

She tried to set her hands in her lap, but the writing desk needed to be steadied on her knees and she held it tightly on the sides. "I can't imagine why you would think that I could accept unsolicited ... advice ... under these circumstances," she spit back with a mixture of sarcasm and fear. The desk was unsteady and she was forced to seize the ink bottle with one hand. He nodded sharply in the direction of the desk and she took that to mean he would permit her to put the pen and ink away. Her eyes never left him as she did so. The unfinished letter was shoved blindly into her valise. She could think of nothing to say.

"Doctor Gantry ..."

"You know me?"

"I know of you. And, we have met, though I doubt you'd recall me out of context. You are Miss Letticia Gantry, of Cardiff, New College of London, Tokyo, but not yet of the Dutch East Indies. 'Lettie' to your intimates. And with any luck, a Professor in the School of Geology." He moved closer to her, recovering the distance she was slowly attempting to put in between them. "You can call me Mr. Turner if you like. It's a good English name, though I'm not a citizen of your country." His eyes were so clear and bright the color was almost ice blue. His mouth was small, with thin lips, but it lent itself nicely to an off center grin. "If you'd like to, you can even call me Tom." Of course she wouldn't.

"Mr. Turner, what are you doing? What do you want?"

"I'm afraid we can't let you go to Java Island."

Lettie drew in her breath. "Mr. Wickham has put you up to this? Where is he?"

"Wickham? What makes you think ..."

"He is the only man who doesn't want me going to Java, unless you count the President of the Weldon Institute, which I do not. He's already offered me his unwelcome 'advice.' Now, sir, where is he? Where is Mr. Wickham?"

He grinned in that slightly lopsided manner and squinted a bit, inspecting her again in an amused way. "Let me better word it; we can't let you go off roaming around the Indies on your own. It's dangerous out there. Haven't you read the news? Very, very dangerous. Anything could happen between here and there." Her eyes must have grown so wide in terror that he felt he had to explain further. "You and I will take another route from northern Italy back to Holland where we can make use of a better mode of transportation. Then to the Indies, considerably faster than you planned. Counter-intuitive I know, but you will be pleasantly surprised. You'll stay with us, but once everything is concluded, you'll be able to go home to enjoy that appointment at New College I'm convinced you'll get. Everything will turn out right. That is, if you cooperate."

"And you'll shoot me if I don't?"

His eyes narrowed, unamused. "I'll do what I have to, Doctor Gantry; please don't force the issue." He looked at the tight grip she held on her desk; she was, like most women, more concerned about her character than she was about her very life, foolish as that was. He resentfully added, "Your reputation will be safe, I assure you. Everything will be done to protect that." The trouble they'd have to go to for such an inconsequential thing.

Lettie didn't appear to believe him. Looking at the thickness of the barrel from the open end, the last thing she was thinking of was her reputation. She was no fool. Something was going to go wrong, she knew it, and he was going to kill her. Whether by accident or purpose, it hardly mattered.

The room grew dark, nearly black, with the exception of the two compartment lamps. Turner casually looked out of the window. "We're in the tunnel. A marvel of engineering, don't you think?"

Lettie didn't reply.

She swung her lap table at him. The corner of the box struck him in the jaw, splitting the skin and knocking him down on the seat. She immediately followed by smashing the box down on his wrist, not dislodging the revolver but seriously loosening his grip on it. It was a sturdy box with sharp edges. She lifted the box a third time, to drop it down on his head.

Turner reached up and blocked her with one arm, grasping the box with his free hand and twisting it down. He barely kept a hold of the revolver as the contents of the box spilled across the floor.

Lettie tried to open the compartment door; he slammed it shut. Turner seized her by the waist and threw his weight on top of her, landing both of them on the padded bench.

He clamped his hand down over her mouth. His weight on top of her, her tight clothing; Lettie could barely breathe. The cut on his jaw dripped blood onto her starched, white collar. "That was not very ladylike," Turner said, catching his breath and trying to hold her still. Lettie kept screaming under his hand, violently rocking her head back and forth to dislodge his grip. "Stop it!" He was becoming angry, perhaps more at himself than at her, but in wrestling with her he couldn't spare a hand to put pressure on his stinging wound. He shifted his weight dramatically, which forced one of his knees down between her legs immobilizing her more-so. Even through all the layers of petticoats, it was an effective maneuver - and threat.

Lettie stopped struggling immediately and stared at him with abject hatred.

Turner couldn't keep a tight grip on the revolver with a sore hand, so he set it up on the top of the bench, out of her reach, and pressed his fist against his cut jaw. "That was bright, though. Didn't see that one coming. Should have, but I didn't. You keep surprising me, Doctor." He drew in deeper and slower breaths until he seemed to be breathing normally. She was still struggling to breathe. He released some of the pressure on her mouth, not meaning to bruise her. "No one's going hear you, with all this racket of the tunnel. So you might as well save your voice."

She didn't indicate specifically that she would stay quiet, but the glare she continued giving him said that words were no longer on her mind. He slowly lifted his hand off her mouth.

"That's so much better now, isn't it?"

She said nothing.

Turner lifted himself off of her, just a bit. Flexing his bruised hand, he then picked up the revolver and put it in his pocket, all the while kneeling inconsiderately on her skirt. Pulling a small square of linen out of his upper jacket pocket, he pressed the cut on his jaw, making certain that it had stopped bleeding. "I personally don't care what anyone might have to say on the matter, you're a real lady."

Fuming at the remark, she tried to sit up and he shoved her back down, with his hand on her throat. "Lady or not, you're coming with me.

241

Nicely, quietly, and obediently. If there was ever any room for argument, we just used it up. Don't count on me knowing what to do with a lady under these circumstances. It's not something I'm accustomed to. But I know how to handle a man."

"Why," she said finally, shoving his hand away.

"Actually, I'm not entirely sure anymore. My employer has taken a fancy to you I guess. And, you've proven smart enough to help us. Take it as a compliment I promise, it's meant as one. You're just too dangerous to leave out there on your own. You might figure out how volcanoes work but never share that information. That would be unfortunate."

"What are you talking about? Why doesn't Wickham want me to go to Java? Doesn't he understand what I'm trying to do? It's not a threat to anyone. And of course I'll share my results. That is why I'm doing this work." She drew in a breath and said to herself, though loudly enough for Turner to hear, "No, not Wickham ..."

Turner looked at her curiously but decided not to reply. Instead, he collected her hands and held them in front of her. "No more fighting." He said each word distinctly, without blinking, and staring straight into her eyes. He held her wrists with one hand, and held up a piece of cotton cloth he'd kept in his pocket.

"Are you expecting to take me off the train like that?" Perhaps he hadn't thought of how would appear her along with her hands tied would appear. That was unlikely yet she was grasping at any possibility.

He sat back, let go of her hands, and smiled, just as the train left the tunnel and light flooded back into the compartment. "I'd prefer not to. The choice is yours." Dislodging himself completely from her he took a seat opposite and looked a little relieved as she calmly set her hands in her lap. Pieces of her hair had fallen into her face and the drops of blood on her collar stood out from her otherwise austere travel suit of midnight blue. He liked the color; it was a military blue.

Lettie squirmed a little, to get into a more comfortable position. She was shivering, and hated that there was nothing she could do to stop shaking. Making matters worse, Turner watched her with what she decided was a look of improper admiration. He suddenly shifted over to sit much too close to her. Reaching over to her, he tucked the stray pieces of hair gently behind her ear or up into her chignon. "Can't have you looking unkempt."

That close, she could smell his skin. She had to maintain her composure; she had no doubt whatsoever that her life depended on how calm she remained. This was not a romantic novel and his ability to harm her was quite real.

There was still the matter of the bloodied collar and the threat of being bound up. She might be able to convince him that the binding wasn't necessary. Think woman, think. Remove each threat, one at a time. Be calm. Be rational. "Mr. Turner, don't you believe it will be obvious that I am not with you willingly? This cannot work. Outside this compartment, your revolver will only serve to draw the attention I know you do not seek. And I would suspect that ultimately you would prefer not to use it."

The surprised expression on his face gave her a moment of hope.

"Sir, I will not leave quietly…"

"Yes, you will." The expression vanished.

"No, sir, I will not. If you are looking for an example of the stubbornness of women, I will provide you with the best."

"Oh, I know that," he said, sliding back to his opposite seat and looking out the door, to see who was in the corridor. "If you force me to restrain you, I'll just put your coat over your hands; it will make it appear you're carrying it. A scarf will cover the collar, and I do apologize, it was rude of me to bleed on you like that. Any difficulty you have physically moving about will be dismissed as womanly weakness for which I will be there to assist you. All very proper. Now, do we have to go that far?" Lettie opened her mouth to argue.

"No, Doctor Gantry. You will make no fuss at all. In fact, you will likely be very, very cooperative." Her eyes stared back at him, terrified and confused. He leaned in and tucked one last strand of loose hair back into place, leaving his hand on her cheek just a bit too long, trying to be comforting.

He pulled his hand back suddenly. Why the hell did he do that? Why wasn't his target a man? Why did it have to be her? Couldn't anyone else in the world do what she was doing? Angry at someone, anyone, he lowered his voice and stared directly at her. "Professor Pierce is not a strong man, is he? Personally, I don't have high hopes he'll hold up in the long run, his nerves are too frail, and my employer agrees." That's it; play on her motherly instinct. And, to hell with caring about what she thinks.

243

Chapter 47

The French Alps
Exiting the Frejus Rail Tunnel
Bardonecchia, Italy

Her eyes opened widely and she tried to find the words. Turner waited patiently for her to thoroughly digest what he had said. "He's with you? Professor Pierce? Willingly?"

Turner shook his head and watched her carefully.

"Then the telegrams ... the messages to his father ... were false?" She was answered with only a nod. "Why would you do anything to Professor Pierce? Of all the people ..."

"That's a good question. We've got him building some damn thing." He paused for a moment, wondering if through all else that was happening he had still accidentally offended her by cursing. That he cared made him all the more angry. "But I don't know if he'll make it. Captivity hasn't been good on his health. He just doesn't have a strong constitution." He carefully repeated what he'd been told to say. You're a damn liar, he thought of himself. Fine, I do care. So what?

Not even honesty would make him feel any better and he knew it.

Oh God, not for me, she agonized. She pictured the Professor, with his narrow hands and slender body. He was not a strong man, as Turner said. His mind was his strength, not his body. "I don't understand any of this."

It was the quiver in her voice that bothered him intensely. This wasn't going as he had anticipated. Everything would have been so much easier if he'd been sent after a man. He was supposed to scare her into compliance, but this was too easy. Before he'd thought about it he added a reassurance, "I think it will be explained soon." Damn it, man, why say anything?

He turned his head and something about the lighting on his face reminded her. "How much have you been following me? I've have seen you many times, not just in Paris?"

He looked over at her and smiled, for the first time, quite warmly. "As I said, we have met. You remember me? I'm flattered, Ma'am."

Turner wasn't a difficult man to remember: he had a very square jaw and those uniquely bright eyes. His teeth were surprisingly excellent for a mid-age American, and better by far than the average Englishman. He liked using his smile, appearing fully aware of the power of his good looks. In a polar difference from Pierce, Turner appeared comfortable in his own skin and very satisfied with it. Almost.

In the returning light of the Italian side of the tunnel, she could see it better … the scar. A horrible scar, which looked old and seemed to nearly encircle his throat just under his chin. She looked away before he could catch her staring.

Brushing any dust off her hat, he handed it to her, motioning that she should put it on. A lady's hat was not something simple to be put on and off easily. Watching her very carefully, he waited while she set the thing firmly on her styled hair and used two long hatpins to lock it into place. The hat pins disturbed him until he was certain they were no longer a weapon for her use. He then took her coat and slipped it over her arm. Last, and with too much deliberate ease, Turner wrapped her scarf around her neck. All the while, she glared at him, almost challenging him to try something more: just one more step beyond the already unforgivable behavior he had shown.

Conductors started calling out the upcoming stop as the decline of the track steepened. Everyone would be expected to disembark from the French rail train and to board the Italian version for the rest of the journey to the Mediterranean. As full as the cars were, it was likely to be a chaotic mess of passengers trying to find the right train going to their destination. Several lines ran straight down to Rome, some diverted directly to Austria along the Alpine foothills, while others crisscrossed the Italian countryside. Exactly why he chose to make his move there.

A five-minute warning was called out in French and Italian. Turner understood at least one of those, as he quickly checked his watch and whistled slightly. "Right on time."

"What about my things? My notes and research … they might not be of value to you but they are …"

"Not a worry, ma'am. That will be taken care of. Believe me; they are of importance to us as well."

"Thought of everything, have you?"

Turner stood up, reached under her arms and pulled her gently to her feet. The train itself jerked and jolted to an uncomfortable stop, for which

Turner had to steady them both. He leaned over and took up her valise. Finally, he opened the door and guided her out of the compartment, his hand clamped tightly above her elbow. She pulled on her gloves clumsily. Waiting on either side of the aisle were three men, dressed more simply, and thus less visibly than Turner. "Pick up the mess on the floor, don't leave anything behind, and meet us as scheduled," he whispered to the closest man.

Very politely, even rather kindly, he led her down the passageway, protecting her whenever another passenger had to slip past them in the narrow space. There was so much noise and chaos around them. Families, businessmen, adventurers and travelers all poured out of the various cars and scrambled to claim luggage or to keep track of one another. Turner had chosen the perfect place to abduct her. In the middle of a mindless, frenzied crowd, who would notice them?

He swung around in front of her as they descended the stairs of the Pullman and made certain she disembarked safely. Sliding his arm around hers, he made it appear they were strolling through the rail station, looking like any other pair. They would doubtless be mistaken for a married couple, probably Americans going the Grand Tour.

The thought of Turner playing her husband made her blush. He saw the flare of color in her cheeks and grinned. "What is it you're finding so … amusing? Or, embarrassing?"

Lettie only looked away. Her thoughts were none of his business.

"Don't look too angry, or everyone will think we've quarreled." He thought it was funny. "I hear it's always the husband who needs to make up. If I buy you flowers, will you smile?"

"Stop it!"

"Shhh."

"This is not amusing."

"Then I apologize. Though I think you should try and find something funny or ironic in this. God knows I'm trying. When everything is over, you'll see the humor of it. It's for your own good, and though I know you won't, I need you to believe me." He drew her in, closer.

Resignation took the strength out of her legs, forcing Turner to hold her up. Pierce: she had to do this for Pierce. Her knees were weak and her head spinning. Alone: not a single face offered her a moment of hope. Her reputation was obliterated in a single event, but that seemed like such a small thing compared to her life and Pierce's. The pounding in her chest echoed throughout her whole body and in her ears; her breathing became labored. In the humiliation of weakness, it was possible she might faint. Her sense of balance was off and her feet were not going where she wanted them to. For the first time ever, her corset was painfully tight, biting deep into her back. "I need to ... to sit down. Just for a moment. Please."

Turner looked her over quickly and realized that she was pale and shivering. "Over here." Damn her; even Pierce was less trouble. He guided her, nearly carrying her, over to a bench neatly tucked away down a corridor between two small buildings. Secluded. People rushed by, never once noticing them.

"I need my valise," she whispered.

"I have it here. What do you need?" Turner opened the over-stuffed satchel and was surprised at the mass of papers, pencils, and other objects. Christ, she was the most disorganized creature he'd known. Or, she was clever and stalling for time.

"You'll never find it." She seized the valise and set it down next to her. Though he held it open for her to dig through, her cold hands made it impossible for her to sort through the flotsam. "Damn," she said, halfway under her breath. It was unladylike. But what other word would suffice? And what did proper behavior mean now? Clenching her hands, she tried forcing the blood back into them and then dove back into the chaos of her valise.

Turner reached into her valise too, making for a scene that should have been funny at another time. "What in God's name are you looking for?"

"Excuse me Madame?" A soldier dressed in a sharp red tunic and wearing the insignia of an Engineer stopped in front of them. "May I be of assistance? I'm traveling in the company of a medical doctor and you appear to be distressed."

Dear God, she thought, no. What would Turner do now? He was still armed, wasn't he? "Thank you," she replied before Turner could speak. "I have exactly what I need here, if I can just find it." She forced a slight smile. "I'm not very organized you see."

"Perhaps if you had a bit more light?" The soldier looked directly at Turner, unthreatening, while making his offer.

Turner and Lettie exchanged glances. "If you happen to have

something that would suffice? My wife is feeling faint." Turner said, cheerfully. Rudeness would only draw attention. Lettie bit her lip, stifling a response to Turner's matrimonial assumption.

"An American! I can tell by your accent. Well then, you will appreciate this. The most important mechanism for a smoker." The soldier leaned forward and held out a small torch, which when the top was opened, was lit by a spark caused by flint in the cap. The whole thing was the size of the palm of his hand, but very convenient in that it was thin. He leaned over Lettie, effectively blocking Turner from her. "Brevet Major Chard, at your service." Such an introduction was only polite and expected.

"From the Zulu Wars?" she replied, grateful for his presence (as brief as it would be) and she wanted to be as long as possible. Be normal, keep calm. This man was a British hero. She recognized the name: Chard. John Rouse Merriott Chard. She'd read about him when he'd been awarded the Victoria Cross in '79. With Turner's revolver still near to hand, she could say nothing. She couldn't ask him for help. Stay calm.

"Indeed," he replied cheerfully. "This gadget too. Not a great deal to do in Natal. Build bridges, invent handy little things. Try not to be shot ..." He was considerably taller than Turner, but with the same breadth of shoulder and a matching head of brown hair. He was younger perhaps. "I probably shouldn't smoke. It'll be the death of me."

Death. The word reminded Lettie why she couldn't let the conversation continue. Selfish and weak, she had no right to endanger the man. "I believe I've found what I need. Major Chard, this was very kind of you," she lied. Each word was spoken as though it were her last. Turner noticed. For a moment, he started to reach for her arm: to touch it comfortingly?

Chard nodded politely, yet he didn't move. He remained wedged between Turner and Lettie. Turner was no longer easy with the man's presence. It was becoming quite clear that he was interfering with what should have been recognized and understood as the business of a husband and wife. Turner was still armed. Her eyes darted over toward Turner's pocket.

"My colleague, Lieutenant Watson of the Rifles, is a fine physician. I'm certain he would be able to assist you if you are still in need ..."

"Oh no, Major, I assure you all will be just fine." Oh God, he wasn't going away. She never should have spoken to him; it should have been left to Turner to handle. She shot Turner a look which demanded he be patient for just a moment more. Lettie desperately wanted Chard's help, but couldn't bring herself to draw him into her mess.

"Then I will bid you both an excellent afternoon."

Lettie had been holding her breath without realizing it. It slipped out of her lungs in a flash of relief.

Chard hesitated for a moment. "Oh, Doctor, are you able to walk?"

He called her 'Doctor.' She almost jumped from her seat. Turner didn't catch it: Chard knew who she was.

Irritated with the man's continued intrusion, Turner finally stepped in between them. "Of course she is. This was very kind of you, sir." His voice was tempered but still friendly. That wouldn't last long.

"Are you, Doctor, able to run?"

"What?" she said stupidly.

"Would you be so kind as to do so ... now!"

Chard moved shockingly fast, slamming a fist into Turner's chest and catching his leg behind his knees. Turner fell over the leg and rolled away from Chard, only to get back on his feet. Lettie grasped her valise and obediently bolted into the crowd with no idea of what she was doing. On the far side of the corridor, she stopped to see what was happening. This was her fault. Turner was focused on the Major, the crowd was now quite alarmed by the fight breaking out, and one of Turner's men was coming straight for her.

He called her 'Doctor.' He knew who she was?

Turner's man reached for her and she made her decision. Screaming 'thief' as loudly as possible, Lettie threw all her hopes on Britain's national hero and the hope of that Physician friend of Chard's being somewhere near by. If Chard knew of her plight, he was the man who could save Pierce as well. Sir Richard: he must have sent them. The shrill screech kept coming uncontrollably out of her mouth. She had no idea she could produce that horrible noise. As though the shriek took away the fear for a brief second, she stopped. Everything slowed down, giving her brain time to think.

She took a swing with her valise at Turner's man and cried out for help, in English, French and what she hoped was comprehensible Italian. Anger filled the void vacated by fear and she wanted to hit Turner's man as hard as she could. Lettie advanced on him, her cry laden with the fury building up inside her.

He wasn't put off by her attack.

Lettie dropped the valise and pulled a hat pin out of her hair. That stopped him. She pulled the other out to have something in both hands. In the tunnel vision that overwhelmed her, all she could see was the man and every place she could wound him. The man backed up several steps. Her comprehension widened as the threat moved back.

Chard was every bit the soldier, unfazed by his own notoriety but clearly not entirely prepared to play the role of hero in the middle of an Italian railway station. Taking on Turner might not have been wise. Chard was a trained officer of British quality; Turner was brawler in the American style. Turner caught him in the nose almost immediately.

Lettie's scream elicited a response from an Italian father of three, who waved aside his family and rushed to Lettie's aid. His wife was suitably impressed as he tackled Lettie's attacker, shoving him into the ground. So was Lettie.

"Are you alright?" he said in broken English.

"Si. Grazie. I'm fine now."

The crowd, behaving much like a school of terrified fish, bolted en masse. Before she could say more to the heroic father, he and his family were swept up and carried away in the chaos. Turner's man lay on the ground, semiconscious and being tripped over. Her hat was swept away, disappearing into the crowd. At least the father and his family were away from the madness. She was glad for that much. Perhaps she hadn't been so clever after all, but at least she was free to worry about it.

Turner was furious. Lettie was escaping and he had to deal with Chard, who had determined that to survive he had to use pounding force to make up for the lack of boxing skills. This was not going as planned. The remainder of his men descended on Chard, ending the fight abruptly and not allowing either man to have satisfaction in winning. "Don't bother with him!" Turner shouted. Picking up his hat he paused, realizing what had just happened and why. He stood very close to Chard and purposely lowered his voice. "Tell your friend Wickham to stay the hell out of this. We're not interested in buying or selling weapons. There's no money for him here."

"Wickham didn't send us, you bloody jackass. Leave off the lady, do you hear me?"

Us? Turner took two steps back. Chard said 'us.'

Police whistles filled the air and the crowd disbursed into the shadows, including Turner and his men, leaving Chard alone to straighten out his uniform and dignity. His best hope was that the lady had enough time to escape. Providing that time was all that he was asked to do: all that he was allowed to do even though he'd had suggested several options. He was a soldier with horrific experience which might as well be useful to something other than his nightmares. He gathered up her discarded coat, blotted the blood from his nose with a linen handkerchief, and waited while the policemen gained control of the situation.

Turner and his men had vanished into the night - which Chard expected to happen. The best scenario he was told to anticipate was that they would flee; being cowards who would try to accost a woman, but Chard wasn't willing to accept such a simplistic viewpoint. That fellow Turner had a record of bravery and cleverness during the American's war. He would be looking for the woman doctor, not fleeing in fear.

The Police Sergeant, clearly the ranking fellow in charge, began demanding information. Chard didn't speak a word of Italian, but the Sergeant's tone translated just fine.

"He wants to know what happened." A man walked out of the shadows, hurriedly, drawing a cigar out of his pocket. He offered it to Chard: a reward for the hand-to-hand combat he'd been in. A few beads of perspiration on his forehead indicated the man been running, and he very quickly blotted them away with a silk cloth. His face was tight and his eyes narrowed; he kept closing them for a moment perhaps in the hope that when he opened them again things would have changed for the better if not less violent. The thumping in his chest only reminded him that all his efforts had not helped him arrive in time to assist Chard.

Chard didn't bother to look at him, but did accept the cigar. "Would you be so kind as the tell him that it was a mistake and that I don't intend to press any charges should the fellow be found."

"You're assuming that you would be allowed to," the man said in a soft, French accent.

"Armand, just tell him, please."

"Certainly." Monsieur Armand Guy d'Saint-Amand, the Frenchman, spoke to the Sergeant in a proper, gracious way.

The Sergeant scowled at Chard, said something vicious that included a word sounding like 'Englishman.' It was anything but complimentary.

"Would you care for a translation?" the Frenchman asked.

"No, sir, not in particular. Did you find your Doctor Gantry? Please tell me after all this, you did."

The Frenchman shook his head. "No. We were searching for her when we heard the fight break out. I must apologize for not getting here sooner. Of course, we were not able to locate her." He stared at the ground, then up at the sky.

"I warned you. Never underestimate an opponent just because they don't look, act, or talk like you."

"That is generally a British mistake."

"You'll get no argument from me. It's what got us into trouble in Natal." The Major double-checked the neatness of his tunic; he was a British Army officer in public, after all. "Do you still need me? I hope so. I would like to find the lady."

"If you can stay, I would appreciate it. How long before your ship leaves for Singapore?"

"Three days."

"Surely we can find her by then?"

"Trust me, Armand, it's going to be as hard for us as it will be for him to find her. She's smarter than we are; the only thing she lacks is combat experience."

"If I may borrow your statement, Major, you'll have no argument from me. Damn shame he's on the wrong side; I'd prefer he was with us. A master killer, that one. You're lucky." He drew heavily on the cigar he'd lit; then thought as he exhaled, Madame, where did you go? Where can we find you?

Chard was doubtless thinking the same thing.

Chapter 48

May 22, 1883
Bardonecchia Rail Terminus
Italy

When Lettie finally stopped running, she was gasping for air against the tightness of her corset. Her head was throbbing.

Like every rail line, the air smelled of tar, grease, and burned coal. The alley was dark and she wished she could simply blend into the safety of the shadows. She needed to find help. This was not something she could handle on her own, which in itself infuriated her. But now she couldn't focus her mind. The little Italian railhead was awash with odd sounds and sights, none of which offered her a familiar comfort. Despite the heat in her muscles, her hands were freezing cold. Georgie's bracelet bothered her skin. She rested her back and head against wall and listened for anything beyond her own labored breath. How high up was the village? The air was so much thinner at an alpine altitude, making breathing even harder. But, it would be the same for Turner, she thought. Wouldn't it?

Every sound made her jump.

She had to find Major Chard. He would be near where he'd fought with Turner? Maybe? Yet, it was also likely that Turner would be near there too, thinking that Lettie might seek out the only friend she had in the foreign village. She had to be careful. Once with the famous survivor of Roark's Drift from the Zulu wars in Natal, she believed he would know exactly what to do. Save Pierce. It was truly the only thing that mattered.

She found a place that was hidden deeply in the shadows and had a pair of rather large boxes to hide behind. Her body hurt and, every now and then she felt sick. Despite this, she lowered herself down behind the boxes, not caring what horrible thing might be on the ground. It was better than being the man's prisoner. Corseted too tightly, and with so many skirts wrapped around her feet, getting up would be difficult. She prayed her dark clothing and hair would make her disappear amongst the shadows. She had to rest. She had to think. She leaned her head against her valise and rubbed the bumps under her sleeve where Georgie's bracelet was stuffed. It irritated her and made her scratch at it, as though her skin was a hundred times more sensitive than usual. Lettie slid it off, reverently and apologetically as she hadn't meant to blame the object for her discomfort, and placed it in her valise.

Worrying became frantic thinking. Thinking quickly turned into exhausted sleeping. Not a gentle, restful sleep but a fitful, semi lucid dozing that gave peace neither to her body nor her mind. Every noise was filtered through her dazed mind. At one point she thought she heard her name called, but as she woke more fully, the calling stopped.

She knew the train to southern Italy was due in at a particular time. Early morning, a couple more hours. That had not been changed by Turner's actions. Looking at her watch, barely able to see the face, she discovered that it had been four hours since she'd hidden herself. Slowly, and with much effort, she climbed back onto her feet and aimlessly dusted her clothing. She still was having trouble breathing. Lettie waited pressed against the wall, listening. If she could make it to the train ...

The village of Bardonecchia had only one real purpose: to look quaint for all the tourists going in and out of the Frejus Tunnel and to get them onto the correct trains. Now that night had come to the alpine town, and the trains had all departed except one, the place seemed deserted.

Catching her breath, barely, she pushed herself off the wall of the alley and strayed out of the shadows. The rail station was oddly lit by few gas lamps. There was a sensible economy to it; no one was supposed to be there. She listened with hyper-awareness. She could have heard an insect a mile away.

Nothing.

She shouldn't have moved from her hiding place. Of course he'd been waiting for her to make such a careless mistake. Had she not read in novels about such things? Naive. Stupid. The silhouette that raced down the alley after her was definitely Turner, his shoes slapping against the bricks with every step. By height, breadth of shoulders and his distinctive hat, she knew it was Turner. Just how angry would he be? Probably angry enough to shoot her or beat her unconscious this time. Or possibly something worse.

Flushed from her safe place like a pheasant, Lettie clutched her valise and ran, hoping to find someone in the deserted station or another hole to hide in.

It was then that she realized that she'd come full circle. It was a new train that sat in the bizarre gaslight, but the location was the very spot where she'd been forced to disembark. A new train, still waiting, might mean people. She raced toward what appeared to be the first class car; where staff might still be working.

Turner careened into her, hurling both of them to toward the side of the car. At the last second, Turner swung himself between the wooden rail car and her, taking most of the impact. A terrible crash accompanied the strangely chivalrous gesture. Wrapping his arms around her, he cursed, apologized, then cursed again. Lettie was almost limp with exhaustion and cried out when he tightened his grasp around her waist. The sound she made was pathetic. "You stupid woman! Damn it!"

There wasn't any real response to be made. He held her arms and body so firmly that she had to bend at the waist to keep him from shouting in her ear. Her corset made it painful, and there was a strong chance he'd bruised her ribs underneath. He was crushing her. But that wasn't the worst of the impact, which he'd taken. What damage had he suffered? Not enough, the opinion slipped uncontrollably out of her thoughts.

"Goddamn it, if you'd just been a man ..."

Lettie's energy returned and she began to struggle violently. "I'm not a man. Get your hands off of me!" The valise slipped from her fingers as she twisted her body in his arms, ignoring the pain.

"Stop it! Just what the hell will make you calm down?"

"Let go of me for a start." She stopped struggling to see what he would do.

He was breathing so hard, she wondered if he would ever catch his breath. She knew the feeling. It was the altitude or, perhaps, he really was injured. Slowly, he rested his head against the back of her shoulders and she felt him wince.

"That hurt, didn't it," she said, a bit too spitefully. "You don't seem to be doing too well. You're being beaten up by everyone today, aren't you?"

Between gulps for air, Turner laughed. It was the only thing he could think of to do, and in the strangest way - it was funny.

"Including me," she finished. Now he really was laughing, and hating it because it must have hurt to do so. Take the moment woman, use that brain of yours. "Mr. Turner, I believe we need a truce."

"What? Now? When I'm winning?"

"Are you? Imagine what it will be like if I really start fighting you."

Turner stopped laughing. Oh God, she isn't really fighting yet?

"Compare that to a truce. What do you think?"

"I think I should have gone with my original plan: stuffed you in a trunk and shipped you back north."

"You're not going to hurt me. You just proved that. Actions can be louder than words, Mr. Turner. Can we now have a truce?"

"What do I get from this truce, other than a little less trouble? And what do you get?"

"Answers, Mr. Turner. Answers. And neither of us can keep this up."

He suddenly reached out to take hold of her face with one hand, and pulled her head back against his chest. "No, I don't think so." His men had finally found them, and were gathering in on them. Lettie's breath quickened. "Aren't you forgetting Professor Pierce? Save your bargaining for the both of you."

"I haven't forgotten him at all. Now let go of me. I can't out run you and you don't want the grief I can cause. Wouldn't this be much easier if we cooperated?"

It was rather risky of her to make a demand from that position. He could feel her jaw under his fingers, her soft skin that was likely to bruise. But as his ribs and shoulders began to throb, he had to believe that her cooperation was the better choice. Part of him wanted to strangle her.

She could feel him pressed up against her back. He was fatigued, injured, still not breathing calmly. His body shuddered with every breath: yes, he had to have been hurt. "As I said, I have not forgotten him. But I can help Pierce just as easily by screaming and fighting. What that won't get me are the answers I want. Don't doubt me, Mr. Turner. Major Chard may not be that far away, with the police. He and I just might rescue the Professor while you are rotting in prison." Turner's body convulsed at the suggestion, and she couldn't quite stop herself. "Or?"

"Or what," he replied with resignation, knowing what was coming next.

"Or, we can discuss this in rational terms. I should like it very much if you would take your hands off me first. I'm certain you can imagine why."

He waited for a moment, hoping she understood he wasn't caving in to her demands, but that at any moment the balance of control could return to him. The less she could predict his actions, the less sure she would be.

"Truce," she asked again, her voice not quite as confident as it had been?

"Yes, truce - for now."

Slowly, he released her head, then her waist. Lettie knew not to do anything drastic or sudden. She stepped away and turned to face him, hands held unthreateningly in front of her.

"So, ask your questions." Out of reflex, he reached out to hold her by her arm when she moved too far. Not nearly so tightly as before but quite firmly. Turner bent over and picked up her valise. His face screwed up as his ribs burned under his skin and he released her, holding his arm across his chest.

She didn't react or attempt to take advantage, which was too strange to ignore. She was staring at something behind him. His men were staring too.

Ah, damn it, he thought. If only he hadn't placed all his attention on her. He was getting slipshod in his old age. "Care to tell me who's behind me," he asked, hoping she might say something. When she didn't immediately answer, he took her by the wrist and began pulling her closer.

"Be so kind as to keep your hands where they can be seen?"

Turner stopped abruptly, his blue eyes wide. He jerked his body in reaction to feeling something pushed into his shoulders from behind.

"And I'll thank you to release the woman." As Turner hesitated, the voice grew more determined. "Now, sir, remove your hands from her. And set down the valise."

Reluctantly, Turner let go of her arm and followed her stare back to a tall man standing close behind him. Elegantly dressed, the man was a perfect image of a gentleman, except …

"Mr. Wickham?" she exclaimed.

… except for that dreadful head of over-greased hair.

With an expression of annoyance at first, Turner finally looked at her in an almost apologetic way. If she saw his expression, he didn't know, because she was ignoring him completely and glaring now at Wickham. Apparently, she wasn't too fond of him either.

Men dressed as porters and baggage handlers descended on the group. One stood guard near Lettie, while others took her belongings from Turner's men and carried them away. When Lettie began to protest her guard grasped her upper arm viciously and yanked her closer to him. She turned on the man with a furious glare and wrenched her arm free. The expression of triumph on her face vanished as the guard seized both of her arms and pinned her between them.

"Mr. Wickham, this is unnecessary. Mr. Turner was ..."

"Do shut up, Miss Gantry."

Turner smiled. "Quite a gent, aren't you? Wickham? Sounds like something from an Austen novel. Somehow you just don't look the way I pictured you." Slowly, compliantly, Turner set down the valise. Each movement was designed to cover his observation and calculations. He needed time to think. Something was wrong. This was not a rescue of Dr. Gantry.

Wickham was staring at Lettie and his revolver was pointed callously in her direction. She didn't appear to understand yet, but Turner knew this was not the stance of a man intent on gallantly saving a lady. Wickham was angry with her: frustrated, it showed all over his face in deepening furrows. His eyes began darting back and forth between Lettie and Turner. Turner realized then that Wickham had not counted on his presence. That meant no contingency plan was in place to account for the dramatic change in situation. Too many unknown players. Wickham would be off balance, but not for very long.

Turner himself had counted on little interference in the matter, but had the advantage that Chard's earlier rescue attempt had forced him to consider several new options. He was, at least for the moment, ahead of Wickham.

Wickham's face hardened into a satisfied expression as though he'd finally pieced everything together. "I'll be damned. You're the Yank. Turner, isn't it? Now why in the world are you here? Certainly not to play a trumpet or to plant flags." The revolver was now pointed at Turner. "Robur must want her more than I thought. I'm afraid I can't let him have her." He gestured casually in her direction. "She is part of a bigger problem, one which I hope to resolve."

He's quick, Turner thought. His chest tightened as he repeated Wickham's statement in his head: 'You're the Yank.' He hadn't thought himself known at all. And Wickham knew about Robur. It was that damn urge of Robur's to shoot down the *Go Ahead*: to get even with the Weldon Institute. They'd been too public.

He forced his smile to stay in place. No sense in giving Wickham signs of weakness or frustration. "Well, now that we've met maybe we can resolve this problem together?" Think fast, Tom.

"It is an intriguing situation. You see, now that I know who you are."

"I doubt that, but you were heading somewhere with that comment." Turner kept his hands away from his body, in an unthreatening gesture. He moved a slow step away from Lettie, curious to see how Wickham would react. The muzzle followed after Turner. That was important to know.

"I wonder just how much knowledge you have. You must be privy to any number of ... of interesting designs. This is a bonus, you see. You might well be more valuable than she is."

"She's worth a hell of a lot more than all of us." The words came out before he could think them through. The threat had scared him; thrown him off balance. His first reaction was to protect the lady. Wickham recognized the weakness. Turner bit the inside of his lip and forced the smile back onto his lips. He looked over his shoulder at her. "I don't think you're being rescued, Doctor Gantry." Good. Give her a reason to escape. He could catch her later. The further away she was, the freer he would be to deal with Wickham.

"No, Miss Gantry, this is not a typical rescue, but then you're hardly the helpless damsel in one of those books of yours. I have to admit, with some reluctance, that I didn't think you capable of the things you've done so far. But if you need my assurance," he said barely glancing at her, "I am not interested in harming you." There was no sincerity in his voice. Nothing, except, perhaps, a film of annoyance over his words. He held out his unarmed hand, signaling for her to come toward him.

Her guard began pushing her in that direction. She looked to Turner, which surprised him. Was she looking to him for help? Did she understand what was happening?

"See here, Turner? Maybe I'll keep both of you."

Turner took another step away from Lettie and Wickham reacted by closing the distance. If he could draw Wickham in, he knew he could get control over the weapon and the situation. He didn't look at the gun but instead stared back at Wickham. To look now would telegraph his intent. "I don't know as much as you seem to think. I'm just an honest sailor, that's all." Come in closer, he prayed. Just a little closer. Almost there

...

"Then perhaps I shouldn't keep you. If you're not valuable."

As far as Lettie was concerned, it was obvious: Wickham was going to kill Turner. No other outcome was possible in her mind. Why it mattered if Turner lived or died, she didn't have time to consider. Someone had to make a decision: to keep everyone alive. "Gentlemen! Please." She swallowed too much air; it actually hurt her throat. "Mr. Wickham, are you going to shoot us," she asked blatantly. "I think not. You would have by now if you were planning on it."

"Plans change," he replied, too coolly. "You're safe with me, Miss Gantry; you have my assurance, now, go inside the car. I've arranged for this entire train to be private; you will be safe."

"No." Lettie twisted her arm free and stepped between Turner and Wickham. Wickham moved several paces back before she could accidentally blunder into the gun itself. He turned the muzzle away from her.

Turner misinterpreted the gesture, thrust his arm in front of her and forced her behind him. "Damn it, stay behind me!"

Wickham stuck out his hand toward her but kept the revolver down at his side. "Miss Gantry, come here."

She stayed in place.

Purposely, and somewhat dramatically, Wickham released the hammer to show his good faith. The grip on the weapon caused his knuckles to be white.

She still didn't move. "He's going to kill you, isn't he," she said, half under her breath, to the back of Turner's head.

Turner didn't reply.

He glanced over his shoulder to satisfy himself that Lettie was still behind him. "Don't be an ass, Wickham, if you shoot me now, you'll shoot her. Then you'll have nothing. Put that thing away. You want to talk; then let's talk." He could feel where she was. "You want to discuss inventions? Fine. Why don't we let her go over there," he said, cautiously pointing away from the railcar. "Doctor Gantry, would you please go over to that bench?" He could hear the urgency in his own voice.

"No. I think you should go inside, Miss Gantry. It's much more comfortable in there."

Turner looked back at her. She didn't understand: she didn't have all

260

the facts. The sooner he got her out of the way, the more quickly he could reassess the deteriorating situation. Damn it, if only she'd been a man. He wouldn't feel so goddamned protective. But that wasn't entirely fair; beyond her were the men he'd hired, in no safer position than he was. This was his doing. He had to make it right. He had to figure out his next move, with all of them in mind. "He's right. Doctor, you should go in."

She looked confused. She was surprisingly rational for a woman and right now none of that logic was applicable. She was lost and completely unprepared for this. He tried not to laugh: who would be prepared for this sort of thing?

"Doctor, please. Mr. Wickham and I will talk this out."

"Yes, Miss Gantry, he and I will talk. You needn't upset yourself, we can take care of this."

She started to move out from behind Turner. "You're both liars." She understood far more than they expected. But what could she do? They were the men, they made decisions, they would handle this for her, just as men had handled things for her before. The thought made her feel ill - weak - worthless.

Nodding reluctantly in agreement, Wickham took a couple of steps back to allow her past him and fully lowered his revolver.

She walked slowly away from them, feeling the failing strength in her legs. She had been dismissed. Sent to go sit.

"Alright Wickham, you said we'd talk." Turner stuck his hands in his pockets with a loud, dramatic sigh of irritation.

"You realize, Turner, I don't have to kill you. I can just wound you. Make certain you don't get away." The three clicks of the hammer were loud.

Lettie had not gone far when she turned back toward them. "No!" she cried.

Turner watched as time slowed down for him. Wickham was turning his head, looking toward Lettie, toward her scream. A perfect distraction. Wickham was reacting to movement like a predator. Turner raised his left hand, dismissing Wickham in a gesture. More distraction. Wickham's eyes and body followed the sweep of Turner's hand. Turner's right hand found and retrieved his gun from deep in his pocket.

Stepping back toward Lettie faster than anyone anticipated, Wickham caught her by her collar, dragged her up against his body and shoved his gun to her head. "Put it down, Turner."

"Christ!" Turner pulled his arm back, pointing the revolver upwards. That backfired. Dear God the man was fast. "Don't be stupid, you need her, remember? You didn't come here to hurt her."

"Not entirely true. I have you, your men, and I know your plans, so I'll soon have your employer. She's probably already done whatever good she was going to."

"Son of a bitch."

Wickham shrugged effortlessly. "I won't be blamed when they find her body. I wasn't the one who forced her off the train. You already garnered witnesses who will attest that it was you trying to abduct her."

Lettie tried to say something, but couldn't make her voice work.

Turner's hands were frozen. It was the Roanoke River swamp, the Landing Party, all over again. He could see her eyes were wide in confusion and fear, just as the Confederate sailor's had been. Turner hesitated. Lettie was another innocent dragged into something she didn't understand and would never really benefit her. The boy in the swamp had died, brutally. He couldn't allow it to happen again, not to Lettie Gantry.

He lowered his gun before Wickham could kill her.

"See, Turner. You just aren't willing to go the distance for your cause. Put the gun on the ground and let's have no more attempts like that one, eh?" As Turner set the revolver down, and held his hands where they could be seen, Wickham pushed Lettie away from him, with some disgust. Well, she'd finally been useful.

Strange, staring at her from behind a flash of memory shot through his head, reminding him of his wife. He mentally shoved the thought away. She was not his wife!

Lettie stood stoically, brushing off Wickham's touch on her clothing and shoving away the feeling left by the muzzle of his gun. "Coward."

Wickham actually looked shocked for a moment. A man's wife shouldn't … he stopped the thought. Gantry shouldn't have called him that. Unable to lash out directly at Lettie, he turned his indignation on Turner. "I'm not the coward here, am I Turner? Your Captain should never have sent you after a woman. They're liabilities, you know."

Turner appeared to agree, if for no other proof than that he smiled lopsidedly and waited, allowing the sailors to swoop down around him. Wickham motioned for the entire party to board the waiting train; where discussions presumably would take place. For his part, Turner made absolutely no effort to escape. He smiled that clever, purposeful, knowing smile as he was directed away from Lettie.

Turner's men were led to a cargo car at the back of the train, herded in, and locked inside. They made no attempt to escape or struggle, either. Wickham uncocked the gun again and handed it to one of his own men. Such an item carried on his own person would cause a flaw in the appearance of his suit. He didn't know what to make of it all yet and simply shook his head in disapproval as Turner was diverted into the private Pullman car. "A weak man ..."

Lettie slapped him, hard. The blow to Wickham's face made such a loud noise that actually produced an echo.

Chapter 49

Turner stopped at the entrance to the rail car to look to where the sound came from before being forced inside.

Lettie had never felt anything so powerful, yet terrible. The energy to physically strike someone was unknown to her. It had come without warning from deep inside her stomach, up through her chest, and had blasted out through her hand. Now she was shaking, disbelieving that she'd been capable of violence and proud that she could.

She wanted to feel that sensation again. She wanted to do it again, now that she could. Now that the taboo of restraint was gone.

Wickham rubbed his sore cheek, adjusted the curl of his pathetic moustache as if the worst thing she'd done was to ruin its waxed shape, and stepped back from her indignantly. "Miss Gantry? I'm here to rescue you, whether you like my methods or not."

"Oh really? Are you? Imagine how I might not see it that way?"

"I assure you, we are."

"Why should I believe you? Besides threatening to kill me, you're holding me against my will - he and a man he claimed as his employer," she said staring directly into Wickham's hazel eyes, "are trying to abduct me. You knew this was going to happen and you let it. I think you would have shot him in spite of the danger to me or to anyone else here... Neither of you is honorable? What man holds a gun to a woman's head? Hostage takers are cowards."

"That's nonsense. It was a bluff as your American father might call it."

"A bluff? Is that what you call that? A bluff?"

"It worked," Wickham said as though the point were obvious.

"Have any of you even bothered to ask me what I should like? Such as not having a gun pointed at my head, bluff or otherwise?"

Wickham rubbed his cheek again, it was still quite sore, and accidentally smudged some of the colored moustache wax. "It is for your own good. Stop acting like a child. I know what is best for you right now." He moved his jaw back and forth. "I'll take that for you," he said reaching for her valise.

She couldn't stop herself. She didn't want to stop herself. Shaking, on the verge of screaming, she focused all that energy into slapping him again. It was closer to punching him this time. Several men around them stopped and stared. The violence felt curiously delicious. And, in that moment she felt a strange mix of shame and exhilaration and justification.

Wickham grabbed her by the wrist and shoved her into the rail car. "Don't do that again, Miss Gantry." His voice was very low and harsh. "I've been known to hit back. This is for your own bloody damned protection and certainly my own satisfaction. Call it whatever you like. The last thing I want is annoyance from you. Sit where you are told to, keep quiet, and we'll get you back to England where you belong."

Unable to hit him, burning with violent energy, she lashed out verbally. "Don't you dare tell me what you've decided is best for me. If you have a good reason for me to not go to the Indies, then tell me. You should have told me about this in the first place. I will assess what you have to say as it best applies to me. I'm a scientist."

"No. You're a foolish little spinster who reads too many romances and thinks the world is full of knights and princes. Honor, my dear, is not something one finds in a book. A man spends his whole life defining it … "

Her eyes narrowed, with satisfaction. He'd made a mistake in thinking such an insult would make her hysterical or weak, certainly not if she'd remained relatively composed through everything that had happened. "Let go of me." She spoke the words quietly; her voice dropped in tone as well. Honor: that bothered him when she questioned it.

"No. I don't think so."

Her voice lowered more. "Then you're no better than Mr. Turner. You are certainly no gentleman; and no man of honor … however you define it. You aren't much of a man."

The sides of his mouth fell into a deep frown. Her declaration clearly bothered him. It was the second time she'd questioned his honor and the second time it disturbed him more than he thought possible. They stared at one another and something in the way her face tightened and the color of her skin deepened in the night reminded him of his dead wife.

She looked too much like his wife. She reminded him of things he'd lost. Damn her, she'd hit a sore on his psyche. "That may be true. Simple good versus bad, it's never so obvious, is it my dear?"

"Is that why you feel nothing in making decisions on my behalf or holding a man prisoner? Or killing? Do you even care about that?"

"What man? Turner? Why should you care about Turner, he's a barbaric American. Nothing but a member of the criminal class ..."

"I'm talking about Professor Pierce."

His eyes widened. "Turner told you where Pierce is being held, didn't he? I knew it." He pulled her hand forcing her to stand closer to him. "Where? Goddamn it woman, what were you told!"

She thought for a moment, while letting Wickham continue grasping her hand. Why didn't he know? It was a long time before her curiosity overwhelmed her anger. "Mr. Turner only said they'd hurt Professor Pierce if I didn't go quietly. Not in those exact words but the threat was clear enough. I'm getting used to that, you know. I can only imagine what any of you want with him, or me. For a while I thought you were the employer he kept referring to."

"Miss Gantry, you clearly don't know me, or you'd know that I would never hire a man like Turner to do what I am perfectly willing and capable of doing myself."

"No, you'd only cower behind a woman."

His facial muscles twitched and his shoulders tightened toward his neck. "You must tell me everything you know, every detail, every word." He pushed her back into the rail car. "Now!"

"And will you tell me what is going on?" she hissed back at him, trying not to show the pain he was inflicting on her.

"The less you know the better. It's for your own good."

"You keep saying that, but only a decent man would mean it." She noted with great satisfaction the sting her words caused him; it showed in his expression and the tightness in his body. It was terrible and wrong, but she liked the power she held over his reactions. She liked it. And he deserved it; he was hurting her. "Besides, I'd hardly call that a conversation."

"With everything that may be at stake, the last thing I want is a conversation. Another time perhaps, but not now. You can't comprehend ..."

She tried to pull her hand free. "Then tell me or are you afraid I might understand and prove you wrong." As his face twitched again, she kept going. "You are certainly afraid of being wrong, aren't you? Coward."

Both Wickham and Lettie contemplated what to say next when a third man walked up to them both. "Perhaps, Mr. Wickham, you should tell her everything and allow her to draw her own conclusions. You're not going to win this unless you intend to beat her into submission. She is a scientist, or so she claims. I recommend her monograph on volcanic ash if you wish to assess her capabilities of logical deduction; I found it interesting if limited in scope. You might also let go of her, I believe you are injuring her in earnest."

"Sir ..."

"I insist!" his voice echoed under the awning. The man was agitated, his voice clipped, as though unused to being questioned. "You are a man of Europe, of an Empire ... so-called civilization. And, of wealth. For you, making decisions for others seems to be a natural extension of your own perceived superiority. But for the rest of us, it is not so acceptable."

Whether or not Lettie's actual opinion played into his argument was doubtful, but it was clear that there was a burgeoning disagreement between the two men. The anger ... no, rage ... lay barely concealed and contained. She could see his lips were pursed, his hands clenched, and his neck muscles tight. His eyes flashed with a brutal contempt and focus toward Wickham that left Lettie with the distinct impression that to this man she was only a part of his argument, an example, and not an actual person. She was a convenient excuse for his angry outburst.

Wickham thought for a moment, then bowed over the hand he was grasping in an attempt to preserve his diminished status as a gentleman and let it drop. Stepping aside, he checked his watch and made some under-breath comment about too little time for this nonsense. Habitually, he smoothed the wax on his moustache, either much too aware of his appearance or due to a nervous gesture he'd never admit knowledge of.

The third man came forward. To say he was remarkable would be an understatement or so Lettie thought. In his late sixties she gauged, and by no means frail or aged, the man carried himself with royal dignity. His clothes, those of a merchant ship's master, were clearly a disguise. Underneath the dark blue woolen coat and captain's cap was a man of Indian descent. A silk scarf was wrapped and knotted stylishly around his throat, as though even in disguise he could not be common; his hands now unclenched were elegant; his black eyes were surrounded by weather formed wrinkles; and his thick, neatly sculpted beard had many bright white hairs. His moustache was waxed and curled in the fashion popular and competitive amongst Indian men of stature, and a far cry more impressive than Wickham's. His very presence was regal and powerful. Age had not stooped his shoulders nor bent his back. He was, in the simplest terms, quite beautiful ... and terrible. He didn't seem to blink often and his expression was hard.

After a moment of staring between them, the man nodded in a respectful but not subordinated way. Lettie couldn't help herself, she actually demurred slightly. It might well have been the burning flush in her cheeks or the suddenly absurd application of proper manners in such a situation as they found themselves, but the man allowed the very slightest upward curve in his mouth. From Lettie's perspective, she felt at last that he saw her as a human being.

Wickham stood between them, straightening himself up to his full height as though that was all he had to compete with. He clearly felt compelled to be formal. Forced. "Sir, if I may introduce you?" When the Indian nodded his approval, Wickham continued quite formally. "Your Highness, may I present Miss Gantry. Miss Gantry, I present Prince Dakkar."

"I know you?" she said, almost to herself.

"Madame?" The Prince raised an eyebrow, but otherwise did not change his neutral expression out of habit.

Wickham's annoyance was quick. "Miss Gantry, I must ask you not to form any opinions based solely on speculations about His Highness made by journalists and inaccurate biographers. You really must improve your reading material."

The Prince allowed a wry smile to form on his lips, turning the curled moustache ends upwards. "Mr. Wickham, I do not believe Miss Gantry is referring to ... my other career." As she continued to look at him, confused, he added, "I have called myself Nemo, in many years past. It was appropriate at the time to be no one and nothing, yet more. Times have changed, and so have I. It is no longer useful to me to be known by only that name."

Lettie's confusion dampened her anger and, in a discouraged voice said, "I don't understand. I honestly think we've met. As inappropriate as this may be for me to say, it is your eyes, sir."

"We have not met. But I need ..." he paused for a moment to force his words past every opinion that they were distasteful, "your help, finding my 'eyes.' I believe you have seen them." He hesitated for a moment, thinking what might be the next correct behavior of a man toward an Englishwoman. It was an interaction he did not necessarily wish but time had forced him to be more practical about his dealings with the outer, terrestrial world. This was not his place in the universe. There were so many protocols to be observed. Finally, he decided simply to offer his arm, hoping to elicit her confidence. It was not a gesture that came naturally to him, but he wanted something of her and was not above manipulation for the greater goal. As few times as he had dealt with women, a Prince did not offer to be touched or to touch – outside of an intimate setting. But Europeans had the cultural habit of touching each other's arms or hands. To them, it was a well-mannered act. For a moment, he could allow the situation to progress as is. The gesture was stiff. Her touch should have been unclean to him, but he had to remind himself that she was only doing what she'd been conditioned to do. It would also, perhaps soften the situation. He'd not seen everything, but suspected by the interaction between Wickham and Lettie that things were not going well.

Lettie took his arm, uncertain she believed that any of this was happening. It was too contrived.

"Allow me, Miss ..." he hesitated again, "... Doctor Gantry, is it not? Allow me to explain the unique circumstances we both find ourselves in. This will, perhaps, relieve you of any concern. I hope in fact it will encourage your willing assistance." He leaned closer and lowered his voice, another tactic used between Europeans when colluding with one another. "If you will excuse Mr. Wickham, I understand him to be very passionate about his work and used to giving commands. This too you may find as one of my failings. I ..." He had trouble forming the words. It had never been in his nature to request assistance or to admit weakness. But he was on land, and here he was only an exotic foreign prince with no real nation or desire to remain land-bound. "You know of a young man, an academic and inventor, named Rajiv?" He got to the point.

"Yes, I do."

"Your Highness," Wickham intervened, again checking his watch. "Time for pleasant explanations is not a luxury we have. She says Rajiv is being held and in immediate danger."

Nemo stopped and harshly turned her to face him. He was considerably taller and stronger than most men, though of a similar stature as Christopher Moore. "Tell me." His voice was so demanding and bereaved that she couldn't keep anything from him. "Mr. Wickham is correct. I was told by that man, Turner," she indicated the car Turner was taken to, "that Professor Pierce," she watched Nemo wince at the name, "is being forced to work on an invention … possibly mine. He is under extreme duress, as I understood Mr. Turner. He meant to use the Professor as leverage against me. And, I admit that his plan was working. He indicated that Professor Pierce was not holding up well in captivity."

"Where!" Nemo held her by both shoulders, all decorum gone. "Where did he say my nephew is being held?"

"I don't know. He didn't tell me where. He spoke only of returning with me to Holland and I believe I was to be kept there for a time. I'm under the assumption that Holland is where the Professor is."

She grasped his forearm for a moment. "Your nephew? Did you say …?"

Nemo pulled his arm free of her, shot Wickham a hateful look and marched directly toward the train. Halfway there, Nemo drew out a small fisherman's knife, typical of sailors and perfect in size to be kept handy. Lettie and Wickham assumed the same thing and ran after him, begging him to wait.

Chapter 50

May 22, 1883
Bardonecchia Rail Terminus
Italy

On board the train, Turner glanced up from where he had been forced to sit, as Nemo stormed into the car. "Where is Rajiv?"

"Captain Nemo, wait," Lettie called from the door. It was the only name she could remember to call him.

"You're Nemo? My God, I've read about you." Turner kept staring, almost uncontrollably. Nemo's face ... his hands ... the demeanor ... everything. Turner shook off a frightening notion he'd seen the man before, and the confusion of not remembering where that had been.

Nemo stopped, knife still in his hand.

Turner looked at it, then up at the Mariner. "Ah, there's no need for that." Then he nodded toward the doorway. "Doctor Gantry, I think you shouldn't be here?"

Nemo swallowed, glared back at the astonished lady, and then turned back to Turner. His face was deepening with a rush of blood, but the woman was there and he couldn't do what he wanted. "Where is the Professor?"

"Professor Pierce?" Turner watched Nemo's face tighten. That made no sense: why would a man made famous by a work of fiction be interested in an inventor his employer just happened to have ... Turner must have had a stunned look on his face.

"Where is he?" Nemo's grasp on the knife whitened his knuckles and his unblinking eyes indicated a man just angry enough to use it.

Turner had to think fast. He glanced up to the left, thought for a moment, then replied, "I wasn't told exactly where Pierce is being kept, only where to go once I'd obtained Doctor Gantry. No threats will get you information I don't have." A lie.

Wickham stepped forward. "Mr. Turner. We, none of us, are interested in games. Where were you talking Miss Gantry?"

"Holland. I'm supposed to take her up to the Port of Rotterdam, to a hotel there." Turner glanced up toward the ceiling for a second.

"Anyway, I was to wait there in Doctor Gantry's lovely company until provided new instructions. My guess was that the plan for us was to go by sea to just about anywhere, but I wouldn't know that until we checked in at Rotterdam. I doubt my employer was planning to come there himself." He had to protect Robur.

Lettie waited for a moment, to see what else might be said. "He's lying." All eyes turned toward her. Her hands were no longer shaking and her voice was very flat. Now, she was in her element. "I am not perfect in my every analysis, God knows, but I remain a good observer of people's behavior. And he is lying. Or he has been given a lie to tell and is aware that it is a lie." When all were waiting on her to explain, she lifted her chin. "It's an understood fact that when one is remembering a truth, their eyes often look right. However, when one is imagining or making something up, the eyes go left. No one really knows why, but it remains a proven statistic. You looked to the left, Mr. Turner. Not at anyone or anything, just to the left."

Well, wasn't that a twist? He'd have to be more careful around her. And he'd have to remember that little statistic, it could prove useful. "The little lady is brighter than all the learned men around her. Rather what I expected. I hope you'll take that as a compliment, ma'am. It was intended as one. I don't know what he has in mind, but that was what I was told to tell you."

"Why wouldn't he tell you what he planned," she asked.

This time Wickham's hands clenched into fists, but the rest of him remained cool and calm. "Because of this very circumstance: in case his American employee couldn't handle one little woman." These games would cost precious time. Too much time. He shook his right hand to loosen it and used it to check his watch. A comforting habit.

Lettie bit the inside of her lip at being called a little woman. For an odd moment, she felt sympathy with Turner, for she was quite certain that Turner had not taken the insult well. But her assessment of Turner was that he could be far more devious than Wickham. She noted that Turner maintained a neutral expression.

"Will your employer trade you for my nephew?"

The look of shock on Turner's face said far more than he would have liked. "Nephew?"

Nemo continued, "Will your employer trade you for the ... the Professor?"

Turner barked out a laugh. "No."

"Then why keep you alive?" Nemo spat out at him.

"Maybe because there's a lady in the room?"

Lettie thought for a moment then whispered to Wickham. "He said he was taking me to Holland. Lying or not, perhaps we should start there."

Wickham nodded reluctantly. "I'll get you on board the next train for Paris. The sooner you are ensconced in a safe hotel ..."

"No, sir, you will not! You've involved me too far in this mess. The decision is no longer yours to make, it is mine. I have been used throughout and I intend upon seeing it to the end. That employer of Mr. Turner is holding my colleague hostage and possibly forcing him to work on an invention of mine ... if he is to be at all believed regarding the Professor."

"I am, this time." Turner added, having listened in.

"And I would imagine that if I am not present in Holland, his employer, who is no doubt watching for us, will suspect danger and not show himself. One need not be an expert in kidnappings to know that the same applies to Mr. Turner. He must be there, as must I."

Nemo tensed. "I will not use a woman as a decoy."

Wickham attempted to cool his temper. "But I will, if Miss Gantry is cooperative. For the Professor's sake, I assume you will?"

"How kind of you to ask this time. Yes," Lettie said before really thinking through what she'd agreed to. She didn't want to think about it too much for fear of panic. "Perhaps this is easier resolved than you think." Before Wickham could comment, she turned to Nemo, speaking to the Mariner with a gentle reverence. "Sir, I believe cold logic will serve each of us best in this situation. Would you allow me to talk to Mr. Turner?"

Wickham tensed and dearly wished to lash out at her with either a cutting phrase or a bruising blow from the back of his hand. How dare she dismiss his presence? He forced his way back into the conversation. "I'll consider that," he replied before Nemo could answer. He didn't sound as though he expected to decide in her favor. "Captain, Miss Gantry, I wish to speak to you both, if you please, outside." He turned to Nemo, waiting to see if the Mariner was willing to acquiesce to his request. "Sir, if you please." It was disgusting to have to kowtow to the old Wog but necessary. Machine. Be a machine, he reminded himself.

Machines do not react emotionally, and following that line of logic, they do not make mistakes. No, he would not allow either that uppity Bitch or the old "Wog" to hold sway over him through his useless emotions. His face began to drain of the flushed color.

Nemo backed away from Turner, deliberately staring at him until he was close to the door. If this caused Turner any distress, he did not show it. In fact, despite the circumstances, Turner appeared amused.

Outside the train car, Wickham offered a hand reflexively to Lettie as she climbed down the steps, which she did not accept, sweeping past him and raking his ankles with her skirt hem.

Nemo was in the process of reining in his anger when she walked up to him. She desperately wanted to rest her hand on his shoulder as a gesture of kindness, but he was so far above her station in life - or too far beneath it - she wasn't sure. Prince or Sailor, Madman or Murderer, she wasn't certain which persona he preferred, or if perhaps he was uncomfortable with all of them. Her mind raced through the pages of the Verne biography, hoping to remember what she'd read. "Sir, is Rajiv Pierce really your nephew?"

"Yes. He is my nephew. He, and his cousin, and his mother ... all gone, or so I thought until I learned of him through his lectures and through Pierre Hetzel. Now I know that he was taken from my family, not dead."

"I have made the acquaintance of Sir Richard Pierce and, by his reputation alone, I know that he would never steal a child from his family. He shared with me some of Rajiv's history. He had no idea that Rajiv's family existed anymore. I can say that Sir Richard has been very kind to him, very loving. In fact, he was greatly distressed over the Professor's disappearance."

Stifling a laugh, the Mariner shook his head. "If Rajiv had not been taken from me, my little prince would be dead like his mother and - my own son. That is the logical truth. No, I do not blame the man for saving a child. Despite my usual opinions regarding the English to the contrary, I think I admire him for such an act of compassion. It is rare in humanity."

Wickham actually wasn't happy to intrude, but intrude he did. "Miss Gantry, do you think Turner will tell you what he will not tell either of us," he said, indicating Nemo, who was still holding the knife.

"Doctor Gantry," she corrected him. If they were going to work together then he would need to recognize her twelve years of brutally hard academic work and social upending. "And yes. He will tell me the same truths and lies that he's planning to tell you. But he may give away information, by reactions or even outright admissions, that he will feel he can get away with - with a woman." She waited to see what Wickham was thinking. His face gave away nothing. "I am a fairly good observer; let me do what I do best. Let me observe Mr. Turner. Even knowing that little statistic about looking left or right, one cannot help themselves or entirely prevent it. That is only one way I can read most people." She narrowed her eyes at Wickham and let the remark stir whatever concern it might in Wickham.

He continued to hide his feelings.

A machine.

Chapter 51

Her hands went cold and her chest shivered with each heart beat. For a long time there was nothing in her vision except Turner and the man beating him. No sounds, no peripheral objects, no depth: a tunnel-like effect.

There were things that were unfit for a lady and she'd never known them before this. She had been protected. Now she couldn't find enough breath to speak. These were things she should never have seen in her life.

In the brief time she had been in conversation with Nemo and Wickham, Turner had been handcuffed in a painful position, with his hands caught high up behind him and the swivel of the cuffs hooked into the highest notches in the tall, carved chair back by his guards. He was forced to lean forward with his hands pulled unnaturally upward. It exposed his neck and she could see the scar from the back. A dreadful inverted 'V' partially disappearing into his hairline. His lip was cut and bleeding, and his left cheek was swollen.

Turner was apparently made of stern stuff. He spit blood on the floor from a pool that had filled in his mouth, unaware that Lettie had returned. Wickham's men had looked startled when she walked back in and gasped loudly. For a long time everyone stared at one another.

The tunnel effect began to wane. "Get out." Her voice was cold and sharp; caught up in her breath. "Now!"

Wickham stepped into the room behind her and, with a sigh of exasperation, rolled his eyes. His hirelings had taken it upon themselves to question Turner. Less than being annoyed by the sloppy and unlikely success of their effort, he was infuriated by the fact he'd been denied the pleasure of doing it himself.

"Mr. Wickham, neither you nor your employees are necessary at this time." She stood stiffly, shaking with every breath. The explicative that waited to be said would do nothing by coming out of her mouth. She'd be ashamed for saying it and for letting Wickham drive her to forget herself.

At first she refused to look at him. "Did you hear me," adding slowly, "sir? You are not needed."

How dare she dismiss him again? It was a habit she had best not develop, he thought. Wickham was about to protest when he found himself staring down at a very determined woman who didn't blink as she glared into his eyes.

In that moment he was afraid of her.

"Mr. Wickham, leave. Additionally, I require that you give me your word, as a gentleman - and if not as a gentleman then as a man if you can manage it ... that you will never lay a hand on him again, except in defense. That goes for those you employ as well. Your word, sir."

He glared back at her, thinking, you stupid woman, do you really think I'd promise you that? "Except in defense." Fine. He could and did agree to that knowing he would break his word without caring.

Lettie held back the urge to see if she could slap him across his smug face before he left, but reason was catching up with her mouth. She considered herself to be a prisoner, like Turner. If Wickham decided not to allow her pushing or bullying, there was little she could do to prevent him from doing whatever he pleased to her. It was possible that Nemo was the force dampening Wickham's violent behavior. Since the Mariner had arrived, Wickham had been more restrained. That might not last too much longer.

Wickham started to say something, looked uncomfortable and angry, but then walked out of the car.

Turning to face the man who had originally held her captive, Lettie saw a curious expression on his face. He seemed confused. Genuinely, confused. It had to be the injuries he was suffering, she decided.

Turner was uncertain whether she had extracted the promise from Wickham to trick him into trusting her or if she really had saved him from further pain. Either way he was relieved. He let her help him sit in a much more comfortable way, disentangling the handcuffs from the chair. He sat back, licking his injured lip and biting on it slightly, hoping the bleeding had stopped. Watching as she turned a well-upholstered chair toward him, he wondered what she was thinking. "Thank you," was all that he could say.

"I'm hoping that you will tell me what you would have told them, but with far fewer threats."

"You're my interrogator now?"

She didn't like the term very much. Her eyes glanced left and right: anywhere but at Turner. In another circumstance, Lettie would have been thrilled to ride in a private rail car such as this one. The floor was covered in a repeating pattern of red, black and beige geometric patterns. The walls were smooth, polished wood – no doubt expensive. Curtains of velvet matched a pair of stuffed benches. There were in fact three other high backed chairs such as the one Turner was seated on. Lit lamps hung from a decorated ceiling.

Of the train itself, she had not had the opportunity to see it very well. Wickham had said this was his train – or at least one he controlled privately. A locomotive designed to climb the Alps, a fuel bogey, one crew car and two passenger cars. It was Wickham's no matter what and he could treat it as a prison if he wished.

She took a long, deep breath. "Not a role I'm used to playing. This isn't a role you're used to playing either, is it, Mr. Turner? You're not a kidnapper, by trade."

"Not of civilians and certainly not women." He shook his head. "You were supposed to be a man." He was a little amused by it. "That's not an insult I promise."

She dropped into the chair, exhausted.

Low voices drew their attention to the far end of the car. Separated by a sliding door, open at that moment, they looked down into Wickham's 'office.' Set diagonally so that both drawers could open up without taking up the entire width of the car, the office desk was an impressive design of folding writing surface, box drawers, and shelves. An empty Trans Pneumatic Tube 'bullet' sat poking out of a drawer.

Wickham looked down toward the pair. Lettie could only see Nemo's feet protruding into the aisle from the chair he'd chosen.

"I don't have a key for those," she whispered, pointing vaguely in the direction of Turner's hands.

"Thank you all the same."

"Perhaps it's not worthy of your thanks. I simply don't accept such violence."

"Ha," he said, laughing at her. "This from a lady who struck Wickham, twice … twice. Well, I won't complain. Since meeting you, I've taken more damage than I have in a whole lifetime, with one notable exception." His expression changed slightly before he caught it and began purposely smiling for her again. "At least you didn't slap me."

"I did hurt you ..." She couldn't quite finish the sentence. From the other end of the car, both Wickham and Nemo leaned out to where they could see them.

"Yes, you did plenty with that writing desk." He settled himself again, looking for a more comfortable position. "You ... afraid of violence?" His voice was sharply sarcastic.

"You know what I mean, Mr. Turner."

"Yes. You don't want anyone you know or are near to be tortured. That's the real word for it, torture." He leaned forward, lowering his voice. "And I appreciate that fact, believe me. But, people are being tortured all the time, all over this world. Some people call it war and find ways to justify it. It's in the nature of humanity to lash out and pick on the weak or the unwary. You did. You succeeded in hurting Wickham because he never saw that coming. Because he thought you were helpless, he let his guard down and you took advantage."

"It was nothing so calculated," she said defensively and swallowed. "I lost my temper. I behaved inappropriately."

"No, you didn't."

"Excuse me?"

"After everything you've gone through? You reacted as naturally as anyone would. I think I would have been disappointed if you'd just stood there and taken it. You'll excuse my frankness, Ma'am, but I find nothing charming in weakness. There's nothing quite as disgusting as a human doormat."

Her muscles tensed. She was in agreement with him and was hardly happy about it. She began to explore the car again, visually. Something to break the bond growing between them. A smaller desk, not too dissimilar from Wickham's, filled a corner opposite the coal burning stove that heated the entire car. If the train were to derail, the car to overturn, the magnificent Pullman would erupt in flame: this was a liability of the elegant, wood paneled rail cars.

Turner was watching her intently.

She stood up and used the straightening of her skirts to conceal her nervousness. "All the same, I shouldn't have."

"Because you are a lady." He wasn't asking a question of her, he was stating a fact he believed.

"I am a scientist. I have spent my life using reason and ... if you will excuse the term coined by Herbert Spencer should you be of a religious mind ... 'social evolution' to behave in a manner that is better than common. Though I will confess, lately, I haven't done very well." She slowly sat down again. "Mr. Turner, I don't know what questions I'm supposed to ask. This is not in my experience. I don't suppose you would make this easier by simply telling me what you've been instructed to say?"

"No, that would make it too easy. But, we could trade." He smiled slyly, acutely aware of his intention even if she wasn't.

"I don't imagine that I have anything to trade that you should want anymore."

Turner waited and thought for a moment. "Promise me that when we're in Holland and free of Wickham's control, we'll think of something?"

She was very skeptical. "You're counting on something that very likely won't happen. I don't think Mr. Wickham has any intention of letting you go. And I'm not entirely convinced we're headed to Holland."

"We can still trade, you and I. I'm sure you'll have something I want." He allowed the salaciousness to cling to the remark. Now what will you do, Doctor, he thought.

"Excuse me!" She had misunderstood him, as a woman in her predicament might. He was making cruel fun of her. He was a cold man.

Angry and ashamed, she stood up, marched directly to the sliding door, and locked both Wickham and Nemo out of the conversation. The door frame rattled as she slammed it closed too harshly.

That was a reaction worth getting, he mused. What else could he do at that moment? She was only going to blunder her way through an art form of intrigue and intelligence gathering that was better left to experts. "Is that such a difficult request? Or do you really need specifics?"

"You are completely, utterly joking. I daresay you're being cruel. For some odd reason I had expected better from you. I find the humor lacking."

"Not joking in the least." His voice lowered to a softer, gentler tone. He'd succeeded: she was off balance. So much for her logical and observational skills. Now he could tell her anything and she would take it at face value.

Lettie couldn't think of a single thing to say.

"It wasn't very funny, was it? A small joke in a hopeless situation? I apologize."

Lettie blushed deeply and looked away.

They sat in silence as the train began grudgingly pulling away from the station, headed back as though heading toward the tunnel into France. Suddenly, the train stopped, reversed direction, and moved through the village to the Great Turntable. There, the entire length of the train would be turned onto one of the many tracks leading away from the Alps. Lettie became nervous and rushed over to the window. She had hoped to see the Great Turntable in action, but not under such circumstances as she was in.

"We're not going north, Mr. Turner. South?"

"No." He thought for a moment. "My guess is that we're going west. To the French coast. Once we're out of these mountains we can get there very quickly. We're going to the nearest Atlantic coastal town. We'll go by sea from there. It's the wise thing to do. Depending on the weather, it could be faster and won't draw attention." He then said more to himself, "I wonder if the *Nautilus* really exists? And what was that about Nemo's nephew?"

The train jerked violently as it was locked into position on the iron and oak Turntable, and continued the jolting motion as the table was turned meter by meter. The entire table was half the width of a London city block. This was what Bardonecchia provided that no other town could. By choosing Bardonecchia high in the Alps, rail lines could be run in every direction.

Hydraulic compressors positioned in the Roundhouse drove enormous double-action stationary engines, most of which could be seen through open, sliding doors, along with cottage sized boilers that fed them. Clouds of blackened smoke and hissing steam spit out of stacks positioned every nine meters on the Roundhouse roof. The roof itself was covered in a layer of soot that had the appearance of a grotesque snowfall.

The Roundhouse gears in turn pumped pistons whose rods were thicker than a human body, effectively rotating the giant table around until it aligned with the appropriate track. The piston Lettie could see drew back so that more than half of it was exposed, then pushed until its length was nearly hidden under the table. Underneath were receiving gears that locked into place with each stroke of the piston, turning the platform.

The table could rotate a four-passenger car train, complete with locomotive. Every other turntable she had seen could accommodate an engine only.

281

The Turntable stopped. Over in the Roundhouse, the boilers were venting any unused steam while idling, waiting for the next train to be turned.

Lettie hurried back to her chair and she could see that Turner was bracing himself.

Again, the train grudgingly pulled forward. After a few moments, Lettie let go of her grip on the arms of her chair and settled back, quite uncomfortably.

"I have no key for those," she said softly, nodding in the direction of his hands. "I said that already, didn't I?"

"It's no matter. I have been worse off ..." he stopped abruptly, thinking that he'd given away some personal detail. Would it be so bad if she knew about the scar? That would allow two people to know what he'd lived through, one being himself. "It's nothing."

A small clinking noise chimed from over at a cabinet. Lettie followed the sound to a pitcher of water, sitting in a ceramic bowl, likely put there to catch any spillage from the rocking of the train car. Other items were in the small pantry, including several, better used, linen napkins. Steadying herself against the rocking of the train car, she took three napkins, along with the bowl and pitcher, and set them at Turner's feet. Soaking one napkin, she leaned over to press it against his swollen cheek. He was startled by the gesture, but eventually allowed her to continue.

She feels guilty, he thought. Good.

He feels confused, she thought. Good.

"You said your employer was meeting us in Holland. Will Professor Pierce be there?"

"What was that Nemo said about his nephew?"

"Nothing that I clearly understand." Well, that was true; she didn't really understand how her colleague Pierce could be related to a man she'd thought was fictional. "I am at a loss to explain it."

Maybe she didn't know. He'd have to be alert for any more on the subject. Nemo's nephew? That could be more than just a problem. "If you can't answer that, then tell me where did the name Makepeace come from? It's an odd name for a lady."

Lettie sighed. "Must we horse trade for everything?"

"It's a long way to the coast," he exclaimed, as if she didn't understand that there was a considerable amount of time to fill.

She glared at him in annoyance. "It was a name my grandfather used, and I honestly don't want to talk about that. We should stay to the more immediate topic."

"Why?" He almost seemed to laugh at her.

"I'm trying to save your life. Don't you understand that?"

"Maybe I don't want you to," he snapped. He did not need or want her to rescue him.

"Well then, how about my life? Would you mind so terribly if I attempt to stay alive? Will we meet Professor Pierce in Holland?"

Turner watched her growing anxiety and frustration. "Since you answered my question, somewhat, I'll answer yours. Yes, yes, we will."

She replenished the cool water, squeezing the napkin tightly in her hands. The water felt deliciously cool. "Thus, we shouldn't bother looking for him, am I right? Naturally, I think Mr. Wickham will want to look for the Professor all the same."

"Naturally."

She carefully blotted the blood off his lip, and rested the cloth on the cut she was responsible for. Oh God, had she really hit him? Had she done some of this? The split in his skin was deep and red. He had a nice face, one she would have noticed in a crowded room. He closed his eyes as she moved the cool cloth to his cheek. She pushed slightly, causing his chin to lift. Hoping to see how deep the cut was, she found herself looking instead at the old, horrific scar. The tissue had long ago healed, but its scope was terrifing. A thick, dark brown line encircled his throat from under one ear to the other. It arched upwards in the back.

Turner's eyes opened and he instinctively lowered his head. "Please don't." He whispered, without looking at her. Damn it.

Lettie lifted the cloth off of his face. "I thought this would help."

He stumbled on his words, wondering what to say that would give him control of the conversation again. Damn her and damn that scar.

"Why me," she asked?

"Is that your next question?"

She nodded.

"Why volcanoes?"

At least he wasn't asking something disturbingly personal, she thought. "I saw what they can do. As a child, my father took me to the Indies, to one of the northern-most islands. We were caught in an eruption. My father was injured and I saw too many people die.

283

Horribly." Lettie abruptly stood up and crossed the room to where her valise had been left. Inside she found the bracelet. Bringing it back to Turner, she held it out for him to see. "This belonged to the man my father was doing business with. His son gave it to me at his funeral. I keep it as a reminder of the horrors we suffer when we ignore facts or remain purposely ignorant." She closed her eyes, remembering. "I want to stop that."

"You can't stop an eruption."

"Of course not. But I can warn people when eruptions are imminent. They can evacuate and survive."

"You really believe you can predict them?"

"Oh yes. And everytime I get distracted or blocked in my work, more people are at risk of dying." She stood up and turned her back on him, fingering Georgie's bracelet. "You really don't understand how selfish these games you and your employer and that Mr. Wickham are playing? Every moment I can't finish my work, time and lives are lost. Don't you see that?" Her voice rose to a high pitch.

"But, we want you to succeed. Don't you understand that?"

"You want to help me?" Her tone was sharply sarcastic and stinging. "For nothing, I presume. No profit."

Turner opened his mouth, but this time had nothing rehearsed or improvised to say.

"I thought so." She finally looked at him again. "How much will you charge a village for evacuation notice? Could you really walk away when they can't afford the information?"

He closed his eyes, coloring slightly. His mouth twitched briefly. "That is not what we have in mind." Opening his eyes to stare at her, he wondered aloud, "what price will you or New College, or the British government place on that information?"

Lettie put the napkin down on the chair. "None. I want this for everyone." Breathing deliberately, slowly, she gathered her thoughts. "Would you really have helped me? What could you possibly do that would make up for all the lost time and research?"

"Everything," he said enthusiastically. He was pleading now, hoping to recover the situation. Turner has hopelessly off-script and she had managed to wreck his original plan. Why couldn't she have been a man? "Doctor Gantry, we are prepared to help you in anyway possible."

"Even if it is my desire to give the prediction model away - to everyone who desires it - no cost involved?"

"Yes." Turner was actually quite pleased to hear her say that.

"Pierce's sampling trolley or whatever it is he's working on for you? Will you let me use it to get my prediction model working?"

"It's partially your invention if I'm not mistaken. It's something Wickham won't let you use or help you with, and you know that."

"The idea has crossed my mind." She seemed to be coming back to her senses. "I'll need space to do my work. Access. Not just any samples. I need first-hand detail. I will need to see it, test it, put it into context of environment."

"Naturally."

"I'll need opportunities to gather that detail, which I assume is the point of your wanting me to go with you. I need unique photographs. An aerial view of craters. Compounding of lava flows..."

Turner said yes, and was about to explain what facilities would be at her disposal, and then he stopped. She had tricked him. He had almost given away too much information too soon. "Brighter than all the men in the room. I did say that earlier, didn't I?"

"You're the only man in the room now," she replied a little too coyly.

"My point - remains unchallenged. Yes, I believe you discussed photography with my employer. Aerial photography."

"And he has designed inventions that challenge the imagination? No wonder Wickham wants him."

"Indeed. Well played, though a bit amateurish. I'm afraid it must be the last time you do that. It's almost not fair. I feel a bit too lightly armed for the battle."

"I'm sorry that I don't know how to play your games properly, Mr. Turner. But if you'd prefer, I can cease my amateur interview and leave it all to Mr. Wickham..."

"You won't do that." Any coy tone to his voice was gone.

"No. You're right; I won't. But Mr. Wickham may just ignore his promise to me about your well-being and extract the rest of your information as he pleases. Don't be stupid, Mr. Turner. And please don't play this game anymore. We're both in too much pain ..." She wrapped a hand around the side of her waist, and felt sore ribs pushing against her corset.

"I hurt you ..." his eyes became wide and in that instant he realized he'd given her another card to play later. He wouldn't have cared it she was a man. Damn her.

Lettie watched him for a moment. "That concerns you?"

"No." he said coldly, looking away from her.

"You're lying again."

"Which of your astonishing skills of observation told you that?" He met her eyes without blinking. "This is a man's game. Tell Wickham that. He shouldn't be hiding behind you."

"He's not."

"This would have been - you should have been a man. You stupid woman, what the hell made you think you belonged here? Men do evil things to each other, and you think you can make it better - with a smile and a volume of meaningless numbers and symbols." His face was quite red now.

Lettie stood up, offended and confused by his sudden anger. "Mr. Turner ..." She hadn't been flirting, really she hadn't. Ladies didn't flirt with strange men. And now he was upset?

"Leave this to the men. Stay out of it. Just stay to what you do well." He stared at different parts of the car, anywhere but at her. "Tell Wickham to go to Holland. That's all he needs to know for now." Turner wouldn't look at her anymore. "And stay the hell away from me. You're bad luck." He bit down on his cut lip, wishing it would bleed again, as if the release of blood would take other pains with it.

Chapter 52

They arrived at the coast two and a half days after leaving the Franco-Italian Alps. From the private rail train – whose ownership was still a curiosity - the group and their goods were bundled into various carriages, carts, and cabs, which took off in different directions. Presumably, this was to confuse anyone who might follow them. Lettie watched as Turner was taken to an enclosed cab, and forced to sit between his two escorts. Throughout, he kept his eyes down, and his mouth tight as though biting the inside of his lip.

Securely ensconced, he then began looking around as surreptitiously as possible, from under his thick brows, and once he spotted the lady doctor, and she him, Turner kept an eye on her until the carriage door was closed. It seemed for a moment that he was actually concerned for her.

Inexplicably, she hoped he was no longer angry with her. She still hadn't figured out what had triggered his outburst.

None of Turner's men were to be seen. They remained on the train and Lettie wondered how they would make it to whatever destination was ahead. If they were to make the journey at all. Would they be killed?

Nemo and his sailors were in a much better mood now that they were nearer the ocean. It had occurred to Lettie that land travel was not a comfortable thing for men used to the sea and their own ship. Nemo did not travel by rail well, and it showed through his royal mask each time the train had to stop for coal, water, or a switch. He gave no other observation nor asked questions, choosing a brooding silence instead.

Wickham, the silent Mariner, and Lettie were then seated in a plain carriage with a pair of semi-matched horses. It was meant to appear uninteresting and likely to belong to a merchant with only so much money to spend on luxuries. A wealthier man would have a fancier rig with matching horses. No doubt Wickham had a set of his own.

The driver quickly whipped the team up to a run, giving Lettie all the more reason to wish they had a better-manufactured transport. Every bump, hole and rock in the road translated into a jarring lurch for the passengers.

Wickham kept an eye on the proceedings through the small, curtained window until they were too far away to see what was happening. Checking his watch several times, he turned his attention to Lettie. Looking over his glasses, he leaned forward to rest his elbows on his knees. "You've had more time to digest your conversation. What else did Turner say?"

"Not a great deal more than I already told you. He wasn't in a very chatty mood two days ago, something I suspect had to do with the beating he received. Nothing has improved over time."

"Not on my orders."

"Pardon me?"

"He was not beaten on my orders." Wickham was irritated by her inference.

"If you say so," she said, not actually believing him. "Mostly he confirmed what I already suspected. I believe without a doubt that this is Robur's doing."

Nemo stirred from his introspection and looked somewhat surprised. "Who or what is Robur, other than the Latin word for 'Oak?'" he asked Wickham.

"A problem."

"A man," Lettie corrected him, harshly, out of exhaustion. "A man you clearly haven't told Captain Nemo about." Her remark caused Nemo to tense. Lettie continued, "A man who has the genius and vision to design an airship. A viable airship."

Wickham barked out a laugh. "A vision only, thank God."

"No, sir, a fact. A design completed and operational." When Wickham stopped laughing, she continued. "I can't guarantee you of it, but the evidence is there."

"Evidence? You mean he's not just starting to build it?"

"Didn't you read about the Weldon Institute?"

"Easily persuaded Americans and sensational journalism."

"You should have believed them. The evidence has been mounting. I believe I saw his ship at least twice, once while I was crossing the Atlantic and once in Paris. Professor Pierce was a witness as well." When neither man commented, Lettie continued. "I believe the Professor is on board Robur's ship. Robur himself offered me passage on it and any assistance I might require in my research. Mr. Turner has reiterated that offer. No, Mr. Wickham, the airship has been built and is in use. I am also of the opinion that it has been for some years."

"Tell me, why didn't you take him up on his initial offer?"

Lettie sat up straight and glared at him. "Because I value my character and could never willingly allow it to be lost as a compromise for a goal that I can well achieve on my own. You may be able to do whatever it is that pleases you but as a woman, I cannot. And I will not!"

"Thus, Turner was sent to abduct you. As you said, you could never risk your reputation or career on willingly setting yourself into Robur's hands." Wickham leaned back, and rubbed the wax of his moustache with his fingers out of habit, neatly smoothing the coated hair into its approved curl. It gave him something to do while he decided what came next. He stared at her for a full minute with an expression that could either be anger or admiration. "Well done," he finally said. "An airship ... a functional airship. Wonderful."

"I believe that we should be aware of the skies above us as well as the terrain. Robur has the advantage of being able to attack us from either the ground or the air."

Wickham nodded in appreciative agreement. "I've considered the place selected for the rendezvous. The whole area is flat, which makes our approach by sea or by land very difficult to hide. Adding now your belief that Robur is capable of striking from above, it makes the area all the more advantageous to him."

"He is able to hide in some sort of cloud, a vapor I believe he is able to create, though I honestly don't know how. If there is enough fog or clouds in Holland, we may not see him at all. And the North Sea is known for its storms and fog."

Nemo shook his head. "There are two very important questions we've not asked ourselves. Why and how? The latter question begs to know how he is able to do any of this. The resources necessary for a heavier-than-air craft are tremendous. Materials, fuel, cost? The effort to conceal such an undertaking in secret is substantial, this I know. And the former question is more philosophical but equally important. Why did he build this airship? Why is he pursuing Miss Gantry and her knowledge of volcanoes? Is there no one else in the field of volcanism more appropriate? Perhaps not, as it would be much less troublesome to abduct a woman foolishly traveling on her own."

"Could a volcano provide anything that he might need?" Wickham asked.

"That is a ridiculous idea," she snapped. Her head still hurt. "Volcanoes are too violent, unknown, unstable ..."

Wickham tilted his head in a knowing way and allowed himself a slight smile. "Unless, of course, you could predict when they happen and how big they might be?"

Lettie's heart pounded. Of course, it made insane sense. "Then you believe that somehow Robur has found a reason to utilize some aspect of volcanism. I don't know what that would be. But, you are correct, if a volcano's behavior is ultimately predictable and proven consistent, as I believe it can be, then whatever resource it provides becomes the more available resource." She began straightening out her skirts in her nervous habit. "That is why I am involved; that's why they have such an interest in my research."

Nemo could hear the disappointment and possible shame in her voice. "Science and discovery have always existed for themselves, but as with all things of value, someone will always desire to use it for profit or gain." The harsh words were well meant, but fell on embarrassed ears.

"My prediction model is entirely imperfect."

"Has it never worked?" Nemo seemed to expect an answer of complete failure.

She shook her head. "It works about half the time. Statistically speaking, I might as well be guessing. I daresay I'd have too large a failure rate."

"Yet, with your Prediction Model in its current state, Robur still stands half a chance of succeeding where he had no chance before. Unlike a geologist, his guesses would not be so well founded." Nemo folded his arms across his chest. "The question of why, continues. Why has he done this? Pure science? Lust?"

Lettie colored deeply and turned to stare out the carriage window. She didn't know. "I have no sense of Robur except from the one time I met him. He is proud, arrogant, brilliant and unaffected by the rules of society."

Wickham leaned heavily on his elbows as the carriage hit a deep rut in the road. "What nationality is Robur? Did he speak with an accent? Did he give you any indication of loyalty to a king or country?"

"He's not doing this out of loyalty to anyone but himself. He plays with people and no monarch or general would put up with that for very long. No, I've not seen a flag or any other indication of nationality. As to race or language, I'm at a loss here as well. He appeared to be European and yet not. He spoke English like an American."

Nemo raised an eyebrow. "Speaking of Americans... what is your take on Mr. Turner's character?"

"Loyal. Brutally loyal. And self limiting. He seems to me to be very intelligent, exceptionally bright, yet he waits for orders and allows another to give him direction. He has very little scientific training but is curious enough to ask and smart enough to understand." Lettie looked up at both men, surprised at a memory. "And he's been traumatized. Something distinct. Time in prison or in a war I think. And, his scar ..."

"But he gave no clear indication of what Robur is up to?" Wickham demanded, taking control of the conversation again.

"None. And other than building the trolley or something, I can't understand why Professor ... Rajiv is involved. He hasn't the slightest knowledge of volcanoes." She smiled at a further memory. "Well, a little, but only what he'd learned from a somewhat outdated book. I was a bit flattered that he'd made the effort so that we could converse on a mutual topic. I didn't have the heart to tell him his information was antiquated."

Nemo smiled then realized he was doing so and immediately settled his expression into his requisite frown. Yes, he had smiled because it was good to hear that Rajiv had a sense of kindness in him. Or, romance? A civilized man needed to marry and reproduce himself. Sadly, Rajiv was a "civilized man" and Nemo was adamant that he had no need - for civilized men or civilization.

Lettie glanced up at Wickham. "How did you know to come to my aid?"

"I became aware of Robur some time ago. The flag planting. The trumpet blowing. Then his attack on the *Go Ahead*. Later, he appeared to be following you, perhaps even studying you. He was seen in London, watching after the Professor too. He is a dangerous man, and clearly we're only just now learning how dangerous he is." He looked at his watch again. "None of this is disturbing you, Miss Gantry?"

"All of this is disturbing me, Mr. Wickham," she snapped.

"Surely you are enjoying the attention and interest?"

Lettie glared at him. "Mr. Wickham, I find this so-called attention quite appalling. And, in some instances, quite insulting."

291

His hazel eyes twinkled a bit as he recognized the discomfort in her response. "Forgive my assumption," he said with absolutely no regret whatsoever.

"You will assume whatever pleases you, Mr. Wickham. I should have hoped that your observations, brief though they are, were more accurate." The tone of her voice changed to aloof superiority. "As a scientist, I find that I must carefully develop and test my hypothesis before declaring a theory or fact. I would recommend to you the same tactic in the future."

Wickham scowled. "How very logical of you."

Nemo shook his head and closed his eyes for what would likely be too long a journey to his ship.

Chapter 53

Lettie was ordered into an oilskin coat, which at first she protested. The texture was odd and it smelled of old fish. The air was warm at the coast and she was already too hot from being trapped in a small carriage with two men and no open windows. She was also too exhausted and irritated to accept orders from anyone, let alone strangers of dubious intent.

Strangers?

Strange men, not of her acquaintance: not properly associated with her.

Her heart began pounding as she was sinking into some sort of abyss, a social abyss, and one she would very likely die in. She pulled the collar of the coat up around her face as if to hide from prying eyes, which of course was foolish, because the likelihood of anyone she knew being in that small Basque fishing town was impossibly small. Nonetheless, she feared it. It was her worst of all terrors bound up in an unending, inescapable series of events now out of her control. If one word of her status as traveling with unfamiliar men, whether compliant or captive, were to reach her colleagues, her character would be ruined. She might as well be dead at that point. Had she not done all in her power to protect herself from such a situation?

No; in full honesty, she had not. If she had meant to be truly circumspect, she would never have left England and the comfort of her father's house. There was no excuse she could use, to explain her actions. She had, by her arrogance to rise above her sex, brought herself to this condition. New College would shun her; the Moores might be forced to choose the loss of a beloved friend rather than be known to associate with a ruined woman; other scientists would only respond politely that her presence on their expeditions was not required. And her father …

Everything she was, that she had so carefully crafted within the strained limits of social acceptability, could be so easily lost. None of the men around her understood that. They would not have to deal with such extreme demands. Even Nemo, if the stories were true, had the freedom to throw every aspect of civilization to the wind and declare it not pertinent to him. Lettie Gantry had to be as Caesar's wife: above reproach. In this respect, she had already failed.

Staring at the tiny boats waiting for them on the precarious, thrashing waves, Lettie allowed the brief thought that dying in the bleak ocean might well be preferable to returning to social destitution - at best, to be buried alive in isolation. The water was rough enough to swamp the boats, leaving her boots soaked and spraying her with thick salt water long before they rounded the seawall that attempted to protect the fishing harbor. One of the sailors in her boat called out to Nemo, pointed toward a place ahead of them, speaking in that strange language she couldn't understand. She watched as Nemo, in his boat, sat up taller and nodded in acceptance of the notification.

At first, all that could be seen of their destination was a bright luminescent glow sitting steadily in place, unmoved by the waves. As the small, tightly clustered boats approached the light, it became obvious that the green phosphorescence was the result of two artificially lit windows, locked in riveted metal frames, protruding approximately a meter above the water. Her first impression was that of a Nile Crocodile, waiting quietly for its prey, eyes only slightly above the waterline so as to see but not be seen, its massive body in readiness below.

The moon provided a reflection off the smooth metal body and enhanced every seam and bolt. The great iron barge, for she decided it must be like the Ironclad warships, generated a small disturbance in the rear, apparently keeping its place against the currents yet not providing enough energy to carry it forward.

A screw propeller, she wondered? Could it be what had been described in Verne's biographies of Aronnax and Nemo?

Closer and closer they steered. Lettie gauged that the barge was made of panels overlapping, welded and bolted. She was also aware that the barge must have been not less than 50 meters in length. Despite being dark in color, and appearing glass smooth at a distance, a proper inspection showed harsh forging violently molded into unyielding lines of grotesque design. The aesthetics were clean but hardly attractive.

A panel in the center unlocked loudly, followed by a hiss of escaping air, and then slid open. Twelve men emerged, three each aligning themselves to receive an incoming boat. From inside the barge a great light shown out. Lettie heard Turner whistle sharply from the boat nearest hers.

Every meter closer gave her cause to reassess the size of the enormous vessel. Gigantic. And, not a barge at all, but a human constructed monster of a fish-like shape. The barge was a submarine, one that she had read about in Verne's books. It was greater in length than 60 meters, she was certain now. How wide or deep she could not tell, but she was sure much more of the craft lay below than above the waves. Five more men emerged from the interior.

Her boat docked against the monster ship, striking it and causing a metallic echo that reminded her of the giant bells found in old fortress churches, ringing out a message of divine and absolute authority.

Each of the tiny craft was steered into a specific mooring and locked into place. Wickham shared Nemo's boat and was in fact in his way, but waited patiently. Nemo climbed past everyone else and stepped up onto the deck.

Nemo was the commander. No foot but his would be tolerated as the first to step aboard. The men nearest him bowed and waited for him to require them to speak in their unique language. To his own men Nemo was regal yet somewhat gentle, a kind dictator and patriarch. They were his men. Turning to the strangers on his vessel he sharply commanded, "Come aboard, Mr. Wickham." Part demand and part invitation, he considered his duties as host solidly initiated. Wickham arose from his seat, surprisingly graceful, and confidently stepped onto the vessel.

Wickham turned and offered Lettie his hand. The little boat was stable, having been secured firmly, but the whole ship was rocking back and forth in the deep swell. She hesitated. This was the last place she could resist and attempt to retain her reputation. As though expecting such a notion to cross her mind, Wickham took her hand without permission and pulled her up onto her feet. Two of Nemo's men took hold of her, in the most inappropriate way, though with little apparent design to harm her. Three men pulled and maneuvered her onto the deck of the vessel and any opportunity to save her character was gone.

Her skirt dragged slightly in the water that lapped up the curved surface but otherwise she managed to stay relatively dry. Her every fear must have shown on her face. Nemo stuck out his hand and offered to provide her with safety on her last few steps.

"Please come aboard Miss Gantry. We have very little time to waste." Then he added uncharacteristically, "As you are already aware."

She liked the feel of his hand, of his skin and strength of his grip. There was no reason for her to do so, but this was a time of brutal honesty for the sake of survival. She would say nothing, of course, about her opinion. The man was very likely stepping away from his own regular behavior to be gallant.

Her voice shook slightly, and she re-started her response to him with a bit more bravado. "Thank you, sir." Swallowing she allowed him to let go of her once she was completely balanced on the deck of his ship. "Am I to understand this is the *Nautilus*?"

He looked at her for a moment, deciding what, if anything, to say. "It is, though perhaps not the vessel you have heard of. This is my second creation. Let that suffice for now. I require that you go below immediately Miss Gantry. You as well Mr. Wickham."

There was a flurry of activity from Nemo's men, many of whom were surreptitiously looking at the woman being led toward the open panels and quietly commenting to one another.

Nemo was suddenly aware and embarrassed by their behavior. Miss Gantry, he noted, was aware of it too but stoically pretending not to notice … a damnable reaction of the British. If it bothered her, she should have said something. He glared at one of the sailors who understood and barked out a command to his fellows, all of whom became entirely focused on their own tasks.

Wickham shook his head slightly and chose to keep silent. He began to show her toward the open panel, a gesture that Lettie believed spoke of Wickham's familiarity with the ship, when a fight erupted from the boat moored immediately behind. Turner was putting up a struggle at last.

"Goddamn it, what is the problem," Wickham demanded under his breath.

"It appears Mr. Turner will not board the *Nautilus*," Nemo replied.

"Afraid of an ocean voyage, Turner?" Wickham's voice was thick with sarcasm.

Turner pushed back on the man who held his collar and braced himself inside the boat. Narrowing his eyes at Wickham, he folded his arms. "I come from a long line of honest sailors and seamen, and was one myself. A man doesn't board a ship without permission from her captain. I hardly expect that a landsman would know this."

Lettie gasped, realizing where she'd first met the man calling himself an 'honest sailor.' The Captain only took note of her reaction as she pulled her coat tighter against her body. The eyes, Lettie knew, how had she not recognized them before on the 'honest sailor' in Calais?

"Go inside Miss Gantry!" Nemo snapped at her. He felt instantly sorry to have been short with her, she was only a woman, but with each moment he was becoming aware that he knew far less about the situation than he aught. Returning to Turner, he focused his frustration on the sailor. "What is this?"

"I'll not set foot on this ship until the captain says so."

"Oh for the love of God …" Wickham started to say.

"You may not think much of the likes of me, but I have my pride too. It isn't done."

Such an odd occurrence, the Captain thought. It reminded him of Ned Land, a feckless Canadian harpooner once aboard the *Nautilus*, someone for whom he had little interest and less reason to recall. But Turner was correct. "Consider yourself permitted to board, under provision. I'll not tolerate any disturbance or disobedience from you Mr. Turner. You are not a guest on the *Nautilus*."

Turner hadn't heard the name of the ship, as he had been too far away to hear Lettie and Nemo's discussion. His blue eyes grew wide. "It's true then. The *Nautilus*."

"From time to time, Mr. Turner, it has proved efficacious to allow my truth to be considered either fiction or implausible. But the *Nautilus* is real. You may come aboard."

"Thank you, Captain." He reached up to where the brim of a uniform cap would have been many years ago and saluted in the appropriate, Naval way. The presence of a cap was not a requisite but regulations held that the gesture was yet essential. Had Turner been wearing a hat of any sort, he would have tugged slightly at the brim out of custom and respect. Whether Nemo appreciated it was hardly his concern and he gave no more resistance to the crewmen who took him toward the open panel.

Wickham and Nemo exchanged glances, curious if not confused. All Lettie could do was shrug when they looked to her for explanation, certain she had no idea what Turner might do next. Perhaps that was what the whole exchange was about? Or perhaps it was genuinely a matter of pride to the man.

She would have to ask Turner if she saw him again. Despite his demand that she stay clear of him, a demand she chose not to share with Wickham, she knew she was quite probably his only hope of staying alive or at least unharmed. Another hesitant moment of honesty left her questioning just why she should even care. She braced herself on her hands, on either side of the open panel, as the brightness of the interior light didn't allow her to see what sort of steps she was attempting to use.

Blast it, she thought, she should have stalled Wickham and Nemo, or withheld information about her interview with Turner. Stupid. Now she would have to come up with excuses for needing to see him, or to bargain for his safety. Perhaps, even, for her own.

The crewmen did nothing to assure her of better treatment. Although they were not cruel toward her they did not treat her as a lady, often manhandling her.

Needing to see Turner again? Had she actually thought that? Yes. Mad as the theory was, Turner was a known quantity. He had said he didn't wish to harm her. He had shown himself unwilling to brutalize her, though scaring her was not beyond him if it accomplished his needs. His needs were clearly on behalf of the employer whom he served with a bizarre honor. Turner was dangerous but predictable. His needs were to see that she remained alive. Wickham and Nemo were unknown quantities. What they wanted and how they would achieve it was unknown. Her stomach turned as the ship rolled and she accepted that for the time being, Tom Turner - abductor and Robur's agent - was her only stable resource.

Her eyes adjusted to the light and she found herself staring down the main hatch and a steep ladder. Clearly, it was not made for a woman in wet boots and petticoats. She would have to be careful. No friendly faces stared up at her, but two pairs of hands reached out to help her down the precarious rungs. Lettie grasped a wide balustrade that curved from the top of the panel to the floor. As one pair of hands held her by her hips, she held back an urge to demand his release of her person. How dare he?

But she couldn't say anything. The second pair of hands seized her waist and she was efficiently lowered to the deck. No metallic sound was caused when her hard heels touched down. She noted thick "phormium" matting that quieted footsteps and prevented a dangerous slickness at the base of the ladder. A short corridor greeted her, illuminated by polished globes set into the walls, glowing with some sort of electrical power such as the type she'd seen at the World's Fair. How Nemo harnessed electrical power in the midst of an iron vessel, sitting in water, was worthy of much consideration and calculation.

She would have time. The crewmen pulled her quickly along, at last leaving her in a sterile room, alone. There was no sign of Wickham, Turner or Nemo.

The bulkhead was cleaner in its appearance, yet still harsh and mechanical. A bed, extended from the wall, was all that provided any comfort. The room was otherwise empty. Even the door lacked a handle by which she could open it for herself. She tried pushing and pressing, searching for some mechanism to give herself freedom.

Suddenly the room shook, a roar of power vibrated the walls and it was clear to her that the *Nautilus* was underway. It was a submarine. Would it dive? Could she stand the concept of hundreds of feet of seawater between herself and fresh air?

The room felt smaller.

A full hour passed before the door opened. A small man, perhaps in his late sixties entered and bowed. He was dressed in a combination of classical Indian tunic and some sort of skin trousers. Around his thin, wrinkled head was wrapped a turban in soft blue cotton. He said nothing to Lettie but brought her a plate of food. Setting it on the bed, and placing simple steel utensils next to it, he bowed again and retreated from the room.

Lettie hadn't even bothered to remove the oilskin coat, fearing that she might be without it at an important moment. But, it was also likely she desired the extra layer of something between her body and her surroundings.

The lights dimmed, scaring her into thinking something drastic was about to happen. When, after another half hour, nothing else changed in the environment, she decided to see what meal had been offered to her.

The door opened again, and the small man stepped in, looked at her then the full plate, in surprise. He then indicated the meal and looked confused.

"I'll eat, I promise," she said, wondering if her non-consumption of the food had somehow offended the man. He appeared so very harmless and even genuine in his desire that she eat something. To make certain he knew she would keep her promise, she took up her fork and pierced a piece of fish, white and flaky, looking to have some finely ground spice on it. She ate a small bit. There was no question that its flavor was exemplary. She smiled, considering that if the man could speak English he would have. He probably only spoke his own native tongue and the language of the *Nautilus*. Lettie was vitally aware of the man's relief and nodded in thanks as he backed out the door, which closed tightly behind him.

The meal was very much a delight and made her feel welcome, if not a bit safer than before. Fish, spiced lightly. Something with a touch of curry. A very rich creamy sauce that tasted of the ocean rather than land based game. Sliced cucumbers, or something rather like them, marinated in a tangy flavor.

Once she finished the meal, having cut each item into ladylike bits and trying to maintain some semblance of the manners her mother instilled in her, she gathered up and organized the plate for removal. It was then, as her vision blurred for a second, that she realized there had been an extra ingredient in the culinary delights. Her fingers, her hands and feet, her leg and arm muscles all began to involuntarily relax and after a moment of internal admonitions, she surrendered to the fact that she had been drugged.

She never made it into the bed, but slipped to the matted floor and drifted off into a series of dreams that moved from sweet and nonsense to passionate: to Tom Turner, Philip Wickham, and the strange Nemo. And, yes, the Frenchman too. The oilskin coat weighed her down all the more, and she had one silly thought that she maintained a modicum of control over during the few lucid moments ... Turner had wanted and perhaps Wickham would accomplish the task of drugging her unconscious, stuffing her into a trunk, and shipping her by freight back to England. Freight... how rude! She deserved at least a second class ticket ...

The glowing globes went out in her room, though she didn't know it.

Chapter 54

Possibly May 26, 1883
Aboard the *Nautilus*
Actual location unknown

In what she presumed was the morning, Lettie awoke in another room. She'd been moved during the night. The oilskin coat was draped neatly across a carved, padded chair. Her valise was set on a desk, open. One of her travel trunks was situated in the corner with the lid raised. Her boots had been removed and set near a heat source to dry. Her collar had been unbuttoned only two places down to give her some comfort in breathing, but otherwise she was fully clothed and 'reasonably' untouched.

Nemo? In Monsieur Verne's biography he'd described such a drug being used on the harmless Pierre Aronnax and his companions. They too had found themselves missing an evening's worth of memories, yet alive and well. And, as she'd read of Monsieur Aronnax's experience, she too was feeling rather refreshed. The fact that she had been moved did not sit well with her, but her new surroundings were much better. Besides the addition of the writing desk and chair, and the recovery of some of her belongings, she had a bed of a regular sort. And the room was far more pleasant, decorated with a hint of Indian style. It was considerably more practical and gentler to the eyes. Yet, why would they insist on rendering her unconscious? Surely she had been calm in her demeanor - well, calm enough under the circumstances.

Lettie walked over to her trunk on somewhat unsteady legs. Resting her hands on the rim and trying not to support her weight on them, she looked for a change of clothing. Her travel suit was stale from being wet and contained under the oilskin coat. She needed to refresh herself and to be attired in a much more sensible way. For all practical purposes, she was now in the field.

At that moment she realized that her belongings had been searched. Nothing was where she had packed it. It was her habit to always set her shoes on the right side as it was often the end that her trunk was turned on when being stored on its side. Lighter or more delicate items went toward the middle and those belongings she might need to find in a hurry were placed on the left. This was not how her trunk was arranged now. Everything was in excellent condition, folded or wrapped, but not where she had left them.

She rushed to her valise and pulled the stiff sides open. Her loose papers and personal effects were there, including the scandalous romantic novel, but not her private letters. She searched twice, dumping the contents on the bed the second time. The letters were missing, as was her journal of notations. They had been taken.

Lettie wanted to hit something, Wickham. He was behind this theft - this violation.

Chapter 55

The ship vibrated occasionally, indicating motion. With no view to anything outside her room, Lettie was beginning to feel nauseous. Disoriented.

A knock on her door scared her. She didn't have time to respond that she didn't desire any company when the small man from earlier entered through the doorway with a plate of food. Lettie stood up from the desk and backed away from him. Not again.

He set the plate down and looked confused.

This isn't his fault, she reminded herself. In four quick steps she went back to the desk, took up the plate and handed it to the man. "No thank you. I shall sleep on my own tonight." She nodded politely then deliberately turned her back as a way to dismiss him. He set the plate down; again she handed it back to him and, containing her anger, pointed toward the door. The man was utterly confused as to why but understood what she wanted him to do. He bowed slightly and left the room with the plate. The door slammed shut and locked.

It was now an opportunity for her to change clothes; very likely it would take them a while to decide just what her intention in sending the food back meant – or if it were to mean anything to them at all. It was either dumb luck or a wise decision on someone's part that the trunk they provided her with had her personal items. She chose a plain jacket and skirt as anything else was ridiculous.

Beside the change in over-clothing, she quickly stripped off her wet and soiled corset cover and petticoats, setting them aside for laundering in the small sink in her room. These she would never allow anyone, certainly not a sailor, to wash or repair. The All-in-One undergarment had served her well in the past when working outdoors. Fearfully she'd rushed this part of her dressing wondering who might barge in at any second. A corset of few spring steel bones was all that was necessary: it was made for working conditions. A fully-boned corset of whalebone or hardened steel would be neither comfortable under the circumstances nor practical. Pulling at her hairpins, she dismantled the fashionable arrangement that had become unruly, brushed her fingers through, and pinned it simply in a tidy chignon.

She estimated that another nerve-wrenching hour passed before the man was sent to her again. Someone had thought the extra hour of hunger might persuade her to eat. They were wrong and the plate of food was sent away again. Hopefully, she thought, this won't keep up all night.

Expecting that she had another hour to wait, Lettie sat down to read some of her papers. They were comforting and kept her focus away from her bizarre circumstances. No more than ten minutes passed before another knock on her door ... a much stronger and determined knock.

Nemo himself entered. "Are you not fond of this food? Or are you unwell?" For a moment he showed that almost fatherly concern she's seen in him earlier.

"I prefer my seasonings to be bereft of sleeping drugs."

He set the plate down before her. "You may accept my word that there are no such drugs or concoctions in this meal."

She looked down at the food. It did look inviting, yet the success of her stubbornness was not a substitute for her growing hunger.

Her hesitation annoyed him. "My word ..."

"... would hold more value to me if I knew why I was treated in such a manner and why belongings of mine have been taken."

He drew up sharply. "I deemed it appropriate, as master of this ship. I was not convinced that your reaction to submersion would be either efficacious or safe. I have known hysterical women before."

"Has any behavior of mine been suggestive of hysteria," she said as coldly as possible, folding her hands neatly. "I believe, sir, it was you who defended my scientific thinking and ability to assess situations with logic and reason. Why change your mind now?"

"The safety of my ship was not in question at that time, Doctor Gantry. I was also not aware of the degree of impact your presence on board would cause. You are the first female to board either of the two *Nautilus*."

"And my notes, personal letters? You do not strike me as someone who lives vicariously through others. The scientific notes I understand, but really, sir: my personal letters from friends and family?"

This caused Nemo to move back and to regroup his thoughts. "That was the decision of Mr. Wickham who needed to be certain of both your science and ... discretion."

She couldn't help it, she barked out a laugh. It startled Nemo. "Mr. Wickham is hardly one to judge discretion, evidenced by his appearance and behavior. And unless he requested your assistance, I doubt very much that he could comprehend my notes or equations."

"He could not," the Mariner replied, allowing a softer expression on his face. "Your model, your Predictive Model, is extraordinarily complex. I was not prepared for the number of variations you allowed. It had been my experience that a terrestrial volcanic phenomenon was divided into only a handful of types. Your model implies far more."

At last, they had something to discuss. It was an opportunity she would be foolish to ignore. "I believe my model's weakness is the limited number of variations I have considered. It would seem that no two volcanoes behave perfectly alike. That will create a number of variables in my calculations that simply defy repetition. How does one develop a concept of predictability when the phenomenon is unlikely to occur in the exact same way again? You see my dilemma?"

"I perceive a need for greater statistical research."

She smiled, hoping to encourage the mutual discourse. "Then, sir, you do understand. If there is no further sign of espionage in my correspondence with my family and friends may I have my letters back? They are dear to me."

"You would choose to live in the past with them?

"No, sir. They merely please me. And they remind me that I do have such people in this world who think lovingly of me and care for my well being."

"Then, Miss Gantry, you must let go of them for they will only draw you back into the past. Your future, your immediate future, is here. You are the singular cause for my only living relative to be in captivity. It is only your feminine birth and possible innocence that keeps me from treating you as a prisoner. I would have every right."

"I have done nothing to directly encourage this lamentable situation. Further, it is my honorable intention to do all in my power to rescue him."

Nemo did not believe her, thinking her entirely lacking in the strength necessary for such bravado and that she surely must have known this too. "Miss Gantry, I only doubt your physical strength and cleverness to achieve your goal."

"Then what in the name of heaven do you want me to do?"

He carefully composed himself and his words. "Your word as a lady that you will submit to my few demands."

Lettie sat down ungracefully and demanded, "And just what few demands do you have? Are they the same as those given to Professor Aronnax? I read about that."

"Yes, Miss Gantry. From time to time certain unforeseen events may force me to consign you to your cabin for some hours. As I do not desire to apply violent means, I expect obedience from you in such a case, which I do not expect similarly from the others. Do you accept the condition?"

"I believe I may, but with one condition of my own. Surely in our short voyage this need will be rarely called upon. If confinement is not required, I desire a respectful freedom of the ship. I presume that the bridge and engine rooms to be unapproachable, as well as crew quarters. But your library is renowned and the collections of information extensive …"

"Yes, I agree." He seemed a bit surprised by his own eagerness to acquiesce. "You may have such liberty, but some limits that allow you little to no contact with my men. I believe such encounters to be disruptive to the functioning of my *Nautilus*."

"There is one more item." She stood up and stepped directly in front of him, staring him directly in the eyes. She knew the action would cause some sort of reaction on his part and she wanted to see what that would be. "I will participate in the rescue of Rajiv. There is no argument that I will accept which can force me to do less. You stand here and accuse me of causing his distress. In that, you are wrong, and you know that you are wrong. The only person to hold accountable is Robur and none other. I intend to rectify the situation with or without you and your remarkable ship."

His eyebrow rose slightly. "Do you intend to swim?"

"What makes you think I wouldn't or couldn't? I've climbed erupting mountains and escaped mudflows that otherwise killed thousands. I've put up with the cruelties of men who disguised their actions in false courtesy and meaningless chivalry. I have accomplished things that every man said I could not. I am resilient and unrelenting."

"You are a woman."

Lettie perked up. "How very civilized of you. Now you sound like all the rest, all those little men who live in their happy, civil ..."

"I am not what you would call a civilized man, I have turned my back ..." his face began to color.

She didn't care, and smiled at him. "So you keep saying, and yet your every action is tempered by old habits from your earlier years. You say and posture one way, then you speak of the great liberty of life. Yet, you have kept me locked in this room."

Nemo glared at her for a moment then his face surprisingly softened. "Hypocrites, aren't we all? Professor Aronnax made a similar observation."

"Did he?"

"I believe it failed to be included in the biography Verne wrote. It is hard to hate a villain when he is as human as the next man. And that was the role I was cast in ... the villain. The evil doer. The monster." His voice saddened. "I was not the man that author wrote about. And I am not that man now."

For a moment, they stood looking at one another, feeling oddly naked.

"Captain. I shall agree to remain in appropriate places on board your ship and, if you see it necessary for my safety, shall willingly retire to my room without argument." The tone of her statement begged him to meet her in compromise. Surely it was possible.

"As for my nephew's rescue, I cannot use you ..."

"Sir," she said with exasperation, "it is not usage when I am volunteering. I care for Rajiv, I respect him highly, and will do anything to help; anything but wait quietly in the dark. Surely you see that I may provide assistance that is valuable. Every possible aspect of his rescue must be taken into account, whether or not it is pleasant or comfortable. We are working against a genius, not an average man."

"You ... you are volunteering, then?" he said with a slight hesitation.

"Yes, sir, I am. I am volunteering to actively participate in Rajiv's rescue, whatever the risk."

He narrowed his eyes a bit. "And what of your Lady's Reputation?"

Lettie laughed with no humor. "Gone by now, I am sure. But not my honor, and it seems to always surprise men that women have honor too. What have I left to do, but this thing, to save a man's life? And please, don't try the argument that my sitting here quietly will serve the purpose as we both know it will not."

"You are a harsh bargainer, Miss Gantry."

"If I told you that one of my grandfathers was a Purchaser for the Chisholm Cattle Company, would you believe me?"

Nemo allowed one half of his mouth to turn up in a smile. How odd, he thought, that neither Verne nor Aronnax ever mentioned in their competing publications about him that he smiled - and he did smile, though not too often. This woman was making him do it far more than ever. Perhaps that was a good thing?

Chapter 56

May ... something ... probably the 27th, 1883
The *Nautilus*
Distance from French coast not known

The cell was simple, but better appointed than the jail he'd known before. While not large by any standard, it was relatively spacious for an ocean-going vessel. And, Turner was the only one in it. It smelled clean, free of human odors and a stench of death. He cynically estimated that any other prison would manage to fit at least five more men in there before he stopped the memory that arose.

A bunk was held perpendicular to the far wall by a pair of chains, yet as austere as it was, there were a comfortable mattress and pillows. Two blankets. An electric light, which the prisoner could adjust for himself. A writing desk and a chair. He wasn't surprised in the least to find the practical use of electricity aboard the ship. Better than gas. A plate of food had arrived. Simple yet generous. Portions of curried vegetables and rice filled the tiny room with delicious aromas.

He wondered if she had arranged it. The generosity seemed to be something she would insist on, even for the man who had shouted at her, called her stupid, and told her to stay away. Even for a man who had pointed a gun at her. It would be just like her to watch out for him despite his behavior. Wickham would protest but ultimately concede. Despite Wickham's reputation for being a cold and calculating bastard, he was concerned about being perceived as a gentleman. He'd give in to her demand, as it was small enough. Turner was grateful to have the food. And ashamed. He didn't like failure and he didn't like what he'd been commanded to do.

This was still a prison cell. The door was locked. And he had no idea if they were headed toward the North Sea, though that seemed the most likely destination. Holland, that's where he told them everything would take place. She believed him. And she probably convinced everyone else that Holland was where they had to go. Good. At least that portion of the plan was going right - he hoped.

Turner poked at his plate of food. It did smell very good, but he longed for meat, especially a steak. But a ship commanded by a Hindu was unlikely to have beef anywhere on board. Tasting the yellow, spicy sauce before deciding he could stomach the foreign meal, Turner wondered why it was that he had been such an ass about boarding the submarine. He was Nemo's prisoner; of course he was expected and permitted to board. It was stupid of him, and yet he felt a tinge of satisfaction. He simply couldn't bring himself not to ask. It wasn't done, it simply wasn't done.

Of course, that he had managed to confuse Wickham and Nemo if for only a moment was a source of victory. A petty victory, but victory nonetheless. And she was there to see it.

Turner pushed the plate away, annoyed at where his thoughts were going lately. His throat felt tight and he loosened his collar. Usually he preferred wearing something that armored his neck against questioning eyes and other forms of attack. Not that fabric would do much to save him, but the thought that he had something between his neck and the world comforted him. His fingers lingered for second on the familiar line of raised scar tissue. No, his thoughts were dangerously unfocused and filled with too many unnecessary memories. Stay on track, man. Eat something, he told himself. Just because she's a woman ...

Letticia Gantry was his target, not someone to show off for. Her opinion was of no consequence, none - no, none at all. He was there to complete his assignment; he was following orders and she was simply a part of that task. Why should he care what she thought - about anything?

And, yet, he did. Damn it. He cared. He tried being angry at her. It didn't help.

Turner couldn't eat anymore. He reminded himself that this meal might be the only one he got for a long time. It could even be his last. He hadn't been given the courtesy of a last meal before. Yet his appetite was gone all the same.

He lay back on the bunk and stared at the rivets in the ceiling. It had been a long time since he'd held a woman. He'd been, to say the least, busy. Robur had no place for women, which made his near obsession with Doctor Gantry just plain odd. On board the train, when he'd first been so close, she had smelled like sweet lavender soap, clean and fresh ...

Fine. She's a woman. Why fight that? I'm already in the middle of the operation. Fine. He needed to accept the real truth of the situation.

To put himself into the right frame of mind to fall asleep and to dream of something other than the dreadful past, he thought about her as his target. He would do so with the every ounce of his training. He would consider her in terms of being an object, not a human being. She was a target just like any; one with specific habits, weaknesses, skills, and patterns of reaction. His target.

His womanly, feminine, softly curved target. His mind visualized her and his holding her; helping her to remove the preposterous layers of gown, corset, bustle and petticoats. Of pulling away the soft leather shoes from her feet and sliding the delicate stockings down the length of her curving thighs and calves. Of tasting her mouth and holding her head gently with his fingers entwined in her black hair. Of that delicious smell of lavender all over her body.

Stupid. So much for falling asleep, this was now unlikely to happen immediately or even soon. Maybe he'd dream about it but to actually fall asleep he needed something less - stimulating.

His face, frankly, hurt like hell. It wasn't swollen beyond recognition, but it hurt as though it was. Again, it had been Doctor Gantry - Letticia - to his rescue. Truthfully, he didn't deserve her efforts on his behalf; after all, he had tried to abduct her - albeit on orders. He was nowhere near done with his assignment, and things weren't exactly going well. The heat in his skin rose as he admitted to himself he'd bungled a few things. It wasn't as though he had experience in abducting women. The fact was he hated the assignment. It was undignified and beneath any man. But, Robur commanded and he obeyed. Now he had to work things out for himself; things his captain hadn't foreseen.

But that was exactly why Robur had entrusted him with the mission. Turner had the experience of laying deep into enemy territory and completing the task. Infiltration. Spying. Obtaining illicit objects. The Federal Navy had made him a master of it and he was born to take the role. Landing Party activities were his specialties during the war and he was damn good at them - until he got caught. Doctor Gantry wasn't the only keen observer of humanity.

Rarely did the average mission go without any problems, and his knack for adjusting to the circumstances and making decisions on the fly were his stock and trade.

He'd only just succeeded in purposely incurring the curiosity of Nemo, a strategy he added on his own. Nemo. He was real. Turner's fingers ran down the sides of the wall: the *Nautilus* was real. Turner had seen the hate in Nemo's eyes when the subject of Professor Pierce, Robur's prisoner, came up. No one would escape Nemo's anger if anything happened to Pierce, that much was certain. Family would trump any argument. Nemo was a man Robur should not meet. It had to be prevented. Despite all, Turner had long since decided he would do whatever it took to protect Robur, the *Albatross* and her crew. That was Turner's decision to make, and had. What to do about it was still impossible to figure out, as so much depended on the events of the next two days. He needed a way out of the cell.

It was also for such things, like difficult but unscientific decisions, that Robur had chosen him. For all he knew, this was a suicide mission, but one he now more willingly undertook upon further assessment as he became increasingly aware of all the players. Besides, how suicidal could it be? He'd already been dead once. And what mission was without risk?

Chapter 57

May 27, 1883 – she decided
The *Nautilus*
Underway to Holland – she also decided

In the depth of the Atlantic Ocean, there was little to indicate the passage of time. The *Nautilus* maintained its own calendar and clock. It had nothing to do with the world outside the ship. It kept up a constant twenty-four hour loop. Despite external days and hours, the crew worked in shifts and ate at regulated times specific to the ship. Large round clocks were to be found everywhere, all tuned precisely to one another.

According to the *Nautilus's* clock, it was morning. Time for breakfast.

Lettie hadn't slept. Every noise caused her to sit up in bed, clutching the dinner knife she'd taken off her food tray. There were so many men around her, none of whom she knew "correctly." If not on their way to Holland, where might they go? At first it felt as though someone was sitting on her chest, then her abdomen. No, that was anxiety.

Nemo had been very reasonable with her, but once he'd gone, the silence took control of her thoughts. The creaking and groaning of the submarine reminded her of the water striving to get into the little bubble of iron-wrapped air. Once she though she heard the sound of rushing water, but she'd dozed off and was semi-lucidly reacting to sounds she simply had no experience with.

Where were Wickham and his gun? The place on her skin where he'd put the muzzle, right at her temple, felt as if the gun was still there. She could never forgive him for that. A bluff it was not. She knew - she could feel how much he wanted to pull the trigger.

Several times, she had to sit up and decide where she might run to if her stomach started to erupt. Nemo may have been right: she wasn't able to cope with the submersion. There was too much water - everywhere.

Now it was "morning." She dressed as simply as she could with what she had. Lacing her corset was nearly unbearable. Her head hurt. She could never bring herself to admit the lost sleep or the need for assistance. She would not be weak!

The older gentleman who had brought Lettie her first meal on board arrived promptly at 0800 with an invitation to join the Mariner for breakfast. The card had been written out in a very legible hand. It was formal and surprisingly "civilized."

Oh God, she would have to eat something or Nemo would know something was wrong with her. The older gentleman, unaware of her growing fears, guided her to an entryway larger than the others on the ship. Its size was necessary considering the contents of the room it led to.

Lettie stopped abruptly in that doorway, stunned by what she saw. For a moment, she grasped the door frame and let it hold her weight. Any feeling of nausea or pain slipped past her awareness.

Floor to ceiling, great bookcases made from black mahogany covered two thirds of the room. Rows of matching sets of books filled them, along with samples, specimens, and various artifacts. The clutter was beautiful. Occasionally an entire row would be bare of literature but filled with a painting of incalculable worth. Nemo's collection favored French authors and artists, but was by no means exclusive. In fact, the room was clearly wide in its range of internationalism.

A heavy oak table was economically fitted up against the far wall and covered with maps and papers. A bookstand held several volumes of work; only the top book was spread open and extended past the width of the stand. Chairs, couches, even the Persian carpets, favored the color red which looked at once unearthly and garish against the blue light reflecting back into the Salon.

Nemo was waiting in front of a window. At first Lettie wondered what optical illusion was being presented for certainly the depth pressure of the ocean would preclude something such as a window in a submersible boat. But as she approached, she began to see that it was a uniquely designed porthole. Dual layers of convex glass resisted the pressure crushing against it and provided a gap of air between them to insulate against the cold water outside. Nemo was not facing her but, through the reflection on the glass, he watched her approach.

The *Nautilus's* engines had cut back, which was easy to recognize by the reduction in noise and vibration. Outside the remarkable porthole was a vague dark shape, like a tall building's chimney, but twisted and bent. A mirrored, focused, electric torch blasted the object with light, but it could only offer so much help to see in the ocean depths. She couldn't make out any distinct features: distance to the object made that impossible. Yet, she found herself thinking that the chimney was in fact smoking. Underwater? Perhaps Nemo was right to try and confine her to her rooms; she was going insane.

"Professor Aronnax found these particularly interesting." Nemo drew on his cigar slowly, still moved by the beauty of the view he'd seen so many times. "We dare not go closer. The immediate water around it is too hot."

"What are they?"

"The Professor thought they were volcanoes, though I dispute that definition. I have been off the Hawaiian Islands and know firsthand what volcanic lava does in water. This does not have the same appearance. The Professor wrote about it extensively: I've set his notes on that podium for your perusal."

Reflexively, Lettie placed her hand on the glass to assess how warm the exterior was. The glass was hot but not scalding. "Thank you." She had not been fully breathing. Several deeply drawn breaths caught her up.

A moment later and the distant geological feature was gone. The torch light was put out. The engines started working harder. Nemo had slowed down to show her that amazing sight. He said nothing more and retired to the oak table that had been set with the morning's fare.

Chapter 58

Wickham had been given his own room if for no other reason than that he could keep to it and stay out of everyone's way. That was just fine with Wickham.

His manservant would have been appalled at the sight of such a mess. Would have been, were he still alive. Papers everywhere, a travel case open and unpacked. It was a mess. He was a mess. Wickham looked down at his watch and wondered how close to Holland they were. They hadn't much time left. Looking again at the clutter, he turned his back on it and began writing a note to himself. The effort settled his mind, which so easily lost its focus these days.

An airship. A functioning airship. It was valuable beyond measure. But, how to get it? How not to let Hetzel know of its existence? No, that was likely impossible. The Weldon incident had proven that this Robur had some sort of ability to travel by air. Thanks to all the newspaper accounts, and the Weldon men's stories, Robur's aerial conquest was too broadly known to keep it as a secret. To control that airship or to have it outright; this was greater than any other endeavor he had undertaken. In some ways it was exhilarating.

Turner was an essential tool for capturing the airship and her inventor. A good thing that Nemo was just as interested in keeping the American under lock and key.

An airship ... goddamn it, what a feat! What genius! What potential!

He'd have to use Gantry as bait, but he'd since taught himself how not to care. No, he couldn't care anymore.

He surrendered himself to profit. In the age of innovation, the most remarkable inventions were being designed and each one was worth something to someone. Weapons were the most prevalent result of technological advancement. People hadn't changed with the industrial revolution; only their methods of killing one another had. And since he no longer cared who won or lost, weapons were his means of support. But not just any gun; weapons of extraordinary design.

Weapons such as Robur's airship.

His right hand sank down to grasp the watch fob hanging from his pocket. It no longer resembled the golden Ganesha, the elephant-headed God and remover of obstacles, the fob that his wife had given him as a gift and talisman. Worn down by his fingers, numerous assaults, and time itself, the figure was almost unrecognizable. He knew what it was and that it was there. After all, the golden idol had done his job and removed Wickham's obstacles before: he was still alive despite himself. And successful. Nothing got in his way.

Chapter 59

The *Nautilus* had entered the English Channel just before the second day's dinner.

Nemo had walked into the salon moments after a minor technical problem had been brought to his attention, and in his usual temper demanded that Lettie accompany him to another part of the ship. Something in Nemo's less rigid posture told her that she was not in any danger or about to be rebuked for some perceived endangerment of the ship. It was simply his way as master of the vessel.

He led her to a round compartment filled with equipment. In the center of the room was a large hatch still dripping with seawater. This was the diving room she'd read about in *20,000 Leagues*. Rows of hooks held sets of helmets, canvas suits, packs with tanks, and seal-skin clothing.

Nemo handed Lettie an apparatus and then stood back, arms folded, to watch her reactions, just as he had done with Aronnax. He was first amused by her difficulty with its weight and bulk. Neither prevented her from inspecting the whole mechanism.

The helmet was made of polished copper with a thick coating of clear varnish to protect it from damage in seawater. Inside was a fitted resin or India rubber mask to go directly over the mouth and nose. She noted it with a calm voice, meaning only to show him that she appreciated the complexity of its creation. Her fingers moved slowly down the India rubber tubing toward the pack. Here was the filter for the tank of air, which was attached inside a half column of coated bronze. The tank, made from riveted steel and by its weight had to be several layers thick, was inserted into hinged hooks and then tilted up into place in its housing. Lashed into place with buckled straps, it was then quickly and easily connected by short tubes to the filtration system in the lower section of the pack. Though it seemed ridiculous, each item was not plain by any means. Where the basic metal was copper, swirling bronze designs decorated it. Where the basic metal was iron or bronze, copper was used to add an aesthetic quality to the design. It was clean and beautifully cluttered all at the same time.

"And the pack itself filters the exhaled air, allowing some re-circulation"

He nodded slightly. "That is correct. However, as I said earlier, I use the pumps here on the *Nautilus* to compress and load the air into these reservoirs. It allows several hours worth of good air. Recirculation increases the capacity of the tank by ten percent only.

She tried not to laugh. "That is a difference between life and death at one hundred meters below the sea?"

He appeared to agree. For a single moment, he seemed lost in a memory, a very unhappy memory. He quickly distracted himself with the person in front of him. "The most important items I believe that will appeal to you are these." He set the pack down, with its air reservoir, and pulled the breathing mask out of the helmet.

On closer inspection, Lettie could see that there were two significant tubes going into the mouthpiece. A loose toggle inside opened or closed each of those tubes.

"One uses their mouth to allow good air to flow in and bad air to flow out," he stated.

"Yes, I see."

"Do you?"

"That this invention, based on some original designs by two prominent French inventors, and increased to its maximum potential by you is essential for ship's maintenance. Yes, Captain, I see."

He shook his head. "It is not about what I ... do you not see applications beyond ship's maintenance?"

Lettie held the mask admiringly. "I know that I would find it useful in places where the quality of the air is dangerous. Oh, say, such as one might find on a volcano. Sulfur dioxide can be fatally disturbing to a volcanologist's plans."

"Then you do see," he replied calmly, turning his back to her while replacing the helmet on its proper hook.

"Your nephew, sir. Rajiv. He will have a great appreciation of this invention."

"And in your romantic mind, Doctor, you expect that I will be able to show it to him. That he will be quickly and easily rescued so that I may do so." Nemo kept his back to her.

" 'Quickly?' No, sir. Not if Captain Robur is as intelligent as he brags to be, and thus far every indication says he is. But I believe Rajiv is alive and will be saved."

Nemo's shoulders fell and his head lowered. "You have hope."

"Yes, I do."

"I have dreamed that - I am not the last of ..." He still would not turn to face her, but instead began running his finger along the decorations of the helmet. "He is all I have left, of my flesh and kin. And for years, I held no hope of such a thing. And I lived as a man with nothing."

Lettie folded her hands in front of her, holding back an urge to touch him. To her own father she could show such affection. Nemo? Was he able to receive such a gesture, even from a member of his own family? Nemo and family: the two terms did not seem to go together at all. Yet there he stood, his back to her to hide whatever outward sign of emotion he feared she would see: Nemo the faithful uncle, not the mad inventor and monster of the seas. "You have no other family members, even distant?"

He nodded, the motion moving his entire body. "None. Rajiv was my little Prince. I had such ambitions for him. My sister's only child."

For a moment, Lettie was feeling confused. "Your nephew? You call him..." She stopped, knowing that she might have intruded too far into his personal life.

After a moment of awkward silence, he looked over his shoulder at her. "You were going to ask why I call my nephew 'my little Prince' when I had a son who should have been - loved by me as well." His eyes were red.

"You did say something about your son. I decided I shouldn't ask after all. It is, perhaps, too painful and intimate for me to be so curious and forward in asking about this." She kept her voice low and calm. But seeing his eyes, she felt tears welling up in her own.

Nemo turned his back on her and said, barely above a whisper, "I deserved no son." His breathing appeared to be labored, as though something dreadful was crushing his chest. "Fate gave to me a beautiful wife. She was French, but loved India and its people. She adopted every custom and became as Indian as any foreigner could ever be. And she gave to me a son. A son I should have loved, I should have ..." His shoulders began to shake. "I honored Rajiv above my own child for the ugliest and lowest reasons. Rajiv was born of two royal parents of Bundlekund. My son, was half French and appeared more like his mother than me."

Lettie stood there, the feeling gone from her hands and legs. Why was he telling her this?

"It was the time of the Indian Rebellion," he continued. "I was so full of hate for the British, for anything European ... I turned my back on my own son. My only son. I gave my preferences - my love - to my pure Indian nephew. What a hateful father I was. What man should use so small a thing as appearance to betray his only child? But, when the Rebellion began to fail and I knew my family was in danger, I sent them away, to be safe in France. I tried to save them, but it was so late, so very, very late."

Nemo suddenly turned around and grabbed her by both shoulders. His eyes were wide with madness. "I sent my wife and son to be slaughtered, do you understand what I am saying? I sent Rajiv with them. And he nearly died. But now I have a chance, to save what is left, for ... for ..." The words failed him.

"Redemption," she said softly.

His body slumped; with that one word, a portion of the weight was lifted from his chest and it was visibly apparent. He hadn't used that word - not once. How could he? How dare he seek forgiveness? He was a bigot who let his only son die. How dare he?

Lettie waited, watching his eyes. "We all seek it."

"What have you to be redeemed for?"

"Not saving the world, when I could? For being born into privilege and not knowing the pains of those who go without? For not forgiving my mother until she was already dead? For giving up what is supposed to be a woman's right of happiness: having a family of my own?" She made a sound that was partially a brisk laugh. "For being born a woman in the first place. How many men think that is a sin or at least a capital mistake? Sir, the list could go on, though I don't believe any of these things to be as significant as your need."

He let go of her shoulders. They stared at each other, trying to gauge through red and blurry eyes what waited in the mind of the other and would it be visible in the other's face?

Lettie didn't smile, as had been her previous habit to soften an awkward or painful moment. "I am your ally, sir. Before, I was only my own and Rajiv's."

"And sometime's Mr. Turner's?"

She blushed slightly. "Yes, sometimes Mr. Turner's as well. I now understand far more than I did. I am, for all that it is worth to you, your ally. And, I shall be discreet. This conversation was between us."

"You still have hope?"

"Yes, sir. I now have the greatest hope."

Chapter 60

He emerged from his quarters, clean shaven and washed, and settled into the salon with too much familiarity. "Well, its official, 'they' know," Wickham said, tapping the ash off a cigar and reading Hetzel's letter. It had pleased him immeasurably to have forced the Mariner to stop his great submarine and allow him to retrieve a message. A courier had delivered it a few hours before to the seaside village home of an employee of Hetzel. It was all very carefully crafted and very secret. Codes had been used before the letter was handed off to Wickham; and all the while Nemo waited impatiently. Quite a pleasure, making Nemo do his bidding and then wait. "Or, at least they think they know."

Nemo didn't bother to look up from the chart he was marking, still irked from the delay. "They, who? And what is it they know that you feel compelled to mention it?"

"Miss Gantry is missing. The whole business at the rail station. Not that I didn't expect it to be reported. The fight alone was going to generate too much attention. According to Monsieur Hetzel, half the newspapers are reporting that she has been kidnapped. Several of the papers are blaming their local separatists or anarchists. The Italian government is tripping over itself trying to assure the British that they are doing everything they can. What a mess, all over one woman." Wickham said the last more to himself. He glanced back at the telegram. "A search has been started in the Alps to see if they can find the missing British 'adventuress.'" He held up the single sheet of paper, written on both sides, as though Nemo could read it from such a distance.

"Was that all there was in the message we had to stop for? We lost hours doing that."

Wickham eyed the Captain with distaste. "It was necessary."

"And are you going to tell her? Will you tell Doctor Gantry that she is presumed a victim of anarchists?"

"And distract her with worry or cause hysteria over her lost reputation? Not a chance in hell. She needs to concentrate on her formulas and calculations."

Finally, Nemo set down his compass and rested both hands on the table. "She is determined to join the rescue."

"No."

"You originally wanted to use her as bait."

"I did. And you said you'd never use a woman. Have you changed your mind? No, I don't need her as bait, certainly not if I can't control her. She's a beast of a problem that way."

"You like to be in control, don't you Mr. Wickham." The comment was not a question.

Wickham made no answer. After a several minutes of silence, Wickham finally said, "I wonder how much of her career has been actually been ruined?"

"You almost sound concerned."

"Don't be absurd. She will be hard pressed to find anyone now who will take her research seriously - as if anyone did in the first place. Unless she suddenly appears in Java unharmed and amazed at all the publicity, she's been reduced from an academic to a helpless victim in the public eye. I can't say as I would want to live with that."

"Positively compassionate, Mr. Wickham. If I have judged her correctly, her work is her life. You suggest that she is academically dead? Then why bother with her?"

Wickham sat up and glared. "It's not as though her work won't achieve something useful. She's the sort who won't give in. Rather like that Aronnax fellow. But, without the usual support from the scientific community, she will have to strive a hundred times harder for her predictive model or turn to someone the likes of Robur which I cannot allow. Thus she will be isolated and unrecognized. But while her name will be lost in time, her work will provide the basis for future successes of others. I wouldn't discourage her. She will simply have to accept that society has abandoned her and that she will be one of the many forgotten. Once she accepts this, she'll be able to live with the situation. Not every one of us will make a mark on history."

"You could help her," Nemo snapped. "You could ask Hetzel to tell a convenient lie to the press, he is very good at that say that she is on her way to Java. That it was all a mistake."

"Why go to the trouble?"

"Because she will succeed in creating an effective model."

"Of course she will. But she needs to be reined in, directed ..."

"Controlled!"

"Yes, controlled. What she does now is for herself, her own needs, her own limited notions of what the world needs. We need her focused on our needs."

"We?" Nemo's face screwed up in anger. "Without choice? She's not being lost to the world, she is being thrown away."

"Not entirely. We'll keep her confined from here on out. It's better for a woman anyway. She'll just have the advantage of being confined with all her equipment. She couldn't ask for more than that."

Nemo's breathing changed. "She will never know freedom again, not for her entire life? And you have the ability to remove her from the world?"

"She's not the first scientist or inventor who has 'disappeared.' If you want to take her in after we rescue your nephew, fine. She won't be able to come off this boat anymore than she'll be able to leave whatever facility she's installed in. I'll want regular reports on her progress ..."

Wickham had barely finished his sentence when Nemo crossed the room and seized him by the clean, celluloid collar and cast him onto the floor. "I am not your informant. Nor your servant. And not your jailer! Do not presume I will do your bidding."

Wickham's eyes grew huge and for a moment he thought they would come to blows.

Lettie, who had been standing in the doorway, invisible to both men, thought it too. She'd heard the discussion. She'd been drawn to the Salon by the sound of shouting. Having heard Wickham's words, she actually hoped Nemo would turn the full brunt of his infamous rage on the man.

"For God's sake, Nemo, do you want men like Robur to succeed? Is that it? Or do you just see too much of yourself in him?" Wickham struggled out of Nemo's reach.

Nemo only glared at him. He turned and started out of the room as Wickham scrambled to his feet perhaps ready for a brawl. He didn't bother to wait; he strode out of the salon. He shouldn't care: he couldn't care. But he did. There was nothing to be done about it. But he cared. It was his ship and no "enemy" of his, invited or not, would have the last word.

Wickham stood there with his mouth open; it was not in his experience to fail to say the last scathing or rebuking words. For a moment, 'the machine' began to break down; emotions were swelling up in him. He shook, almost violently, trying to maintain his composure.

Nemo was a problem waiting to become a drastic situation. Gantry was a lost cause, mostly due to her own actions. Wickham was just being practical. It wasn't as if she would go out and commit suicide. For all her foolishness, she wasn't really stupid. She would go on.

Wickham looked up suddenly, his thoughts frozen, and found himself face to face with Lettie. How much had she heard? He couldn't bring himself to speak. All he could see were her eyes and her black hair. He couldn't tell what she was thinking and she was saying nothing. Fear? Anger? Hate? Sadness? Strands of black hair spilled over into her face, reminding him of his wife's hair - her beautiful hair.

And he remembered his wife's eyes.

Lettie turned from him, in more than physical terms - he was now sure - and walked back into the corridor. He'd lost control. Even Nemo knew too much now, which was likely due to something Hetzel had told him. He'd lost control.

He'd lost control of himself; taking the box of cigars he pitched it across the room and walked out of the salon and down the corridor after her.

Chapter 61

May 28, 1883
The *Nautilus*

Turner woke to a very sharp sound and lay awake with every creak caused by changes in pressure on the hull. Energetic voices echoing against the metal walls melded with his semi-lucid dreams. Had there been a fight, or had he dreamed it?

Finally, the ship must have reached its depth for optimal movement against the currents it would encounter in the English Channel. Or, so he estimated. Turner rolled over and tried to find a position that didn't remind him of prison, of sleepless nights waiting for death. Try as he did to fill his head again with visions of damn close to anything but death, the room's elements kept dragging him back to the War, the Confederate prison, the pain. Twice he awoke in a terrible sweat, gasping for air, tearing at an invisible rope around his neck. Unlike reality, in his dreams General William T. Sherman did not arrive in time.

A moment of head clearing later, he knew he'd had another worthless total of an hour's sleep. It served him right – they had used sleep deprivation on Pierce to break him down, to make him more malleable and cooperative. It served him right not to get any rest now that he was the prisoner. What was the cliché? No rest for the wicked?

He was relieved when all that came for him was a meal.

Chapter 62

She looked at the door briefly as she ran to her own quarters next door. A brief notion crossed her mind: that was the room where Turner was being kept. Why - why did she feel better knowing he was close to her? It made no sense.

Instantly her mind returned to the moment. Wickham wanted to lock her away: to slave in her science for him. She couldn't allow it. God no, it couldn't happen. No freedom? No life outside a golden prison? Surely Nemo wouldn't let him do that to her? Turner was locked away. Robur was as bad as Wickham. No, Captain Nemo was the only man who could save her.

She stopped at her door, disgusted by the thought. She climbed volcanoes, for Christ's sake. She was one of a handful of women who endured the pain of becoming academics. She was capable ...

Damn it, she was!

She was a woman, and a lady. Nothing in her experiences prepared her for this. Her mother had kept newspapers away from her, thinking that what was printed was too harsh for a young woman to read. Family told her to get married and stop with the foolishness of becoming an unseemly scientist. It was her father, then Christopher Moore who had saved her from the limits forced on her life. Always she had had a man to turn to. Even in the rail station, she had been rescued by Brevet Major Chard. Always a man. So of course it would be a man she'd turn to. Nemo. But why was she so incapable of saving herself? Why?

Because it wasn't done. Her reputation depended, relied, on her being a lady in every possible way. That meant demurring in public and deferring to men, always. Or leaving a room when she was insulted rather than stand up for herself.

The memory of being shamed out of the lecture hall in Paris flooded back. She stepped into her unlit quarters. She shouldn't have left the lecture hall. To hell with what those old men were trying to say about her. Like a lady, and perhaps a coward, she allowed their rudeness to force her from a place she dearly wanted to be. With scientists and thinkers. Innovators and curiosity seekers.

She was a coward. Truthfully, she had to admit she was hiding behind her reputation. Now that her reputation was likely ruined and worthless, she still sought protection. Coward!

What little light entered the room from the corridor was blocked. She knew who it was. "Mr. Wickham, get out. There is nothing we have to say ..."

Wickham plunged into the room, seizing her by the neck and forcing her against the bulkhead. Shadows covered his face. One of his hands gripped her mouth and held her head back against the cold wall.

"Control, Miss Gantry," he said in a harsh whisper that sent droplets of spittle onto her face. "I will have order and control. We have no time to play games or to pretend that this will end any other way. Nemo will get his nephew, who is likely dead, and I will get Robur's ship. You will retire to a place of safety, of my choice, to live your life in service to a better cause."

He almost said something else then stopped.

Lettie was standing, not struggling, and he wondered. She was shaking though. Her eyes were wide and trying not to look at him. Wickham shook her head roughly and drew her gaze back to him. Her hair was falling down. Down, in long strands of silky black. Her face was dark in the unlit room and her skin appeared deep in tone. Silky black hair. Dark skin. Delicate shoulders and round breasts forced into a corset. She looked like his wife. How dare she!

His free hand moved to the high collar of her blouse and he pushed the button back through its hole. The first time his wife had worn English clothing, she'd looked so out of place he had insisted on helping her remove the constrained garments. He had pushed each pearl button out of its buttonhole and they had laughed at each step.

At first, Lettie did not move and could not make a sound. He held her mouth too tightly. And what would she know of sex or intimacy? Of course she didn't know what to do.

Slowly she pushed at his free hand, trying at once to stop him firmly but without angering him. He didn't care.

He'd opened her blouse to the top of her corset and pushed it to the side - away so that he could see the skin underneath. Soft. Round. Touchable. Yes, touchable. He ran his fingers down the curve of her throat, her collar bone, her breast. He pushed his long fingers deeper into her clothing and felt the hardness of her nipple. He could imagine it rosy pink against her pale skin. He could see how his mouth could engulf it and suckle it.

Squirming, she twisted her head away from his grip and screamed.

Wickham stepped back. This wasn't his wife.

He raised his hand to her but stopped when noises were heard in the corridor. He grabbed her neck and spoke closely to her ear. "Speak of this, one word to anyone, and I will find ways to punish you you've never thought of. I hate you, and Nemo, and this whole goddamned world. I'll have control and order or I'll see to it nothing survives."

Wickham quickly walked out of the room, looked both ways before choosing which way he would flee.

Lettie sank to the floor and failed to respond when the old gentleman, who had brought her food, tried to learn what had happened. She barely heard him.

For the rest of the morning, she remained alone in the dark room.

Chapter 63

By the time the *Nautilus's* clock declared it late afternoon, Lettie had allowed herself to leave her room, pushing back tears that were trying to fall, hardening herself, and finalizing her plans. She was exhausted and emotional, two things that were of no use to her.

Her plan was complex, which meant it would work or fail miserably. No in between. Failure would mean imprisonment for the rest of her life: or worse. For all her attempted understanding and observations, she hadn't anticipated what Wickham was willing to do. Success or failure? She prayed for the former and expected the latter.

First she had to do the sensible things. All but the bare essentials would have to be left behind. Fight or flight? Flight. There was no sense in trying to become courageous now.

The crew had stored the bulk of her luggage in a locker. It was easy enough to get into the storage room. Digging quickly through the luggage she pulled out a leather box. In it she kept her tools: a hammer, a jeweler's lens, gloves, binoculars, recent maps, goggles, and a long cloth tape measure. There was also a celluloid bottle for the collection of gases in water. Pencils, scraps of paper, a knife, and a rubber eraser. The tools of a volcanologist. Added into the box, with its cross-the-body bandolier strap, went the two packages of Mr. Winchester's .44 caliber, centerfire, brass cartridges. It made the kit outrageously heavy, but she couldn't do without protection. Over her arm she also slung her beloved rifle: in case she had to fight.

Lettie relocked the storage door, having made everything inside look undisturbed. A sharp ping and the sound of a dropped tool froze her to the spot. She pressed her back to the locker door, not sure what she would say if a crewman found her there.

She waited, quietly, listening only to her own shallow breathing. The ship was so small, it was any wonder she didn't have ten men walking past her at any given moment.

No one walked by. Astonishing, considering how many men lived on board the submarine.

She began breathing heavily again. Her next stop was, in her own estimation, dishonorable but necessary. Were she stealing from Wickham, frankly she wouldn't care. And she just might have to take something of Wickham's; she actually had something in mind. But stealing from Nemo? He had been so intimate. She knew things now that elicited her compassion. And, certainly she respected Nemo's scientific knowledge. He would understand, wouldn't he? This was for Rajiv; surely he'd understand and forgive that? This was for her freedom too, and that he had to comprehend.

Two crewmen left the diving room, conversing in the Nautilus's language. It was empty now. Lettie stepped in, half anticipating that men in dive suits would spring out of the hatch.

Quickly she found the seal-skin coats and gloves.

Carefully detaching a connecting tube between the underwater pack and the helmet, she detached the mouth piece as well. She then inserted one of the empty reservoir tanks into the pack and started to sling the whole unit over her other shoulder. It was too heavy; it couldn't be done. Reluctantly, she set the apparatus back on its hook, but allowed her hand to linger on the helmet and its decoration.

"You would not be able to refill the reservoir, so you are wise not to take it."

Lettie didn't turn around ... mostly out of shame.

"Without the helmet," Nemo continued, "you cannot go underwater. You would also want the canvas suit for protection."

"It's likely just as well, the helmet is not the appropriate material or design for protection as I should like to use it ... as you suggested I use it. Copper, after all, conducts both heat and static electricity."

"This is, in an essence, stealing from me?" Somehow he didn't sound as angry as he should have; in fact, he didn't sound angry at all.

"It is no worse than stealing my future from me. But if you think I do this lightly, you would be in error. I have to do what I must. I cannot live out my life in a prison."

He began stuffing the gloves into the pockets of the coats. "I swear that I did not know what Wickham planned for you and never sought to cause you harm. If you wish to trade with me instead of simply taking ..."

She turned to face him then. "I'd prefer that by far. But in trading, you will become entangled in my little plan. I don't think you should be so exposed, so involved."

"I know what it is you are planning to do, though how I might be curious enough to ask. Yet, I think I should remain ignorant for the time. Bring me back my nephew. Do what you must; just bring my nephew to me."

"Wickham?"

"Wickham is using us all and presumes too much." Nemo's eyes began to grow narrow in rage. "I'll see to Wickham as much as I can. Promise me you'll help Rajiv." His face began to redden.

"I can only promise you to do everything I can. I don't know if I'll be successful. You should consider what to do if I fail. I barely have a plan now. For the moment all I intended was to gather these things."

"Do more than gather, Doctor. Leave. As soon as possible."

She stopped for a moment, a freezing wave sweeping over her body and leaving her stomach queasy. "Captain. What about Mr. Turner? You know what Wickham will do to him, or at least what he claims he will do?"

"Turner has made his bed."

She shook her head, hoping the vigorous movement might warm some part of her. "I cannot look the other way."

"You're too soft," Nemo spit at her. "Harden yourself. You cannot afford to be a woman. You must be like a man." His blood was up.

"Since men claim logic as their exclusive realm, allow me to apply it here. Mr. Turner must go with me. I'll need to take him with me. He's the only one who will know where to find your nephew."

For a long silence, he stared out at nothing in particular. The blood raised now faded from his face. Nemo sighed and nodded in one gesture. He half expected that she would require Turner. He was sorry that she had. Turner was not worthy but he could spend no more time on that. He quickly pulled a second sealskin coat off a hook and handed it to her.

"And I must ask about his men."

"You are being a woman again. They are not his men. Merely hirelings from Paris. We left them behind. You needn't spend another moment thinking of them." He seemed annoyed that she'd asked after such inconsequential persons.

"Thank you, sir. I shall, therefore, remain focused on the task at hand." She hesitated. "I have one more thing to ask of you." Lettie drew a folded, addressed letter from her pocket. "I ask this of a man who knows the pain of losing family. This is a letter I was going to send to my father from Brindisi. Can you arrange to have it mailed? It will relieve his suffering if Mr. Wickham is correct and I am believed to be missing. He will take it as a sign that I am alive and well. I finished it today in order to suggest that the report of my abduction is false. I know what he is feeling. I know what I would feel if he were the one who had disappeared. Please. Will you do this?"

He nodded, his temper cooled considerably. He accepted the letter, holding it for a moment. Quickly he pocketed it, looked up at her with a renewed officiousness and said, "In two hours we will dock against the shoreline. Mr. Wickham will take several of my men to secure the area. Two hours." He said nothing else but turned and walked from the room.

Chapter 64

Her last step was an act of madness. She assured herself it was Nemo who arranged for the *Nautilus* to be so close to a shoreline and Wickham to be "off ship." Were the *Nautilus* further out to sea, she would need to use one of his boats. She would have neither the skill nor the opportunity to use the boats as all would already be in use by Wickham. Being up against land allowed her a better chance of escape. Very rational. Very simple.

The island where it was suspected they would find Robur was remarkably flat, with only some natural changes in elevation. The highest points on the island were connecting levies and dykes. Plodder, they called it: reclaimed land from the sea.

Small, slightly submerged rock formations provided natural stepping stones to the sandy, grassy beach, behind which the locals had built their famous dykes against inundation by the North Sea. Some small piers were also built along the interior shore of the island. The *Nautilus* was able to settle herself into an area where she was free to move forward and backward at will so long as the tide was in. With tide out, the submarine would have to float away, stranding its crew on shore. Planks of iron plating were positioned from the ship to a pier, allowing Wickham and the others to disembark without getting too wet. However, as the men marched off toward the village, the planks were not withdrawn as they should have been.

She stopped in her hiding place, pulled one of the boxes of cartridges out of the pack, removed ten, and loaded them into the rifle. Each one slid down the magazine tube crashing into the bottom with a noise that surely everyone on the ship could hear. Half of Holland must have. No. It was her imagination. She was still hidden, invisible, a state of being she never desired before now. The rod was pushed back down, twisting it to lock the bullets in place. Her heart was pounding so much that her whole body rocked with each beat. Three more cartridges she slipped into her skirt pocket before putting the box back into her pack. For an emergency.

There would be an emergency. There was always an emergency.

It was time to go.

Chapter 65

Lettie unlatched Turner's door and forced herself inside. One of Wickham's pretty revolvers was in her hand and pointed directly at Turner. Only fair. And, Wickham would miss it. It was one of the fancy, pearl-handled guns he kept so neatly in his cabin and was sure no one, especially not Lettie, knew about. She'd seen it through his open door, lying on his desk where he'd just cleaned it, and she'd taken it for several reasons; mostly because the rifle was unwieldy in the cramped spaces of the *Nautilus*, and because she needed another weapon. She had chosen the one she was sure had been shoved into her head at the rail station. It hardly mattered if she was correct.

The weight of the gun and her heart made her hand shake.

Turner stood up, confused by what he was looking at. She came dressed in a practical fashion and laden down by a number of things worn on her back and shoulders. The silly woman also clutched in her left hand that damned overstuffed valise. Setting down the valise, she un-pocketed a pair of hand cuffs, which he recognized as those used on him earlier.

"Put those on," she ordered, throwing them down on the bed where he'd been sitting and pointing the gun again with both hands, trying to steady it.

"What the hell are you doing, woman?"

"Put them on or I am leaving you here. I'm not staying and you may come with me, but not in a condition that continues to threaten me. Put them on."

"Nemo won't let us off ship."

"Nemo is helping us," she replied with limited composure.

"Not if he wants his nephew."

"Because he wants his nephew. He doesn't believe that Mr. Wickham can be relied upon to outwit Robur."

Turner smiled slightly. "Then he's right about that. But what does he expect you to do?"

She bit her lip. "To make a trade."

"He's trading you?" Turner sounded entirely unconvinced.

"At my insistence, Mr. Turner. He knows Wickham will fail because Wickham is too indifferent to the lives involved. That indifference keeps him from understanding all the nuances of the situation. He neither knows nor cares what motivates each of us. Nemo is well aware of problems. So he is allowing me - us - to escape. Now, put those on." She carefully chose not to tell him about Wickham's plan to imprison her in a laboratory.

Slowly, Turner locked one cuff over his left wrist, looked up hopefully to Lettie. It was only reasonable as there were two ladders between Turner's cabin and the shore. Surely she understood that he couldn't climb, let alone be helpful in their escape with his hands behind him? She only scowled and indicated that his hands could be in front of him. He was only moderately relieved at her reaction. He was hoping she'd give up on the whole idea of his having to wear them at all. He pulled on his navy jacket, a short blue item with practical pockets, a number of well mended patches, and looked at the hat he had brought from Paris. It would have to stay. So would most of the contents of his one piece of baggage. Perhaps Nemo wouldn't destroy the hat; it was a damned fine thing. "Give me that pack, or the rifle. You're carrying too much and you will slow us down." She reacted to his demand with pale skin and wide eyes. What did he say that frightened her so immediately?

Reluctantly, she handed him the tool box, which he pulled on over his head. "Oh hell, and the rifle, too. Come on, that's heavy. I'm not going to get killed because you were bogged down." He wanted to see if he could generate the reaction again, to see what caused it. It would be a handy thing to know.

Like the lady she'd been taught to be, Lettie regained her composure and erased any expression of fear. "May I remind you who has the pistol?"

Damn. "The person who won't be handcuffed. I'm clear on that point. I'm just in the same mood you are, I want to get out of here." He took one of the seal-skin coats and tucked it through the tool box strap.

Terrifying herself and surprising Turner, she forced him back into the wall and pointed the Colt directly at him. "Tell me Robur will help me do my work and then let me go. Promise me." Her voice was high pitched.

Turner's face softened. Something had changed, radically, in his favor. "Yes, I can promise you that we will help you. I'll help you." As she continued to point the revolver at him, he finally clamped the other cuff down on his right wrist. Holding both hands up so that she could see them locked together, he looked at her with an expression that demanded to know if she was satisfied yet. "And I have his assurance that he has no intention of keeping you indefinitely on board his ship." Her face changed so fundamentally that he had to wonder what it was that was driving her from Nemo's boat. Nemo clearly favored her. He wouldn't harm her. Was it Wickham?

Lettie un-cocked the Navy Colt pistol and slid it into her overburdened valise. With surprising speed she twisted out the key from the handcuffs and put it in her waistcoat pocket.

"How much water and food do we have, Doctor?"

"Not a great deal. We'll have to be careful with it."

"Well, I suspect we won't be out there for very long."

Weakness in her knees followed by a wash of cold over her skin stopped her at the door. "Robur is waiting for us? Of course he is. Your job was to kidnap me in Italy, but that didn't go right. So, you've been hoping to escape with me, once Nemo and Wickham provided transportation to the place you were already planning to go to."

"That was the plan." Seeing her brief reluctance, he whispered to her with a slight lift in his voice, "but you were supposed to be in my custody, not the other way around. Either way will do, I suppose, so long as we escape this floating madhouse. Doctor Gantry, we will help you finish your model. To save lives."

Her fingers tightened on the door frame as she looked out, seeing who was hopefully not there. "When we're no longer in such a hurry," she whispered sarcastically and bitterly, "will you be so kind as to tell me why the lot of you men are so very interested in me and my prediction model? I daresay it isn't to save lives."

Turner started to say something, decided it was neither witty nor important enough to risk being heard, and remained quiet.

Everything was wet. Of course it was wet. Yet every drop that hit the floor sounded like cannon fire to both of them. Turner struggled to keep all the equipment he carried from crashing into the endless pipes and beams. The combined weight keep him off balance, a feeling he wanted rid of.

No one was near the entrance as they quietly climbed up to the open hatch. The glare of sunlight was making one last attempt at reaching the ground through a break between the clouds and the flat Dutch landscape, and painted the great iron ship in dark orange. It was too quiet. The sea only made enough sound as required by its presence breaking against the shore. Turner's hyperawareness made the silence nearly unbearable and he felt an urgent, nagging paranoia about the whole situation. It felt like Georgia. It smelled like Georgia. It wasn't, he reminded himself.

They quickly made it across the slick metal planks and dragged themselves up the sandy shore.

Their feet sank deeply into the sandy mud, pulling and grasping at their limbs as though it meant to drag them back to the ship. Grasses and shrubs helped to keep them from falling or losing traction in their steps but hardly erased the feeling that safety was behind them. The whole landscape seemed to cry out, "Go back!"

The artificial channel between earthen levies was filled with a strange fog that could not escape over the pair of dykes on either side. The white and brown wisps roiled and brewed as though something beneath it was boiling. They would have to go through it.

Climbing up the closest dyke, they had their first look at Holland, and perhaps freedom.

"Are you still sure, Doctor?"

Lettie shook her head. "I'm a coward, by nature and training. This is not something I have any knowledge of. But I have to do this. I cannot tell you every reason why, but I'm certain you can guess."

He waited, to see if she would say more. "Letticia Gantry, you are many things. You are not a coward. If you were, we wouldn't be having this conversation." He pointed to a spot at the base of the dyke that would offer some brief shelter. "We'd better get going."

Turner started down the slope toward the layer of fog.

Uncertainty. That was what she knew was waiting before her. Turner's assurances aside, she had no idea what was waiting for her in the dark. She didn't trust him. But she did know that waiting for someone to rescue her would accomplish nothing. Behind her was imprisonment or death. And who else would be dragged into that danger? This was her responsibility. Cowardice or no, this was the only path she could take.

This was her responsibility.

For the reader's enjoyment:
From Volume II of The Volcano Lady
(Pre-edit)

May 31, 1883
Holland

Dry grass and shrubbery was trampled by several pairs of feet, all too near to them. Turner rolled over onto his knees. Lettie struggled with her tangled skirt as she worked her way over and crouched next to him, her valise in one hand and the pistol in the other.

Voices whispering to one another, in the concocted language of the *Nautilus*, were coming toward them. Turner indicated to her that silence was required and nodded toward the gun. After pulling the boxes and equipment quietly up against his body, not making a sound, he hauled Lettie to her feet. Very ungentlemanly. She didn't care. They backed away from the voices, looking around frantically in the increasing light for shadows where they could hide. There were still enough dark places as dawn had not entirely arrived. But where?

Suddenly, five men stepped out of the brush and into the small clearing that had been Turner and Lettie's sleeping place. One held a lantern that was not entirely needed while another knelt down to an impression in the dirt, touched it, and said something to his comrades that included the recognizable word "Turner."

The man was right: it was where Turner had slept and Turner, watching from inside the bushes, was moderately impressed. He hadn't heard them approach until the very last second. Motioning to Lettie, he decided that they couldn't afford to wait and see what else Nemo's men might do to impress him. They carefully worked their way around several large, half barren shrubs. Lettie was wisely keeping control over her skirt so that it wouldn't snag in the bramble. Her finger rested on but not in the trigger guard, another bright action on her part. An accidental gunshot would give their position away or do worse.

With Lettie behaving rationally, Turner focused instead on the stability of the ground beneath their feet. They were off the worn path, with not enough light yet to see or indicate a dangerous bog. He would have to be twice as careful. He listened for the voices, which remained behind them in the clearing. It wouldn't take long to find where they had entered the bushes and to follow their footsteps in the mud. They had to keep moving with cautious speed.

The strap of her geological tool box caught on one of the branches. Turner stopped and backed up to free himself. The branch was too old and brittle and broke off with a horrible snap.

Nemo's men heard it and thrashed their way wildly into the brushes toward them.

Lettie began to run but Turner stopped her, pushing her down onto the ground, all the equipment he carried landing on top of them. "We lost them once this way," he whispered into her ear. "Stay down. It'll work again."

He picked up a large stone with both hands, still handcuffed, and lobbed it ahead of them. The stone hit the ground with a thud and a slight splash. Lettie and he looked at one another, noting the luck they had in stopping where they had. Ahead was a bog.

"We can't let them fall into ..." she began.

Turner clamped a hand down on her mouth as one of Nemo's men burst past the broken shrub to stand right next to them, oblivious to them. Only one man, the others were spread out, searching.

Turner grabbed her valise and swung it up into the face of the man. The blow was considerable and Turner's momentum with all the equipment he had strapped to his shoulders spilled both men into the dirt. The attack was loud but fast. Lettie scrambled onto her feet, picked up the valise next to the unconscious man, and tried her best to help a slightly dazed Turner to stand up.

Retracing their steps back to the clearing, Lettie knew that they had been lucky. Turner pointed to the path the men had made through the bushes and they used the footprints of their pursuers to hide their own in their escape.

It had been too close.

Too close.

"The man you hit is going to come to in a moment and be able to tell the others where we were and likely where we've gone," she said between gulping breaths.

Nodding, Turner added, "then we'd better keep moving."

Two hours of cautious maneuvering through the bushes and mud, and neither of them could detect their pursuers. It had surely been too close. Turner was showing a bit of fatigue at carrying all the equipment. He constantly shifted it around as much as he could.

The sky had changed to a hideous black, with rain falling in mourning veils. It might as well have been night again.

As they walked, crept, or hid from potential dangers she couldn't help looking at Turner. He was still young enough to restart his life and smart enough to choose any direction he wanted. She didn't hate him, even though she had every right to. The feeling tore at her as she realized she envied him. A North Sea storm was approaching and time had run out.

Lettie stopped, contemplating the swirling clouds above her. She pulled a long, cylindrical object of out of her pocket. It was the key to his shackles. She reached out and took hold of his right hand, pushed the key into the slot and frantically began turning it. Her hands were shaking as she did it. The lock loosened and opened the handcuff enough that he could pull his hand through. With his hand free, Turner took off the equipment, giving his shoulders relief. Lettie took his other hand and began unlocking that cuff. "Robur isn't coming, is he?"

About the Author

T. E. MacArthur is an author, artist, and historian living in the San Francisco Bay Area with her constant companion, Mac the cat. She received her Bachelor's Degree in History from Cal State University and spent many an evening in subsequent Anthropology, Geology, Criminal Investigation and Art classes. Writing remains, however, her passion. She has written for several local and specialized publications and was even an accidental sports reporter for Reuters with three national bi-lines. T.E. is the artist and author behind *Shamanka: Oracle of the Shamaness* (www.shamanka-oracle.com.) *The Volcano Lady: A Fearful Storm Gathering* is the first of two volumes to follow the adventures of Victorian lady scientist Lettie Gantry, and is her first novel in publication. To put it mildly, T.E. has a love for all things Victorian (history and clothing from 1870 – 1890 in particular) and is having a lifelong affair with the writings of Jules Verne.

Visit T. E. MacArthur on her blog:
http://volcanolady1.wordpress.com/

Made in the USA
Charleston, SC
16 May 2012